Australia

HANDSOME HEROES

Marion
LENNOX

Alison
ROBERTS

Lilian
DARCY

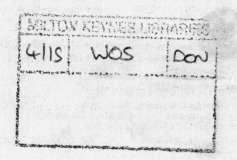

Mills & Boon, an imprint of Harlequin (UK) Limited, Eton House, 18-24 Paradise Road, Richmond, Surrey TW9 1SR

AUSTRALIA: HANDSOME HEROES
© Harlequin Enterprises II B.V./S.à.r.l 2013

His Secret Love-Child © Marion Lennox 2006
The Doctor's Unexpected Proposal © Alison Roberts 2006
Pregnant with His Child © Lilian Darcy 2006

ISBN: 978 0 263 90609 7

010-0813

Harlequin (UK) policy is to use papers that are natural, renewable and recyclable products and made from wood grown in sustainable forests. The logging and manufacturing processes conform to the legal environmental regulations of the country of origin.

Printed and bound in Spain
by Blackprint CPI, Barcelona

HIS SECRET LOVE-CHILD

Marion
LENNOX

THE AUSTRALIA COLLECTION

March 2013

April 2013

May 2013

June 2013

July 2013

August 2013

Marion Lennox is a country girl, born on an Australian dairy farm. She moved on—mostly because the cows just weren't interested in her stories! Married to a 'very special doctor', Marion writes Medical romances, as well as Mills & Boon® Cherish™ novels. (She used a different name for each category for a while—if you're looking for her past Mills & Boon romances, search for author Trisha David as well.) She's now had well over ninety novels accepted for publication.

In her non-writing life Marion cares for kids, cats, dogs, chooks and goldfish. She travels, she fights her rampant garden (she's losing) and her house dust (she's lost). Having spun in circles for the first part of her life, she's now stepped back from her 'other' career, which was teaching statistics at her local university. Finally she's reprioritised her life, figured out what's important, and discovered the joys of deep baths, romance and chocolate. Preferably all at the same time!

CHAPTER ONE

THIS old house had seen it all.

He should find somewhere else to live, Cal decided as he sat on the back veranda and gazed out over the moonlit sea. Living in a house filled with young doctors from every corner of the world could sometimes be a riot, but sometimes it was just plain scary.

Like now. Kirsty-the-Intern and Simon-the-Cardiologist had disappeared into the sunset, protesting personal concerns so serious they needed to break their contracts. They'd left a house agog with gossip, two bereft lovers and a hospital that was desperately understaffed.

Crocodile Creek, Remote Rescue Base, for all of far north Queensland, was notoriously short of doctors at the best of times. Two doctors were away on leave, a third had somersaulted his bike last week and was still in traction, and a fourth—unbelievably—had chickenpox. The two doctors who'd left so hastily hadn't considered that when they'd started their hot little…personal concern.

Dammit, Cal thought. Damn them. Now there was a bereft and confused Emily, and Mike, whose pride at least would be dented. Both were wonderful medics and fine friends. In such a confined household even Cal would be called on for comfort, and if there was one thing Dr Callum Jamieson disliked above all else, it was getting involved. All Cal wanted from life was to practise his medicine and commune with his beer.

And not think about Gina.

So why was he thinking of Gina now? It had been five years since he'd seen her. She should be forgotten.

She wasn't.

It was just this emotional stuff that was making him maudlin, he thought savagely. The old bush-nursing hospital that now served as Crocodile Creek's doctors' residence seemed to be a constant scene for some sort of emotional drama—and dramas made him think of Gina.

Gina walking away and not looking back.

He had to stop thinking of her! Gina had been his one dumb foray into emotional attachment and he was well out of it.

Maybe he should find Mike and play some pool, he thought. That'd clear his head of unwanted memories, it'd stop him swearing at the sea and maybe it'd help Mike.

But there wasn't time. He'd have to take another shift tonight. There might be no surgery to perform, but with the current shortage of doctors Cal could be called on to treat anything from hayfever to snake bite.

That meant he couldn't even have another beer.

Damn Simon. Damn Kirsty, he thought savagely. Their sordid little affair was messing with his life. His friends had loved them and he didn't want his friends to be unhappy. He wanted the Crocodile Creek doctors' house to be as it had been until today—a fun-filled house full of life and laughter, a place to base himself without care while he practised the medicine he loved.

The door opened and Emily, of the now non-existent Simon-and-Emily partnership, was standing behind him, pale-faced and tear-stained. Emily was a highly skilled anaesthetist. He and Emily made a great operating team.

Right now Emily looked about sixteen years old.

He didn't do emotional involvement!

But he moved on the ancient settee to let her sit beside him, and he put an arm around her and he hugged. OK, he didn't do emotional involvement but Emily was a sweetheart.

'Simon's a rat,' he told her.

'He's not.' She hiccuped on a sob. 'He'll come back. He and Kirsty aren't really—'

'He and Kirsty *are* really,' he told her. It wasn't helping anything if she kept deceiving herself. 'He really is a rat, and you can't love a rat. Think about the life they lead down there in the sewers. Gross. Come on, Em. You can do better than that.'

'Says you,' she whispered. 'You lost your lady-rat five years ago, and have you done better since Gina left? I don't think so.'

'Hey!' He was so startled he almost spilled his beer. How did Em know about Gina? Then he gave an inward groan. How could she not? Everyone knew everything in this dratted house. Sometimes he thought they were even privy to his dreams.

'We're not talking about me,' he said, trying to sound neutral. 'We're talking about you. You're the one who needs to recover from a broken heart.'

'Well, I'm not going to learn from you, then,' she wailed. 'Five years, and you're still not over it. Charles says you're just as much in love with Gina as you were five years ago, and for me it's just starting. Oh, Cal, I can't bear it.'

Gunyamurra. Three hundred miles south. A birth and then…a heartbeat?

No. It was her imagination. There was nothing.

Nothing.

Distressed beyond measure, the girl stared down at the tiny scrap of humanity that should have been her son. Maybe he could have been her son. Given another life.

How could she have hoped this child would live? She was little more than a child herself, so how could she have ever dared to dream? How could she have ever deserved something so wonderful as a baby?

Now what? Living, this child might well have made her life explode into meaning. But now…

It would all go on as before, the girl thought drearily. Somehow.

Her body ached with physical pain and desolate loss. She was weighed down, sinking already back into the thick, grey abyss of the last few months' despair.

She put out a tentative finger and traced the contours of the lifeless face. Her baby.

She had to leave him. There was no use in her staying, and this quiet place of moss and ferns was as good a place as any to say goodbye.

'I wish your father could have seen you,' she whispered, and at the thought of what might have been, the tears finally started to flow.

Tears were useless. She had to get back. The cars were leaving. She'd slip into the back seat of the family car and her parents wouldn't even question where she'd been. They wouldn't notice.

Of course they wouldn't notice. Why would they? Her life was nothing.

Her baby was dead.

'There's a baby behind my rock.'

Gina closed her eyes in frustration and tried hard not to snap. CJ's need for the toilet was turning into a marathon. The coach left the rodeo grounds in ten minutes and if they missed the coach…

They couldn't miss the coach. Being stranded at Gunyamurra in the heart of Australia's Outback was the stuff of nightmares.

'CJ, just do what you need to do and come on out,' she ordered, trying hard for a voice with inbuilt authority. It didn't work. Dr Gina Lopez might be a highly qualified cardiologist who worked in a state-of-the-art medical unit back home in the US, but controlling one four-year-old was sometimes beyond her.

CJ was just like his daddy, she thought wearily. Even though those big brown eyes made her heart melt, he was fiercely independent, determined to follow his own road, whatever the cost.

Like now. CJ had taken one look at the portable toilets and dug in his heels.

'I'm not using them. They're horrible.'

They were, too, Gina conceded. The Gunyamurra Rodeo had come to an end, the portable toilets had accommodated a couple of hundred beer-swilling patrons and CJ's criticism was definitely valid.

So she'd directed his small person to where the parking lot turned into bushland. Even then she had problems. Her independent four-year-old required privacy.

'Someone will see me.'

'Go behind a rock. No one will see.'

'OK, but I'm going behind the rock by myself.'

'Fine.'

And now…

'There's a baby behind my rock.'

Right. She loved his imagination but this was no time for dreaming.

'CJ, please, hurry,' she told him, with another anxious glance across the parking lot where the coach was almost ready to leave. She was too far away to call out, and she hadn't told the driver to wait. If they missed the coach…

Stop panicking, she told herself. It'd come this way. If the worst came to the worst, she could step down into its path and stop it. She might irritate the driver but that was the least of her problems.

She should never have come here, she thought wearily. It had been stupid.

But it had seemed necessary.

Back in the States she'd thought maybe, just maybe she could find the courage to face Cal. Maybe she could find the courage to tell him what he eventually had to know.

But now she was even questioning that need. Was it even fair to tell him?

She'd started out with the best of intentions. She'd arrived at Crocodile Creek late last Thursday and she'd left CJ with her landlady so she could go to find him. The house she'd been directed to was the doctors' quarters—a rambling old house on a bluff overlooking the sea. At dusk it had looked beautiful. The setting should have given her courage.

It hadn't. By the time she'd reached the house, her heart had been in her boots. Then, when no one had answered her knock, things had become even worse.

She'd walked around the side of the house and there he'd been, on the veranda. Cal. The Cal she remembered from all those years, with all her heart.

But he wasn't her Cal. Of course he wasn't. Time had moved on. He hadn't seen her, and then, just as she had been forcing herself to call his name, a young woman had come out of the house to join him.

Gina had stilled, sinking back into the shadows, and a moment later she had been desperately glad she had. Because Cal had taken the woman into his arms. His face had been in her hair, he had whispered softly, and as Gina had stood there, transfixed, the woman's arms had come around Cal's shoulders to embrace him back.

This wasn't passion, Gina thought as she watched them. Maybe if it had seemed like passion she could still have done what she'd intended. But this was more. It was a coming to-gether of two people who needed each other. There was some-thing about the way they held each other that said their relationship was deep and real. The girl's face looked pinched and wan. Cal cupped her chin in his hand and he forced her eyes to meet his, and Gina's heart twisted in a pain so fierce she almost cried out. This girl had found what she never had.

She'd fled. Of course she'd fled. She'd treated Cal so ap-pallingly in the past. Now it seemed that he'd found love. Real love—the sort of love they'd never shared. What right did she have to interfere with him now?

She'd gone back to her hotel, cuddled CJ and tried to re-group, but the more she thought about it the more impossible it seemed. How would Cal's lady react to her appearing on the scene? How could she jeopardise this relationship for him?

She couldn't. CJ had been born in wedlock. Paul was his father and that was the way it had to stay.

But she'd invested so much. She'd come so far. Surely she couldn't simply take the next plane home, though that was what she frantically wanted to do.

She'd promised CJ they'd see Australia. She had to make good that promise.

So she'd made herself wait a few days. She'd booked her-self and her young son onto a crocodile hunt—a search by moonlight for the great creatures that inhabited the local es-tuaries. Thy hadn't found a crocodile but they'd met a real live crocodile hunter and CJ's wide-eyed enjoyment of his stories had helped ease the ache in her heart. They'd taken a tour out to the Great Barrier Reef and had tried not to be disappointed when the weather had been wild and the water cloudy.

Then she'd heard about the Gunyamurra Rodeo. CJ's pas-sion was for horses. There'd been a coach going via the rodeo to the airport, and the last day of the rodeo was a short one, so they'd decided to spend their last morning in Australia here.

CJ had loved it, so maybe it hadn't been a total waste of time, but now the thought of leaving was overwhelmingly appealing. Crocodile Creek was three hundred miles away. She was never going to see Cal again. Their coach was due to leave to take them back to Cairns Airport, and it was over.

All she had to do was get her son from behind his rock.

'CJ, hurry.'

'I can't do anything here,' he told her with exaggerated patience. 'There's a baby.'

'There's no baby.'

CJ's imagination was wonderful, Gina thought ruefully, and at any other time she encouraged it. Her son filled his life with imaginary friends, imaginary animals, rockets, battleships, babies. He saw them everywhere.

Not now. She couldn't indulge him now.

'There's not a baby,' she snapped again, and, dignity or not, she peered around CJ's rock.

There was a baby.

For a moment she was too stunned to move. She stood and stared at the place between two rocks—the place where her son was gazing.

This was a birth scene. One fast glance told her that. Someone had lain here and delivered a baby. The grass was crushed and there was blood…

And a baby.

A dead baby?

She moved swiftly, stooping to see, noting his stillness and the dreadful blue tinge of his skin. He was so pale under his waxy birth coating that she thought he must be dead.

She touched him and there was a hint of warmth.

Warmth? Maybe.

He wasn't breathing.

She fell to her knees and lifted him against her. His tiny body was limp and floppy. Where was his pulse?

Nothing.

Her fingers were in his mouth, trying frantically to clear an airway that was far too small. She turned him over, face down, using her little finger to clear muck from his mouth and then using a fold of her T-shirt to wipe his mouth clear.

Then she pulled him up to her mouth and breathed.

She felt his tiny chest lift.

Yes!

Heartbeat. Come on. There had to be a heartbeat.

Her backpack was where she'd dropped it, and CJ's windcheater was drooping out of the top. She hauled it onto the grass and laid the baby down on its soft surface. It was almost one movement, spreading the windcheater, laying the little one down and starting cardiopulmonary resuscitation.

She knew this so well. Cardiology was her specialty but to practise CPR here, on a baby this small…

She wanted her hospital. She wanted oxygen and suction equipment. She wanted back-up.

She had to find help. Even if she got him breathing, she needed help. Urgently.

CJ was standing, stunned into silence. He was too young to depend on but he was all she had.

'CJ, run to the side of the parking lot and scream for help,' she told him between breaths.

Breathe, press, press, press…

'Why?' CJ seemed totally bemused, and who could blame him?

Could she take the baby and run for help? She rejected the idea almost before she thought of doing it. How long had the baby been abandoned? How long had he not been breathing? Even if she got him back… Every second without oxygen increased the chance of brain damage.

She needed every ounce of concentration to get air into these little lungs. She breathed again into the baby's mouth and continued with the rhythmic pumping that must get the heart working. Must!

'This baby's really ill,' she told CJ, fighting to get words out as she concentrated on CPR between breaths 'You have to get someone to come here. Scream like there's a tiger chasing you.'

'There's not a tiger.'

'Pretend there is.' She was back to breathing again. Then: 'Go, CJ. I need your help. You have to scream.'

'For the baby?'

'For the baby.'

He considered for a long moment. Then he nodded as if he'd decided that maybe that what his mother was asking wasn't too crazy. Maybe it even appealed to him. He disappeared around the other side of the rock. There was a moment's silence—and then a yell.

'Tiger. Tiger. Tiger. There's a tiger and a baby. *Help!*'

It was a great yell. It was the best. He'd put his heart into it, and it sounded for all the world like a tiger was about to pounce, and a baby, too. But the end of his yell was drowned out.

The coach they'd come in was huge, a two-level touring affair. It had a massive air-conditioning unit, and even when idling it was noisy. Now, as it started to move and went through its ponderous gear changes, it was truly deafening.

Gina heard just one of CJ's yells before the sound of the coach took over. The second and third yells were drowned out as the coach turned out of the parking lot, growing louder and louder until nothing could be heard at all.

Gina made to stand—she made to get herself out in front of the coach to stop it—but then there was a tiny choking sound from the baby. Her eyes flew back to him. Was she imagining it?

No.

If he was choking… His airway must still be slightly blocked. She had to get his trachea clear.

Once more she lifted the baby and turned him face down, and her fingers searched his mouth. The coach was forgotten. She desperately needed equipment. There might well be liquor or meconium stuck in his throat or on his vocal cords. How to clear his tiny airway without tracheal suction?

She shook him, carefully, carefully, supporting his neck as if it were the most precious thing in the world.

He choked again.

Something dislodged—a fragment of gunk—and she had it clear in an instant.

She turned him back over and breathed for him again.

This time his chest rose higher.

It fell.

It rose—all by itself.

Again.

Again.

She was breathing with him, willing him to breathe with her. And he was. Wonderfully—magically—he was.

She wiped his mouth again, using her T-shirt, and then searched her bag for a facecloth. She was cradling him against her now. She had to get him warm. Once she had him breathing, heat loss was his biggest enemy.

At least the outside air was warm.

She had to get help.

The coach was gone.

As if on cue, CJ appeared back from his tiger yelling. 'I think they heard me,' he told her, uncertain whether to be proud or not. His expression said he was definitely uncertain about the baby his mother was paying such attention to. 'One of the ladies on the coach waved to me as it went past.'

Fantastic. She could hear it in the distance, rumbling down the unmade road, starting its long trip to Cairns.

To the airport. To America. Home.

She couldn't think of that now. All that mattered was this tiny baby. His breathing was becoming less laboured, she thought, or was it wishful thinking? She wanted oxygen so badly.

She didn't have it. She had to concentrate on the things she could do.

Swiftly she checked the baby's umbilical cord. It looked as if it had been ripped from the placenta. Now that his heart was beating strongly, the cord was starting to ooze.

How long had the cord been cut? she asked herself, a bit confused. Obstetrics wasn't her strong point, but surely the cord shouldn't still be bleeding?

How much blood had he lost?

Where was the nearest hospital to Gunyamurra?

She couldn't depend on a hospital. She was all this baby had.

She tugged the drawstring from her backpack and tied the umbilicus with care, then hauled the backpack wide and found her own windcheater—a soft, old garment that she loved. It'd do as a blanket.

Once again she checked his breathing, scarcely allowing herself to hope that this frail little scrap of humanity might survive.

But as if he'd read her mind and was determined to prove her wrong, he opened his eyes.

And even CJ was caught.

'It's a real baby,' CJ breathed, awed at this transformation from what must have seemed a lifeless body to a living thing, and Gina could only gaze down at the baby in her arms and agree.

More. There were no words for this moment. For this miracle. She was suddenly holding a little person in her arms. A baby boy. A child who'd one day grow to be a man, because CJ had found him and her lifesaving techniques had blessedly worked.

How could missing a coach possibly compare to this? How could being stuck in this outlandish place possibly matter?

He was so tiny. Four, maybe five pounds? Premature? He had to be. His fingernails had scarcely started to form and he was so small.

His lips were still tinged with blue. Cyanosis? The tips of his fingers were still blue as well, and she started to worry all over again. As he'd started to breathe, his little body had suffused with colour, but now...

She checked his fingers and toes with care, trying not to expose him any more than she had to. It was a hot day, so the wind was warm against the baby's skin. How long had he been exposed?

Maybe the warm wind had helped save his life.

But there were still those worrying traces of cyanosis. His heart wasn't working at a hundred per cent.

It wasn't his breathing, she thought. He was gazing up, wide-eyed, as if wondering where on earth he was, and his breathing seemed to be settling.

So why the skin blueness?

She wanted medical back-up. She wanted it now.

'How will we get home?' CJ asked, and she held the baby close and tried to make herself think.

'We need to find someone to help us.'

'Everyone's gone,' CJ said.

'Surely not everyone.'

But maybe everyone had. Gina's heart sank. The rodeo itself had finished almost an hour ago. A group of country and western musicians from down on the coast had booked the coach to transport their gear. They'd played at the closing ceremony, then organised the coach to stay longer, giving them time to pack up.

The timing meant that the crowd had dispersed. The rodeo had taken place miles from the nearest settlement—which itself wasn't much of a settlement. There'd been mobile food vans and a mobile pub, but they'd gone almost before the last event.

CJ might well be right.

'Someone must be here,' she said, trying to sound assured. She tucked the baby underneath her T-shirt, against her skin, hoping the warmth of her skin would do the same job as an incubator. 'Come on, CJ. Let's go find someone.'

CJ was looking at her as if he wasn't quite sure whether he wanted to accompany her or not. 'Is the baby OK?'

'I think so.' She hoped so.

'You've got blood on your shirt.'

She had. She grimaced down at her disgusting T-shirt but she wasn't thinking of her appearance. She was thinking of how much blood the baby had lost.

Why had he bled so much? And newborn babies had so little… He couldn't afford to have lost this much.

He whimpered a little against her and she felt a tiny surge of reassurance. And something more.

Once upon a time—four and a half years ago—she'd held CJ like this, and she'd made the vows she found were forming again in her heart right now. She'd loved CJ's daddy so much. Cal had taught her what loving could be, and she'd pass that loving on to CJ.

And even though Cal no longer came into it—even though Cal was no part of her life and had nothing to do with this baby—she found herself voicing those same vows. She'd protect this baby, come what may.

What mother could have left him here? she wondered. How much trouble must a woman be suffering to drag herself away from her newborn child?

She thought of how distressed she'd been when CJ had been born—how much she'd longed for Cal and how impossible it had seemed that she raise her son without him. But the bond to her tiny scrap of a son had been unbreakable, regardless.

He'd been her link to Cal.

She'd thought of Cal so much as her son had been born, and suddenly, achingly, she thought of him now.

But it was crazy. She couldn't think of Cal. Neither could she think about the coach growing further away by the minute. Her ticket out of here—away from Cal for ever—was gone.

She needed to find help.

'Come on, CJ. There must be someone still around.' She cradled the baby with one hand, took CJ's hand with the other and went to find out.

The rodeo had been held in a natural arena where a ring of hills formed a natural showground. There was scrub and bushland on the hills but the rodeo ground was a huge, dusty area that now looked barren and deserted.

But not everyone had gone. As Gina and CJ crossed the parking lot back into the rodeo grounds, they found one solitary person—an elderly, native Australian. Gina had seen him before, working on the sidelines during the rodeo. Was he some sort of ground manager? He must be. He was staring around at the piles of litter and scratching his head in disgust. As he saw Gina and CJ, he shoved back his hat and smiled, obviously pleased to be distracted from the mess.

'G'day. Come to help me clean up?'

'We've found a baby,' Gina told him.

He stared. His smile faded.

'Um…say again?'

'Someone has abandoned a baby in the bush. I have him here.' She motioned to the bulge beneath her stained T-shirt. 'We need medical help. Fast.'

'You'll be kidding me.'

'I'm not joking.' She outlined what had happened and the man's jaw dropped almost to his ankles.

'You're saying some woman just dropped her bundle behind the rocks—and left it for dead?'

'She may have thought he was dead already,' Gina told him. 'I had trouble getting him to breathe.'

The man cast an uneasy glance at the bulge under her shirt. He took a step back, as if maybe he was facing a lunatic. 'So he's under there? A baby.'

'He's under there. Can you take us to the nearest hospital?'

The man stared at her for a moment longer, took another step backward and then motioned uncertainly to an ancient truck parked nearby.

'There's no other way of getting out of here than that. How did you get here?'

'Coach.'

'The coach has left.'

'Yes,' Gina said, trying to hold her impatience in check. 'Will you take us to the hospital? We need help.'

'Nearest clinic's at Gunyamurra, twenty miles from here,' he told her, still really doubtful. 'But there's no one there now. The Wetherbys and the Gunnings—the two families that live near there and the workers on their stations—they were all here today so there won't be a clinic operating. Maybe you need a doctor.'

'Yes, please.' To tell him she was a doctor herself would only confuse matters.

He cast another glance at her bulge. His mouth tightened as if he was becoming sure of his lunatic theory.

'How can I contact medical help?' she snapped, and he blinked.

'We had the Remote Rescue Service on call during the rodeo,' he told her, totally bemused. 'They flew Joseph Long out with a broken leg an hour or so back. That was near the end with only the novelty events left, so they didn't come back. Word is that they're short a couple of doctors back at base.'

'I need a doctor now,' Gina told him. She was still holding

CJ's hand tight and using her other hand to cradle the baby. But the baby didn't seem to be moving. He was so limp.

He couldn't die. He mustn't.

'I s'pose I could call them back.' There was another doubtful look at her bloodstained T-shirt—a look that said he accepted there was blood and maybe there had been a baby but he wasn't too sure that he mightn't be dealing with an axe murderer. 'You sure it really is a baby? A live baby?'

She released CJ and held up the T-shirt—just for a moment, just so he could see.

They all looked at the bulge.

At the windcheater-wrapped baby.

He was surely real. He was surely a baby. He was incredibly tiny—more, he was incredibly beautiful. His crumpled little face was now becoming the flushed crimson of most newborns. His eyes were wide, dazed and unfocussed.

And he moved. It was a slight movement, but he definitely moved. He whimpered a little and a hand—a hand the size of a man's fingernail—broke free from his makeshift blanket.

Gina didn't say anything. She tucked the little hand back into the warmth of her windcheater, and she waited for this man to make his decision. She needed his help so much.

And it seemed that she had it. The man stared down and his face twisted into an expression she could scarcely read,

'Will you look at that?' he whispered. 'He's just like mine were at that age.' He stared down at the baby for a moment longer and then he looked up at Gina. His old eyes met hers and held.

'You really found him?'

'We found him. We're tourists on the coach but we found him just as the coach was leaving. I've been trying to get him to breathe. So far, so good, but if he's to live we need your help. We need outside help. Fast.'

'I'm moving,' he told her, and he turned and started to stride swiftly across the dusty arena to his truck.

He took three long strides—and then he started to run.

'Mommy,' CJ said, in the tone of a patient man whose patience was being tested to the limit.

'Yes?'

'I still need to go to the toilet.'

'Cal?'

He jumped. Cal had been placing a scalpel in the steriliser, but Charles's voice from right behind him startled him into dropping it. He swore, then stooped to retrieve it with a sigh. 'Will you cut that out?' he demanded of his boss. 'Quit oiling that damned wheelchair so we have a chance.'

Charles grinned. Charles Wetherby was the medical director of Crocodile Creek Medical Centre. He'd been confined to a wheelchair since a shooting accident when he'd been eighteen, but his paraplegia didn't stop him being a fine doctor and a medical director who missed nothing. Charles knew his silent approaches startled his staff but he didn't mind. It never hurt his young doctors to believe their medical director might be right beside them at any time.

Not that he had any need to check on Cal. Callum Jamieson was one of the best doctors they'd ever been blessed with.

Normally doctors didn't stay at Crocodile Creek for too long. The work was hard, the place was one of the most remote in the world and doctors tended to treat it almost as a mission. They spent a couple of years here working with the Remote Rescue team, they got their need for excitement out of their system and then they disappeared.

Not Cal. He'd come four years ago and had made no attempt to move. There was something holding him, Charles had decided long before this. Something that didn't make him want to face the real world. Woman trouble? Charles didn't know for sure what the whole story was, but he knew more than Cal ever admitted—and he'd met Gina. For now, though, he wasn't asking questions. Cal was a fine surgeon, and he went that extra step with patients. He really cared. Also, Cal was more gentle and painstaking with the indigenous people than any of the younger doctors who struggled with—and often didn't care about—their culture. Cal was invaluable to this Remote Rescue Service and Charles was deeply grateful that he had him.

Especially now.

'I need you in the chopper,' he told him.

'Trouble?'

'Out at the rodeo.'

'Didn't Christina and Mike just bring someone in?'

'Yeah. Joseph Long, with a fractured femur. You'd think kids would have something better to do than to risk life and limb sitting on a steer that doesn't want to be sat on.'

'How old were you when you got shot pig-shooting?' Cal asked mildly. 'Eighteen? Don't tell me. Joseph's…what? Eighteen? You're telling me that kids should learn a lesson from you and stop being risk-takers?'

'Don't play the moral bit on me.' Charles's craggy features twisted into a wry grin. There weren't many people who could joke with Charles about his background, but Cal had been around long enough to become a firm friend. 'Just get on that chopper,' he told him. 'Fast.'

'What's up.'

'Newborn. Breathing difficulties.'

Cal came close to dropping his scalpel again. 'A newborn at the rodeo?'

'There's a woman there says she found him.'

'A woman?'

'Hey, I don't know any more than you do,' Charles said, exasperated. 'I know it sounds crazy and if I could, I'd be in the air right now, finding out what's going on. But Pete Sargent—the rodeo groundsman—has radioed in, saying there's a baby and a woman and for some reason they don't match. He says the woman found the baby. The baby's certainly in trouble and he wants a doctor out there fast. Mike's refuelling the chopper as we speak. You're the only doctor available. So what are you standing here for?'

Gina was just about frantic.

The blue tinge to the baby's fingertips and lips was becoming more and more pronounced. Cyanosis in a newborn had to mean heart trouble—but she didn't even have a stethoscope. She was sitting in the rodeo judges' stall and as a hospital ward it made a great judges' stall. There was no equipment whatsoever.

Pete—bless him—had taken CJ in charge. Out on the grounds the pair of them were collecting litter. Pete had supplied CJ with a pair of work-gloves that were longer than his arms, and CJ was enjoying himself immensely.

That left Gina free to concentrate on the baby, but there was so little she could do. She kept his airway clear. She watched his breathing. She kept him against her skin, curving in so he had as much skin contact as possible, cradling any exposed parts into her soft, old windcheater. She was using herself as an incubator.

She willed him to live, and she waited.

Help came so slowly she thought she might well lose him.

But finally the helicopter came in from the east, low and fast and loud. It hovered for a moment above the car park as if the pilot was checking for obstacles. But Pete had already checked. There was no problem with its landing, and before it reached the ground Gina was running toward it.

She stopped just out of range of the rotor blades. Pete had come up behind her. The elderly groundsman was holding

CJ's hand and he gripped her arm, too, as if warning her that the rotor was dangerous.

Maybe he still thought she was deranged, Gina decided. He must think there was a possibility she might run into the blades.

She wouldn't. She knew about helicopters. She'd flown with the Remote Rescue Service before.

So she stood and she waited, but she didn't have long to wait. A man was emerging from the passenger seat, his long body easing out onto the gravel. He hauled a bag out after him, then turned.

Her world stopped.

Cal.

CHAPTER TWO

FOR how long had she dreamed of this moment? For how long had she thought of what she might say?

Her prepared speech was no longer appropriate. She'd accepted that three nights ago when she'd seen him back at Crocodile Creek, so maybe it was just as well that there were things to say and do now that had nothing to do with their past.

He was past the slowing rotor blades. He was almost by her side.

He stopped.

And he saw who he was facing.

'Gina.'

The word was a blank expression of pure shock.

He'd had less warning than she. She at least knew that he was in the same part of the world as she was. She'd seen him only three days ago. But Cal hadn't seen her for five years.

He'd hardly changed, she thought. He was a big man, long and lean and tough. He always had been.

Information about Cal's background had been hard to glean, but she knew enough. His parents had been farmers on a holding that had been scarcely viable. His mother had abandoned them early. Cal had been brought up to hard times and hard work, and it showed. His bronzed skin was weathered, almost leathery. His deep brown eyes crinkled at the edges,

26

and his strongly boned face spoke of the childhood he'd talked about reluctantly, a childhood where his first memory had been of gathering hay in the blazing sun before a storm on Christmas morning, heaving bales that had been almost as big as he'd been before he had been old enough to stop believing in Santa Claus.

Before he'd been old enough to stop hoping that one day things could change.

But they hadn't. He hadn't. He hadn't changed a bit.

Yet she still loved him. She looked into his shocked face and she felt her heart break all over again.

How could she still love him?

Five years of heartbreak.

She had to move on. He had a life to lead and so did she. There was no room here for emotion.

But... His burnt red, tightly curled hair was just the same as her son's.

Concentrate on medicine, she told herself fiercely. Use the medical imperative. Medicine had been her lifesaver for five long years and it would be her lifesaver again.

And as for loving?

Get over it.

'Cal, there's a baby.'

He was staring at her as if he were seeing a ghost. She might be moving on, but he hadn't yet. How could he?

'What the hell are you doing here?'

The harsh words were like a blow and she found herself physically flinching.

But she had to move past this. The baby's life was too important to waste time on non-essentials.

'I've been at the rodeo,' she told him. Somehow. It was almost impossible to make her voice work at all, but when she managed it came out expressionless. Businesslike. 'I found a baby,' she managed.

'You found a baby.' Shock was still the overriding emotion.

'It's wrapped in a windcheater, under her T-shirt.' Pete had moved into helpful mode now. He was looking from Gina to Cal and back again, as if he couldn't figure out why they weren't moving. As indeed they must. 'She says some woman must have dropped it in the bush.'

'What—?'

'I need oxygen,' Gina told him, hauling herself even more into medical mode and willing Cal to follow. 'Cal, the baby needs urgent help if he's to survive. He's badly cyanosed. His breathing is way too shallow—he's tiring while I watch.'

She still hadn't pulled the baby from under her T-shirt so he was just a bulge under her bloodstained clothing. No wonder she didn't have Cal's belief. She must look crazy. 'He's only hours old. He's lost blood. He's prem, I think, and he's not perfusing as he should. Blue lips, blue fingernails. Heartbeat seems far too rapid. Do you have equipment?'

She watched as Cal caught himself. As he finally managed to flick an internal switch.

'A baby.' His eyes dropped to the bulge and his deep eyes widened. He was taking in the whole scene, and it wasn't pretty. 'Not yours?'

'Not mine.' A little blood could go a long way and she was aware that she looked so gory she might well be a mother who'd given birth only hours before. And maybe she looked shocked and pale to go with it.

'I need oxygen, and I need it fast.'

'We have an incubator on board. Everything we need.' The pilot of the chopper—a guy in a flight suit—was coming toward them now, carrying more equipment.

Medical mode won.

'Let's move.'

* * *

They moved.

The next ten minutes were spent working as once they'd worked together long ago. The pilot—a youngish guy Cal referred to as Mike—was a paramedic and he was good, but with a baby this tiny they needed every ounce of skill they all possessed.

She and Cal were still a team, Gina thought fleetingly as she searched for and found a tiny vein for the intravenous drip. Newborn babies had such a tiny amount of blood that even a small loss could be catastrophic. He had to have replacement fluid. Meanwhile, Cal had a paediatric mask over the tiny face, using the attached bag to assist breathing. His breathing slowed almost at once. From an abandoned baby with nothing, this little one was suddenly being attached to every conceivable piece of medical technology they could use.

Maybe he'd need them all. Because when Cal hooked him to the heart monitor and she watched his heart rate, she winced.

'There's something going on,' she murmured. 'That heartbeat's too fast and with this level of cyanosis…'

'You're thinking maybe pulmonary stenosis?'

'Maybe. Or something worse, God forbid. We need an echocardiogram.'

'Yeah.' He cast her a doubtful look. 'We've done all we can here. We need to get him back to the base.'

She hesitated. Yes. They needed to get the baby to help. But…where did that leave her?

For the first time since she'd found the baby, there was a tiny sliver of time to consider. The baby was being warmed and he was hooked to oxygen and an intravenous drip. He was as stable as she could make him—for now. Somehow she made herself block out the fact that Cal was watching her as she forced herself to think through what should happen next.

Should she stay involved?

Now was the time to step back—if she could.

There were three factors coming into play here.

First, she badly needed transport. Once she reached Crocodile Creek, she could get a coach to the outside world. Maybe she could even still catch her flight home.

Secondly, more importantly, this baby needed her. Or he needed someone with specialist training.

'Is there a cardiologist at Crocodile Creek?' she asked, and Cal shook his head. He was thinking exactly what she was thinking. She knew it.

'Our cardiologist has just left,' he said abruptly, and she nodded. But the way he'd spoken… It brought her to the third factor.

Despite the fact that it was sensible for her to go with him to Crocodile Creek—despite the fact that medical imperative decreed that she go—she didn't want to get in the helicopter with him. It had been a mistake to come. To drag out the moment…

This baby needed a cardiologist if he was to survive. He needed her.

She had no choice, she told herself fiercely. Focus on medicine. Ignore the personal. The personal was all just too hard.

'We need to think about the mother,' she managed, and Cal nodded in agreement. They'd always been apt to follow the same train of thought and it was happening all over again.

'We do.' He turned away to where Pete was kneeling a few yards away in the dust. Pete had obviously decided that his best role was in keeping CJ occupied and they were etching huge drawings of kangaroos in the dust. 'Pete, have you no idea where this baby could possibly have come from?'

'There's been three or four hundred people through here over the last couple of days,' Pete said, looking up from his kangaroo and shaking his head as he thought it through. 'It could be anyone's kid.'

'This baby was born here only hours ago. Did you see anyone who was obviously pregnant?'

'Dorothy Curtin's got a bulge bigger'n a walrus but she and Max took off with the kids at lunch time.'

'There's no way Dorothy would abandon one of hers. But anyone else? Maybe someone who's in trouble. A kid? Maybe someone who's not a local?'

'There were a few out-of-towners on the coach. But I dunno.' He scratched his head a bit and thought about it. 'I dunno.'

'I didn't see any pregnant women on the bus,' Gina told them.

'I'll need to get the police involved.' Cal looked uncertainly across at Gina and then he seemed to make a decision. 'I want the mother found. But we need to take Gina—this lady—back to Crocodile Creek with us,' he told Pete. 'Will you stay on and show the police where the baby was found?'

'Sure thing,' Pete said. 'I gotta clean up anyway. '

'I'll show you exactly where I found her,' Gina told him, and then hesitated, thinking it through. 'Cal, we need to check the birth site anyway. We might have a girl somewhere who's in real trouble.'

'We might at that,' Cal said grimly—and then added, more enigmatically, 'And that's only the start of it.' He motioned to Mike. 'Mike, you go with Gina. I'll stay with the baby.'

Mike nodded. Until then the paramedic had worked almost silently alongside them, but he was obviously aware of undercurrents. He looked at Gina now, a long, assessing glance, and then he looked across to where CJ was intent on his drawing.

'Is this your son?' he asked her. 'Will he be coming back with us, too?'

Cal hadn't noticed CJ. He'd been preoccupied with the baby and with Gina, and CJ had had his head down, drawing dust pictures. Now his eyes jerked over to where the little boy knelt in the dust.

CJ was totally intent on the task at hand, as he was always intent on everything he did. Pete had been showing him the traditional way aboriginals depicted kangaroos and he was copying, dotting the spine of his kangaroo with tiny white pebbles. Each stone was being laid in order. His drawing of the kangaroo was three feet high—or three feet long—and it'd take many, many pebbles to complete it, but that wouldn't deter CJ.

So for now he knelt happily in the dust, a freckle-faced, skinny kid with a crop of burnt red curls that were coiled tight to his head. With deep brown eyes that flashed with intelligence.

With hair and with eyes that were just the same as his father's.

They all saw Cal's shock. Gina watched his eyes widen in incredulity. She could see him freeze. She could see the arithmetic going on in his head.

She could see his life change, as hers had changed with CJ's birth. Or maybe before that.

As it had changed the day she'd first met Cal.

'Hey, the kid's hair is just the same as yours,' Pete said easily—and then he fell silent. He, too, had sensed the tension that was suddenly almost palpable.

'It's great hair,' Mike said, with a long, hard stare at Cal. Then he recovered. A bit. 'OK.' He stared at CJ for another long moment—and then turned back to Gina. 'You said your name is Gina? I'm assuming you're a doctor?' Cal had been working with her as an equal and her medical training must have been obvious.

'That's right. I'm a cardiologist from the States.' But Gina was hardly concentrating on what she was saying. She was still watching Cal.

'Then let's get this birth site checked, shall we?' Mike said, taking charge because neither of the two doctors seemed capable of taking charge of anything. 'There are questions that need answers all over the place here.' He directed another long, hard stare at Cal—and then he took another look at CJ. 'So maybe we'd better start working on them right now.'

The flight back to Crocodile Creek was fast. They put CJ in the passenger seat next to Mike—helicopter copilot was a small boy's dream—and Gina and Cal were left in the back to tend to the baby.

But there was scarcely room for both of them to work, and for the moment there was little enough for both to do. It was Gina who opted out, Gina who sank into a seat and harnessed herself in for the ride and Gina who said, 'He's your patient, Cal.'

Which was fine, Cal thought as he monitored the little one, adjusting the oxygen rate, listening to the baby's heart, fighting to keep him stable.

The baby was his patient.

Gina's son was…was…

Hell, he couldn't take it in. It was overwhelming. The sight of the little boy had knocked him so hard he still felt as if he'd been punched.

How could Gina have borne a child—his child?—and not told him?

Could it be a mistake? Was he jumping to conclusions? Somewhere there was a husband. He knew that. A husband with coiled red hair the same as his? And eyes that looked like his?

He glanced across at Gina. She looked older, he thought. Much, much older than the last time he'd seen her.

He remembered the first time he'd seen her. She'd just arrived in Townsville, a young doctor from the States come to try her hand at Outback medicine. She'd been thin—almost too thin—her green eyes almost too big for her pinched, white face, and with her riot of deep brown curls tied back in a casual knot that had accentuated her pallor. He'd thought she seemed too young, too frail to take on the job she had applied for.

But over the year she'd been with the Remote Rescue

Service, she'd proved him wrong. She'd fast become an important member of the service. She gave her all. She'd thrown herself into her work with total enthusiasm and skill. With basic training in cardiology, she'd proved an indispensable member of their team, and the rest of the doctors had only been able to wonder what had driven her from her high-powered training to life in far north Queensland.

'I had a relationship that didn't work out. It was…a bit of a drama.' It was all anyone had been able to get from her. She didn't talk about her past.

But finally she did talk, though still not of her background. As they'd worked together over the ensuing months, the pinched, wan look had disappeared and she'd blossomed. She'd gained weight, her eyes had lost their haunted look and had filled with life and laughter, and she'd brought life and joy to…

To his world.

He'd thought her the most beautiful woman he'd ever seen.

He glanced again at her now. Her hands were clasped on her knees. She was staring straight ahead, unseeing.

She seemed haunted again, he thought. She was too damned thin again. The bloodstained clothes made her look like the victim of some disaster, and he had a sudden feeling that she'd look like that even without them.

He didn't know her, he thought bleakly. He had no idea what was happening behind that blank mask. She'd walked away from him five years ago and he hadn't seen her since. His only phone call had elicited a brutal response.

'I'm married, Cal. My husband needs me. Absolutely. I can't talk to you any more.'

Married. *Married.*

He needed to concentrate on his job. His fingers were lying lightly against the baby's neck, monitoring his vital signs by touch as well as by sight, but there was still time and still room for him to look at her again. She wasn't looking at him. She was staring down at her hands. She was wearing a plain gold wedding ring. Her fingers had clenched to white.

Why had she come?

Questions. There were questions everywhere. But for now only one mattered, he told himself.

Would this little one live?

He dragged his eyes away from Gina, back to the baby.

Needful or not, he'd continue to monitor him by sight, he decided. And by every other sense—because there was no way he could bear to look at Gina.

And he hardly dared to as much as glance at the little boy sitting next to Mike in the copilot's seat.

Questions. Too many questions.

They scared him to death.

CJ was fantastic.

Over and over Gina how thought how lucky she'd been to have a little boy who demanded so little. CJ lived in his own small world, where his imagination ran riot. His requirements from his mother were for security and for hugs and for the basic necessities of life, but as long as those were provided whenever required, he was prepared to accept the assorted childminders he'd met in his short life. He even welcomed them as a wider audience for his incredible stories.

Now, as the helicopter landed at Crocodile Creek and the baby was wheeled into the hospital, as the emergency team sprang into action, Cal motioned to one of the nurses to take care of him.

'Gina's a doctor,' he said briefly—brusquely. 'She's a cardiologist, right when we need one most. We need her help with the baby. Grace, can you find someone to take care of Gina's little boy?'

'Sure.' Grace, a young nurse with a wide smile, held out

her hand to CJ and beamed a welcome. 'I hear you guys have been out at the rodeo. Did you see many horses?'

'I saw lots of horses,' CJ told her, ready to be friendly.

'Will you tell me about them while we find you some juice and some cake? Come to the kitchen. Mrs Grubb is making chocolate cake and she loves hearing about horses. If we're lucky, I think there might even be an icing bowl to lick.'

CJ was sold. He cast an enquiring glance at his mother for approval, then tucked his hand into Grace's and disappeared cakewards.

'He's a great kid,' Mike said as the paramedic wheeled the trolley through into Paediatrics, and Gina gave him a glance that she hoped was grateful.

She looked back at Cal. There was no gratitude there. His face was set and stern.

Maybe she should have phoned him four years ago.

Or not.

Maybe she shouldn't be here now.

If she hadn't been here now, this baby would be dead.

'We need an echocardiogram,' Cal said. He hadn't paused as they moved through the hospital. He was intent only on the baby. Or he acted as if he was intent only on the baby.

'You said you don't have a cardiologist? No one with cardiology training?'

'No.'

'A paediatrician?'

'Hamish is on leave. We're trying to contact him now.'

'We're dead short of doctors,' Mike said, and smiled, but then his smile faded a little. 'There's been a couple of…disasters. Just lucky you're here, huh?'

'I guess,' she said dubiously, and cast an uncertain look at Cal. His face said there was no luck about it.

But she couldn't look at his face. She needed to focus. This baby needed skills that she possessed.

* * *

He certainly did.

When the results of the echocardiograph were in front of her she felt her heart sink. Any thoughts she had of flying out of this place tonight were completely gone.

'It's pulmonary stenosis.'

With the stethoscope she'd been able to hear the characteristic heart murmur at the left upper chest. That and the fast heart rate had made her fairly sure what was causing the cyanosis. And now... Her fears were confirmed. There was a huge pressure difference between the right ventricle and the pulmonary artery. Blood flowing in one direction and unable to escape fast enough in the other. Recipe for catastrophe.

'We can't risk transfer to Brisbane,' Cal said slowly—reluctantly. 'We'll lose him.'

'What's happening?' Mike asked. He'd come in and watched as they worked, but he'd been on the sidelines. Another nurse was there now—a woman in her thirties who'd been introduced as Jill Shaw, the director of nursing. Jill was wheeling the baby back under the nursery lights, with instructions to keep warming, keep monitoring breathing, while the three of them were left staring at the results.

'We operate,' Gina said, staring down at her fingers as if there were some sort of easy answer to be read there. There wasn't. They really needed a paediatric cardiologist, but the nearest available would be in Brisbane and to transfer the baby...

They would have had to if she hadn't been here. They'd have been forced to. Cal was an excellent general surgeon, she thought, and his additional physician training made him a wonderful all-rounder in this place where multi-skills were vital. She knew that. Cal's skills were one of the things that had attracted her to him in the first place.

But the operation for pulmonary stenosis on such a tiny child...

The heart valve they'd be working on—the pulmonary

valve—was thin, even in adults. Composed of three coverlets, like leaflets, it opened in the direction of the blood flow. With pulmonary stenosis those leaflets were blocked or malformed in some way. In the baby's case it was a major blockage. His heart was being forced to work far too hard to force blood through.

What she needed to do was to perform a balloon pulmonary valvuloplasty—a tricky manoeuvre even in adults—forcing the valve to open. With babies this size…

She'd normally advise waiting, she thought bleakly. She'd normally advise keeping him on oxygen. She'd try and get him fitter, older. She'd operate at a few weeks.

To operate on such a newborn…

But this was no minor blockage.

'Do you have the equipment?' she asked. 'I'd need to monitor catheters by fluoroscopy.'

'I'd imagine we have all you need,' Cal told her. 'Simon, the cardiologist who's just left, had the place well set up for heart surgery.'

Gina nodded. She'd worked with this service before, and she'd expected this answer.

Many of the population around Crocodile Creek would be indigenous Australians, and she knew from experience how reluctant they were to leave their people. For a tribal elder to come to Crocodile Creek for an operation would be hugely stressful, but here at least here they could still be surrounded by their own. To be flown to Brisbane, where there was no one of their tribe and no one spoke their language, was often tantamount to killing them. The cultural shock was simply too great for them to handle.

That would be part of the reason Crocodile Creek would be set up so well, she knew. This base would do surgery which would normally only be done in the big teaching hospitals.

Death rates would be higher because of it, but the population would accept it. The doctors involved had to accept it.

But this doctor in particular didn't have to like it.

'So we have no paediatrician and no cardiologist.'

'We're not normally this short-staffed,' Cal told her. 'We've had a couple of dramas.'

He sounded defensive, she thought. Good. It stopped her thinking about all sorts of things she should be defensive about.

'Do you have an obstetrician?'

'Georgie's mother died last week. She's flown down to Sydney with her little boy, and we don't want to pull her back unless we have to. She had back-up—Kirsty was an obs and gynae registrar—but there was a bit of a dust-up and Kirsty and Simon left in a hurry. Emotional stuff.'

'Emotional stuff?' she demanded, astonished, and he looked even more discomfited.

'Um, yeah. We don't need to go there.'

Of course not. When had he ever?

But she had a baby to take care of. Cal's emotional entanglement, or lack of it, had to wait.

Mike was waiting for her to make a decision. He was looking interested—as interested in the chemistry between them as he was in the baby—and that made her flush. She remembered how intimate working in this sort of environment could be. She even remembered enjoying it, but she didn't relish the questions she saw forming in Mike's eyes now.

'I'll wait for an hour and reassess,' she said, trying to make her voice calm and professional. 'We need to get him fully warmed and make sure the shock of delivery has worn off. Maybe once he's settled we might get better circulation.'

'But probably not,' Cal said.

'No,' she said heavily. 'Probably not.'

'So Gina'll need to stay.' Mike wasn't sure what was going on—his eyes were still asking questions—but he was certainly

prepared to be friendly while he found out. He gave Cal a rueful smile. 'Just lucky we have plenty of room in the doctors'
quarters, eh?'

Cal's face tightened. 'She can't stay in the doctors' quarters.'

'Why not?' Mike was confused.

'I'll stay in town,' Gina said hurriedly, but Mike shook his
head. He was obviously a skilled paramedic, accustomed to
making hard decisions, fast decisions, and he made one now.

'No way. I'm sorry, Gina, but this baby is sick.' He cast a
dubious glance at Cal—as if he thought Cal might just be losing his mind. 'We all know this baby's high risk. It seems to
me that we need our cardiologist on hand, right here. Wouldn't
you say, Cal?'

'Of course.' The words were tight and blunt. Cal turned
away to pack equipment and Mike shook his head at his
friend. He was obviously still confused.

'Cal's being a bore,' he told Gina, with another dubious
glance at his friend. 'He's tired. Too much work. But there's
plenty of us around here who are gentlemen.' He tried a smile.
'Especially me.' He waited to see if he'd teased a reaction
from Cal, but a reaction wasn't anywhere in sight. 'OK.' He
sighed. 'Let's find your son and find you a bedroom.'

'I'll stay here and monitor the baby,' Cal told them, still
without turning around.

'Of course,' Mike said politely. 'How did I know you were
going to say that?'

'The baby needs monitoring.'

'Of course he does, Dr Jamieson,' Mike agreed. He com-
pressed his lips in disapproval and then he turned to Gina.
'OK. There's obviously just me being a gentleman, but I'm
all yours. Take me or leave me.'

Charles entered the nursery silently, wheeling his chair across
the smooth linoleum until he came to rest against the incuba-

tor under the overhead lights. Cal was gazing down at the baby and, seeing the look of his face, Charles thought, Uh-oh.

'Will we lose him?'

Cal turned and stared, almost unseeingly, down at his friend.

'I don't know. He has a chance.' There was a moment's silence. 'Gina's here.'

'I heard.' Charles hesitated. He'd met Gina before, just the once. He'd been astounded by the change the relationship had wrought on his reserved friend, and when it had gone pear-shaped he'd felt ill. Now Mike had given him a quick update on what was happening, and he was even more concerned. He'd suspected Cal's past would catch up with him sooner or later but, damn, he didn't want him to be presented with it now.

From a selfish point of view they were too many doctors down already. He couldn't afford to have another of his staff in emotional crisis.

'Are you coping?' he asked, and Cal shrugged.

'I'm coping. You've seen the kid?'

'I've seen the little boy, yes.'

'Dammit, Charles, he looks like me.'

'Could you be his father?'

It was a direct question and it jolted Cal. He stared at the question from all sides and there was only one answer.

'Yeah,' he said heavily. 'I could.'

'And that makes you feel—how?'

'How do you suppose it makes me feel?' Cal turned and faced his friend square on. 'If it's true… She got pregnant and left? Went back to the States to her husband?' He closed his eyes. 'Hell, Charles, I don't want to think about it. I can't think. I don't have time. We need to get this baby viable. He needs urgent surgery and we're stuck with Gina to do it. No one else has the skills.'

He stared down into the crib and his mouth twisted. 'We'll

do the best for him, poor little scrap. He's been abandoned, too. People…they play games. They have kids for all sorts of reasons. Who knows what the reason is behind this little one and who knows what the reason is behind the child who's out in Mrs Grubb's kitchen, waiting for his mother to take him home? I can't face any of it. Just… Let's stick to medicine. It's all I know. It's all I want to know.'

There was a moment's silence. Move on, Cal willed Charles, and finally he seemed to decide that was all there was to do.

'Emily will do the anaesthetic,' Charles said mildly, his voice carefully neutral, not giving away any of the anxiety that someone who knew him well could detect behind his eyes. 'She's contacting a paediatric colleague in the city who'll stay on the phone throughout. Do you want to assist, or will I find someone else?'

'Who?' He was the only surgeon, and both of them knew it. But he shrugged. 'It's OK. I want to assist.'

'So you can bear to be in the same room as her?'

'I thought I loved her,' Cal said heavily. 'Once. I was a fool—but sure I can stay in the same room as her. I need to be able to. If that's really my son…' His voice trailed off.

'Well, let's get on with it,' Charles said, and there was still heavy anxiety behind his eyes. 'We need to save this life. For now, Cal, that's all we can think about.'

CHAPTER THREE

SHE was good.

There was no doubting Dr Gina Lopez's skill. Cal could only watch and wonder.

Not that there was much time for wondering. To operate on a child so young, to insert catheters into such a tiny heart, putting pressure on the faulty valve—that was something that in an adult heart would be tricky but in this pint-sized scrap of humanity seemed impossible.

Emily, the anaesthetist, was at the limits of her capability as well. This procedure should be done by an anaesthetist specialising in paediatrics, but Emily was all they had. She was sweating as she worked, as she monitored the tiny heartbeat, treading the fine line of not enough anaesthetic, or too much and straining this little body past more than it could bear.

Jill, the director of nursing and their most skilled Theatre nurse, was assisting Emily. She was sweating as well.

It was Cal who assisted Gina.

He watched her fingers every step of the way, trying to figure what she was doing, trying to anticipate so there was no delay between her need for a piece of equipment and the time she had it. He was organising, swabbing, waiting for the pauses in her finger movements to reach forward and clear the way for her. Holding things steady. Watching the monitor when she couldn't, guiding her with his voice, and holding catheters steady when she had to focus on the monitor herself.

Grace, their second nurse, was behind him, and she was anticipating as hard as he was.

There was so much need here. Something about this tiny wrinkled newborn had touched them all.

They needed him to live.

They willed him to live.

All that stood between him and death was Gina.

They were lucky that she was here, Cal thought grimly as he helped her painstakingly introduce her catheters from the groin, monitoring herself every inch of the way. No matter why she'd returned after all these years—she'd been in the right place at the right time and this baby could live because of it.

Maybe.

'He's bleeding too much,' she muttered into the stillness, motioning with her eyes to the catheter entry site. 'There has to be an underlying problem.'

'Haemophilia?' Cal asked, and she shook her head.

'I don't think so. It'd be worse. But it's not right. The cord bled too much and we're having trouble here. I want tests. A clotting profile, please, including full blood examination, bleeding time and factor eight levels. Fast.'

'What are we looking for?'

'I don't have time to think. You think. Something.'

He went back to sorting tubing, his mind moving into overdrive. Sifting the facts. She was right. The bleeding was far more severe than it should be. They were fighting to maintain blood pressure.

Why?

'Von Willebrand's?' he said cautiously.

Was he right? Von Willebrand's was a blood disorder that impeded clotting. Like haemophilia, it was genetically linked, passing from parents down to children. It usually wasn't as life-threatening as haemophilia but it did have to be treated. He watched as Gina frowned even more behind her mask. Her fingers were carefully manoeuvring, she was fully absorbed in what she was doing, but he could see her mind start to sort through the repercussions of his tentative diagnosis.

'You could be right,' she said at last. 'It fits.'

'I'll run tests straight away,' he said. 'There's not a lot more we can do about it now, though. And at least it takes away the risks of clotting.'

'Mmm.'

Silence. The tension was well nigh unbearable. She was measuring the pressures in the right ventricle and the pulmonary artery by placing the catheter tip in each area. It was a tricky procedure in an adult, but in a newborn…

'My face,' Gina muttered, and Jill saw her need and stepped forward to wipe sweat beads from above her eyes.

She was good, Cal thought grimly. Good enough?

The work went on. The child's tiny heart kept beating. Emily was fighting with everything she had. She had a paediatric anaesthetist on the line from the city, and she was working with a headset. Her soft voice asking questions was the only sound as they worked.

Cal had seen this done in adults, but he'd never seen the procedure in one so tiny. As a general surgeon he would never think of doing such a procedure himself. He couldn't, he acknowledged. Somewhere along the line Gina had acquired skills that could only make him wonder.

Gina was working out diameters now, her eyes moving from fingers to monitor, fingers to monitor, and he could almost see her brain doing the complex calculations as she worked out the next step forward.

She was brilliant. An amazing surgeon.

The mother of his son?

'Now the wire,' she said into the stillness, and the sound of her voice almost made him start.

Back to silence.

The balloon valvuloplasty catheter was threaded over the wire, painstakingly positioned so its centre was just at the valve. That was the hard part.

Now came the hardest.

Please…

'Let's try,' Gina said into a silence that was close to unbearable. 'I think…'

The balloon was inflated, showing on the monitor under fluoroscopy, with Gina watching that it remained centred all the time. The balloon had been manoeuvred right to the valve. Now it was stretching the valve, much as a shoe was stretched by a cobbler, hoping that once the stretching was done the valve would self-correct. The pressures would equalise.

If it didn't happen, then the build-up of pressure could mean instant heart failure—instant death.

This was no time for panic. The procedure called for infinite patience.

The balloon was inflated once. Twice. Three times the valve was stretched.

'Enough,' Gina said, and Cal heard exhaustion in her voice.

But she couldn't stop now. She had to check the pressures again. If the pressures weren't equalised the whole thing would have to be repeated, using balloons of different lengths and diameters, and this tiny heart was under so much strain anyway…

The catheters were reinserted, once more measuring the pressures in the right ventricle and the pulmonary artery.

Please.

The figures…

'Hey,' Jill said in a tiny tremulous voice that didn't sound the least bit like the efficient director of nursing they all knew—and, if truth be told, they often feared. 'We have lift-off. Isn't that right, Houston?'

'I… Maybe,' Gina said. She glanced up at her anaesthetist. 'What do you think?'

'I think maybe you've done it,' Emily said in a voice that was none too steady. 'Oh, Gina, that was fantastic.'

'Fantastic? It's a miracle,' Gina whispered. 'If we have indeed won. He's not out of the woods yet.'

He wasn't. They all knew that. To operate on such a tiny baby was asking for post-op complications. Indeed, there might well be complications already. He'd stopped breathing that afternoon. He'd had a birth in circumstances that were appalling. And now maybe he was facing a new threat. Von Willebrand's?

For him to pull through…

'He'll make it,' Cal said, and he wasn't sure why he knew or how he knew, it was just definite, absolute knowledge. 'I know he will. You've done it, Gina.'

'Thank God for that, then,' she whispered. 'I'm not as sure as you as to the outcome here, but he has every chance. Maybe…maybe for once in this country I've done something right.'

Three hundred miles away the girl lay beneath her bedcovers and shivered. It was hot out here—so hot—and for her family to afford air-conditioning was unthinkable. But despite the heat, she couldn't stop shivering.

Her baby…

Dead.

'Sweetheart?' It was her mother, knocking on her door for what must be the sixth time since they'd got home from the rodeo. 'Are you OK?'

She sounded worried. That was a laugh. When had her mother ever worried about her?

'Go away.'

'What's wrong?'

'I've got my period. I feel sick. Go away.'

Her mother hesitated and Megan could hear the fear in her voice. 'You're not well enough to feed the poddy calves, then?'

'No. Go away.'

'But your father…'

She roused herself—or she tried to—but the tiredness washing over her body was overwhelming.

'I know Dad's sick,' she whispered, loudly enough for her mother to hear through the battered farmhouse door. 'I know you've got too much to do to manage. But, Mum, I can't. I just can't. For tonight you'll just have to manage without me.'

When she'd done all she could do, Gina stepped away from the table. Her face said it all. Her eyes were drained, her expression slack with exhaustion. She'd called on every resource she had, and then some.

'Can I leave it to you now?' she asked, unsteadily into the stillness. 'I'll be outside. Call me on the PA if you need me. I won't go away. But I need…some air.'

'You deserve some air,' Emily said warmly. 'You even deserve something a bit stronger, like a stiff drink or a cigar. Off you go, Dr Lopez. Cal and I will take it from here. But thank God you were here.'

'Thank you,' Gina whispered, and with a last, uncertain glance down at the table she started to move away.

Then she paused. Her finger dropped for a fleeting moment to trace the tiny cheekbone, to just touch…

'Fight, little one,' she whispered. 'Fight.'

And then she was gone.

'That's one amazing doctor,' Emily said as she left, and Cal could only agree.

'Yeah.'

'Charles said you knew her five years back.' Em was still concentrating but she had room to cast a curious glance at her friend. 'He's saying she's your lady-rat.'

'Leave it, Em.' Dammit, he couldn't think of what else to say. And it was none of her business.

Since when did privacy considerations ever stop anyone in this place sticking their nose in anyone else's business? It certainly didn't stop Em now.

'Charles says there's a little boy.'

'Leave it, Emily,' Cal snapped again—harder—and Emily had the temerity to grin.

'Yes, sir.'

'Is he yours?' Grace asked from behind them, and Cal groaned.

'Look, this is my business.'

'Hey, we're your housemates,' Emily told him. 'And Mike says there's something really funny going on. He's laying odds on this being your son—but no one's taking bets until we've seen him. So tell us, Cal. Save us our betting money. Is it true?'

They were still working, but the atmosphere in the room had lightened by about a thousand per cent. Something about a tiny heartbeat that was steady and growing stronger by the minute was making even such a serious subject sound frivolous.

'You might as well tell us. You know we share all your dearest concerns,' Emily told him, and Grace choked.

'That's another way of saying we have a right to stick our nose into whatever we like.'

'I don't know how you do it, Cal.' For once Jill was also smiling, the nursing director's tight personality unbending a little in the face of this shared triumph. 'Having all your concerns shared. Ten medicos living in the same house…'

'Eight as of Tuesday,' Grace reminded her, and Emily winced.

'Thanks very much.'

'He was a creep, Em, and you know it,' Grace retorted. 'I refuse to concede that you can possibly mourn the guy.'

'I'll mourn anyone I like.'

'Why don't you have an affair with Cal?'

'Cal's got an affair,' Emily retorted. 'As of now.' She managed a smile. 'Actually, an affair and a bit. A bit about three feet high. So concentrate on Cal's love life. Leave mine alone.'

'OK,' Grace said obligingly. 'If you insist. And Cal's affair is fascinating. A woman and a son arriving out of nowhere, when we all thought he was a fusty old bachelor…'

'Thanks a lot,' Cal managed, and even Jill chuckled.

'But here he is, with a son…'

'Is he really your son?' Jill asked, wondering, and Cal groaned.

'Jill, at least you can keep out of what's not your business.'

'We love you, Cal,' Emily said solidly. 'Get used to it.'

'I don't think I ever will.'

'It's called living,' Em told him, and she turned from the monitor to look down at her little patient. 'Something this little man is about to do. Oh, well done, us. Now all we need to do is find you a mummy and a daddy.'

'And find out whether Cal's a daddy, too,' Grace said mischievously.

'Enough.' Jill had been jolted out of clinical efficiency but her flashes of humour never lasted long. There was levity in her operating Theatre and levity was to be squashed. 'Back to work.'

'Yes, ma'am,' they said in unison.

Where was Gina? All Cal wanted to do was to find her, and he couldn't.

There were myriad things to do before he was finished. Blood tests to order. Harry Blake to be contacted—the police sergeant who'd be in charge of trying to find the mother. A mass of paperwork that had to be done—now. 'Because this case will hit the national press unless I'm mistaken, and I want everything done right,' Charles had growled.

Charles himself wheeled into Theatre at the end and stared down at the little one in concern.

'Do we have any clue who the mother could be?'

'None at all,' Cal told him. 'We're sifting through obs and gynae records now, looking at who's pregnant in the area.'

'One of our tribal people? Maybe some kid who's got herself pregnant out of tribal boundaries?'

'Take a longer look, Charles. I'm guessing this baby's all white. Mum and Dad both.'

'Surely we have pregnancy records.'

'Unless it was someone who's itinerant. Someone who came for the day.'

They stared at the baby for a moment longer, searching for answers.

There were none.

'I guess we have to leave that to Harry,' Charles said reluctantly, spinning his chair in a one-eighty-degree turn and shrugging as he talked of handing things over to the police. 'I hate not knowing as much as you do. Harry's just rung in to say they're searching the area and I'll tell him to increase the manpower. To think there's a kid out there who's only hours from giving birth…'

'And she may be suffering from von Willebrand's disease,' Cal told him, outlining his concerns.

Charles's face stilled. 'So she's likely to be bleeding. She could be in huge trouble.

'Von Willebrand's could be inherited from the father. If indeed I'm right. It's only that the baby's bleeding too much, too fast. I'm only guessing the diagnosis here.'

'Then keep on guessing,' Charles said heavily, 'Guess as much as you can and as fast as you can. I want her found.'

'Right.' Cal hesitated. 'Do we move him down to Brisbane?'

'Not yet,' Charles said heavily. 'I'm calling in Hamish from leave. If the mother's found I want this little one right here, where she has the best chance of bonding with him—or making any decision she needs to make. It's a risk, but if I can persuade Gina to stay then it's a risk I'm prepared to take.'

Cal nodded. Hamish, Crocodile Creek's paediatrician, was out game fishing but it should be possible to call him back. If this base had both a paediatrician and a cardiologist, then it was reasonable to leave this little one here. Good, even.

But would Gina stay?'

'Charles, I also need to find Gina.'

'Sure you do, Charles agreed. 'Get these tests organised, talk to Harry and then go find her. She's over at the house, out on the veranda.'

Of course. Charles knew where everyone was, all the time.

'I'll go, then.'

'You do that.'

She was alone.

Cal walked out the back door of the doctors' residence and Gina was sitting on the back step, staring out over the sea.

The old hospital used now as doctors' quarters and the new state-of-the-art Remote Rescue base were built on a bluff overlooking Crocodile Cove—a wide, sandy beach with gentle waves washing in and out of the gently sloping shallows. In the foreground lay the Agnes Wetherby Memorial Garden. The garden was fantastic—a mass of tropical plants such as the delicately perfumed orchids, creamy, heady frangipani, crotons with their vividly coloured leaves, and more. A wide natural rockpool lay off centre surrounded by giant ferns, and from the veranda Cal could hear the soft croak of tree frogs enjoying its lush dampness.

Beyond the garden was the rock-strewn slope leading down to the beach—thick grassland dotted with moonflowers, their fat leaves looking just like butterfly wings. The sunlight glinted through the garden, the soft wind shifting the dappled shade. It was beautiful.

Gina was beautiful.

He'd thought that the first time he'd seen her, and nothing had changed. Not a thing.

She wasn't dressed to attract. She never had. Now, in faded jeans, a stained T-shirt that was truly horrible, battered sneakers…

Yep, she was beautiful.

He walked over, sat down beside her and stared out over the sea, as if trying to see what she was seeing. This was a beautiful setting.

'Sorry.' She winced and moved sideways. 'It's been too big a day. The rodeo. The baby. Surgery. I…I need to find a shower.'

'You definitely need to find a shower,' he told her. 'But it was blood gained in a battle worth fighting. Well done.'

'Thanks.'

They stared some more at the sea. Trying to figure out where to start. Where was he supposed to start? Surely it was up to her. To do this to him…

She kept her silence. Seemingly it was up to him.

'Would you like to tell me,' he said finally into the stillness, 'just what is going on?'

'We may just have saved a baby.'

'Gina…'

'Sorry.'

'Is CJ…mine?'

She glanced at him then—and then looked away as if she couldn't bear to see him. Which was maybe exactly how he'd expect her to feel.

'Yes,' she whispered.

More silence.

'Hell,' he said at last, and she nodded as if that was no more than she'd expected.

'I guess it is.'

There was anger building now, an anger so overwhelming it was all he could do to stay still, not to stand up and crash his fist into the veranda pole, not to yell...

Yelling would achieve nothing. He had to stay calm.

'So.' He stared out to sea some more, not looking at her, not wanting to look at her. 'So I got used.'

'I— What do you mean?'

'You and your husband used me as a sperm donor.'

'Cal, it wasn't like that.' She turned to him, her face puckering in distress. 'It wasn't. I need to tell you...'

'That's what it seems like to me,' he said savagely. 'You come out here, you say you love me, you con me into taking you to bed—'

Her breath drew in, shocked, stunned. 'Cal, I never did. I wouldn't.'

'And then you leave. You just leave.' His anger was clearly apparent in his voice and there was no way he could disguise it. 'You just disappear.'

'I wrote.'

'Yeah, and told me that your husband—who I'd thought was no longer in the picture—needed you and you were going back to him. You wouldn't answer questions. Nothing. And when I tried to phone you—when I eventually found you through your hospital—you wouldn't talk to me.'

'I couldn't answer questions,' she told him. 'I just couldn't.' Her voice trailed away. 'I couldn't bear to.'

'You couldn't bear to tell me you'd used me?'

'Please, don't, Cal,' she whispered. 'It wasn't like that. You know it wasn't. What we had was amazing.'

'Yeah, it was, wasn't it?' he said heavily into the stillness. 'Mind-blowing. It was sex. Was that all it was? Great sex, Gina, followed by pregnancy, and then back to your husband so you can play happy families?'

'You're not going to let me explain?'

'Mom?' The voice came from behind them. CJ. The little boy stood in the doorway behind the screen door, looking from his mother to Cal and back again. 'Mrs Grubb said you've finished saving the baby. Have you?'

'Yes, we have, CJ,' she told him, visibly gathering her wits. As he came through the door she held out a hand to tug him close. Then she gestured to Cal, took a deep breath and performed introductions. 'CJ, this is Cal. CJ, this is the very special Australian friend I've been telling you for about all these years. The man I hoped we'd get to visit while we were over here.'

'The man with my name?' CJ asked, and Gina nodded.

'That's right.'

'Hi.' CJ put out his hand, man to man. 'I'm Callum James Michelton. I'm very pleased to meet you.'

Callum James.

CJ.

Cal swallowed. His hand was still being gripped so he shook the child's hand with due solemnity and then released it.

'My mom says you're the best doctor in the world,' CJ told him. 'And she says you can juggle better than anyone she knows.'

It was hard, getting his voice to work. Cal swallowed again and tried harder. 'Your mom told you that?'

'She told me lots about you. She says you're terrific.' CJ eyed Cal cautiously, as if he was prepared to give his mother the benefit of the doubt for a while but Cal just might have to prove himself. 'You've got the same colour hair as I have.'

'Is it the same colour as your dad's?' Stupid question.

Stupid, stupid question, and he felt Gina flinch, but he'd asked it and now he had to wait for an answer.

'My dad's dead,' CJ told him. 'He was in a wheelchair and he had black hair and a big scar down the side of his face.' He sighed. 'My dad watched TV with me and he read me stories but then he got so sick that he died. I miss him a lot and a lot.'

'I... I see.'

He didn't see. There were so many unanswered questions.

'Are we talking about Paul here?' he asked—feeling his way—and Gina nodded.

'That's right. Paul.'

'So when you said your marriage was over...'

'CJ, do you think you could bring me out a glass of water?' Gina asked, and there was a note of desperation in her voice. 'Would Mrs Grubb give you one for me?'

'Sure,' CJ told her. 'We've made choc-chip cookies with twice the number of choc chips in the recipe 'cos Mrs Grubb let me tip and I spilt them. They're warm.' He turned to Cal. 'Would you like one, sir?'

'Yes, please,' Cal managed. 'Um...call me Cal.'

'Yes, sir. I mean Cal. I'll be an aeroplane. I haven't been an aeroplane all day.' He was off, zooming along the veranda, arms outstretched.

'CJ,' his mother called, and he stopped in mid-flight.

'Yeah?'

'This is a hospital and some sick patients might be going to sleep. Do you think you could be a silent glider instead of an aeroplane?'

'Sure, I can.' CJ put his lips firmly together. 'Shh,' he ordered himself, 'If you make one loud noise up here, you'll scare the eagles.'

And off he glided, kitchenwards.

Cal was left staring after him.

'Great kid,' he said at last—cautiously—and Gina nodded.

'Yeah. He takes after his daddy.'

'Paul…'

'You.'

He sighed. The anger had gone now. All that was left was an ineffable weariness. A knowledge that somehow he'd been used and somehow this child had been born and there'd been four years of a child growing in his image that he'd known nothing about.

'Tell me,' he said.

She shrugged. 'In a nutshell?'

'Take your time.' His voice was heavy. He hardly wanted to know himself. If she didn't want to tell him…

But it seemed she did.

'Some of it you know,' she said, her voice distant now, as if repeating a learned-by-heart story. 'I told you the bare facts when we first met. That I'd been married and that I was separated.'

'But—'

'Just let me tell it, Cal,' she whispered, and he stared at her for a long minute, and then nodded.

'I'm listening.'

'Big of you.'

'Gina…'

'I married Paul when I was eighteen,' she told him, and there was a blankness about her voice now that hadn't been there before. 'He was the boy next door, the kid I'd grown up with. We decided to marry when we were twelve. We went through med school together, we were best of friends—and then suddenly he just seemed to fall apart. There'd been huge pressure on him from his parents to become a doctor. To marry. To be successful in their eyes. Maybe I was stupid for not seeing how much pressure he was under.'

'You weren't sympathetic toward him when you were here,' he said, and she nodded.

'No. I was young and I was hurt. We'd made it as doctors, we had the world at our feet and suddenly he didn't want any part of our life together. He wanted to find himself, he said, and off he went. And to be honest it wasn't until I decided to come here…until I met you…that I realised that he was right. We'd been kids, playing at being grown-ups. We'd married for the wrong reasons.'

'So?' He wasn't going to get sucked into the emotional bit here, he thought. He couldn't afford to.

'So then I fell for you,' she said softly. 'And I got pregnant.'

He closed his eyes, trying to think back to all that time ago. But it didn't make sense. He'd never been stupid. He of all people knew the risks. 'How can you have got pregnant? We took precautions.'

'Are you saying I'm lying?' Anger flashed out then, bordering on fury. 'Do you think I planned the pregnancy?'

'I don't know what to think.'

'Well, think what you like,' she snapped. 'But I didn't plan it. I was on the Pill. I knew how much you didn't want children, and I was hardly in a position to want them either. So we were careful. But I guess there's truth in the saying that the only sure contraceptive is two brick walls with air space between. Whatever we used didn't work. Anyway, I couldn't believe it. I discovered I was pregnant when you were upcountry on a medical evacuation flight. You were gone. I was down in Townsville, staring at a positive pregnancy test. Thinking I couldn't tell you. I couldn't.'

His eyes opened at that and he met her look head on. Challenging. 'Why the hell not?'

'What would you have said?' she whispered. 'Be honest, Cal. How would you have reacted?'

'How do I know?'

'Well, I know,' she said drearily. 'You'd said it over and over to me. You didn't want family. Your family life was the pits. You never wanted commitment. Sure, what we had was special and we both knew it, but it wasn't enough to make you want marriage. Or children. The thought appalled you. You said it over and over. It was like a warning. Love me despite it—and I did. I was willing to accept you on your terms. But then I fell pregnant. I sat there staring at the test strip and I thought, I can't get rid of this baby. Maybe I did my growing up right there. I wanted this baby. I wanted our baby.'

He shook his head, bewildered. 'Gina, if I'd known—'

'You might even have done the honourable thing,' she said heavily. 'I knew that. But honour wasn't what I wanted from you, Cal, and you were capable of offering nothing more.'

'I might have—'

'No.' She shook her head. 'I knew your background, you see, though I heard much of it from others. Not from you.'

'My background has nothing to do with this.'

'It has everything, Cal,' she said heavily. 'If I don't accept it, at least I can understand. Your mother walked out on you when you were still a kid yourself, trapping you into caring for your two little sisters. Your father was a drunk. You had to leave school to support everyone and then, just as your sisters started being independent, your mother reappeared and offered your sisters a home in the States with her new man. But not you. After all you'd done, they left you without a backward glance. Your dad died and you had to regroup and work your butt off to get yourself through medical school. You learned in the hardest way to be independent. Do you think I was going to trap you again?'

'Hell…'

'It was hell,' she whispered. 'For both of us. For different reasons.'

'So you just ran.'

'Strangely, I didn't,' she told him, and her chin jutted, just a little. Finding her feet again. This part of the story was easier. 'While I was trying to sort some sense out of the mess the phone rang and it was Paul's mother. It was…as if it was meant. It was horrible but it was real. She rang to tell me that Paul had been injured—dreadfully injured—in a motorbike accident in Kathmandu. She was distraught. She couldn't go herself. Could I go? she asked. She pleaded. There was no one else. I had medical training and that was what Paul desperately needed. Family and western medicine. So…' She paused and stared blankly out over the sea. 'So I just went.'

He stared at her, still disbelieving. 'Without waiting for me to get back?'

'You were gone for two days. Paul's mother thought he was dying. I had to move fast. As it was, I only just got there in time. I found him in a tiny village outside the capital and he was dreadfully injured. From then on the drama of the situation just took over. Getting him stabilised. He'd smashed his spine, and the convolutions to evacuate him back to the States took weeks. And then…by the time I'd caught my breath, somehow I was three months pregnant and I was back to being Paul's wife again.'

'That was what your note said,' he said heavily, remembering. 'That Paul had been injured and you were still his wife and you were staying with him. That your marriage had resumed.'

'I didn't lie.'

'No,' he said. 'I guess you didn't.'

There was a long silence then. There wasn't tension here. It was as if the world had somehow paused and was regrouping.

But finally the questions started again.

'How badly was Paul hurt?'

That was easy. 'Break at C1/2. Complete quadriplegia. No function below the neck and barely speech,' she told him. 'No unaided respiration. The guy he crashed into had basic medical training so they were able to establish an air supply. Maybe that was a good thing. Sometimes I don't know. But

Paul had almost five years of life before the infections became too frequent and his body shut down.'

'You don't think,' Cal said carefully into the stillness, 'that it might have been fair to tell me this?'

'What? That I still loved you but I'd decided I needed to stay with Paul? How could I tell you that? It wasn't even fair. If I had to stay with Paul, what was the use of telling you I loved you? Besides,' she said softly into the stillness, 'you knew that I loved you. I'd told you that over and over. But you'd never said it back to me. Not once, Cal. Not ever.'

'I…' He paused and she shrugged, moving on.

'It doesn't matter,' she told him. 'Not now. And it couldn't matter then. Cal, Paul had no one except his elderly mother who was incapacitated herself. He needed me so much. And when CJ was born…'

'Yeah, that's what I can't understand,' he snapped. 'How he accepted another man's son.'

'CJ gave him pleasure,' she told him. 'Huge pleasure. You know, when Paul learned I was pregnant he didn't even ask who the father was. I said I'd had a love affair that hadn't worked out and he didn't want to know more. But the pregnancy itself made him…joyful. It was as if something good had come from the mess he'd created. For the few years left of his life, CJ was the centre of Paul's life. And Paul had been my friend for ever. I couldn't take that away from him.'

'You took it away from me.'

Her eyes flashed at that. 'You didn't want it,' she said, steadily now, as if she was on ground she was sure of. 'When I found out that I was pregnant I was appalled. I knew you didn't want a child. I knew you didn't want a family. Am I right, Cal?'

Was she right?

He stared at her and he couldn't answer.

Of course he didn't want kids. He never had. Damn, with

his family, how could he? Kids were a disaster. Commitment was a disaster.

'Maybe,' he said—grudgingly—and she winced and hauled herself to her feet.

'There you go, then. So I kept my son where at least some-one wanted him. Paul was his daddy, and Paul loved him more than life itself.'

'And you,' he said softly. 'Did you love Paul?'

'Don't be stupid, Cal,' she said heavily. 'To ask a question like that… Don't be so daft.'

He stared at her, wondering where to go from here. Where…

'Here are the cookies! I have cookies.' There was a trium-phant stage whisper from behind them. The glider was flying cautiously back through the screen door, bearing two glasses of water and four choc-chip cookies, all balanced precariously on a plastic tray.

'Bruce is in the kitchen,' CJ told them in satisfaction, hand-ing over his burden with care. 'He says he's really pleased to see us and can he take us out to dinner?'

'Bruce?' He was almost grateful for the interruption, Cal decided. For something else to focus on. Emotions were threatening to overwhelm him.

'It'll be Bruce Hammond,' Gina told him. 'We met Bruce while we were staying here. He took us on a crocodile hunt but we didn't find any.'

'We did,' CJ retorted. 'It was only the grown-ups who said it was a log.'

'You were staying here?' Cal asked, dazed. How could they have been staying here? This wasn't making sense.

'We've been staying at the Athina Hotel for the last three days,' she told him. 'Just near here. When Paul died, I thought…well, I thought that maybe you had the right to know about CJ. So we came to see you. But on the night we arrived you were out here on the veranda with—Emily, isn't it? I thought…' Her voice trailed off. 'It just seemed like such an imposition after all these years.'

'It *is* an imposition,' he muttered, and his voice was almost savage.

She nodded, as if she'd expected nothing less. 'So I decided to go again.'

'Without seeing me?'

'You didn't want this, Cal,' she told him, lifting her chin again and meeting his look full on. 'I always knew what you thought of family. Anyway, Bruce was nice to us. He wanted us to go out with him again and try to find more crocodiles, but I said we were leaving town. I guess he's heard we're back.' She took a deep breath, moving on, and glanced at her watch. 'I guess we could go out for a quick dinner with Bruce.'

'There's dinner here,' Cal growled. 'And you might be needed for the baby.'

'I won't go far,' she said, steadily, as if she was fighting to keep control on her temper. 'I imagine there's a cellphone I can borrow.'

'Bruce says he knows where crocodiles really love to be,' CJ told her, and she managed a smile.

'No crocodiles tonight, CJ. I think we've had enough adventure. But Bruce will tell you about them.' She turned again to Cal. 'Cal, I'm sorry to land this on you. I never meant to. I never wanted… But, anyway, now you know. I won't be an imposition. I won't make any demands. We'll stay until the baby doesn't need us any more. We certainly won't interfere with what's between you and Emily, and then we'll go.'

She hesitated, and then, as if determined to do something that she wasn't sure would be welcomed, she suddenly leaned forward. She kissed him lightly, a feather kiss, fleetingly on the lips, and then she backed off. Fast.

'I've owed you that for a long time,' she whispered. 'Regardless of what's been between us in the past. This is

what I need to say. Thank you for my son, Cal. CJ's been the
only thing that's stood between me and madness for the past
few years. For both Paul and me. I love CJ so much and Paul
did, too. I hope you've found that loving with Emily. Believe
me, I'm not here to interfere. If you've found your true
home… I won't put that in jeopardy for anything.'

And before he could reply—before he could even think
about replying—she'd risen and taken CJ's hand, and turned
and walked inside.

Leaving him staring after her. With two glasses of water
and four truly excellent choc-chip cookies.

By the time Cal left the veranda it was all over the hospital.
Cal had a son. Cal's son and Cal's ex-girlfriend had gone out
to dinner with the local crocodile hunter. Everyone wanted to
know more.

Cal tried for a little privacy at dinner by glowering at everyone who asked questions—but that created even more questions.

At least Gina wasn't there. She'd spent time with Emily,
stabilising the baby. Then she and CJ had disappeared with
Bruce, and watching them go had made Cal glower even
more. Em had found her a cellphone. Bruce promised to have
her back here in minutes if was needed.

But he still glowered. His friends prodded and laughed
and then finally they backed off, realising that information
wasn't going to be forthcoming. But he knew the questions
were still there.

He had unanswered questions himself.

After dinner he headed back to the veranda, looking for
some peace. He had medico-legal paperwork to do but it held
no attraction. It was eight o'clock and then eight-thirty. They
should be back, he thought, and tried not to look up every time
a car approached.

Finally he gave up car-watching and headed next door to

the hospital. Surely there was something that needed doing. Something that could distract him. Where was work when you needed it most? These last few days had been crazy.

Now there was nothing. Even the baby didn't need him. They'd decided to keep a doctor within arm's reach and Em was taking first shift.

But still he visited the nursery. This little one was so small. Things could go either way here, Cal thought, jolted out of his preoccupation with the personal by the sight of their tiny patient. The baby was hooked to tubes everywhere. He was the fragile centre of a huge spiderweb of technology and all of it might not be enough to save him.

They'd discussed again the idea of sending for the neonatal evacuation team to take him to a specialist facility, but Em wasn't happy with the idea. Gina had concurred and the paediatrician in Brisbane had agreed. There was nothing a specialist facility could do that wasn't being done here, and the flight itself would be a risk.

As Cal entered the nursery Em looked up from checking the oxygen level and managed a faint smile.

'Hi.'

'Hi, yourself. How's he doing?'

'Holding on. It's all we can hope for. We're calling him Lucky, because he's lucky to be alive.' She hesitated. 'And maybe because he needs still more luck.'

Cal grimaced. He reached in to touch the soft skin of the baby's tiny face and felt his gut twist in sympathy for this fragile little life.

'You live, Lucky,' he told him gruffly.

He had to.

'Is there any news of the mother?' Em asked.

'There's a search party scouring the bushland around the rodeo grounds, but there's nothing. The current thinking is that whoever it was left with the crowd.'

She flicked a glance up at him. 'And left her son.'

'She probably thought he was dead. He was so flat… He may well have appeared dead to someone who had no med training. Someone who was distressed and desperately ill herself.'

She nodded bleakly and then turned her attention back to the baby. 'He almost was dead,' she whispered. 'He came so close. Oh, Lucky. If not for Gina. And now… Another little boy.'

'Em…' He knew where she was going. The way he said her name was a growl, meant to deflect her, but it didn't work.

'Did you know you had a child?'

'No. Em, I—'

'I can't believe you have a son,' she told him, and Cal hesitated. And then he shrugged. This was Emily. His friend. He knew from long experience it was no use to try and deflect her, so why not vent a little spleen? He surely had spleen to be vented.

'If you can't believe it, imagine how I feel!' he demanded, but he didn't get the reaction he wanted. He expected indignation on his behalf—that was what he wanted. Even sympathy. Instead, Emily had the temerity to smile.

'Yep, I can see how it might leave you flabbergasted. A child out of left field. Does she want child support?'

'No!'

'Then why has she come?'

'She just thought I had the right to know.'

'After all these years? Why not sooner?'

'She's been married,' Cal told her. 'She was married when I knew her. She got pregnant and went back to her husband.'

'Whew.' Em whistled, then lifted the drug sheet beside the crib and studied it. Giving him a bit of personal space. 'That's heavy stuff,' she commented. 'Did you know she was married?'

'Yes, but I thought it was over.'

'But it wasn't.'

'Apparently not.'

'So what's happened now to make things different? Marriage break up?'

'Her husband's dead.'

'Dead?'

'Quadriplegia. Complications.'

She winced. 'Oh, Cal, that's really tough.'

Tough? He didn't want to think about tough, he thought bitterly. He didn't want to think about what Gina must have gone through over the last few years.

He didn't want to think about Gina.

'Did she use you to get pregnant?' Em asked, adjusting the drip stand so she could get a clearer view of the baby's tiny face. 'Because her husband was a quad?'

'No!' It was his turn to wince. OK, that was what *he'd* thought initially, but somehow…that someone else should think that of Gina was unbearable. 'He was injured just after she discovered she was pregnant.'

'Ouch.' She flicked another glance up at him and then looked away. 'So that's why the loyalty. That's why she went back to him.'

'Em, could we leave this?'

She looked at him steadily then, her intelligent eyes turning thoughtful. 'Maybe we can and maybe we can't. So now her husband's dead and she comes back—'

'Em…'

'It puts a different complexion on things,' she said, unperturbed. 'I always wondered how the guy would feel in such a situation. To be unexpectedly a full-fledged dad. And for Gina to front you now… It'd be so hard. But maybe she's right.' She cocked her head to one side, considering. 'I wonder. Even if you'd done this via a sperm bank, maybe there's a moral obligation to tell you that your sperm's successful? That's there's a kid out there in your image?'

'He wasn't the result of any sperm bank. Em, we need to write up these notes.'

'Yeah, Charles told me it was a really hot affair.' Em grinned, refusing to be deflected. 'Not a sperm bank at all. This is the one that gossip says broke your heart. Charles said she really cracked your armour and it's the only time in your life it's ever been cracked. Well, now.'

'Em…'

'Hey, but she's here and you don't have an excuse to be heartbroken any more.' Em even looked cheerful. 'You've been using the excuse that you loved and lost for five long years. You've been using it to keep the world and commitment at bay. Now you can take up where you left off. And she's not married. You know, I'll bet that was one of the things that attracted you to her in the first place. I can see letting yourself fall for a divorcée with as jaded a view of commitment as you have. But now… I wonder what you'll decide to do now?'

'What the—?'

'She's been an excuse, hasn't she, Cal?' Em said softly, boring right to the heart of the matter. There was something about this time, this place—the dim light of the nursery with only this one tiny baby between them—that made a conversation like this seem possible. Or less impossible. 'All these years, you've been telling yourself that you haven't got involved with anyone because Gina broke your heart. You've been letting us all think you still love Gina.'

'I don't,' he snapped. But… Did he?

'Then why haven't you gone out with other women?'

'I have. Look, can we leave this?'

'Of course,' she agreed. 'But as for going out with other women… Sure you do, until they get the first idea that they might be able to expect some emotional return. Then you drop them like hot coals. And if you think the rest of the staff in the house will leave it, you're very much mistaken. Are you taking over here at nine?'

'Nine till twelve. Yes.'

'There you go, then.' She turned back to her little patient. 'We'll just have to keep you alive until then, won't we, Lucky?' Her face softened. 'And then it's Dr Cal's turn to keep you alive. Or Dr Gina's, or whoever else is on duty. But we will keep you alive.'

The intensity of her voice shocked him.

'Of course we will,' he told her, and she looked up and met his eyes. Her own eyes welled with tears.

'There's a mother out there who doesn't have a son,' she whispered. 'It's our job to keep our Lucky safe until we find her. But isn't it strange that on this day, when we've found this unknown baby, you've found your own son?' She smiled at him, a wavering smile that said as much about her own fragile emotional state as it did about her uncertainty over the little boy's fate. 'Go on, now, Cal. I have a job to do. And maybe you do, too. See if you can find CJ before you come back on duty. You have years of catching up to do.'

CHAPTER FOUR

THE house was still when Cal returned. Unusually still. Everyone must be out, he decided. Or busy.

Half their luck.

He grabbed a beer but then replaced it. With regret. He could really use a beer, but if he was to go back on duty at nine he had to leave it.

Why was the kitchen empty? And the lounge? Where was everyone? This house was always full of people. He needed people.

He needed people now.

The door swung wide and he turned, but it wasn't the people he wanted. Or maybe it was.

'Hi.' It was Gina. And CJ. His son.

They'd been laughing, he thought. CJ was still smiling broadly and there was a trace of a smile fading from Gina's face. Gina had showered and changed since he'd last seen her. Apparently her luggage was on the coach to Cairns, but someone had lent her jeans and a soft blue and white gingham blouse. She'd brushed her dark curls until they shone and she looked…she looked…

'Did you have a good evening?' he managed, but then he had to think for a minute to figure out what his words meant. Everything seemed disoriented.

70

Luckily CJ noticed nothing strange. He was more than prepared to chat. 'Bruce took us to Athina's for dinner 'cos he says Mrs Poulos makes the best food in town,' he told him. 'And tomorrow he says he'll take us crocodile hunting again.'

'I'm not sure whether we can go,' Gina told him.

'But we have to go. And he gave me this hat.' This was obviously the highlight of the evening. The little boy was wearing a vast, battered Akubra Cal would have recognised from a mile away.

'Bruce gave you his hat?' Here was another astonishment. Cal knew Bruce well, and he knew the croc hunter lived in this hat.

But apparently no longer.

'He says it's time he got a new one,' CJ said proudly, lifting it off his head to poke his finger through a hole, centre-front. 'I asked him if this was from a bullet and he said it might have been.'

'Bedtime, CJ.' Gina was steering CJ firmly toward the door. CJ balked, planting his feet. Bracing himself.

'Can Cal read me a story?'

'Cal's busy.'

'He doesn't look busy.'

'CJ…'

'I'll read him a story.'

'You—'

'Have you told CJ anything about me?' He was angry, he decided, sorting through the myriad emotions he was experiencing and choosing the one in the forefront. He hadn't met this kid until now, and CJ—*his* son—was wearing another man's hat.

'I've told CJ that you've been a friend of mine for a long time.' Gina's voice was carefully neutral. 'I guess…if you do want to read to him then it's fine.'

'I do want.'

'Then I'll help him brush his teeth and put on his pjs. Jill's found us some gear to keep us going until I can retrieve my luggage. So… His bedroom in five minutes?'

'Fine.'

Why had he done that? This was a crazy situation. He didn't want to get involved.

He *was* involved.

CJ had beamed up at him from underneath Bruce's hat and…

And he was involved right up to his neck.

It was Gina's turn to sit alone on the veranda.

The big French windows leading to her son's bedroom were wide open. She could hear everything that was going on inside. So she sat, staring out at the moonlit sea, listening to Cal's deep voice reading her son a story.

This was CJ's favourite book, carried everywhere in his backpack, and she must have read it to him a thousand times. Paul had read it to him even more.

Now his father was reading it to him.

She blinked. Hard.

No tears. No tears!

This is an unsentimental journey, she told herself fiercely, staring into the deepening darkness. Just come, introduce the two of them and get out of here.

So why did you tell him you'd loved him, she asked herself, sifting through the conversation she'd had with the man she was listening to.

She hadn't meant to admit that. But telling him about CJ…there hadn't seemed any way to explain her little son's existence without acknowledging love. CJ had been conceived in love and she was proud of it. The fact that Cal would never acknowledge it—that he'd admitted that the pregnancy would have seemed a disaster to him—had the potential to hurt.

It hurt now.

'The pirate's little boat started creeping out of the harbour. Creep, creep, creep.'

It was too much. Cal reading to her son. Cal reading to *his* son.

This was dangerous territory. Maybe she should leave in the morning. Fast.

The baby wasn't stable. She'd put her hand up as a cardiac expert. If she had to go in again, put more pressure on the valve…

He was too little for her to contemplate further surgery, she thought. Far, far too frail.

So what was she doing, staying here?

The baby needed her.

Right.

'"Where's my boat?" roared the pirate, and out to sea the little boat chuckled.'

Where's my plane? Gina thought. Where's my way home?

Where was home itself? She was no longer sure. She sat and tried to think about the beauty of the night, tried to think about something other than Cal—but how could she?

'Gina?' It was a yell from the far end of the path. She rose, welcoming the distraction—any distraction—and Charles was spinning down the garden path, his wheelchair moving at speed.

'Is Cal there?'

'He's inside. I'll get him.'

'I need you both.' Charles's voice was clipped and urgent. 'His damn phone's ringing out. What the hell is he thinking of, turning it off? I need him. You, too, Gina. If you'll help.'

Her heart stilled. 'The baby?'

'The baby's OK.'

That was good news. That was great news. For a moment she'd stopped breathing. But Charles was still speaking with urgency. It seemed one drama had been overtaken by another.

'Em will extend her watch and I'll take over if needed,' Charles was saying. 'But there's been a car crash.'

From through the open windows Cal had heard the medical director's voice. The pirate story had reached its conclusion. Now he appeared behind her. 'Where?' he snapped.

'Out past the O'Flattery place. The chopper's out on a call already, but it's only ten or so miles, so you can go by car. By the sound of it, kids have been drag racing. Two cars have hit head on. Deaths and multiple casualties. I've sent one car already. You'll take the second road ambulance and I'll send anyone else as they become available. Gina, it's either you or Em who has to go, and Em's concerned at Lucky's intravenous drip packing up. She's saying she has a better chance of re-establishing a line than you, and that's the biggest risk at the moment. She'll stay close and we'll set up the Theatres in readiness for what's coming. Right?'

'Right,' Gina said, dazed. 'But CJ?'

Charles was there before her. He wasn't the medical director of this place for nothing. Fast planning was what he did. 'I've asked Mrs Grubb to come across and look after the littlie,' he told her. 'If that's OK, then that leaves you free.'

'Who else is available?' Cal asked.

'Mike and Christina have taken the chopper out to pull a suspected heart case off a prawn trawler,' Charles snapped. 'It's probably a false alarm but we have to check. That's where the chopper is. Hell, Cal, weren't you listening at dinner?'

'Maybe I wasn't.'

But Charles wasn't listening now. He was focussing on Gina.

'I know we have no right to ask more of you than you've done for us already,' he told her. 'But we're desperately understaffed and we need you. Can I ask you to help?'

There was only one answer to that. 'Of course I'll help.' She was already moving toward CJ's bedroom door. 'I'll explain what's happening to CJ and come straight away.'

'He won't mind?'

'He's learned not to mind,' she said, and if her voice was bleak, who could blame her?

The ride south was at a speed which would normally have made Gina's hair curl all by itself.

Cal was driving. The first ambulance had left the moment the call had come through, the two available paramedics leaving Cal and Gina to follow. So now they followed. The siren screamed, Cal rode the corners like a racing driver and Gina gripped her seat and held on for dear life.

'Um…I have a son,' she said over the sound of the siren.

'I'm taking no risks.'

He wasn't. He was an excellent driver. He had to be. Training for remote medicine meant everyone had to be multi-skilled, and the longer you stayed in the job the better you got. Cal was fantastic.

Just at the job, she told herself fiercely. Just at the job.

Charles's voice crackled from the radio. 'Cal? Gina?' Cal nodded to the receiver.

'Press the button to speak.'

She knew what to do. She'd worked with Remote Rescue before and she'd loved it. If she was to stay here there was so much she could do, she thought, and then gave herself a fast mental slap. She wasn't staying here. Why would she?

'Charles?' Back to medicine.

'The first ambulance has reached the crash site,' Charles told her, and by the tone of his voice she knew the situation was appalling. 'Two dead, seven injured, some still trapped in the wreck, and the injuries sound major. We're calling in everyone we can, but essentially you're the only two doctors available.'

'OK.' She glanced across at Cal and saw his face setting in lines of grim determination. They both knew what lay ahead.

'One of the local farmers will stay with the bodies until we can get them brought in. We'll send the chopper out as soon as we can but meanwhile use the ambulances for casualties. Let me know if I need an evacuation team from Brisbane.'

'Will do.' Any patient with trauma requiring complex intervention—such as major burns—would need to go straight to a city hospital, Gina knew. 'But you have great Theatre facilities.'

'By the sound of the injuries they may not be enough. And Cal's our only surgeon. You'll help if needed?'

'Of course.'

'Good luck, then.'

'Thanks, Charles,' she said, and replaced the receiver with a sinking heart. She glanced across at Cal again but she didn't say anything and neither did he.

He tried so hard not to care, she thought, but it didn't work. His armour was eggshell thin.

They went round a corner and she thought about where she'd left her stomach for a bit. Then they straightened and she thought about Charles. She needed some sort of diversion. Anything.

'Charles must hate that he can't come on calls like this,' she tried.

'Yeah.' Cal was concentrating fiercely on the road but it had straightened now. They were out of town, heading into flat hinterland.

'Tell me about him.' Anything to get rid of this tension, she thought, and Cal flashed her a sideways glance. He understood exactly she was doing, she realised. Maybe he even agreed with her.

'Charles is a great doctor,' he told her. 'The best. Charles's family—the Wetherbys—own a station near where you were today. Wetherby Downs. They endowed the hospital. Charles was injured when he was about eighteen—his best mate's gun went off when they were pig-shooting. Charles went to the city, learned to be a doctor and has come back and put everything he knows into this place. He's built up the best rural medical centre in Australia. The flying doctor base, the helicopter rescue service, the hospital—he runs it all and he has a mind like a steel trap.'

He hesitated for moment and Gina thought he might stop—but then his voice continued. He was staring out into the night, staring out at the road, and Gina knew he was seeing far more than the dusty track ahead.

'But I suspect on a night like tonight, Charles would change that all if he had a body that'd take him into the heart of the action,' he said slowly, reflectively. 'To be stuck back at base, waiting…'

'At least he can do something. To be injured like that, but to still go on and do something you're proud of…'

'Paul couldn't?' He asked the question gently, as if unsure that he had the right to ask, and it was her turn to stare ahead.

'The only good thing that Paul could do for the last few years was to raise CJ,' she said at last. 'Be with CJ. I kept working to support us all, but Paul was never lonely. We paid a nurse to stay during the day—but the nurse looked after Paul *and* CJ. If you know how much that helped…' She hesitated. 'Cal, that's why I'm here. It's most of the reason I've come. To tell you how grateful we both are.'

There was a moment's silence—and then a blaze of anger. She could feel it before she heard it. 'So even your husband was grateful to me. How's that supposed to make me feel?'

'I don't have a clue,' she told him honestly. 'I'm in uncharted territory. I don't even know whether I'm doing the right thing—admitting to you that CJ exists.'

'How can you question that? You should have told me five years ago.'

'You didn't want him.'

'No, but now he exists…'

She felt a tiny flare of panic. 'But now he exists, what?'

'He's my son.'

'No more than if you were a sperm donor.'

'You know it was far, far more than that.'

'Yes.' She nodded and only she knew that her hands were clenching on her lap. Her fingernails were digging into her palms and they hurt. 'Of course I know that.'

Silence. Then. 'You're planning on staying for how long?'

'Until tomorrow.'

'You need to stay longer.'

'Cal, let's not…'

'Let's not what?'

'There's no obligation on your part to care for him.'

'He looks like me.' It was a flat, inflexionless statement of fact but there was pain behind it. She could hear it.

'That's still no reason for you to be involved.'

'Dammit, Gina, he's my son.'

She thought about that while a mile—maybe two—disappeared under their wheels.

'Yes, Cal, he is,' she said at last. 'But you need to think of the whole picture. CJ's happy thinking Paul is his daddy. Are you sure you want to change that?' She hesitated. 'And I don't want to upset what's between you and Emily.'

'There's nothing between me and Emily.'

She sighed. 'Of course there's not.'

'What's that supposed to mean?'

'There's nothing between you and anyone.'

'You and I—'

'Were lovers,' she said flatly. 'But we weren't committed.'

'Because you ran.'

'I had no choice and you know it. Don't play the abandoned lover on me, Cal. You know you don't need me emotionally. You never have and you never will. And CJ…'

'What about CJ?' He was practically glowering.

'If you acknowledge him now, then you need to do commitment. There's no way you can say proudly you're his daddy and then not see him again.'

'You think that's what I want?'

'I don't know what you want. Do you?'

No answer.

Cal needed to concentrate now. They were approaching a rocky outcrop and the road was no longer clear. The country was growing rougher.

Kids were drag racing *here*? Gina thought, flinching inside at what lay ahead.

'Little fools,' Cal muttered, and she knew that his thoughts had veered back to what lay ahead as well.

'Locals, do you think?'

'Nothing surer,' he said grimly. 'There is a settlement just inland from here. Many of the local indigenous people are tribal—they live as they've lived for thousands of years. But the ones in the settlements...'

He broke off and concentrated on another corner. But then he started again.

'They're so disadvantaged,' he said savagely, and all at once his hands were white on the steering-wheel. His voice was passionate. 'Loss of their culture has left them in no man's land. There's nothing for them to look forward to, nothing for them to hold to. And they're self-destructing because of it.'

'I know,' she whispered.

'Yeah,' he said roughly. 'I remember that you do. When you were in Townsville you had such plans. You seemed to care so much. But off you went, back home to be a cardiologist.'

'That's not fair.'

But he wasn't listening. 'You know, your breakfast group disintegrated as soon as you left. The medics were stretched as far as they could go already. There was no funding and no enthusiasm for taking it forward.'

'You're blaming me that it ended?'

'You never should have started it.'

'Maybe I shouldn't have,' she said through gritted teeth.

It had been a small enough thing that she'd done. She'd taken a group of teenage girls—some pregnant, all in danger of being pregnant—and she'd invited them for breakfast. They'd met in a local café down by the river twice a week. Boys had been excluded. They'd swum, they'd eaten the huge breakfast Gina had managed to scrounge from local businesses—a breakfast of things the kids hardly saw for the rest of the week, such as milk and meat and fresh fruit. Then they'd played with cosmetics and beauty products, also provided by the businesses Gina had badgered. She'd worked really hard to keep their interest, inviting guests such as hairstylists, models, cosmeticians—anyone the girls would have thought cool.

She'd also sneaked in the odd gynaecologist and dietician and welfare support person, all selected for their cool factor as well as for the advice they'd been able to give.

The girls had thought it was wonderful—an exclusive club for twelve- to sixteen-year-olds. It had been working brilliantly, Gina thought. Too brilliantly. Only Gina knew what a pang it had cost her to walk away.

But she hadn't been alone in her enthusiasm. 'You had a boys' group,' she said softly. 'Did you walk away, too?'

'I moved up here.'

'You mean you did walk away.' She bit her lip. 'Cal, I had an excuse. I was going home to care for Paul. What about you?'

'That's none of your business.'

'No,' she whispered. She stared out into the darkness, thinking of what she and Cal had started. What they could have achieved if they'd stayed together.

Maybe Cal was right. Don't get involved.

'These kids in the crash,' she said tentatively into the silence.

'I know who'll they'll be,' he told her. 'The younger teen-agers on the settlement up here are bored stupid.'

'So bored they kill themselves?'

'They drive ancient cars. Wrecks. They get them going any way they can, and they drive like maniacs. This won't be pretty.'

'You think I don't know that?'

'I think we both know it.'

It wasn't the least bit pretty.

They rounded the last bend and knew at once what they were in for. Two cars had smashed into each other, with no last-minute swerve to lessen the impact. The vehicles were compacted, a grotesque accordion of twisted metal.

They'd have been playing chicken, Gina thought dully. She'd seen this happen before. Two carloads of kids driving straight at each other, each driver daring each other to be the last to swerve.

No one had swerved.

The first ambulance was already there and more cars were pulling up beside it. People were clutching each other, staring in horror as they stumbled out of their cars to face the crash. Bad news travelled fast. Parents would have been wrenched out of their quiet evening and were now staring at tragedy.

Two dead? There were two shrouded bundles by the road-side. A young policeman was trying fruitlessly to keep peo-ple back. Voices were already keening their sorrow, wailing distress and disbelief.

'Cal!' The older of the two paramedics who'd come with the first ambulance was running over to meet then. 'There are two still trapped in one of the cars and I'm scared we're los-ing them. And there's a kid on the roadside with major breath-ing problems. Plus the rest.'

'You take the breathing,' Cal told Gina. 'I'll take the car.'

He was bracing himself. Gina could see it. His eyes were withdrawing into the place he kept his pain. He'd do his job with efficiency and skill, and he'd care while he worked, but he'd not let himself become involved.

'I'll do whatever needs doing,' she said, in a voice that wasn't too steady. 'But maybe I'll feel pain along the way.'

'And I won't?'

'Who knows?' She was hauling on protective gear with speed. 'I knew this job once, and I thought I knew you. But we've come a long way. How thick have you grown your armour now, Cal?'

She didn't wait for an answer.

It was a night to forget.

Gina worked with skills she'd almost forgotten, but her skills returned because if they didn't then kids died.

The girl with breathing problems appeared to have fractured ribs, with a possible punctured lung. She was Gina's first priority. Gina set up oxygen and manoeuvred her into a position where she seemed to be a good colour with normal oxygen saturation. She left her with the younger paramedic—Frank—and moved on to the next priority.

There were fractured limbs, deep lacerations, shock... That was bad enough, but Cal had allocated himself the true horror. Two kids still trapped.

One of them died under his hands five minutes after they arrived.

There was a moment's appalled silence—a moment where she glanced across and saw Cal's shoulders slump in defeat and despair—and then they all had to keep working.

How thick was his armour? she wondered. Not thick enough.

Head-on smash. Three dead now. One dreadfully injured. Three more with severe injuries, some of those injuries requiring skills that weren't available in Crocodile Creek. One in such deep shock that she wasn't responding.

There was a girl still trapped in the car. Cal was in the car with her, somehow inching his body into the mass of tangled metal, and he was fighting with everything he had.

All the emergency services had arrived now and machinery was being prepared to slice the cars apart. When floodlights lit the scene Gina saw that Cal was holding a tracheostomy tube in place. The second paramedic, Mario, was helping. IV lines had been established. A tow-truck driver had been co-opted into being a human intravenous stand.

She worked on. She had too many troubles of her own to be distracted by what Cal was doing.

'Dr Lopez?' Gina was splinting a compound fracture that was threatening to block blood supply when suddenly Mario was kneeling beside her. The too-young paramedic had the horror of the night etched on his face, but he was competent, moving swiftly to take over.

'I can do this,' he told her. She had the boy's leg in position and was about to start binding. 'Dr Jamieson needs you over at the car. Can you go?'

'Sure.'

Do what comes next, Gina thought bleakly, trying not to flinch as she approached the wreck. Do what comes next.

Cal's patient—Karen, a girl of about fourteen—was still firmly trapped and she wasn't moving. The guys with the cutting machinery had paused.

Why did Cal need her?

She did a fast visual assessment of what she could see. Massive facial damage. What else?

'Her leg,' Cal told her as she reached him. 'I can't reach and I can feel blood. It was oozing, but we shifted her a bit when we tried to free her and now it's spurting. Mario tried to get in but he can't reach under me and I can't move. You're smaller. If we don't get the bleeding stopped...'

She didn't answer. She was already bending into the mass of twisted metal, crawling under Cal's legs.

Someone—Frank?—handed her a torch.

'There's a tear.' She could see it. 'It's pumping. I want pressure.'

Frank pushed a pad in her hands.

'Can you stop it?' The fear in Cal's voice was unmistakable. Armour? He didn't have any at all, she thought. It was all a façade.

She was right underneath him, her body somehow under his legs. There were pieces of metal digging into her from all sides as she bound the leg as best she could, hauling the jagged sides together and dressing it so the worst of the bleeding eased.

But had the bleeding eased because of what she'd done— or because the girl's blood pressure had dropped so far the bleeding would have eased anyhow?

She wriggled back out, but she didn't ask the question.

'We'll be getting you out of here now,' Cal was murmuring to the girl, holding her as he supported the tracheostomy tube, his arm around her shoulders, willing her to hear him. She seemed unconscious but both of them knew there was no way they could assess her level of consciousness here. She might well be able to hear every word.

Gina stepped back, but her eyes stayed on Karen's face. Was this a winnable battle? From what she could see, no.

But Cal wasn't giving up.

'OK, guys,' Cal was saying to the men working around them. 'Now Gina's fixed the bleeding, there's nothing stopping us cutting her out. Karen, we're with you every step of the way. Gina and I won't leave you.'

Gina and I.

Gina backed, moving out of the way of the men with the machinery, but the image of the girl Cal was treating stayed with her. The girl's pupils weren't responding to light. Her face was badly damaged, and there was a deep indentation behind her ear. Fractured skull. What damage was underneath?

Cal wasn't moving clear. The cars were having to be wrenched apart to get her out. There'd be splintering of metal; there was danger in him staying where he was. It was probably a hopeless task—but he wouldn't leave.

Gina and I.

She loved him. He was so desperately needful and she loved him so much, but he wouldn't see it.

Numbly she went back to the kids who still needed her. Her girl with the punctured lung seemed to be stabilising. The boy with fractured legs was drifting into unconsciousness but part of that might well be the morphine she'd administered. The girl who seemed to be in deep shock wasn't taking anything in, and Frank called her over to help. She went, but a part of her stayed achingly with Cal holding the girl to him, fighting against all odds.

Cal battling the odds as he'd done all his life.

Medicine. Concentrate on need.

'The chopper's on its way,' one of the policemen told her.

That meant she could arrange to get the girl with the punctured lung and the one in shock into the road ambulance. She sent them off with the two paramedics. They'd need the helicopter for Karen. If…

If.

The vast pliers-like equipment nicknamed the Jaws of Life was working now, the noise blocking out any other. It stopped for a minute and she heard Cal.

'Breathe for me, Karen. Come on, love. Breathe.'

Love. He was fighting with love, she thought, and he didn't even know he was doing it.

She needed time to think things through.

There was no time here.

Then the helicopter landed, and Gina was so busy she hardly noticed. One of the boys was vomiting and it took all her skill to stop him choking. She had him on his side, clearing his airway, and when Cal's hand settled on her shoulder she jerked back in surprise.

He was clear of the wreck, but she glanced up and saw that he wasn't clear. Karen…

Not dead. Not yet.

Cal was looking at the boys she was treating, doing fast visual assessment, trying to figure priorities.

'I'll take Karen back to base in the chopper,' he said, briefly, dully, as if he was already accepting the outcome. 'Her parents will want to come with us, and by the look of…things, I think that's wise.' He stooped to feel the pulse of the boy who'd just vomited. Both boys were seriously injured but not so seriously that their lives were in immediate danger. But both of them needed constant medical attention. It wasn't safe to leave either without a doctor.

Which left them with a dilemma. Only one of these kids could fit in the two-patient chopper, but if one of them went, Cal's attention would be divided. Or Gina would need to go, too, leaving one boy untended.

Impossible. They'd have to wait.

'I'll send the chopper straight back,' Cal told her, and she understood.

'Fine.'

Fine? To be left on the roadside with three dead kids and two seriously injured kids and so many distraught relatives?

'No one else can stay,' Cal told her helplessly. 'Damn, there should be another doctor. We're so short-staffed.'

'Just go, Cal,' she told him. 'Move.'

'I'll send someone back to cope with the deaths,' Cal said. There were adults keening over the bodies and the scene looked like something out of a nightmare. Worse than a nightmare. 'Charles said he'd send back-up. Where is it? But, Gina, I need to go.'

'Of course you do. Go, Cal. I'll manage.'

He touched her hair, a fleeting gesture of farewell—but then, before she could begin to guess what he intended, he bent and kissed her. Hard. It was a swift kiss that held more desperation than tenderness. It was a kiss of pure, desperate need.

Maybe it had been intended as reassurance for her, she thought numbly as she raised a hand to her face, but it had ended up being a kiss for himself. For Cal.

Cal had never kissed her as he'd just done then.

But he was already gone, stepping away from her. Stepping away from his need.

Into the chopper, back into his medicine, and away from her.

Somehow she organised order from the chaos at the roadside. She couldn't work miracles—there were still three dead kids. But she sent relatives to start the drive into town so they could be at the hospital when the kids were brought in. She worked with the police sergeant who'd come to assist the white-faced officers who'd been first on the scene, getting details from shocked relatives. The bodies had to stay where they were until the coroner arrived.

She worked.

Finally the helicopter returned and by the time it did, she had her two remaining patients ready to go. She'd hauled the stretchers from the road ambulance she and Cal had come in, so the moment the chopper landed she had them ready to carry on board. Mike was the pilot. He swung out to help her. There was another paramedic or doctor in the back, receiving the patients, but there was no time for introductions.

'Let's go,' Mike told her.

She glanced one last time at the mess left for the police to handle—the detritus of wasted lives—and then she concentrated on the living. She climbed up into the chopper herself. Moving on.

If only it was that easy.

Someone—a big man with a Scottish accent that was apparent the moment he opened his mouth—was organising the securing of the stretchers. He talked over his shoulder to Gina as Mike fastened himself back into the pilot's seat.

'You'll be Gina,' he said briefly, hanging the boy's drip from the stand built into the side of the chopper. 'I'm Dr Hamish McGregor. Call me Hamish.'

'William's IV line's not stable. And his leg…'

'I'm noticing that, and it's my problem.' Hamish was making a calm assessment of each patient. And of her. 'You look like death and I'm taking over. If I need you, I'll say so. Meanwhile, sit back and close your eyes.'

'But—'

'Just do it.'

She did. She buckled her seat belt and closed her eyes, and suddenly nausea washed over her in a wave so intense that she needed to push her head down between her knees to stop herself passing out.

Hamish eyed her with concern but he left her to it. Every doctor in the world had these moments. They came with the job.

So for a while Gina simply concentrated on not giving way to horror. On not letting the dizziness take over.

Finally, though, the nausea passed. She took a few deep breaths and ventured—cautiously—to open her eyes again. The helicopter was in the air. The two kids seemed settled and Hamish was focussing on her.

'So you're Cal's Gina,' he said softly.

'I… No.'

'No?'

'I'm just a doctor tonight,' she said wearily, and then, because she couldn't think of what else to say, she added, 'Where's Cal?'

'Last time I saw him he was about to drill a burrhole to try and relieve raised cranial pressure,' he told her. 'It's desperate surgery he's doing. We're damnably short-staffed. Every doctor at the base is doing two jobs or more tonight.'

'So where did you come from?'

The big Scot managed a lopsided smile. 'I'm supposed to be on leave,' he told her. 'However, I made the mistake of telling people where I was. Charles radioed the skipper of the game-fishing boat I was on and they hauled me back to town with the boating equivalent of red lights and sirens. To be met by this.'

'So you're another doctor with the Remote Rescue Service.' She frowned. 'Hamish. The paediatrician?'

'Yes, ma'am.' He gave a rueful smile. 'Or I'm the best we can supply in the paediatric department. I have a post-grad qualification in paediatrics, as well as my accident and emergency training.'

Great. That was another small weight lifted from her heart. All the time she'd been out here she'd been conscious of the tiny baby she'd left back at base, and now they had someone with paediatric training to take over. 'You've seen Lucky?'

'I have,' he told her. 'He's looking stable. I'll be heading back there fast to spend some more time with him. But you and Cal and Emily seem to have done a fine job. He has a fighting chance.'

'I would have thought you'd have stayed while Em came out,' she said, puzzled, and he grimaced.

'Em's in Theatre with Cal. He needs the best anaesthetist we have. Christina and Charles are with the two kids who arrived by road. That means we're right out of doctors—apart from Alix, our pathologist, who's just recovering from chickenpox. And we've even pulled her out of bed. So we had to take a chance on Lucky. Grace is specialling him. I came here. Sometimes in this place there's not enough skill to go around and you need to make a hard call.'

'I guess,' she said, thinking bleakly of the number of times she'd had to leave her own son as she was leaving him now. As she'd have to walk away from Cal. So many choices…

Think of something else, she told herself fiercely. Anything.

'Do you know Cal well?'

'Cal's a friend.'

'I didn't think Cal had friends.' Why was she asking this, she wondered, in the midst of this horror? But the boys they were transporting now were the least injured. They were heavily sedated and they both had parents gripping their undamaged hands, as if that link alone could keep them safe. There was time and space for the two medics to talk.

And surprisingly Gina found she wanted to talk. In truth, she was desperate to talk. Anything but face the horrors of the night.

Anything but Cal?

But she'd asked.

'Our Cal certainly keeps to himself,' Hamish was saying. He cast an assessing look across at their patients but it appeared their respite could continue. 'But… Gina, there's things going on that I'm not understanding. I was barely back in town for two minutes before I was told you've produced Cal's son. Cal's son! Would that be right? Have you done that?'

'Yes. But I'll take him away again,' Gina whispered. 'I just wanted Cal to know he was alive. You don't think I'm intending to cut in on his precious independence, do you?'

His eyes grew thoughtful. 'You know,' he said softly, 'it wouldn't be such a bad thing if you did.'

'He's getting along fine without me,' Gina snapped. 'He's got a relationship with Emily.'

'Has he, now?' Hamish sent another assessing look across at their patients but both boys were breathing deep and evenly and there was no need to worry. One of the fathers had his head on his son's hand, as if love alone could bring him through. 'I wasn't aware that he had such a thing,' Hamish said softly. 'And I know both Emily and Cal very well. Cal doesn't have a relationship with anyone.'

'But I thought… On the day I arrived here I found him… cuddling Emily.'

Hamish thought about that for a bit. 'Emily's fiancé has just walked out on her,' he said at last. 'He's saying he wants space, but in reality he's found another woman. Em knows in her heart what's happening, no matter how much she's denying it. If Cal was cuddling Emily, I'd be guessing that it was just Cal picking up the pieces.' He hesitated. 'You know, picking up the pieces is what Cal's best at,' he remarked thoughtfully. 'It's what to do with them afterwards where he doesn't exactly shine.'

Gina blinked, and stared. Astonished. 'You're a paediatrician,' she said slowly. 'Not a psychiatrist.'

'Everyone does everything at Crocodile Creek,' Hamish told her, giving her a rueful smile. 'There's no such thing as delineation of roles. If we need a psychiatrist then I'll be one. And I do consider Cal a friend. Even if it is a bit one-sided, if you know what I mean.' He cast her a long, questioning look. 'And I'm imagining you know very well what I mean.'

They fell into silence again. So much had happened in the last few hours. This sort of life-and-death drama always left her drained, Gina thought wearily, and tonight was no exception. She was exhausted. In a few minutes they'd land and they'd be thrust back into the hospital atmosphere where there'd be surgery to perform, appalled relatives to counsel and treat, Cal to face…

This was her two minutes to catch her breath and look squarely at her future.

She couldn't. Cal…

'I don't know what to do,' she whispered, and Hamish had to lean forward to hear. 'I don't know how to break through that barrier.'

'It's one heck of a barrier,' Hamish told her. 'You know his family history.'

'I know what I've been allowed to know.'

'He's been betrayed by just about everybody in his life. It's a miracle he's a functioning human being.'

'He's not a trusting human being. So that makes him…'

'Dysfunctional?'

'Maybe,' she whispered. 'Yes.'

'Then how far are you prepared to go to get him functioning again?' Hamish asked, and Gina stared at the metal-plated floor and shook her head.

'Not far at all. I'm just here to tell him of the existence of his son.'

'You know, I doubt that,' Hamish said gently. 'I've known you, what—for about fifteen minutes? And even now, I doubt that very much.'

She'd been right when she'd assumed the hospital would be in chaos. The casualty entrance was mad.

Gina stood between the two stretchers that had just been wheeled in and took three deep breaths, trying for triage, trying to get some sort of priorities formed in her head. Grace appeared in the doorway, looking just as frazzled as she was feeling.

'Where is everyone?' Gina demanded.

'Both Theatres are occupied,' Grace said briefly. 'Karen's intracranial pressure is life-threatening. She has signs of a blood clot in association with her fractured skull and Cal's drilled a burrhole to try and reduce pressure. Melanie has a collapsed lung and Christina and Charles are working on her. Alix is looking after path. needs and blood supply. That's taken our full complement of doctors, except you and Hamish. Hamish, you need to check on Lucky. I came out to see if you needed any help here.' She gazed around the mess that was the emergency ward. 'I guess you do, huh?'

'I guess we do,' Gina said, mentally saying goodbye to the rest of the night. What a day. What a nightmare! 'I guess we all do.'

They worked for two hours straight. Evacuation in the morning would see the compound fractures taken to Cairns for attention by orthopaedic specialists, but meanwhile blood supply had to be ensured, adequate pain relief had to be given, wounds had to be stitched. With only paramedics and nurses to help her, Gina had three incredibly sick and traumatised kids in her care. To say nothing of their parents.

But somehow she coped, and when Charles finally arrived to take over she was able to greet the medical director with a faint smile of reassurance.

Charles's face twisted as he looked around the room. She had each patient settled and ready to be transferred to the wards—or to a flight out. Their appropriate relatives were settled with them. The inappropriate relatives or the onlookers who were simply there for drama had been sent home.

'Is everything OK?' he asked.

'I'll go through the case notes—'

'There's no need,' Charles told her. Christina appeared in the doorway behind him and the complement of doctors had suddenly grown to three. Charles spun across to the desk and lifted the folders she'd started out at the crash site. 'Christina and I can take over here.'

'Lilly?'

'She'll be fine,' Christina told her. 'We'll fly her out for plastic surgery tomorrow morning but she's stable.'

'And... Karen...?'

'That's your next job,' Charles said grimly. 'I'm sorry, Gina, but I can't let you go to bed yet.'

'You need help with Karen?'

'Karen died twenty minutes ago,' Charles told her. 'Cal and

Emily worked with everything they had, but they failed. Cal's just talked to her parents.' He hesitated. 'Gina, when things like this happen, Cal withdraws. He's out in the hospital garden right now, and he needs someone.'

She stared at him, appalled. 'What are you asking? I don't… I can't…'

'Yes, you can,' he told her, and his voice became stern. 'You've thrown a hell of a shock at our Cal this afternoon. The least you can do is mop up the mess.'

'It's nothing to do with me.'

'Who are you kidding?' he said roughly. 'But you choose. Go to bed or go and see if you can get through to Cal. But if you go to bed now…well, I don't see how you can.' He stared around the room and his face grew even more grim. 'There are things that all of us can't walk away from. You know that as well as everyone here.'

CHAPTER FIVE

SHE should go to bed. She'd do more harm than good if she approached Cal now, she thought, and CJ needed her. She made her way resolutely across to the doctors' quarters, avoiding the garden, sure that she'd made the right decision.

CJ wasn't in bed. Instead, there was a note pinned to his pillow.

Dear Dr Lopez

CJ couldn't sleep and he seems a bit upset. We've got a new puppy at our place. Me and Mr Grubb are in the little blue house over the far side of the hospital and hubby's just come over to tell me the pup's making a fuss. So I thought I'd take CJ home. I'm guessing he and the pup might sleep together in our spare bedroom. I asked Dr Wetherby and he reckons you'll be busy till late and us taking the littlie will give you a chance to sleep late tomorrow—but come over and get him if you want him back tonight. Or telephone and we'll bring him straight back. I'll let you know if he frets.

Dora Grubb

So CJ didn't need her, Gina thought as she stared down at the letter. This was a note written by a competent woman who

Charles trusted. CJ would be overjoyed to be asked to sleep with a puppy.

But where did that leave her?

She wanted to hug CJ, she thought bleakly, acknowledging that her ability to hug her small son in times of crisis was a huge gift. But to wake him now, to wake the Grubbs and the puppy as well, just so she could be hugged...

Grow up, she told herself, and tried to feel grown-up.

She glanced at her watch. It was three in the morning. She should shower and slide between the covers and sleep.

She knew she wouldn't sleep.

Damn, she wanted CJ.

Cal was... Cal was...

Go to bed!

She took a grip—sort of—and walked over to pull the curtains closed. Then she paused.

Cal was down at the water's edge. The shoreline was two hundred yards from where she was standing but his figure was unmistakable.

He was just...standing.

So what? she demanded of herself. She should leave him be.

But he was Cal. She stared down the beach at his still figure and she felt the same wrenching of her heart that she'd felt all those years before. It was as if this man was a part of her and to walk away from him would be tantamount to taking away a limb.

She'd had to walk away before, she thought dully, for all sorts of reasons. And she'd survived.

But CJ was safely asleep and there was nothing standing between herself and Cal.

Nothing but five years of pain, and a desolate childhood that had destroyed his trust in everyone.

He'd never get over it, she told herself. He was damaged goods. Dangerous.

But still she couldn't walk away. Not now. There was only so much resolve one woman was capable of, and she'd run right out of it.

She opened her door and she walked down to the beach to meet him.

He sensed rather that saw her approach. What was it about this woman that gave him a sixth sense—that made him feel different, strange, just because she was on the same continent as he was? he wondered. She was walking along the beach to reach him and he braced himself as if expecting to be hit.

She'd hurt him.

No, he'd hurt her, he thought savagely. She'd been pregnant and he hadn't been there for her.

He would have been there if she'd said…

Liar. He would have run.

'I'm sorry, Cal,' she said gently behind him, and he flinched. But he didn't turn.

'What do you want?' It was a low growl. He sounded angry, which was grossly unfair but he was past being fair tonight.

Maybe she sensed it. She sounded softly sympathetic—not responding with her own anger.

'It's been a dreadful day, Cal. To have CJ thrown at you, and then copping such deaths…'

'I couldn't save her,' he said savagely into the night. He'd left his shoes back on the dry sand and rolled up his jeans before he'd come down the water's edge. The water was now washing over his feet, taking out some of the heat but not enough. Still he didn't turn and Gina came and stood beside him and stared out at the same sea he was seeing. She was wearing jeans and T-shirt and sandals, but she didn't seem to notice that she was wading into the shallows regardless. Neither did he. 'I worked so damned hard and I couldn't save her. Of all the useless…'

'You can only do so much, Cal. You're a doctor. Not a magician.'

'The pressure was too much,' he said, picking up a ribbon of kelp that had washed against his legs and hurling it into an oncoming breaker. It didn't go far. He walked further into the waves to retrieve it and then hurled it again. 'Did you know we actually split her skull, trying to save her?' he demanded. 'We drilled a burrhole, but the whole brain was so bruised we realised the pressure was killing her. So we split…'

Gina was beside him—but not too close. They were up to their knees in the surf and the rolling breakers were reaching their thighs. She didn't touch him. They were standing three feet apart, and she was staring out to sea, and he knew that she was seeing what he was seeing. A dying child.

'That's heroic surgery, Cal,' she said softly. 'Performed as a last-ditch stand in a hopeless case. But it was hopeless. You can't blame yourself when something like that doesn't work. Medicine has limits.'

'Yeah.'

She took a step closer and laid a hand on his arm. He flinched.

'Don't.'

'Don't touch you, do you mean?' she asked. 'Cal, that's what you've been saying for years. You're so afraid of people being close.'

'What do you know about what I'm like now?'

'Hamish says your friendship with Emily is platonic,' she murmured softly, and her hand stayed on his arm, whether he willed it or not. 'He says you're still driving people away.'

'I didn't drive you away.'

'No?'

'Gina—'

'OK, let's leave it,' she told him, her voice softening in sympathy. But instead of removing her hand from his arm, she linked her fingers through his and tugged him sideways. Cal had such shadows but he'd earned them the hard way. For him to move past them must be a near-impossible task. 'Let's leave the lid on it.'

'What are…?' She was tugging him through the shallows. 'Where—?'

'Cal, there's one thing I have learned in the last few years,' she told him, still tugging so he had no option but to follow. 'Reinforced by stuff like tonight. And that's the reality that you can't spend your life dwelling in the shadows of what's gone. If you do that, then you might as well finish it off when you lose the ones you love. But I only have one life, Cal. I intend to make the most of it.'

'So what's that—?'

'It means I'm going for a walk in the moonlight,' she told him, refusing to let him interrupt. 'CJ's safe with Mrs Grubb and the new Grubb puppy. This water is delicious. It's a full moon and it's low tide. We have miles of beach all to ourselves and there's no way either of us is going to sleep after today's events. So let's walk.'

He stopped. Firm. Planting his feet in the shallows. Holding himself still against the insistent tug of her hand.

'I don't think that's a good idea.'

'I think it's a splendid idea,' she told him, sounding exasperated.

'I don't want to get close to you, Gina.'

'You know, I have news for you,' she told him, linking her arm through his and keeping on tugging. 'You're the father of my son. You're here now. You don't want to get close? Cal Jamieson, you already are.'

He was walking. Gina started down the beach through the shallows, and Cal let himself be tugged beside her, and as he relaxed and started to walk without being tugged she knew she'd achieved a significant victory.

He'd always taken deaths personally, she thought. It was one of the things she loved about him. Most doctors developed personal detachment from patients, but she'd never seen that in Cal, no matter how hard he fought to find it.

He'd never succeeded in personal detachment. Except in his personal relationships.

Except with her.

But for now he was walking beside her, fighting the way he was feeling about her and about CJ, and at least that meant that he wasn't internalising Karen's death, she thought. The hours after such a death were always dreadful. Going over and over things in your mind, wondering what else could you have done, what you'd missed…

She could distract him for a little while, she thought, and if by doing so she could distract herself from…things, great.

Or at least good.

Given the staffing in the hospital, they both knew they couldn't venture far, so they confined their walk to the end of the cove. But as they reached the headland, Gina decided it was not far enough. So they walked to the opposite headland. Then they turned again—and again. Walking in silence.

So many things unsaid.

'We'll wear the beach out,' Cal told her, breaking the silence on their third turn, and Gina kicked up a spray of water in front of her and smiled.

'Good. I like my beach a little world-weary. You have no idea how much I miss the beach.'

'So where are you living?' It was almost a normal conversation, Gina thought. Excellent.

'Idaho. Same as when you first knew me, Cal. Some things don't change.'

'But you love the beach.'

'Mmm, but my family and friends are in Idaho. So sure I miss the beach but where I live is a no-brainer.'

'You always intended to go back?' he asked, and she felt the normality fade as anger surged again. Deep anger. This water wasn't cold enough.

'Strangely enough, I didn't,' she told him. 'Five years ago I came out for a break after Paul left me. Yes, I intended it to be brief, but then I met you. And then I thought about staying permanently.'

'So you considered deserting your family and friends.'

'I had hoped,' she said softly, 'that in you I might have found both. I was dumb. But I was young, Cal. I've learned. So it's back to Idaho for me.'

'You must know that I'll want to see CJ.'

'I'll send photographs.'

'I didn't mean that.'

'So what do you mean?'

'I don't know,' he said, exasperated. 'He's my kid.'

She thought about that for a minute, trying to figure out a response that didn't involve anger. 'Do you think,' she said softly into the night, 'that because your mother and your father were your biological parents, they had automatic rights over you?'

'Not rights,' he said, in an automatic rejection of an idea he clearly found repugnant, and she grimaced.

'No. They had obligations, which they didn't fulfil. But rights... You have to earn rights. If you love your kid then maybe you have the right to hope the kid will love you back. You're at first base, Cal.'

'He looks like me,' Cal said inconsequentially, and his words sent a surge of disquiet through her. Like something was being threatened. Her relationship with CJ?

'So do you love him?' she managed to ask, and he seemed startled.

'Hey...'

She kicked up a huge spray of water before her, so high it

came back down over their heads. Enough. This conversation was way too deep and she didn't know where it was going, and she wasn't sure how she could handle it wherever it went. And she was so tired. She kicked again and then suddenly on impulse she dropped Cal's hand and waded further out into the sea. Her clothes were already wet. They were disgusting anyway after this night, so a little more salt water wasn't going to hurt them. The moon was so full that she could see under the surface of the shallow water and…and what the heck.

Walking forward to the first breaker, she simply knelt down and let the water wash right over her.

It felt excellent. Her anger, her uncertainty, the way she was feeling about Cal…the way her hand had felt as if it was abandoning something precious when she'd released Cal's. The waves had the power to soothe it all.

This had been some day. The trauma of the baby, and then the accident, and Cal as well. It was simply, suddenly overwhelming. Now her brain seemed to have shut down as her body soaked in the cool wash of the foam. She knelt and let wave after wave wash over her and she just didn't care.

She didn't know where to go from here.

She wasn't sure how long she knelt there, how long was it before she surfaced to the awareness that Cal was still with her. He was kneeling behind her. A wave washed her backwards and his hands seized her waist so that she wasn't washed under.

Maybe he'd sensed that she'd reached a limit where it was no longer possible to support herself, she thought dully in the tiny part of her mind that was still capable of thought.

Or maybe he needed contact, too?

It didn't matter. It couldn't matter, for there was no space in her tired mind to make any sense of anything. She was grateful that he was here and she leaned back into him but still her focus was on the water, on the wash of cool, on this minute.

'The sea's great,' Cal murmured during a break in the

waves, and she thought about answering but another wave washed up against her and she had to concentrate on getting her breath back. She spluttered a bit and thought, Well, that served her right for trying to think of something clever to say. Of anything to say.

'Where do you go in Idaho when you feel like this?' he asked some time later, and that was a reasonable question to ask, she decided. There was no danger down that road.

'I drive,' she told him. 'The night Paul died I got in the car and I drove and drove. A friend took CJ home with her for the night and I think I drove five hundred miles before I stopped.'

'I wish I'd known.'

'Do you?' she asked. She tried to shrug but his hold on her waist tightened.

'Believe it or not, yes, I do,' he said softly.

'Your friend Hamish said you were really good at picking up the pieces,' she murmured. 'He also said you didn't know what to do with them after you've picked them up.'

'He's got me tagged.' But he didn't sound angry. He sounded defeated.

'I guess he's a friend.'

A wave or two more washed over them and they had to wait for a bit before they could talk again. But she was feeling the tension in him and it wasn't going away.

'Does Hamish being my friend give him permission to talk about me?' he asked at last.

She thought, No, this wasn't about Hamish. But she answered him all the same.

'It gives him permission to worry about you. Like with kids, commitment gives rights.'

'Hell, Gina…'

'Just leave it, Cal,' she said wearily. She tried to pull away but another wave, bigger than usual, propelled her harder against him. His arm tightened even further.

'I don't think I can,' he said unsteadily.

'We need to go back to the hospital.'

'We have unfinished business.'

'I can't think what.' She tried to sound cross—but it didn't come off.

'Gina...' Things had changed suddenly. The feel of his hands. The feel of his body...

Once she and Cal had been lovers and suddenly the feel of his hands touching her had brought it all flooding back. The way she'd once felt about this man.

The way she still did.

Cal. He was her Cal. She'd fallen desperately in love with him five years ago. She'd spent five years trying to forget how he felt but now all he had to do was be here, touch her, and it was as if those feelings had started yesterday.

No. Not yesterday. Now.

And he could feel it, too. She half turned and he was looking down at her in the moonlight, the expression on his face something akin to amazement.

What was between them wasn't one-sided. It was a real and tangible bond, and five years hadn't weakened it one bit.

'Cal, don't,' she whispered, but it was a shaken whisper.

'How can I not?'

She should have struggled.

Of course she should have struggled. She didn't want this man to kiss her.

She mustn't let him kiss her. To rekindle what had once been...

But she was so tired. The part of her brain that was used for logic had simply switched off, stopped with its working out of what she should do, what was wise, what the best path was to the future.

All she knew was that Cal's closeness, the feel of his hands on her body, the sensation of his mouth lowering onto hers, was transporting her into another space.

Another time?

Five years ago.

She knew this man. She'd fallen in love with Cal Jamieson the first time he'd smiled at her. She'd told herself it was crazy, that love at first sight was ridiculous, that she wasn't even divorced yet—but it had made no difference at all.

This was her man. Her home. He was the Adam to her Eve, the other half of her whole, her completeness.

Six, seven years ago Paul had walked away from their marriage because he'd sensed that there had been something more. She'd been devastated. She hadn't understood.

And then she'd met Cal and all had become clear.

Paul had been right. That it had gone so horribly wrong for them both hadn't been Paul's fault. He'd gone in search of something he'd sensed had been out there. He'd been injured before he'd found it, but Gina had found it here.

Cal.

She was holding him tight. Tighter.

What was it between them? She didn't know. Pure, uncomplicated lust? There was certainly that, she thought. Her body was reacting to his as if there was some switch that sent heat surging in a way she hadn't felt for five long years.

He made her feel…

What?

Who was asking for explanations? Why waste this moment? She surely wasn't going to.

Her lips opened to his and she hadn't wanted to be kissed—or she was almost sure she hadn't wanted to be kissed—but she was numb and past rational thought and she was wet and his body was so close and their clothes were soaked, so soaked that they might as well not have existed, and his hands were wonderful and she could taste him and she was sinking against him and…

And he was her Cal.

The heat was overpowering. She was melting inside, turning to liquid jelly as wave after wave of pure hot longing surged through her body. She was responding to him with every nerve ending she had, from the tips of her ears to the tips of her toes. The waves were washing against them and at times they were up to their necks in the water, but it made it more wonderful. It didn't take away the heat.

Nothing could take away this heat.

'Gina…'

He was holding her close. Closer. She was merging into him under the water, her body curling against him as if two melting objects were merging into one. Her lips widened, her tongue was searching… She wanted this man so much.

The kiss deepened, lengthened, strengthened, and with it came a strengthening of the bond that had been forged five years ago. It was a bond she'd thought she'd broken but she knew now that she never could.

This man was her son's father.

This man was her love.

But he didn't know it. Not as she wanted him to know it, in a glorious acknowledgement that they could be a family.

'You're beautiful,' he managed in a voice that was husky with passion. She'd drawn away as a wave had crashed against them but he'd tugged her back into him again and she had no power to resist.

'You're not so bad yourself,' she whispered, before his mouth lowered again. She even managed a shaken laugh. 'A bit soggy…'

'Soggy's good. Soggy's great.'

'Shut up and kiss me, Cal.'

'Yes, ma'am.'

What was she doing? she wondered in the tiny fraction of her brain available for such thought. But she knew very well what she was doing. She was taking what was offered right now because this moment was all she had. Even if Cal wanted to forge something from now on, there was no way he was offering himself. He'd hold himself independent, regardless. He'd drilled that hard lesson into his heart and he intended to stay that way.

But just for now, just for this minute, she told herself desperately, there was no such thing as independence. Cal was a part of her and she'd take what comfort she could before she moved on.

Tomorrow.

For some reason the word slammed through her tired brain, smashing against the love and the heat and the joy, and she felt her body shudder. He felt it, as he'd feel a wave crashing against them, and he drew away again, holding her at arm's length and looking at her in concern.

'What is it, my love?'

Doctor picking up pieces, she thought dully. Then not knowing what to do with them. Cal would always act with honour. He was so kind, so caring…

He just couldn't take the next step.

'I'm not your love,' she said, in a voice that was none too steady.

'I've loved you from the first time we met.'

'Have you?'

'Of course I have.'

But the bubble had burst. Reality was slamming back and with it a kind of sense.

'Then what, Cal?' she said, knowing exactly where this was headed. 'What? If you do indeed love me, then what? Do you want us to stay together?'

His face shuttered. 'Don't, Gina,' he whispered. 'Not yet. I can't. Just let's take this moment.'

'Like we did five years ago? That ended up with CJ.'

Where had that come from? She hadn't wanted to say it. This moment could well be all she had, and to spoil it…

But desire was being replaced by an anger that couldn't be ignored.

'I'm not suggesting we go to bed,' he told her, and her anger grew.

'Good. Neither am I.'

'We have to figure something out.'

This was ridiculous. They were chest-deep in water, discussing their future. Or their lack of a future. The waves were washing in and out, Cal's hands still held her firm around the waist, protecting her from the waves' force, and she was so close. But his face, his eyes…they said there was still a distance between them.

Of course there was a distance between them.

'Gina, do you have to go back to the States?' he asked, and she stilled.

'What are you suggesting?'

'We need to work things out.'

'Maybe.' Be careful, her head was screaming. Be very careful. But there was a tiny hope…

'Gina, you loved working in Townsville.'

So I did, she thought. Because you were there.

'What if I did?' she asked, and managed to keep her voice steady.

'You had your kids' club. You enjoyed it. You loved the emergency work.'

'That's right.'

'If you were to go back there… Townsville's only an hour's flight from here. I spend a lot of time there.'

The world seemed to have stopped breathing. She tried to make herself think. 'So…why would I go to Townsville?'

'I could see you,' he told her. 'I work a roster of three

weeks on, one week off. I could spend a week at Townsville and get to know CJ.'

'I guess you could.' Her glimmer of hope had faded into nothing. Her voice sounded leaden, defeated. What else had she expected? she asked of herself. Fairy-tales were for storybooks. Not for her. 'But where would that leave me?'

'You liked Townsville.'

'My family and friends are in Idaho.'

'I'd be in Townsville.'

'Once a month.'

'Gina, we could see how it went.' His voice was softly persuasive and he bent to kiss her again.

But she was having none of it and she shoved him away.

'Yes, we could,' she said. Anger was her only aid now, but she had it in spades. More than anger. Pure, blind fury. 'I could give up my very good job in the States. I could abandon my friends. But why, Cal? So you get to see CJ once a month?'

'He's my son.'

'Prove it,' she snapped. 'What makes a father? A one-night stand?'

'We never had a one-night stand. You know that.'

'I know it. Do you?'

'Gina, I'm saying that I've loved you.' He put a hand through his sodden hair, raking it with the air of a man past his limits. He was as exhausted as she was, she thought, and had to fight an almost overwhelming compulsion to reach out to him. But no way. No way! 'These last few years have been hell.'

'But not enough to reach out now and say let's be a family. Not enough to even want me to stay in the same town as you.'

'I don't do—'

'You don't do commitment,' she finished for him, almost cordially. 'So what's new?'

'You know as well as I do what happens down that road,' he told her, and he was drawing away from her now. 'Look

at what happened tonight. One minute these people had loving, laughing teenagers, the next they had nothing. You had
Paul and he's dead. And me... I learned that lesson over and
over again. The only way of sanity is independence. You can
love someone and stay independent. You must.'

'Can you? Can you really love them?'

'That's what I'm saying,' he told her, as if explaining something to a child.

'Then you're talking nonsense,' she managed. 'I can love
CJ and stay independent? I don't think so.'

'That's what I mean,' he said wearily. 'You're caught. If
anything happened to CJ, you'd break your heart, and why put
yourself there?' His eyes grew bleak and distant. 'Of all the
stupid, irresponsible acts. Stuffing up birth control. Us! Two
doctors. We should never have messed up like that. For me to
have put you through that...'

And that was the limit. Her anger had boiled straight over
to full-blown fury, a fury mixed with desolation, rejection
and loss.

She stared at him for a long, baffled minute—and then she
reached out and hit him.

A wave caught her just as she did, knocking her sideways
into the surf. She'd hit his face but her slap had been deflected, much of its force lost. But she no longer cared. She
lay where she'd been knocked, letting the water wash over her,
thinking about not even bothering to surface, and when Cal's
hand reached down to grab her and haul her up she reacted
as if his touch burned.

She kicked out, a futile act in three feet of water, smacked
his hands away from her and backed out of the waves. Dumb,
useless tears were mixing with the salt water.

'You low-life! Get away from me.'

'Hell, Gina, I didn't mean to say...' Cal sounded horrified.

'You did say,' she spluttered, backing further away from

him. 'Get lost, Cal Jamieson. You say you loved me. That's ridiculous. You don't know the meaning of the word. Leave me be. I'm going back to the hospital. I'm going to check on our baby in the morning and the minute he doesn't need me I'm out of here. I'm out of your life. I'll send you a photo of CJ every year on his birthday. I'm sure that's all you want, Cal Jamieson, and it's all you deserve. Get lost.'

Three hundred miles away another drama was being played out. Another consequence of loving.

'Megan?'

'Go away.' The girl's voice dragged as though there was no strength left in it and her mother's surge of fear grew even stronger. What was happening?

Honey had hoped this day could be different. When she'd persuaded her husband and daughter to go to the rodeo she'd almost allowed herself to be optimistic. She'd hoped it could be time out from the depression that draped this sad old farmhouse and the people in it.

But Megan had been silent and sullen all the way to the rodeo, and as soon as they'd arrived she'd disappeared to be by herself in the bush. Well, what was new? Honey had wondered sadly. For the last few months Megan had glumped round the house in her oversized men's clothes, she'd worked in sullen silence, she'd eaten like there was no stopping her, not caring care how much weight she put on...

Honey Cooper had been concerned about her nineteen-year-old daughter for months, but then she'd also been terrified about her husband's failing health. More. She'd been terrified that the bank would finally foreclose on the farm. She'd been terrified that Jim would kill himself. There was only so much terror one woman could hold, and Megan's depression had seemed the least of it.

But today there'd been something new. Worse. On the way

home from the rodeo Megan had huddled into the back of the car like a wounded animal. She'd stayed there until Honey had got Jim inside and then Megan had scuttled into her bedroom and locked the door behind her.

Now she'd been in the bathroom for an hour and as Honey had lain beside Jim she'd heard searing, racking sobs that had terrified her past all the rest.

And things she'd been trying hard to ignore had suddenly refused to be ignored a moment longer.

'What the hell's going on with Megan?' Jim asked, and she laid a hand on her husband's arm to stop him getting up. His heart was so bad. He mustn't get upset.

'Hush. I'll go and see.'

'It's not that boy?' Jim rolled over in the dark and stared bleakly at his wife in the moonlight streaming in through the dust-streaked window. 'He wasn't at the rodeo, was he? If he's been seeing her again... If he's hurt her...'

'I'm sure he wasn't there,' Honey said soothingly. 'You know Megan promised she wouldn't see him again. I'm sure she meant it and I'm sure he hasn't tried to see her. Hush. I'll go and see what's wrong.'

But now she stood outside the locked bathroom door and she knew that there was no quick fix available here. Megan's sobs were truly frightening. Megan, who'd held the family together. She'd leaned on her far too much, Honey thought as she asked again that her daughter unlock the door. But what choice did she have?

Megan was nineteen and clever and she'd ached to go to university—but if she'd gone then the hard work here would have killed Jim. So Honey had pressured her to stay. Megan had worked and worked, even after that boy...

'Megan, love, you need to unlock the door.'

'I'm fine.' The words were spoken on a hiccuping sob. 'Go away. I'm fine.'

'You're not fine and I'm not going away until you open the door. Please, Megan. Your father's worried.'

Your father's worried. Your father's sick. Your father needs you. Here it was again, Honey thought. Emotional blackmail. But it was all she had.

And it worked now as it had worked before. There was a ragged gasp, a scuffle—sounds of cleaning up?—and then the door was opened a crack.

'I'm fine,' Megan said again, harshly into the stillness of the darkened house. *'Tell Dad he doesn't have to worry.'*

'Come into your room and we'll talk about it.' She was still whispering. Jim mustn't hear.

'Why?' Megan whispered back, just as fiercely. *'There's nothing to talk about.'*

She turned, and as she did, Honey gasped.

Megan was wearing a faded chenille dressing-gown, the sort of shapeless garment she'd been wearing for months. But as she turned against the moonlight streaming in from the window at the end of the passage, Honey had caught her profile.

For months she'd been looking at that profile, thinking no, surely not, that would be the one thing that would kill Jim, please no. It was just weight gain. Megan had been overeating. It had to be the reason.

And now...

'Oh, God, you've lost it,' she whispered. *'Meg, you've lost the baby.'*

'What baby?'

'You were pregnant.'

'So what?' Megan said wearily, and Honey grabbed her shoulders and propelled her back into her room and shut the door behind her.

'You really were.'

'Yeah, but I'm not any more.' The girl's voice sounded exhausted. Defeated.

'What…what happened?'

'It was dead,' Megan whispered, still in that awful, inhuman voice. 'It came early and it was dead. A miscarriage. I miscarried a baby and now it's over. So you don't have to worry. I'm fine.'

'Oh, my dear…' Honey reached out to hug her daughter but Megan flinched away.

'Leave me alone,' she said dully. 'Go back to Dad. Tell him there's no need to worry. I'll go on being his good little girl and he doesn't have to have a heart attack.'

'Megan, that's not fair.'

'My baby's dead,' Megan flashed at her. 'Is that fair?' Then she crumpled back onto the bed, sinking her face into her hands. 'Nothing's fair. The whole world isn't fair.'

'I'll take you to the hospital,' Honey said uncertainly, and Megan's hands dropped from her face so she could stare at her mother in fury.

'You think I shut up for all these months for you to tell Dad now?' she snapped. 'Protect Dad at all costs? Well, I have and there's nothing to do now but go to bed and forget about it.'

'You'll need to be checked.'

'I'm fine.'

'Love…'

'I'm not going anywhere,' Megan whispered. 'I'm not doing anything. You tell anyone and I'll deny it absolutely. The whole thing is over, Mum. Go back to bed.'

She sat, rigid and unmoving, waiting for Honey to leave. Waiting to be alone again. Waiting.

Honey was left with nothing to do. With nowhere to go.

She stared down at her daughter for a long, long minute and Megan glared back, unflinching.

'The baby's dead and it's over,' she whispered. 'There's an end to it. An end to everything.'

'Oh, my love…'

'There's no love about it,' Megan said bleakly. 'Leave me be.'

'Honey?'

It was Jim's voice calling from down the hall, and with a last desperate glance at her daughter Honey turned away.

Megan flinched again.

But she sat unmoving. Then, as the door finally closed behind her mother, the girl hauled herself under the covers—and she started to shake.

CHAPTER SIX

IT WAS almost noon when Gina woke and for a moment she didn't have a clue where she was or what was happening.

Then remembrance flooded back and with it horror.

The events of the day before were a jumbled kaleidoscope of surging emotion. A desperately ill baby. Dead children. Appalling injuries. Cal…

CJ. She reached out and his warm little body wasn't beside her. Of course. He was with the Grubbs.

Still?

She checked her watch and gasped. What was she thinking of, sleeping this late? The baby, CJ—she'd have been needed and no one had called. She threw back her covers and then gasped again as a man's silhouette blocked the sun.

'You might like to reconsider getting out of bed,' Cal drawled. 'Unless you're wearing more than it looks like you're wearing from out here.'

He was on the veranda. She'd left the door open last night to let in the sea breeze, and he was blocking the doorway. And as for what she was wearing… Last night—or early this morning—she'd simply stripped off her sea-soaked clothes, stood under a cold shower until her burning body had cooled and then fallen straight into bed.

And now here was Cal, right in the doorway.

'Go away,' she snapped, and hauled her sheet up to her chin.

'I brought you your luggage,' he told her, not going away at all but walking into her room and dumping her gear at the foot of the bed. 'You could at least sound grateful.'

'I'm grateful,' she told him, glaring enough to give the lie to her words. But then she looked at the single red bag he was carrying and was distracted enough to be deflected. 'I had two bags. A red and a green one.'

'The red one's heavy enough.'

'I had a small green one.'

'It didn't come back, then,' he told her. 'The coach-line people delivered one red bag this morning but that was all there was. Problem?'

She caught herself. 'Um...no.' No problem. She was staying next door to a hospital after all.

Right. Where was she? Glaring.

'There's no problem if you go away,' she told him, and he had the temerity to smile.

'OK. But I've also brought you your son.'

CJ. She sat up, cautiously, still holding her sheet. 'What have you done with CJ?'

'You sound as if you expect that I've corrupted him by just existing.'

'Don't be ridiculous,' she told him, still trying to hold her glower. Drat the man, why did he have to smile like that? 'Where is he?'

'He was right behind me but his puppy escaped into the garden. I can see them from here. The puppy seems to be investigating the lorikeets in the grevillea and CJ is supervising.'

She tried to sort this information but found it even more confusing. 'His puppy?'

'The Grubbs have given your son...our son...a puppy.'

There was a lot in that statement to consider—so she stuck to the easiest bit. 'CJ can't have a puppy,' she said blankly.

'I would have thought that.' Cal stood at the end of her bed and looked at her, speculation and amusement lurking in those deep eyes. 'But you did leave him with the Grubbs for the night.'

'I didn't mean to.'

'No, but you did, and the Grubbs are warm-hearted people who maybe lack a little in the grey-matter department. They have a puppy they don't want—their bitch has a habit of finding all sorts of unsuitable partners and the Grubb puppies are legion in this place—and they've seen a little boy who falls in love. So they've done the obvious thing.'

Still too much information. She couldn't figure it all out. And why was he standing there, just…smiling?

'We're going back to the States,' she told him.

'I guess the puppy is, too, then.'

'Oh, for heaven's sake.' She went to toss back the covers, remembered and grabbed them back again. 'Go away so I can dress.'

'I'll wait on the veranda.'

'Wait anywhere you like. Just not here.'

'I'll watch CJ, shall I?'

'Watch him all you want.'

'Gina…'

'Yes?'

'You're not being very kind.'

'Why should I be kind?' she demanded. 'Just go away, Cal Jamieson. You don't make me feel kind at all.'

By the time she'd showered and dressed she'd simmered down a little—but not much. Not enough. She walked out onto the veranda wearing her own clothes, a soft linen skirt and a T-shirt that didn't look businesslike but at least made her feel clean and normal and almost in charge of her world. It was great to have her own gear. Or almost all her own gear. Then she saw Cal with her son and she forgot about her luggage and she wasn't in charge of her world any more at all.

They were so alike it was breathtaking. Heartbreaking.

From the time CJ had been born she'd seen Cal every time she'd looked into her son's face, and now, seeing them side by side, it was almost too much for her. When she walked out onto the veranda CJ was wearing Bruce's hat, but the pup bounced up and knocked it off. Cal retrieved it and together they carefully inspected it for damage. CJ's wiry curls, the intent look in his eyes, the way his forehead puckered in concentration… Their heads were almost touching, the sound of Cal's grave voice telling the pup to leave the hat alone, CJ's higher voice raised in a copied command—and then a low chuckle and a high-pitched giggle as the puppy bounced up and raced off with the hat again…

Practicalities, she told herself fiercely as she dug her hands deep into her skirt's side pockets and walked steadily down the steps to meet them.

They heard her sandals on the steps and Cal turned—but as he turned, the pup saw a new pair of legs coming toward him, dropped the hat and bounced over to investigate.

For the first time she focussed on the dog. What was it?

A cross between a Dalmatian and a boxer with a bit of cocker spaniel thrown in, she thought. It looked half-grown, long and gangly and all legs. White with black spots. A face that looked like it had just been punched flat. Great ears that dangled past his collar.

He reached her and jumped up, his large paws landing on her thigh and darned near knocking her over. He looked up at her, and she could swear his big stupid canine face was grinning, and his black and white tail was wagging so fast it could have made electricity.

'What sort of a dog is this?' she gasped, trying to back off. But the pup wasn't having any of it. He was leaping up and dancing around her, barking and grinning and grinning, and despite herself she had to grin back.

'His name is Rudolph, after a ballet dancer Mrs Grubb saw on TV,' CJ told her, looking at his mother with a certain amount of anxiety. 'Mrs Grubb says he's going to be the best dog in the world and he prances just like a ballet dancer. Can we keep him?'

Rudolph had raced back down to his new would-be owner. Now he squatted in pounce position, leapt at CJ, knocked him down, licked his face, then galloped back to Gina. Gina backed fast but he jumped up, the backs of her legs caught the veranda steps and she sat down. Hard.

Rudolph licked with a tongue that was roughly the size of a large facecloth.

'Ugh,' Gina said, stunned. She wiped her face and watched the dog gallop over to Cal.

'Sit,' Cal said.

Rudolph sat.

The tail was going ballistic.

'CJ, we can't keep this dog,' she said, and if her voice sounded desperate, who could blame her? 'For a start there's no way we can take him home. He can hardly sit on my lap on the plane.'

'He can sit on mine,' CJ said stoutly, and Cal choked.

'You laugh and I'm going to have to kill you,' Gina said conversationally, and focussed on CJ. Or tried to focus on CJ. 'I'm sorry about last night,' she told him. 'Did you mind sleeping at Mrs Grubb's?'

'No, because of Rudolph,' he told her. 'Mom, Mr Grubb says he has to take a dead tree to the rubbish tip and I can go in his truck if I want, and Rudolph can come, too, but I have to ask you first so Cal said we should wake you up.'

'Gee, thanks, Cal,' she said, and glowered.

'Think nothing of it,' Cal said, smiling blandly. 'But Mr Grubb's waiting. Can CJ go? Grubb's very reliable.'

There were three faces looking at her in mute appeal. CJ's, Cal's, Rudolph's. She was so out of her depth she was drowning.

'Fine,' she told them all, and was rewarded by a war whoop and the sight of her small son—and dog—flying away across the lawn to the dubious attractions of Crocodile Creek's rubbish tip.

'I haven't even thought about when we're leaving,' Gina said, staring after her son in dismay.

'Good,' Cal told her.

'You're not still on about Townsville?' she snapped, and he had the grace to look a bit shamefaced.

'No. Gina, I'm sorry about last night.'

'Good.'

'I pushed you for my own ends.'

'So you did.'

'And I never meant that I didn't want CJ to have been born. Of course I didn't.'

'Fine.' She glowered. It seemed to be becoming a permanent state.

'But it would be good for CJ to be raised where I could have some access.'

'So move to the States.'

'My base is here.'

'No,' she said, and her anger faded a bit as she turned to face him square on. 'You don't have a base.'

'I've been here for four years.'

'Yes, but you don't love anyone here.'

'That's irrelevant.'

'No, it's not.'

'Gina…'

'You don't need any of these people,' she said. She'd gone to bed last night thinking of Cal, thinking of what was happening with him, and this discussion seemed an extension of that. It might be intrusive—none of her business—but him pushing her last night seemed to have removed the barriers to telling things how they were. 'Cal, you're spending your whole life patching people up, picking up the pieces, in medicine and in your personal life. Like with me. I came out here five years ago desperately unhappy and you picked up the pieces and you patched me up and I fell deeply in love with you. But then you don't take the next step. You never admit you need anyone else. Is there anyone here you need? Really, Cal?'

'I…'

'Of course there's not,' she said, almost cordially. 'Because of what happened with your family, you've never let yourself need anyone again.'

'What is this?' he demanded, startled. 'Psychology by Dr Lopez?'

'I know. It's none of my business,' she told him, gentling. 'But it's why I have to go home. Because I've admitted that I need people. I need my family and my friends.' More, she thought, and the idea that swept across her heart was so strong that she knew it for absolute truth. She needed Cal. But she wouldn't say that. She'd said it years ago, and where had that got her?

'For me to calmly go and live in Townsville would hurt,' she told him. 'Sure, I'd have a great job…'

'You'd meet people.'

'So I would,' she told him. 'But not the people I love.'

'You'd learn…'

'You really don't understand the need thing, do you, Cal?' she said sadly. 'I need my friends and I need my family and I'm not too scared to admit it.'

'You're saying I am?'

'I'm not saying anything,' she said wearily. 'But Townsville's not going to happen.' She regrouped. Sort of. 'And Rudolph's not going to happen either,' she told him, 'so stop encouraging CJ.'

'I'm not.'

'Just stop it,' she said. She closed her eyes for a moment, still trying for the regroup. 'The baby. Lucky. How is he?'

'He's still holding his own,' Cal told her. They'd both moved back into the shade of the veranda—in this climate you moved into the shade as if a magnet was pulling you. 'There doesn't seem any sign of infection. His heartbeat's settling and steady.'

'I'll do another echocardiogram now.'

'We thought you'd say that, so we waited for you to wake up.'

'You should have—'

'There was no need,' he said gently, and she flushed. She hated it when he was gentle. She hated it when he was…how she loved him. 'What about the bleeding?'

'The results of yesterday's blood tests should be in soon,' he told her. 'Alix, our pathologist, is working on them now.'

'I haven't used any clot-breaking medication,' she said. 'Usually after a procedure for pulmonary stenosis I'd prescribe a blood thinner but I've held off. There's a fair risk of blood clots in infants this tiny, but if he's a bleeder…'

'Hamish concurs,' he told her. 'He's saying von Willebrand's is a strong possibility.'

She nodded, flinching inside as she thought through the consequences.

Von Willebrand's was a treatable condition. A similar disorder to haemophilia, any cut or major bruising could be life-threatening, but treated it was far less dangerous. In fact, given this baby's condition, it was a bonus in that it made it less likely that Lucky would get a clot.

But it left an even deeper sense of unease about the mother. A woman, or more likely a girl, who'd had no medical help during a birth, who had possibly told no one about the birth, who was on her own.

Was she right in her surmise that the girl wasn't a bleeder? If she'd haemorrhaged afterwards...

'Has there been any news about the mother?'

'Nothing,' Cal told her, and she could see by his face that he was following her train of thought and was as worried as she was. 'The police and a couple of local trackers have been right through the bushland round the rodeo area. They're sure that she's no longer in the area. She must have come by car and left by car.'

'Or by bus.'

'Or bus.'

'And maybe she has von Willebrand's disease. Maybe she's a bleeder.'

'She or the father,' Cal said.

'I'm not worrying about the father right now,' Gina told him. 'I'm worrying too much about the mother. To give birth in such a place, to leave thinking your baby was dead... What she must be going through.'

They fell silent. Each knew what the other was thinking. Suicide was a very real possibility. If only they knew where she was. Who she was.

'There's no matching prenatal mothers in our records at all,' Cal told her. 'No clues.'

'I thought everyone knew everyone in this district.'

'No one knows who this is.'

'Someone must,' Gina said, and Cal nodded.

More silence.

'Charles says his father had von Willebrand's,' Cal said, and Gina frowned.

'Charles?'

'Our medical director. The guy in the wheelchair.'

'I know who Charles is,' she snapped. 'Charles's father has von Willebrand's?'

'Had. He's dead.'

'Charles is a local?' Gina was still thinking it through. 'Von Willebrand's is a rare blood disorder. In such a small community there has to be some connection.'

'We talked it through last night,' Cal told her. 'After you and I...' He broke off. 'Well, when I came back to the house Charles was still awake and we ended up talking things through till almost dawn. Like you, when he said that I thought there must be a connection. But it seems unlikely.'

'Why? Tell me about his family.'

'Charles is a Wetherby. The Wetherbys own one of the biggest stations in the state—Wetherby Downs. Charles's brother runs the station now.' Cal hesitated. 'I'm not sure why, but Charles and his family don't get on. Charles was hurt in a shooting accident when he was eighteen. He went to the city for medical treatment, ended up staying to do medicine and only came back here to set up this service. He hasn't had much to do with his family for years. But as for the von Willebrand's.... Charles himself doesn't have kids. His brother doesn't have von Willebrand's, and his brother's two kids are only fourteen and sixteen.'

'The sixteen-year-old?' she said quickly. 'That'd fit. A girl?'

'Yes, but—'

'A teenager in trouble and desperate not to tell her parents?'

'Charles checked it out this morning,' Cal told her. 'She's in boarding school in Sydney and hasn't been home for a month.'

'So we'll cross her off the list,' Gina said reluctantly. 'Is there no other family?'

'Charles's only other sibling is a sister who moved to Sydney over twenty years back,' he told her. 'It was a lead worth following but it's going nowhere.'

'It just seems such a coincidence,' she murmured. 'It's so rare.'

'Charles's father was not exactly a man of honour,' Cal told her. 'Charles volunteered that last night. The man was filthy rich, and used to get what he wanted. There's more than an odds-on chance that he played around.'

'But he's dead,' Gina said. 'So we can't ask him if he fathered anyone who might or might not have fathered someone who's just had a baby. We're clutching at straws here.' She sighed. 'OK. Enough. I'll go and see the baby now.' She hesitated. 'But last night… The accident, the repercussions…'

'Will be felt throughout the district for ever,' Cal told her heavily. 'I'm going out to the aboriginal settlement later this afternoon.'

'Do you want me to come with you?' Now, where had that come from? She hadn't meant to offer. It had just slipped out.

'I'd like that,' he said gravely, and she cast him a sideways look of suspicion.

'Maybe I shouldn't.'

'Gina, you would help,' he told her. 'You're good with people. You know what to say.'

'So do you,' she said bitterly. 'The Dr Jamieson specialty. Picking up the pieces.' She shook her head. 'Sorry. I'm not going there any more. But I will come to the settlement with you. I might as well be useful now I'm here. OK, Dr Jamieson. Let's move on.'

Cal had patients booked to see him. He had to leave her—for which Gina was profoundly grateful. Sort of. With CJ happily carting junk and Cal disappearing, she was left on her own.

She spent a few minutes calming down and then went to find a pharmacist.

She wanted to see the baby but she had priorities of her own first.

The hospital dispensary was deserted. Open at need, she

thought, and tried to figure who to ask. Not Cal. But as she turned away Charles was behind her in his wheelchair and she jumped almost a foot.

'Do you mind?' she asked breathlessly, and he grinned.

'Sorry. I've tried to get a wheelchair that does footsteps but they don't make them.'

'I'm sorry.'

'Don't be. My speciality's scaring people. And I'm sorry about last night. Talk about throwing you in at the deep end…'

'It was awful,' she admitted. 'But maybe less awful for me who doesn't know the people and who won't be round to cope with the consequences.'

'Cal reminded me you used to run a kids' group at Townsville.'

'So I did,' she told him.

'You don't fancy doing it again?' he asked mildly. 'There's a screaming need here.'

'Cal suggested that,' she told him. 'But he suggested I do it at Townsville.'

Charles's face stilled. He looked at her for a long minute and then he grimaced.

'Cal's a fool.'

'No.' She shrugged. 'Not a fool. And I'm going home. There's no place here for me.'

'There's always a place here for you,' Charles told her forcibly. 'Your reputation from Townsville was that of a splendid doctor and we'd be honoured to have you stay. Apart from really, really needing a cardiologist.'

'And where does that leave Cal?'

'Having to face what he should have faced five years ago,' Charles told her.

She shook her head and closed her eyes. 'Leave it, Charles.'

He looked up at her for a long minute—and then he sighed.

'OK, We'll leave it.' He glanced up at her face once more

and then through to the empty dispensary. 'Were you looking for something?'

'A pharmacist.'

'We don't have such a thing. We get what we need when we need it. Do you need something?'

'Insulin.'

There was an even longer pause. 'For you?' he asked at last, and Gina thought, Yes, the man was fast. He'd have figured it couldn't have been for CJ. She'd never have been able to leave him with strangers if it had been CJ.

'Yes. For me.'

He frowned. 'Does Cal know you're diabetic?'

'Cal doesn't know the first thing about me,' she told him. 'But that's irrelevant. I had my main supply of insulin in my second suitcase, which still seems to be lost. I carry enough for two or three days in my hand luggage but I'll be needing more by tomorrow.'

'I'll organise it for you,' he told her. 'Is there anything else you need?'

'An air ticket home?'

'I'll organise that, too,' he told her, but then he hesitated. 'Gina, can you give us another forty-eight hours? I'd like to have Lucky really out of the woods before you go.'

'With Hamish and Emily, you hardly need me.'

'I know I hardly need you,' he growled. 'But it's the *hardly* I don't like. I don't want to lose this kid. And neither do you.'

'No.'

'So you'll stay two more days?'

'I guess.' There was a lot to be sorted, she thought. She had to come to some arrangement with Cal by then. She had to figure out what sort of father he was prepared to be.

Then there was the added complication of Rudolph.

She sighed.

'I do need another couple of nights,' she told him.

'A couple of years would be good.'

'Don't push it.'

Next on her list was Lucky. Gina walked into the nursery and found not one but two doctors clucking over him. Hamish was checking a drip and Em was consulting patient notes, but both of them looked up with such guilty starts as she walked in that she smiled.

'Don't tell me. Both of you should be somewhere else.'

'We're just looking,' Hamish told her, and smiled. His smile was a bit forced, though, and Gina knew exactly what was happening. After a night like last night, there was a huge need for at least one happy ending and she had a feeling that she wasn't the only one to have an urge to hug. Babies were excellent therapy. As if he was reading her thoughts, Hamish continued. 'You've just missed Cal.'

'And Charles before him,' Emily said ruefully. 'Anyone who's anyone has been in to check on our little Lucky this morning.' She moved aside. 'Now it's your turn. Go right ahead. Do your checking.'

She did.

He looked different today, Gina thought. A little...fuller? Yesterday he'd been barely alive. Now, even though he was still a tiny scrap of crumpled babyhood, Lucky's eyes were wide, his tiny fists were flailing, and she had the strongest urge to pick him up and gather him to her.

She couldn't. Hamish had him wired for everything—the technology surrounding this baby was far, far bulkier than the baby himself. It almost seemed ridiculous. So much technology on something so small.

Her hands slid into the incubator port and she stroked the little one's cheek, and then she slid her little finger into the palm of the tiny hand. His fingers curled around and held, and Gina had to fight back a sudden, stupid surge of tears.

'You don't need me here,' she said blindly, gently releasing her finger and starting to turn away.

But Hamish caught her shoulder and turned her back.

'We do need you, Gina,' he said softly. 'You did a wonderful job here. I've only read of the operation you did on Lucky yesterday. I haven't even seen it. I rang the paediatric cardiologist in Sydney this morning and he's stunned it's gone so well.'

'That's...good. I was lucky.'

'Lucky was lucky,' Hamish told her, and smiled. 'And last night we were lucky to have you again. And Cal... Cal's lucky that he met you.'

'We think he loves you,' Emily said, and Gina blinked.

'Um...excuse me?'

'He's been faithful for years.'

'Sure.'

'He has.'

'Because I'm an excuse.'

'Yes, but you're more than an excuse,' Emily told her. 'He really fell hard. Charles said—'

'You've all been talking about me.'

'It's the doctors' house,' Hamish said, as if that explained everything. 'We all talk about everyone. And we worry about Cal.'

'He's big enough to worry about himself.'

'But if he had a son—' Em started, but Gina had had enough.

'Look, leave it,' she said, more roughly than she'd intended, but Hamish looked at Emily as if for confirmation and then went in anyway.

'Gina, you fought for Lucky,' he said gently. 'Emily and Charles and I think you should fight for Cal. He's worth fighting for.'

'I've been fighting for years,' she said bitterly. 'I'm past fighting.'

'But Cal—'

'Sure, Cal's had it hard,' she snapped. 'But I haven't exactly had it easy. I've been fighting for my husband's life, for my son's welfare and for my own health.' She caught herself and bit her lip, angry with herself more than them. These were Cal's friends. Sure, they were interfering more than she liked—a lot more than she liked—but she wasn't in familiar territory and what she should do now was back out.

So she backed out. Fast. Letting her eyes drop again to Lucky as she did.

He was so perfect.

'I'm going out to the settlement with Cal,' she said, and Emily smiled.

'That's great.'

'It's not great. But…keep Lucky safe for me while I'm away.'

'We will, that,' Hamish told her softly. 'Of course we will. And in return, can we ask that you keep an open mind?'

'An open mind and an open heart?' she demanded, meeting his look head on. 'Is that what you mean? If it is, I tried that five years ago and it didn't work. What makes you think it'll work now?'

Megan woke and for a moment she'd forgotten. She lay in her sweat-soaked bed and let herself stay blank. Just for a moment.

But then her mother was there, holding her hand, sitting on the bed, terror flooding her face.

'Dad,' Megan whispered. She was accustomed to that terror. 'Something's happened to Dad.'

But it seemed that the terror had been redirected. The terror was for her.

'Sweetheart, we need to get you to a doctor,' Honey was saying, and yesterday flooded back in all its horror. Megan cringed.

'No.'

'You're ill. You're soaking in sweat.'

'I'll get over it.'

'Megan, you must let me take you—'

'There's no must about it,' Megan told her, fighting for strength to sound sure. 'OK, I'm ill, but I'll get recover. Tell Dad I've got the flu. Don't let him near me. Tell him he'll catch it. I'm sorry, Mum, but you'll have to do my chores…'

'Oh, sweetheart…'

'Just for a day or two,' Megan mumbled. The effort she'd made saying just those words had been too much for her and she was wilting. 'But you don't want to tell Dad anything else. Do you?'

'Of course I don't.'

'There you go, then,' Megan said wearily. To tell Jim was unthinkable. Protect him at all costs. 'Leave it. Leave me be. I'll be just…fine.'

CHAPTER SEVEN

WHY had she said she'd go out to the settlement with Cal? She must have been mad. But after a couple of hours of staying back at the doctors' residence, watching CJ play with a pup he couldn't keep, seeing every other doctors' eyes on her, staying started to seem a pretty bleak alternative.

After the chaos of yesterday the hospital was quiet. Gina had thought she'd be needed for Lucky but Emily had been hovering over the little one, almost possessive. 'Emily's had a bad time lately,' Charles told her. 'She needs distraction and if that distraction's the baby then we'll let her be.'

This hospital was more of a family than a medical clinic, Gina thought, and Charles's speculative gaze on her made her feel intensely uncomfortable. Who knew what he was deciding that she needed?

She'd offered to help with the kids from the night before, but she was stymied there as well.

'The worst of the cases are being transferred to Cairns,' Charles told her.

There was another pang as Gina saw the plane take off. She should be on it.

'But you've offered to go out to the settlement with Cal,' Charles said.

'I could change my mind.'

133

'Cal needs you.'

'He doesn't need anyone,' she snapped, but Charles just smiled his wry smile and told her that in a medical capacity she'd be useful and he'd be delighted if she stayed. As she'd agreed to.

So she agreed. She'd run out of excuses. CJ and Walter Grubb had decided they were friends for life and there was more trash to cart. There was nothing for it but to decide this afternoon was just something to be worked through.

But it was hard. She sat beside Cal as the miles disappeared under their wheels and thought she'd been mad. She tried to think of something to say and nothing came.

Silence. Cal's face was set and grim.

Silence, silence and more silence.

Then, out of nowhere, Cal snapped 'How long have you been diabetic?'

It was almost an explosion. His knuckles were white on the steering-wheel and she stared at him in astonishment.

'How did you know?'

'Charles told me. Just now. He asked me how long you'd been diabetic, whether you were type one or two, how your control was—and you know what? I didn't even know you were diabetic. You couldn't have been one five years ago. Were you?'

He wanted her to say no, Gina thought. He sounded almost desperate.

'I've been diabetic since I was twelve,' she told him. 'Type one.'

'You weren't diabetic when you were here.'

'Of course I was.'

'You were living with me,' he said explosively. 'Sharing my bed. Sharing my life. How can I have not known you were diabetic?'

'No,' she said softly. 'You weren't sharing my life. We were lovers, Cal. We hadn't taken it further.'

'We were living together.'

'Cal, if we'd been really living together—really sharing our lives—do you think I could have kept something like that from you?'

'You must have hidden—'

'I hid nothing,' she said wearily. 'But you were so contained. I was hopelessly in love with you but you never shared your life. I had to drag your family history from you. You'd come home after a dreadful day—after some trauma or other—and you'd take my body as if you were desperate, but you'd never talk to me about what you were feeling. And me... You saw what you wanted to see, Cal. I remember at the end, when I was just starting to suspect I was pregnant. I was feeling ghastly and my blood sugars were all over the place and I was desperate. You came home that last night we had together and said I looked pale and what was wrong, and I told you I'd had a tummy bug. "Do you need medication?" you asked. When I said no, you hugged me and told me to go to bed and you considerately didn't touch me for the rest of the night. When I was crying out to be touched. Then next morning you asked if I was fine, and you believed me and went off to your urgent medical call. Even though I was shaky and white-faced and sick. Because you wanted me to be fine. You wanted me to slot into the edges of your life—the parts that were available.'

'But you're diabetic,' he said, sounding confused but also exasperated. 'Why hide it?'

'Because that would have made me way too needy,' she said, knowing that he wouldn't understand but not being able to think of any other way of explaining.

'Needy...'

'I was already in need,' she told him. 'I came to Townsville after Paul had asked for a separation and I was a mess. And you picked me up and put the pieces back together. Then... then you couldn't figure out where to go from there.'

'I don't know what you mean.'

'I don't suppose you do,' she said sadly. 'Because what I needed was for you to need me, and that was never going to happen. It was so one-sided. You fell for me because I leaned on you, and as soon as I didn't need you in a way you understood then you got uncomfortable. I sensed as much really early. I thought that I'd been stupid in the first place, letting myself lean on you, and if you knew I was diabetic then you'd figure I needed you still more, and the relationship would never go past being you the rescuer.'

'This isn't making sense.'

'It's not, is it?' she said. 'But I hate people feeling sorry for me because I'm diabetic.'

'I wouldn't have felt sorry for you.'

'No, but you would have supported me, and it would have felt more as if I needed you, and there was no way our relationship was going to work out that way. I was fighting so hard to get through to you on a personal level. And then I got pregnant and Paul was injured and it didn't matter any more anyway.'

He shook his head, obviously still trying to work things out.

'Your diabetes,' he said at last, and she Gina knew he was returning to medicine because that was an easy route. When in emotional crisis, turn to what you're good at.

Well, why not? 'What about my diabetes?'

'It's obviously well controlled.'

'Why obviously?'

'Because I never knew.' Once again he seemed to be fighting to contain anger.

'It wasn't, actually,' she told him. 'I've struggled for years and my pregnancy was a nightmare. But there's a new background insulin that was released last year and it's fabulous. I haven't had a hypo since I've been on it.'

'You never had a hypo when you were with me.'

'Of course I did.'

'When?'

'It mostly happened at night,' she told him. 'I'd wake feeling dizzy and sick and I'd head to the kitchen for juice. I did my injecting in the bathroom.'

'I never heard.'

'Of course you didn't.'

'What's that supposed to mean?'

'After we'd made love,' she said softly, remembering, 'you'd sleep on the far side of the bed so I didn't disturb you. You needed space, as I remember. You always needed space.'

More silence. Loaded silence.

'I'd have seen your injecting sites,' he said at last.

'Would you?' She shrugged. 'That needs real intimacy, Cal. Making love in the daylight with our eyes open. We hadn't reached it. I'm not sure we would have.'

'Why are you telling me this now?'

'I'm being honest. I don't know where else to go.'

'You don't need to go anywhere.'

'Meaning what?'

'Meaning you have to stay here.' The anger was growing, she thought, and the anger was self-directed. Fury at himself for not noticing?

Just plain fury.

'You can't go back to the States,' he told her.

'Why on earth not?'

'Hell, Gina, you need—'

'I don't need anything,' she flashed at him. 'Get that through your head, will you? I don't need you. CJ doesn't need a father. He's got great memories of Paul and they'll last him a lifetime. I don't need a husband. I have family and friends back in Idaho. I have a great career. I'm not a lost soul here, Cal.'

'I can look after you.' It was as if he wasn't hearing her. He was gripping the steering-wheel so tightly it was likely to crack at any minute.

'I can look after myself.'

'Look, Townsville was a bad idea,' he said. 'I know that. It was a dumb suggestion. At least, by yourself it was a bad idea. But together maybe things could work as they did last time you were here. We could set up house here.'

'You're not suggesting I marry you?' she said, astounded.

'We're good together.'

'No, we're not. Have you been listening to a thing I've been saying?'

'How did you cope with a pregnancy and type one diabetes and a quadriplegic husband?' he demanded, and she sighed.

'I'm sure I don't know. And I did it without you. Astounding, isn't it?'

'It's not astounding,' he said, catching the sarcasm in her voice and his own voice gentling in response. 'But it must have been hell.'

'Maybe. But that's got nothing to do with the here and now. Or with what I do in the future.'

'You say you love me.'

'That has nothing to do with it either,' she told him.

'Hell, Gina, if I'd known... If you knew how much I'd wondered about you...'

'You would have come galloping to the rescue,' she whispered.

'Of course I would. Gina, I love you.'

'See, that's the problem here.' She bit her lip, aware that her hold on the thread of this conversation was growing tenuous. She was barely making sense to herself, much less to him. 'I'm not sure you've really figured that out. You think it was dumb not telling you I was diabetic. You don't know why I didn't tell you.'

'No, but—'

'Shut up, Cal,' she told him. 'Just shut up.'

The country around the car was changing now, the bush-land near the coast giving way to the rocky country where they'd driven last night. They were nearing the site of the crash. Cal slowed, but there was no need. There were a couple of deep gashes in the gravel, a pool of spilt oil but nothing else. Everything had been cleared.

They drove in silence for a couple of minutes more, and Gina knew Cal was thinking exactly what she was thinking. What an appalling waste. And how quickly life could be snuffed out.

Was she crazy, throwing away Cal's offer? she wondered. He was saying marry him. Live here. Happily ever after?

Maybe she was just plain dumb, but she glanced across at Cal's set face and knew she was exactly right. She had no choice.

'Cal, I don't want a relationship based on need,' she told him. 'Or…not just my need. Sure, I love you but…'

'Well, then—'

'Let me explain,' she snapped. Honestly. Maybe a letter would be easier. She had to get her tongue around the right words.

'Even if I needed you—which I don't—that's no basis for a marriage,' she told him. 'Paul taught me that. He worked out the hard way that marriage was a really special thing. He sacrificed a lot to try and find it, and he didn't find it for himself, but I know exactly what it is and I'm not prepared to opt for second best. Cal, I love you, and all right, in one sense—in the sense of never being really happy apart—I need you. You say you love me and you want me, but you're only admitting that to yourself because you believe that I need you. You'd never in a pink fit say that you need me.'

'I don't need anyone.'

'There's the rub,' she said sadly. 'There's the reason the whole thing's not going to end in happy ever after. Because you won't let yourself need. You won't cuddle me to comfort yourself because you might get dependent. You say you didn't know I was diabetic? That's because you were so busy preserving your private space that you didn't notice that I had mine. I'm sorry, Cal, but CJ and I need more than that.'

'Gina, I'm asking you to marry me.'

'Am I expected to be grateful?'

'No. Yes. But—'

'I am grateful, Cal,' she said, softening in front of the anguish in his face. 'And I would love to be married to you. But I need to be needed, too, and I won't spend my life being grateful.' She thought about it—or tried to think about it. They were approaching the settlement now and time was running out.

'Cal, I want you to sleep with me and hold me and miss me desperately when I'm not there,' she told him, speaking almost to herself rather than him. 'I don't want you to train yourself to sleep on the other side of the bed in case one day I disappear. I want a relationship that's based on us being together for ever. Sure, one day it'll end and it'll hurt like crazy when that happens, but your way, hurt will be there all the time. Why let that happen when we could have forty years of cuddling?'

She caught her breath and blinked. Whoa, she was being too deep for comfort.

'Unless you snore,' she added, trying frantically to retrieve the situation. 'Then you're off to your side of the bed so fast you'll probably be ejected to the middle of next week.'

He didn't smile He didn't even try to smile.

'Gina, I can't do that,' she said slowly. 'You know I can't. What you're asking…'

'Is too much. I know that. That's why I'm going home.' She took a deep breath and tried to regroup. 'So let's cut out the talk of marriage, Cal Jamieson,' she told him. 'Let's see what this community needs. Move back to medicine. It's the only sanity in a world that seems often to be nuts in every other department. Tomorrow Bruce has asked that CJ and I go croc spotting with him, and the day after that I'm going home. We'll exchange Christmas cards and birthday cards and leave it at that. Your precious independence won't be compromised at all.'

'There has to be a middle road.'

'There isn't,' she said bluntly. 'Get used to it.'

Jim Cooper stood at the back step and watched Honey usher the house cow into the bale. And frowned. Megan did the milking. She'd done the milking since she was eight years old. To see his wife doing it...well, something was wrong.

'What's wrong with Meg?'

'She's not well,' Honey said in a clipped, strained voice that was unusual for the determinedly cheerful Honey.

That was when Jim felt the first shiver of fear. Or maybe it was more than a shiver. Maybe he knew that this was the end.

Honey had lost her optimism.

It was Honey's hopefulness that kept this family together, he thought. No matter what happened, Honey had always said things would be fine.

When the Wetherbys had cut off access to the creek at the crossing, meaning their stock were at the mercy of the district's notoriously unreliable rainfall, Honey had said they'd cope. There wouldn't be a drought. The rains would be reliable, at least until they'd got Megan through university and had saved enough for retirement.

When the drought had hit she'd said they could weather it. They could sell some stock and Megan didn't have to go to university quite yet.

When he'd had his heart attack she'd said it had just been minor, hadn't the doctor said? And, yes, he needed bypass surgery, but if they couldn't afford it then that was that, and surely a minor heart attack meant that the bypass could wait until after the rains came.

Meanwhile she and Megan were strong and they didn't mind doing more than their share of the work.

Then when Megan had fallen in love with that boy, she'd said she'd get over it, she was young, there were lots more boys, but, please, God, she wouldn't find one until after the rains because they needed Megan so much, and wasn't it lucky Megan was such a good girl?

Honey. The eternal optimist. But now... Honey's face was pressed against the cow's warm flank and she looked...defeated.

'What's wrong with Megan?' Jim asked again.

'Women's troubles.'

'Yeah?'

'And maybe she has some sort of infection,' Honey added reluctantly. 'Yeah, that'll be it. Women's troubles and flu. Don't go near her, Jim. I don't want you to catch it.'

Jim stared down at his wife for a long time. Honey kept on with her milking, methodically clearing the teats, her face carefully expressionless.

'I will check Megan,' Jim said at last. 'Sorry, Honey, but you can't protect me from everything for ever.'

The afternoon was a long one.

Cal came out to this settlement once a week. They rotated this duty, so three different doctors visited, with three different specialties. The settlement had a population of two to three hundred but the numbers changed as the various nomadic tribes arrived and stayed for a time before taking off on walkabout again. The nomads were generally healthy, Cal knew. It was those whose tribes had dwindled so far as to make the nomadic lifestyle untenable—those whose backgrounds had hauled them out of the ancient ways and left them with nothing to replace it—they were the ones who were in trouble. They stayed in these camps with no plan for the future, and in many cases they had drifted into despair.

Cal came out here once a week and he worked through medical problems, but every time he came here he tried to figure out how he could help.

Without getting involved.

His first patient for the afternoon was a teenager with a ragged gash from a fight involving broken bottles. His second patient was the kid's opponent. The cuts had been roughly patched but they needed deep cleaning, debridement, an administration of fast-acting antibiotics and a lecture on care.

The lecture would fall on deaf ears.

Five years ago he'd started a club for kids like these back at Townsville. Gina had talked him into it. But after she'd left… He'd gone down to the club and he'd realised that these kids had given him comfort. That helping kids like these had felt good.

That he'd cared.

And the knowledge had had him backing off as if he'd been burned. He'd told himself he needed to move to Crocodile Creek. He needed to concentrate on his medicine, and he couldn't do that if he was emotionally involved.

Work.

'Why the hell,' he asked the boy he was stitching, 'were you fighting with broken bottles? I thought you and Aaron were mates.'

'We were on the petrol,' the boy said, a bit shamefaced. 'I was off me head, like. Aaron was, too. After the accident…all our mates dead…we didn't know what else to do so we started on the petrol to kill time till the olds got back from the hospital. Aaron must'a said something to set me off, but dunno what. Just lucky it hurt, like, before we got too far.'

'Before the community had someone else to mourn,' Cal said grimly. 'Slicing like this could have meant you bled to death.'

'Nah.'

Cal sighed. Petrol sniffing was endemic here, used to alleviate boredom, loneliness, dissociation. There were so many problems.

He looked over to where Gina sat under a stand of eucalypts. She was in the midst of a group of women and their distress was obvious. Karen's grandmother was over there, Cal saw. Mary Wingererra. As he watched, Gina put her arm round the old lady's shoulders and hugged her.

She went in fast and hard, Cal thought. Maybe he should, too.

Could he? She thought he should. Her accusation was that he didn't care. It was unfair. That was the problem. He cared too much.

'When did you last go to school?' he asked Chris, the kid he was stitching, and the thirteen-year-old looked at him as if he was joking.

'School?'

'It's an option.'

'No one goes to school. It's not cool.'

It was the only option, Cal thought. Education was the only way out of this mess.

Yeah, but how...?

It was too hard. Once he'd thought he might try, but then Gina had walked away and he'd abandoned his kids' club when he'd left Townsville. It had hurt like hell and he wasn't putting himself through that again.

Don't get involved. Treat what's hurting and move on.

Gina was getting involved. Her body language was obvious. He could see her distress.

They were working outside—a hygienic option when the weather was good. It took a long time to get a room clean, and outside the rain periodically cleaned things up. He was sitting at a table and chairs they'd brought themselves. That was his surgery.

Gina didn't even have that. She was sitting on the grass twenty yards from where he was sitting. He couldn't hear what she was saying, but that they were talking through last night's accident was obvious.

She'd be expecting him to do something. She'd be judging...

No.

She didn't expect anything, he reminded himself. She was going home the day after tomorrow and he didn't have to answer to her. He had nothing to do with her.

Together they had a son.

'Will I have a scar?' Chris demanded, and Cal thought if he wasn't careful, yes, he would have.

'It's not too deep.'

'I don't mind having a scar.'

'I can count six already. That's enough for any kid.'

'Men have scars.'

'Only if they live long enough to be men,' Cal told him. 'Which you won't if you keep sniffing petrol and fighting with glass. Scars in the tribe you come from are supposed to be a sign of wisdom. There's not much wisdom in a scar like this.'

'No,' Chris admitted, and he cast a shamefaced glance behind him at his mate. 'I got a bit scared when Aaron bled. And...' He swallowed. 'I don't like it that they all got killed last night. I reckon they'd been sniffing petrol, too.'

'So stop it,' Cal said gently.

'There's nothing else to do.'

Gina was rising now. She still had her arm round the old lady's shoulders. Mary was weeping, Cal saw, and Gina's face was creased in concern. Gina was upset.

She didn't know these people. She didn't have to get involved.

Neither did he.

Gina looked across at him and gave him a half-smile, as if she expected that he share her distress.

'You need a swimming pool,' Cal said, and where the words had come from he didn't know. But he knew where the idea had come from. Something he'd heard on the radio— something he'd heard happening at a remote settlement a thousand miles from here and had thought a great plan.

Someone who might get involved might grab a plan like that and run with it.

'A swimming pool.' Aaron and Chris were looking at him like he was stupid.

'That's right,' he said, and it was too late to retract now. 'It's fifty miles to the coast from here, and even then you can't swim during the hot six months. Too many stingers. You guys need a pool.'

'Yeah, but how would we get a swimming pool?' Aaron demanded. Cal had been dressing Chris's leg while he spoke and now he motioned to Aaron to take his friend's place in front of him. Aaron's face had a long, vicious scratch. It didn't need stitching as Chris's leg had, but it needed to be scrupulously cleaned if it wasn't to be infected. Cal started work with care but the boys' attention was caught.

'You mean one of those paddling pools you blow up,' Aaron said scornfully. 'We had one. It lasted a whole day and a half before it got a hole in it.'

Gina was in earshot now. She was walking Mary over to see him, Cal realised, and he wished he could stop this conversation now, but both boys were staring at him in half-resentful expectation that this was nothing. It was definitely too late to back out.

'If I could talk the politicians into building a swimming pool here, would you guys go to school?'

'Nah,' Chris said scornfully. 'Why would we?'

'Because Mr Robbins and Mrs Cook run classes every day here, and they never have any more than six or so kids. They have heaps of room, they're great people, and if you guys learn to read and write then there's so much you could do.'

'Like what?' Chris demanded.'

'Well, you could get put up for selection for the national footy teams for one thing,' Cal said. 'They won't look at you unless you can read.'

'Yeah, but that's not till we're sixteen,' Chris objected. 'We might be dead before then.'

Which was the absolute truth, Cal thought grimly. It was even a probability.

OK.

OK, what?

Gina was watching him now. His conscience. And back at home was a little boy who looked like him—whose very existence seemed to make him aware that he ought to be doing more

He had to get involved. Just a bit.

'I'm going to work on getting you guys a swimming pool,' he told them.

They stared at him, disbelieving.

'You gotta be joking.'

'I'm not joking.' He glanced up at Gina but his eyes were caught instead by the little lady she was holding. Mary's face was swollen with weeping but her eyes were arrested. Her face was still. Waiting.

What was he doing? He didn't get involved.

He was involved.

'I was reading about a place like this near Darwin,' he told them, thinking it through as he talked. 'The locals started a collection, they got a government grant to help and they've built a swimming pool. They feed it from an underground bore. There's bore water here.'

'No one would do that for us,' one of the boys muttered.

'If they did it there I don't know why they wouldn't do it here,' Cal said. 'All it needs is some pressure.'

'No one here'd be a leader enough to put pressure on anyone,' Mary said slowly, and the old woman's voice was husky from weeping. 'We're so…' She searched for an appropriate word and didn't find one. 'Stuffed,' she said at last. 'Finished. We keep getting hit and the more we're hit the more we can't get up again. Now…all our young 'uns are dead…'

'Not all your young 'uns,' Cal said gently. He was clearing every trace of dirt and broken glass from Aaron's face. 'I'm so sorry about last night. But there's kids left and we need to move forward for them. We need desperately to move forward. I'm prepared to fight on your behalf.'

'You,' the old woman said, and Cal grimaced inside. He'd been coming out to this settlement for years, and until now he'd never got personally involved. It was no wonder the woman's tone was incredulous.

'Yeah, me,' he said ruefully, and tried not to look at Gina—who was looking as incredulous as the old lady. 'It's not only a way to give you some pleasure, but it's a way to get the kids to go to school.'

'How?' Aaron said belligerently.

'Stay still,' Cal told him, and Gina moved in to help, cutting a dressing to size so he had it ready as soon as the antiseptic was in place.

'Easy,' Cal said. 'Once we get the pool, there'd be a rule in place. If you miss a day's school without a very good reason, you'd be excluded from the pool for a month.'

'You're kidding me,' Aaron said. 'That's not fair.'

'That'd make 'em go to school,' the old lady said, thinking it through. Deflected for a moment from her tragedy. 'It's so hot and dusty here all the time, and the kids are bored stupid, and if they got to stay outside a fence, watching other kids swim…'

'Not fair,' Aaron said again, and Cal grinned.

'Fair or not, you'd go to school.'

'It'd be a start,' Gina said, and he glanced at her and glanced away again. Fast.

He wasn't doing this for her. He wasn't.

'You say you'd get it going?' Mary whispered, and he nodded.

'I'll come out next week and we'll have a community meeting. Next Wednesday?'

'So soon?'

'It might help,' he said diffidently. 'You need it, Mary.'

'Mary has been having what seem like panic attacks,' Gina told him. 'I thought maybe we could give her a script for something to help over the next few days.'

'There's no need,' Mary muttered, and she fixed Cal with a look that said now he'd offered there was no way he could back down. 'I couldn't see a way past this mess we're in. Now, though…a pool… If you really think it's possible…'

'I do.'

'Then I don't want no tranquillisers,' she told him. 'I just want a plan forward.'

'Do you mean it?'

They were in the car, headed back toward Crocodile Creek, and Gina was looking at him as if he'd grown another head.

'Of course I mean it.'

'You'd build a swimming pool out here.'

'It's possible,' he said, and he knew he sounded defensive but he couldn't help it. 'I've been thinking about it ever since I read about the other place. It seemed such a good idea. How to bribe kids to go to school in one easy hit.'

'And you'll get the money? These people don't look like they have anything.'

'I might have a route through Charles,' he told her.

She frowned. 'Charles is rich?'

'Charles's family is rich. The Wetherby station is vast. Old man Wetherby was a nasty piece of work. After Charles's accident he couldn't bear looking at him. Disability disgusted him. That seemed fine by Charles—he couldn't stand the old man either. Anyway Philip, Charles's brother, now runs the place. Charles refused to take anything personally from the farm but he's not above touching his brother's conscience when he needs something for the hospital. Or in this case, if he needs something toward a pool. Philip can well afford it.'

'But will he?'

'There are things going on between Charles and his brother that I don't understand,' Cal told her. 'All I know is that Philip is a weak reed but an incredibly rich weak reed, and a contribution for a pool wouldn't touch his huge financial base. As long as he doesn't have to commit any effort…'

'It'll be you who has to commit the effort. '

'So it seems.'

'Why are you doing this?' she said, so softly he hardly heard.

Why was he doing this? Good question. 'It has to be done,' he said, trying to figure it out for himself. 'Those kids last night shouldn't have died.'

'No, but they're just more in a long sequence of tragedies. Mary was telling me. The death rate among the adolescents out here is horrific.'

'So it is.'

'So why today?' she whispered 'Why today did you get out of your comfort zone and offer to do something about it?'

'I don't know.' And wasn't that the truth?

'Was it because of me?'

'Gina…'

'Because I accused you of not letting yourself care?'

'I care.'

'Of course you care,' she told him. 'You care and you care, even when you try so hard not to. It's impossible not to care, Cal. It's impossible not to expose yourself to get hurt.'

'Can we do without the life lesson?'

'Sorry.' She relapsed into silence but she still seemed uncomfortable.

'We could still get married,' he said, and she jerked into rigid awareness.

'I beg your pardon.'

'You could stay here. We could marry. I could care for you and CJ.'

'Care…as in look after.'

'Of course.'

'Why would I want you to look after me?'

'Hell, Gina…'

'I might agree if it was mutual,' she told him.

'How do you mean—mutual?'

'Well, if you, for instance, told me that what happened out there today moved you to tears and you felt just dreadful and you needed a hug in order to get the strength you need to keep going.'

He froze.

There was a long silence. Her words played over and over in his head.

It was like there was a huge carrot in front of his nose— no, a wonderful, amazing dream, enticing him, sweetly singing its siren song. All he had to do was take a step forward.

And fall into a chasm so deep he could never get out of it.

He'd fallen before. He couldn't. He just…couldn't. He'd taken one small step today and he hadn't fallen, but this wasn't a small step. This was huge. Vast. Overwhelming.

To admit he needed someone.

He needed Gina.

He didn't. He couldn't.

'No.'

'Of course, no,' she said softly into the stillness. 'Of course, no, Cal Jamieson. So I guess that means we're stuck. You're here working your wonderful medicine—and taking one tiny step into caring that might or might not destroy you. And me returning to Idaho. And never the twain shall meet.'

'If you weren't so pig-headed…'

'Not pig-headed. Sane.'

'Why?'

'Because I've broken my heart over you once before, Cal,' she said steadily. 'I'm not going down that route again.'

'I'm not asking you to break your heart.'

'You think living with you and loving you and watching you not need me for ever and ever and ever would do anything but drive me crazy?' she asked. 'Cal, you're a doctor short in this wonderful hospital of yours, and Hamish's make-do medicine won't cut it. You definitely need a psychiatrist.'

CHAPTER EIGHT

CJ WAS waiting for them when they got back, sitting on the veranda steps, licking the world's biggest ice cream, while Rudolph Mutt sat adoringly at attention beside him. Hamish was watching them, and as they appeared he uncoiled his long legs from the veranda seat and smiled.

CJ was still wearing Bruce's hat.

Tomorrow his son was going to spend his last day in Australia with the man who had given him the hat, Cal thought.

Not him.

'Here they are, CJ,' Hamish was saying. 'The world's best medical team, home from sorting out the problems of the world.'

'How are things here?' Cal wasn't in the mood for smiling. He was feeling like things were out of his control and he wasn't sure how to get them back.

Hamish's smile faded. 'We've had the coroner working through the autopsies, and one of the kids' dads has had a heart attack.' He hesitated. 'Gina, we were wondering whether you'd see him. You looked after the prawn fisherman last night...'

'He just had indigestion,' she said. 'It didn't take a cardiologist to work that out.'

'Yeah, it was a pity we had to take the chopper two hundred miles out to sea when all he needed was antacid.' He hesitated. 'But this guy's a definite case. Charles wants to send him down to Cairns but he won't go. And maybe I wouldn't either if I had a kid to bury.'

'I'll see him,' Gina said. CJ had risen for a hug and she was hugging him, hard—ice cream and all—and that was doing something really strange to Cal's insides.

Damn, he wanted to be in that hug.

No, he didn't. What was he thinking?

'Our baby?' Gina asked, her face muffled by small boy. 'Lucky?'

'Lucky's good,' Hamish told her. 'His heart rate's settled beautifully. A couple of minor prem hassles but I'm thinking he's no more than three weeks early. We have him on oxygen but it's more a precaution than a necessity.' He eyed Cal and then stooped to pat Rudolph. 'We might be seeing a happy ending with Lucky.'

'The von Willebrand's?'

'Tests came back positive,' Hamish told them. 'It's a hassle but properly treated it should be no more than a minor inconvenience as he goes through life. And it does mean we called it right in not giving him heparin now.'

'What of his mother?' Cal asked.

'No news. Harry has every cop in the state looking for her, and every medical clinic within a thousand miles. I told him about the von Willebrand's thing and he's scared we have a bleeder.' He stooped and hugged the dog as if he needed some comfort himself. 'I guess we all are.'

'I'm not sure. I'm guessing it may well be the father,' Gina said.

'Why do you say that?'

'I am just guessing. But I saw the birth site. If the mother had been a bleeder as well, there would have been a lot more.'

'Maybe you're right,' Hamish said, relaxing a little. He looked from Gina to Cal and back again and he stopped relaxing. He looked interested. 'So, out at the settlement…bad?'

'Bad,' Cal said.

'Cal's going to organise them a swimming pool,' Gina told him, still hugging CJ, and Hamish stared.

'The hell you are.'

'Yeah, well, I'm going to take a shower first,' Cal said, and tried to push past him to go into the house, but his friend blocked the way.

'You're going to organise them a swimming pool?'

'To bribe the kids to go to school.' Gina smiled. 'It sounds a fantastic idea.'

'I read about that,' Hamish said. 'I remember showing Emily and saying what a great idea. And Em said what we needed was someone to get enthusiastic and organise it here.'

'Cal's enthusiastic.'

'Not now I'm not,' Cal said. 'I'm not the least bit enthusiastic. Hamish, move over, mate. I want to get past.'

'When I've finished asking questions,' Hamish told him. 'So you're going to organise a pool.' He glanced across at Gina. 'And you're going to help?'

'Not me. I'm going back to the US.'

'I don't understand,' Hamish complained. 'No one's making sense.'

'My ice cream's squashed,' CJ told them all conversationally. He pulled back from his hug and eyed his mother's cleavage. 'I think some of my ice cream's dropped down there.'

'Great,' said Gina. She peered down. 'Oh, goody. Chocolate.'

'I guess that means you get first crack at the shower,' Hamish told her, and grinned. 'Want some help?'

'CJ will help,' she said with dignity.

'I was offering Cal's services.'

'Butt out, Hamish.' Cal was feeling like so many things

were being thrown at him his head was spinning. He needed space. He needed to get away by himself and sort his head out. And the chocolate ice cream had gone *where*?

'Will you look after my dog?' CJ was asking him, and he tried to think of something useful to say. Hamish was chuckling.

'Hamish is a paediatrician,' he told CJ. 'He's good at handling babies. Rudolph is a puppy and therefore—'

'CJ, Rudolph isn't your dog,' Gina told her son, tugging him up the steps.

'The Grubbs can't keep him,' CJ said, distressed. 'He has to be my dog.'

'We can't take him home, honey.'

'I'm going back to the hospital,' Hamish said. 'I'm needed.' He gave them his most virtuous look and disappeared. Fast. Before he ended up with a dog.

'I need to keep Rudolph,' CJ said urgently, not even noticing Hamish's exit in his distress. 'What will happen to him if I can't keep him?'

'Cal will look after him,' Gina said, 'Won't you, Cal?'

'I don't want a dog.'

'Of course you do,' she told him. 'Everyone wants a dog and he's splendid. You won't have to need him at all.'

'What's that supposed to mean?'

'Figure it out, Einstein.' She tempered the words with a smile but the smile was strained. 'He's a fine dog, Cal. You offered to take us because you thought we needed you, but we don't. But Rudolph needs a home and CJ needs to know that he's in good hands.'

'But…' Cal stared down at Rudolph. He really was the weirdest mutt. His huge, long face looked lugubrious already and he was only a pup. Imagine what he'd look like when it got some age on.

The dog was staring right up at Cal and suddenly the

bounce had gone right out of him. He expected to be kicked. His tail was right underneath him and he whimpered.

'See. He knows his life hangs in the balance,' Gina said.

'What are you looking at me like that for?' Cal demanded of the dog. 'The Grubbs aren't planning on putting you down.'

'What's putting down?' CJ asked, and Cal knew he was lost.

'Fine,' he said. 'Fine,' he told the dog. 'I'll keep him,' he told Gina. 'You walk back into my life and suddenly I'm organising swimming pools and taking care of manipulative dogs and…'

'And what, Cal?' She tilted her chin and met his look with one of defiance.

'And nothing.'

'That's what I thought,' she whispered. 'Nothing. CJ and I are off to have a shower and then I have patients to see. You have a dog to care for and a swimming pool to organise. Separate lives, Cal. But that's the way you want it. Isn't it?'

'And the damnable thing is that I now have the Grubbs' dog, which they've been trying to palm off onto unsuspecting victims for the last two months and they didn't even try me, and now look!' Cal was in Charles's office, and Rudolph was beside him. The mutt had cheered right up. He was leaning—hard—against Cal's leg and his tail was sweeping the carpet as if he'd found paradise.

'He looks quite a nice…personality,' Charles said cautiously, and Cal grimaced.

'If you grin, I'm going to have to slug you.'

'Hey, I'm in a wheelchair.'

'I'll tip you out of the wheelchair and then I'll slug you.'

Charles grinned.

'You know, it's not such a bad thing,' he told him. 'You need someone to love and Rudolph sure looks like he needs someone to love,'

'I do not need someone to love.'

'Which is why you're sending Gina home.'

'I'm not sending Gina home either,' Cal snapped. 'I offered to marry her.'

Charles stilled. 'You did what?'

'I offered to marry her. She refused.'

'You offered to marry her,' Charles said cautiously. 'Gee, that was noble of you.'

'It was not noble. And she refused.'

'Why?'

'How would I know?'

'Did you tell her you love her?'

'Yes!'

'You're kidding.' Charles was still staring at Rudolph, who had rubbed against Cal so hard that Cal had put his hand down to push him away. Now, though, the hand had become a scratching post. Cal's fingers were running along the dog's spine and Rudolph was arching in ecstasy. 'I don't believe it.'

'I've never loved anyone else.'

'No,' Charles said cautiously. 'Maybe that's the trouble.'

'Look, it's academic anyway,' Cal told him. 'She's going home to the States the day after tomorrow. Our baby's looking good. Gina could leave tomorrow but apparently she's got some date with Bruce, crocodile hunting.'

'So your son's last day in Australia will be spent with someone else,' Charles said, still carefully watching the dog. 'You know, if you want tomorrow off, we'll cover for you.'

'You know you can't. We're so short-staffed.'

'I see it as an imperative,' Charles said, and he did look at Cal then. 'You have a son, Cal. A son. Do you know how fantastic that is?' His voice was rough with longing and there was a loaded silence. A silence that made Cal rethink. Charles wore his disability lightly but there was suddenly such pain on his face that Cal knew a nerve had been hit.

'I'm sorry, Charles,' he said at last, and Charles gave a bitter laugh.

'You should be sorry, you lucky sod. I can't have kids, and if you know how much that hurts… But you. You have a son appear out of the blue and you don't make the slightest effort to keep him.'

That was a bit much. 'Hey, Charles, I asked her to marry me,' he protested. 'I want to marry her. She needs me. She's diabetic, a single mum, trying to raise a kid by herself…'

'And that's how you proposed.'

'Of course it is.'

'You're a fool.'

'What?'

'I had a proposal once,' Charles said, the pain on his face replaced by a look of reflection. 'A nurse. Abigail. Abby. I went out with her a few times and we had a ball. I even thought I was in love. And then before I got around to proposing, she proposed for me. She said she wanted to spend the rest of her life caring for me. That she thought I was really brave, the way I faced life, and I had so much courage and she'd never let anything hurt me again. She said she loved me. And you know what? I ran a mile.'

Cal stilled. 'You're saying…'

'I'm saying need's no basis for a marriage. If ever I fall for anyone, it will have be someone who needs me as much as I need her. Do you see that, Cal?'

'Yeah, but—'

'But you won't let yourself go there. Because of your past.'

'You know, I really should get myself my own house,' Cal said, raking his hair in disbelief. 'You and Hamish and Emily and Grace. And who else? Even Mrs Grubb's had a go at me. Let's sort out Cal's problems.'

'Well, you won't sort them out yourself.'

'I don't have any problems.'

'Yeah, you do. You have a kid out there who's desperate for a dad, and you have a fantastic woman who you've held in your heart for years…'

'I don't need her.'

'The household says you do,' Charles said with a wry grin. 'And who are you to go against the decision of your housemates? You'd be a very brave man to try. Now, tell me about this planned swimming pool of yours. Hamish says you need Wetherby money. How are we going to organise that?'

She should have organised to leave tomorrow, Gina thought over and over again as the night stretched out. She was lying in bed and she could hear people out in the living room. They were playing billiards. Cal was there. She could hear his voice, raised in protest at something Hamish was saying, laughing with Emily, and there was such a surge of longing in her heart that it was all she could do not to get up and join them.

Did they know how lucky they were—to have such friends?

She'd told Cal she was going home to Idaho to her family and friends, but in truth her family and her friends were few and far between. Paul's illness had isolated them. Friends had dropped away and Paul's mother had died. Gina's parents were divorced and remarried with more children and grandchildren, and Gina was only a tiny part of their lives.

The laughter from the living room was unbearable.

Maybe she should marry Cal, she thought bleakly. It'd be better than going back to Idaho. And maybe it could work. Maybe in time…

Maybe in time she'd break her heart. To love with Cal but to never be allowed close. To always be the taker. The dependent one.

No.

So she should leave now.

But she'd thought the baby might need her and so she'd promised to stay and now she'd told Bruce she'd come with him on his crocodile-hunting expedition, and she'd told CJ and he was wearing Bruce's hat and he was so excited...

Bruce was definitely interested.

So what? She wasn't interested. Not while Cal was alive in the world.

It was an impossible situation. Crazy.

One more day. One day spent hunting crocodiles and then it would be over.

It would never be over and she knew it.

Midnight. Cal was staring down at Lucky's incubator, watching the tiny chest rise and fall. Over and over. One tiny baby taking the first step toward living.

He slipped his hand through an incubator port and touched the tiny hand. The little fist opened and the fingers clung around his finger.

'He's fantastic.'

He was startled but he didn't jerk. Not with that tiny hand holding him with such trust. It was Emily coming up behind him.

'Your dog's blocking the entrance to Casualty,' Emily told him. 'I thought I'd find you here.'

'He's not my dog.'

'CJ says he is,' Emily said, and smiled. She looked down at the baby and her smile faded. 'Poor little one.'

'He'll live.'

'But where's his mother? His family? He has no one.'

'He's tough,' Cal said, trying not to let the sensation of one tiny hand clutching his finger make him sound emotional. 'He's a survivor. You don't need people to survive.'

'Of course you do,' Emily said, startled. 'We need to find him a foster-family. They'll have to be the best. Special people to love a special little boy.'

'He'll survive,' Cal said again into the stillness, and Em shook her head.

'There's survival and survival, Cal. We need to find this little one someone who'll love him to bits.' She smiled. 'What about you?'

'Me?'

'Well, you're in adoption mode. First Rudolph and now…'

'Don't be ridiculous.'

'I'm not being ridiculous,' she said thoughtfully. 'If you can't have CJ…well, I think a son is just who you need.'

'I don't need anyone.'

'Now, why do I think that's a nonsense?' she said. She watched as he reluctantly released the grip of those tiny fingers. 'Why are you here?'

'I thought I'd check—'

'Hamish and I are well able to look after him and Gina's only a call away.'

'I thought—'

'You thought your bedroom seemed really, really empty,' Emily said softly. 'Well, mine is, too. It's a really bleak feeling but it's something we're going to have to get used to. Meanwhile, can I suggest you go remove your mutt from the door of Casualty before someone falls over him and sues the hospital for zillions? We've all had just about as much drama as we can stand in the last few days—and then some.'

'She won't talk to me. She's got her head in the pillow and she won't even look up when I go in.' Jim sounded as shaken as his daughter and Honey pulled out a kitchen chair and motioned him into it.

'Hush. You're not to upset yourself.'

'But what's going on?'

'She's menstrual and she has the flu,' Honey told him. Then because he clearly wasn't satisfied she added a rider. 'And

she's been thinking of the boy you sent away. Dwelling on it. What she needs is something to take her mind off it but it's a bit hard where we are.'

'Why is she thinking about him now?' Jim was astounded. 'I thought she'd forgotten all about him.'

'When you're feeling poorly, things mount up in your head.'

'That's why she won't talk to me. She blames me.'

'She knows why you hate the Wetherbys,' Honey told him. 'We all do. She doesn't blame you. It was just unfortunate. For her to fall for him...'

'Then why isn't she talking to me?'

'She's not talking to anyone,' Honey said miserably. 'I guess we have to sit back and wait for her to get better. All by herself.'

Breakfast at the house was very, very strained. There were six medics sitting around the breakfast table. The huge toaster on the sideboard was working overtime; they were onto their second pot of marmalade but there wasn't a lot of conversation. Everyone was watching Gina and Cal—and Gina and Cal were very carefully trying not to look at each other.

How had Cal lived in this house for so long under these watchful eyes? Gina thought. Friends or not, she'd have gone nuts.

'Why isn't anyone talking?' CJ demanded through toast, and Gina ruffled his curls—more a reassurance to herself than a reassurance to CJ.

'They're all busy eating,' she said, 'I expect they'll start talking when they finish their toast.'

There was a general regroup. Talk started.

'The weather's looking good,' Emily said, and they all nodded.

'You don't call scorching hot and no rain in sight good, do you?' Hamish demanded. 'I want to go back to Scotland.'

'Are you hunting crocodiles today, CJ?' Emily asked with a desperate look at Hamish, as if she was pleading for support.

'Yes,' CJ said, adjusting his hat and swelling a little with importance. 'We are.'

'You could go, too, couldn't you, Cal?' Emily asked brightly, and everyone at the table looked at Cal.

'That's dumb,' Cal snapped. 'You know how short-staffed we are.'

'Just a thought,' Em said.

'Is Rudolph going?' Hamish asked.

'Rudolph isn't my dog any more,' CJ said mournfully. 'He's Cal's dog.'

'I wouldn't be the least bit surprised if Cal offered to lend him to you,' Hamish told him.

'Hamish!' Em said, shocked. 'You know they've only had one day together so far. Cal and Rudolph need to bond. And, besides, dogs are crocodile bait.'

'Maybe I could lend him…' Cal started, but got such a glare from Gina for his pains that he backed off.

Good, Gina thought. Back in your box, buster. And don't come out till I'm gone.

'You're sure you're happy for me to go today?' she said, addressing herself solely to Hamish. 'If you're the least bit worried about Lucky…'

'Lucky's fine,' Hamish said. 'Isn't he, Emily? Emily's been up half the night with him.'

'Why?' Gina frowned. 'I thought he was settled.'

'He is,' Hamish told her. 'But there's a lot of people in this place who don't seem to be sleeping. Isn't that so, Mike? Emily? Cal?' No answer.

'Mr Narmdoo's stable,' Gina said, to no one in particular. 'He's pain-free this morning. The ECG changes are settling and cardiac enzymes are only minimally raised. It seems to have been a relatively minor infarct, but he's going to need follow-up. Angiography will show whether he needs bypass surgery.'

'He won't have it even if he needs it,' Hamish told her. 'Most of the people from the settlement refuse to go to the city. That's why we had Simon…' He paused and looked at Em. 'Um. Simon was our cardiologist.'

'He may come back,' Em said stoutly. 'He just…needed to go.'

'If he doesn't then we're in trouble,' Hamish told her. 'A cardiologist and a surgeon—like, for instance, you and Cal—can save a lot of lives up here.'

'I think I hear Bruce,' Gina said abruptly, and rose from the table. 'Coming, CJ?'

'I haven't finished my toast.'

'I'll meet you on the veranda,' Gina told him. 'It's getting a bit hot in here.'

Cal watched them go from the veranda.

Gina and CJ and Bruce the crocodile hunter.

'We can manage without you.' Charles was right beside him and he swore.

'One day you'll give me a heart attack.'

'Then you'll need a cardiologist.'

'Leave it, Charles.'

'I'm serious,' Charles told him. 'Miraculous as it seems, everything here seems quiet. If you want to go croc hunting with your son…'

'Charles, leave it.'

'He is your son, Cal. He's going back to the States tomorrow.'

'I don't need a family,' Cal growled.

'You're a fool, then,' Charles said cheerfully. 'You know, if that was my son, if that was my woman…'

'They're not.'

'They'll find someone else.' They watched as Bruce solicitously helped Gina into his ancient croc-spotting truck. 'Maybe they already have.'

'What, Bruce?'

'He may not look much, but his tours are earning him a for-tune. He has twenty guides on the payroll now. And you have to admit he's good-looking.'

'The people Gina loves are in Idaho,' Cal said, but there was a trace of uncertainty in his voice.

Charles looked up at his friend's face and his own face grew thoughtful.

'Things change,' he murmured. 'People change.'

'Not me.'

'Then you're a fool.'

CHAPTER NINE

WHAT was she doing out on a river, looking for crocodiles, when it was her last day ever close to Cal?

He didn't want her.

Gina sat in the bow of the boat and listened to Bruce chat to CJ about the mating habits of crocodiles. Bruce really was a nice person. He had three other tourists in the boat, an American couple and their teenage daughter, and he was including them all in his chat. He was making them laugh, making sure they all had fun.

He was very interested in her.

She knew it. She knew it in the way he watched her, the way he touched her.

She wasn't the least bit interested.

Cal...

He had to unbend. He had to.

He wasn't.

She was going home.

The day stretched on. It was the quietest of days, there was no trauma at all.

Cal was almost longing for the radio to burst into life, bringing action, bringing something to keep his thoughts occupied.

Nothing.

167

In the nursery Em was sitting by Lucky's incubator and he knew she was feeling exactly as he was.

'He doesn't need specialling,' he said gently, and Em flashed him a look of anger.

'He needs someone to love him.'

'We'll find his mother.'

'Yeah, right. And meanwhile I'll love him for her.'

She'd fallen for Simon, he thought bleakly. This was the consequence.

Gina would never treat him as Simon had treated Em.

Cut it out.

Jill was in the nurses' station. Rigid, uncommunicative Jill, who took her job as director of nursing with all care but as little humour as possible. He walked in to look up patient notes before doing a ward round, and she met him with a rueful smile.

'This place is like a tomb.'

This, from Jill? Things must be really bad.

'Too much has happened too fast,' he said softly. 'All these deaths. And Simon and Kirsty…'

'Em still doesn't believe he's not coming back. Even though Kirsty told Mike what the situation was.'

'I think she knows in her heart,' Cal said. 'She's hurting.'

'And how about you, Cal? Are you hurting?'

He sighed, dug his hands into the pockets of his coat and glowered. 'Jill, I thought I could depend on you to butt out of what's not your business.'

'It's my business if everyone in my hospital is going around with a face as mournful as that stupid dog of yours. Speaking of which, Rudolph is now draped across the entrance to the kitchen. Will you ask him to move?'

'Sure.' A marrow bone should do it, he thought. He and Rudolph had rather enjoyed sitting on the back step and communing over a marrow bone at three that morning.

She eyed him with caution. 'So you're going to keep him?'

'CJ wants me to.'

'CJ won't know anything about it when he goes back to the States.'

'Jill?'

'Yes?'

'Leave it.'

'Sure,' she said, and smiled, which for Jill was unusual all by itself. 'I'll leave it. But do cheer up.' She shoved a clipboard at him. 'This'll help.'

He stared down at the name on the chart. Albert Narmdoo. Mild coronary. Father of one of the boys who'd died.

'Right,' he said. 'Great. What's happening?'

'Nothing.'

He raised his brows in query.

'Just nothing,' Jill repeated. 'He's not eating. He's just staring at the ceiling. His wife came in this morning and the rest of his kids, but he didn't even speak to them. He's just…lost.'

His heart sank. 'I'll see what I can do.'

'Of course you will,' she told him. And then, before he could begin to imagine what was coming, she leaned forward and hugged him. Jill. Hugging. Unbelievable.

'Go on, Cal,' she said softly. 'Let go. There's a life out there, just waiting.'

As Jill had said, Albert was motionless. He was a big man, one of the elders of his community, his skin so dark his face seemed almost a chasm on the pure white pillows.

Cal walked forward and touched him on the shoulder, but the man didn't register.

'Albert?'

Albert turned eyes that were dulled with pain toward him, and the pain behind them made Cal's heart wrench in pity. 'The kids say you're going to build us a swimming pool,' he whispered.

'I'm going to try.'

'Won't bring…anyone back.'

One of the hardest parts of the indigenous culture was the rigid rule that the names of the dead were no longer spoken. Cal gripped Al's shoulder and watched the agony on his face, and thought they should be able to speak of his son.

He was right. This was what loving was all about, he thought bleakly. Loss. He watched the raw pain on Albert's face and he thought, no, he was right, it was better to do as he'd learned to do. Not to love…

But as if he'd spoken the words out loud, the man reached up and gripped his hand. Hard.

'I've had so much,' he whispered. 'Six kids. Six kids and their mother, and this is the first I've lost. It wrenches you apart, losing, but I've been lying here thinking what if I hadn't had him. You know, when I was a young 'un I didn't want any of it. I wanted to be by myself.'

'You would have missed out,' Cal said, seeing where Albert was headed, seeing where he wanted to head.

'Too right I would have missed out.' His face twisted. 'You know, two days ago, me and…well, we went outback to where we buried his grandfather. Spent the night out there. We woke at dawn and we sat and watched the sun rise over the ranges, just him and me…and it was…well, it was worth everything. And now there's death and my ticker's playing up and maybe it won't be long for me either, but that moment… Hell, to have lost that… If I'd had my way and not had him…' There were tears streaming down the man's face and he gripped Cal's hand, hard. 'You just grab it, boy,' he told him. 'You just never know…but you just grab it now, 'cos the pain will come regardless, but those moments…no one can take them away from you, ever. Me and my boy, that morning. It'll stay with me for ever and it's my gift and I'll love him for life.'

Enough. He released Cal's hand and he turned his face into

the pillow. Cal stood, motionless, his hand on the man's shoulder. He stood until Al's face eased a little. He checked the chart, he wrote up medication and then he hauled a chair up beside the window and sat.

'No need for you to stay,' Albert said.

'I'd like to, if you don't mind,' Cal said. 'I can see the sea from here.'

'Got your own thinking to do?'

'I have.'

He could go down to the beach and do his thinking, he knew. But he wanted to be here.

He needed company.

He needed…

The afternoon was hot and humid and there were no crocodiles. They drifted slowly down the river. The Americans were talking to Bruce, swapping yarns, intent on outdoing each other in travel tales. CJ had Bruce's binoculars, checking out every floating log, every mound in the mangrove swamps on the riverside. Imagining jaws.

Gina let her mind go blank and she drifted.

Tomorrow she'd leave.

For ever.

She was empty, desolate and she was turned into herself so she didn't hear the boat until it was almost on them. A speedboat, blasting along the river far faster than was legal or safe. A group of people on board with beer cans waved in greeting, yelling, yahooing, blasting past them with a wash of white water in their wake.

Bruce shouted a warning and she swerved around, reaching automatically for CJ. But CJ was rocking, falling. He clutched the side and held on, and she thought he was safe, but his hat, his dratted hat, fell overboard.

With a gasp of distress he was up, leaning over, trying to hold it.

She grabbed for him but the second wave of the speed-boat's wake hit, knocking her sideways.

Her hand just touched CJ—just touched, but couldn't hold him. Her fingers closed on thin air and her son was gone.

Cal was in the radio room when the call came through. He'd been sitting with Albert until he'd drifted off to sleep. Longer. He'd sat and stared out the window until he'd lost track of time, until his mind had told him it was time to move forward.

Where to?

He still wasn't sure. He needed to find Gina, he thought, and he went to find Charles first to tell him he needed the rest of the day off. But he walked in the door as the call came.

'Crocodile Creek Rescue Response.' Charles himself was taking the call. 'Harry. What's the problem?'

Harry. The local police sergeant. Maybe they'd found Lucky's mother, Cal thought, and he sent a silent prayer that that was the case.

But it wasn't good news. He watched Charles's face and he knew this was trouble.

'The chopper will be in the air in minutes,' he snapped. 'Hell, Harry, you know that river…'

But the line was already dead. Whatever was happening, Harry was moving fast.

Charles spun round. Then he saw Cal and his face froze.

'You.' And something about the way he said it…

'What?'

Charles took a deep breath, regrouping. Or trying to regroup.

'Harry's just had a call,' he told him. 'From the northern reaches of Crocodile Creek. Faint call, just about out of range, from an American tourist who's out with Bruce Hammond.'

With Bruce Hammond. The croc hunter who'd taken Gina and CJ out.

'What?' he asked, and his voice sounded disjointed. Strange. Like someone else was speaking, not him.

'It might be nothing,' Charles warned. 'Harry can't get back to them. No one's answering.'

'What?'

'The boy's been washed overboard,' Charles said bleakly. 'That's all we know. CJ's missing.'

It was a ten-minute flight but even so it was the longest flight Cal had ever known. Mike was at the controls. Cal was beside him, straining the machine to go faster, and Hamish was in the back.

'Because I want a doctor there who's not emotionally involved,' Charles had said.

'Don't send me, then,' Hamish had said. 'I'm emotionally involved.'

'Just go, the lot of you,' Charles had snapped. 'And bring CJ home.'

Charles was emotionally involved himself. CJ had been at the base for a whole two days and already he'd wriggled his way into everyone's heart.

Bring CJ home. The words rang over and over in Cal's head. Home.

Home was here. Home was with him. He had to find him. He had to bring CJ back to Crocodile Creek. They needed to stay here. They needed…

It wasn't working. The line he'd been using all this time to try and persuade Gina to stay was ringing hollow. CJ might well not need him at all.

His son might be dead.

The vision of the bereft Albert slammed back into his heart and stayed there.

*You just grab it now, 'cos the pain will come regardless,
but those moments...no one can take them away from you,
ever. Me and my boy, that morning. It'll stay with me for ever
and it's my gift and I'll love him for life.*

What had *he* had? Cal thought grimly. One bedtime. He'd
read his son one story and now he was gone.

One story was never going to be enough. He wanted more.
He wanted so much.

He needed his son.

He needed Gina.

He sat rigid in the helicopter with Mike staring grim-faced
ahead, and Cal did his own staring ahead.

What a fool he'd been. What a stupid, hopeless, inadequate
fool. So many people had tried to tell him, but he'd done it
his way. He'd tried to make himself self-contained, but to do
that...it was just plain dumb. He could share his life with Gina
and with CJ and with Rudolph and whoever else came along,
and he could love them to bits and he could let himself need
them, and why not? Because whatever disaster happened in
the future, he could never feel any worse than he did right now.

'For God's sake, how much longer?' he exploded, and
Mike glanced across with sympathy.

'Five minutes, mate.'

'And there's no news.' Why was the radio dead?

'You know there's transmission dead spots on this part of
the river.'

'Then they should move to where they can transmit.'

And move away from where CJ had fallen in? It was a
dumb suggestion. Both of them knew it and Mike was kind
enough not to say it.

'I'll kill him,' Cal was saying, directing impotent fury at
the absent Bruce. 'To take my kid on that part of the river...'

'It's safe enough. They were in a high-sided boat.'

'He should have roped him in.'

'Yeah, I can see CJ agreeing to that,' Mike retorted. 'No one gets roped into tourist boats. There's usually no need. How he fell…'

'Can't you make this machine go faster?'

'We're almost there,' Mike told him, and the big chopper swooped down in a long, low dive. They'd reached the fork where the main tributary turned northwards. 'We're assuming they're on the main branch. Let's just keep our eyes peeled until we see them.'

There was no need for him to say it.

Three pairs of eyes were scouring every inch of the river. With dread.

Gina heard the chopper first. She glanced over her shoulder and she could just make it out, low on the horizon and half-hidden by the canopy of the boat.

'That's the Rescue Response helicopter,' she said, and everyone turned.

'There must be another drama along here somewhere,' Bruce muttered. He was sounding a bit shaken, as indeed they all were. 'It'll be that blasted boat, come to grief. They come here doing ten times the legal limit—they'll have hit a log. They'll be lucky if they haven't killed themselves, the fools.'

'Oh, no,' Gina whispered, hugging CJ closer. His wet little body was dripping against her, making them both soggy, but she didn't care. He was still tear-stained and shaking against her, but the worst of his sobs had died. 'We don't need any more drama.'

But the corpulent American in the back of the boat was suddenly looking uncomfortable.

'We might…we might just have a problem here,' he admitted.

'What?' Bruce raked his bare head and looked exasperated. His expedition to show Gina the river wasn't going to plan.

He hadn't wanted to bring tourists but the Americans were wealthy and prepared to pay a premium if he took them today, so he'd thought he could include them. Now this had happened, and he'd like to be comforting Gina, but he still had to be a tour operator. And on top of everything else, he'd lost his favourite hat!

'When the little guy fell overboard...' the man said.

'Yeah?'

'Well, everyone was screaming and you guys were real busy trying to haul him in and then Marsha screamed about the crocodile and I saw it and I just... I just...' He lifted his cellphone and looked sheepish. 'I knew your emergency code here was 000 so I dialled it.'

'You dialled the emergency services,' Harry said slowly.

'Well, I did.' The man beamed, recovering. 'And, of course, after we got the kiddy back...after seeing those great jaws chomp on that hat...but we had him safe... Well, I guess I clean forgot that I'd phoned, but I'd imagine that's why they're coming, to look for us.'

'I guess they are,' Gina said, and all of a sudden she cheered right up.

The sight of CJ floating downstream on a log, and then the huge teeth rearing up and snapping down on Bruce's hat wasn't something she'd forget in a hurry. She was holding CJ tight and he was still shaking, and she'd been thinking she badly wanted to go home. But suddenly the helicopter was overhead and she thought maybe, just maybe, home was coming to her.

Don't hope, she told herself. It wouldn't be. It wouldn't...

But Bruce was winding the canopy back so they could see up, and the helicopter was right above them, the whirling of its rotor blades causing white water. She could see...

Cal.

He was looking down at her and his face—dear God, his face.

What had he thought?

She knew exactly what he'd thought. The expression on his face matched how she'd felt as she'd seen CJ slide overboard.

Well, why wouldn't he look like that?

He was family.

Home had come to her.

CHAPTER TEN

IT TOOK them ages—ten minutes at least—before the boat could reach a place where the helicopter could land. They steered back along the river, and the helicopter stayed with them every inch of the way.

Up in the chopper, the crew were all crowded into the cockpit, probably breaking every safety rule in the book, Gina decided. Mike and Hamish and Cal. They were watching CJ. The moment the little boy had looked up at them and given a tentative, shaken smile and a tiny wave…well, the expression on all of their faces would stay with Gina for ever.

How had she ever thought she could go back to Idaho?

Home was here.

And then they were mooring at a jetty near a picnic ground. The helicopter was landing. Bruce and the tourists were climbing off the boat, but Gina didn't move. She sat still, holding CJ. The vision of the croc coming toward her son was still with her. Her legs weren't moving. She couldn't get her legs to move.

But she didn't need to.

Cal was out of the chopper and running toward them. He was climbing down into the boat, oblivious of the Americans climbing upward onto the jetty, oblivious of Bruce.

He was gathering her into his arms. He was gathering his

178

son into his arms, and by the way he held her she knew that
this man would never let her go again.

'I thought I'd lost you,' he murmured.

'It was CJ who fell.'

'It makes no difference which,' he told her, pressing his lips
into her hair. 'You and CJ. My loves. My two loves. I thought
I'd lost my family.'

The nursery lights were dim when they returned.

Equanimity restored, CJ had headed to the hospital kitchen
to tell Rudolph and Mrs Grubb all about the very exciting ad-
ventures of his hat. Hamish and Mike had disappeared to tell
everyone the good news—though the radio call to Charles
would have done the same thing. Cal and Gina fell behind,
but somehow, because it seemed the right thing to do, the obvious thing to do, for this was who had brought them together
in the first place, Cal and Gina ended up beside Lucky's crib.

Lucky was the only baby in the nursery, and he certainly
had medical attention. Em, Mike, Hamish, Charles, Jill, and
now Cal and Gina. They were all there.

'There's nothing wrong?' Gina asked, startled at the mass
medical gathering.

'No,' Jill said, and tried to look busy. 'I was just checking
Lucky's obs had been done.'

'And I was doing the obs,' Em said.

'And I was checking that Jill had checked that the obs had
been done,' Charles said, and grinned.

'Hey, I'm the paediatrician,' Hamish said. 'I'm in charge
of all of this. You can't trust underlings these days.'

'And I'm here in a paramedic capacity,' Mike told them,
also smiling. 'When there's so many people packed into a
small room, there's a risk of crush injuries and fainting.
Especially when emotions are running high.' He smiled across
at his friends, his brows rising as he noted their linked hands.

'And emotions seem suddenly to be running a notch higher. Well, well.'

Gina blushed and tried to haul her hand away. Cal held it tighter.

'But the baby's OK?'

'Lucky's great,' Jill said, smiling across at the pair of them. 'He's…lucky. And we were just talking…'

'You were talking,' Charles said. 'Well, bossing, more like.'

'I do not boss.'

'Tell me what you were talking about,' Gina said, taking pity on her.

'We thought, seeing as this hospital has been so miserable…'

'We're not miserable,' Cal said, and Gina gave her love a quelling look.

'Shut up, Cal. You were saying?'

'Tonight's been declared a fire night.'

'A fire night?'

'We do it often,' Cal told her, and there was such a smile in his voice that everyone heard it. Everyone saw it. Gina saw every one of their friends register his happiness, and her own joy increased because of it. 'When we need to celebrate or commiserate or patch up a misunderstanding or whatever, we plan a fire night. We gather all the driftwood we can find on the beach and light it, like some sort of great tribal ceremony.'

'Um,' Gina said faintly. 'Don't tell me. You make sacrificial offerings and dance to the sound of didgeridoos, naked apart from three stripes of ochre on each cheek.'

'Hey, I never thought of that,' Hamish said, brightening.

'We barbecue sausages,' Jill said, quelling him with a look. 'Much more civilised.'

'Or prawns,' Mike said, smiling down at their linked hands, 'In times of high celebration we give sausages a miss and we barbecue prawns.'

'I guess we are celebrating tonight,' Em said softly. She put her finger through the access port in the incubator and stroked Lucky's face. 'We've had these awful deaths. We've had such awful...' She paused for a moment. 'Such awful things. But life goes on. CJ's safe, and Lucky's obs are completely normal. He's wonderful. He really has been... Lucky.'

'For more than just himself,' Cal murmured, and Gina looked at her love and smiled.

'He has.'

'He'll be loved to bits,' Em said stoutly. 'We'll find his mum. I know we will. This little one was born to be loved. He's just fine.'

'Everything's fine,' Cal said. 'Everything and everything and everything.'

Megan woke, unsure for a moment where she was. Moonlight was streaming in over her coverlet. The shivering had stopped. Her bed was warm and soft, and for just a moment she felt safe and secure, as if everything was OK.

She'd been dreaming. And what a dream...

She'd been holding her baby. Her little son. She'd leaned down and let her face rest against the soft down of his cheek and she'd smelt the new-baby smell of him. It had been so real it was with her still, a reality in a world that had gone mad.

A reality.

It was real. She could see him clearly, and she could sense that he was loved and cared for and at peace.

Her baby was OK.

She was no true believer. Somewhere along the way Megan had lost what religion she's had, had lost it in despair and bleakness and the sheer desperate grind for survival.

But now...

Her baby was dead, she thought, but her arms still cradled him, her heart still held him.

Her baby was loved.

Her little son...
He was waiting for her. Her tiny boy.
Her baby.

Away from the fire the beach was deserted. The last of the bar-
becued prawns had been eaten. Hamish was sitting on a mass
of driftwood, strumming a guitar and humming something
soft and sweet. Maybe dreaming of a girl back in Scotland?
CJ and Rudolph had fallen asleep at his feet, a warm and con-
tented bundle of small boy and dog, and when Cal looked que-
ryingly at his friend, Hamish grinned and paused in his
strumming long enough to indicate that his friend should go
ahead. He'd take over child- and dog-minding duties.

So Cal was free to lead Gina along the beach, out of the
pool of light cast by the fire. Out of earshot of their friends.

The night was still and warm. The tide was coming in and
Gina and Cal were barefoot, soaking up the cool of the sea
between their toes. Soaking up the serenity of the evening.
The serenity of certainty—the knowledge that from here
they'd move forward together.

'I can't believe I've been so stupid,' Cal said softly. They'd
been swinging their hands as they'd wandered toward the
headland but now he paused and twisted so he was facing her.
'What you've gone through alone, because of my stupidity...'

'No.' She took his face between her hands and smiled up at
him. 'Cal, if five years ago you'd wanted me, if you'd begged
me to stay, if you'd wanted CJ as your son, there'd still have been
Paul. And Paul was my husband. He was my friend. I've been
thinking about it. If that phone call had come to say he'd been
injured, and you'd loved me and wanted me, maybe I still would
have had to go. And how much harder would it have been?'

'You'd let me off...'

'There's no letting off,' she told him. 'Five years ago you
weren't ready for loving and I wasn't free to return that love.'

He thought about that for a moment and still found it unsatisfactory. 'OK, then,' he said, grudgingly. 'But no matter how you look at it, we've still wasted two days.'

'Um…right.'

'I don't want to waste any more time.'

'No.'

'So will you marry me?'

She thought about it.

'There's a few conditions,' she said at last.

'Like what?'

She tried to make her face stern. She tried to keep the loving laughter at bay—the joy from showing in her response. This was important.

'You're never to ask what my insulin levels are,' she managed. 'You'd be my husband, Cal Jamieson, not my doctor. I've already asked Charles if he'll be my physician and he's agreed.'

'But—'

'No negotiation, Cal. I don't need you as my doctor. Take it or leave it.'

'I'll take it.'

'You're never to sleep on the opposite side of the bed.'

He grinned. 'That's a given.'

'You're to tell me when you're worried or when you're sick or when you're frightened.'

'So you get to know my insulin levels but I don't get to know yours?'

'I have the upper hand,' she said serenely. 'It may be the last time it happens so I'm making the most of it. Promise me, Cal.'

'You drive a hard bargain.'

'I know,' she said smugly. 'But it has to start now. So start. Are you worried about anything now?'

'Um…yes.'

'Why?'

'You might not promise to marry me.'

'I have to think up some more conditions.'

'What about loving?' he said softly. 'And needing. If I promise to need you every day of my life, every hour of every day, every moment…if I promise to need you…'

'As much as I need you,' she whispered. 'I don't think that's possible.'

'How can you still need me?'

'My son loves your stupid dog,' she said, and her hands slipped to his waist and tugged him into her. 'CJ loves your dopey dog. I love him and the only way I can get this whole crazy family together is to agree to marry you. So you see…' But she was forced to pause as his lips met hers, and the pause lengthened and lengthened. When finally she managed to speak again her voice had grown breathless. 'So you see,' she whispered. 'I do need you.'

'You'll be my family?'

'Of course I'll be your family,' she said, really, really unsteadily. 'I think I already am. Maybe I've been your family for five long years and you haven't even realised it. Even Paul…'

'I owe Paul,' Cal said, and the laughter suddenly disappeared as he tried to speak of what he'd been thinking. 'Paul was your husband and his death has brought you back to me. But Paul's decision—to face life, to search for what love truly was—was what brought you to me in the first place. He'll always be honoured in our home.'

'Oh, Cal…'

'Will we have more kids?' he asked, and she stared up at him in such astonishment that he leaned back to see what she was thinking.

'What? What's surprising about that?'

'You want to extend our family?'

'Family's good,' he said, tugging her back to him again. 'Family's great. Three days ago I was alone. Now I have you, I have my son and I have a dog. And I was wondering…' He smiled against her hair. 'Gina, if Lucky's parents aren't found…'

'You'd want him?' She could scarcely speak. This was so much how she'd been feeling herself.

'I guess I've learned that love expands to fit all comers,' he whispered. 'Lucky brought you back to me. We could love him. Couldn't we?'

'Of course we could,' she whispered. 'Of course. Oh, Cal…'

'And if we do find his parents…'

'Then we'll just have to work on making our own babies,' she told him. 'How about that for a good idea?'

He didn't answer. And she didn't speak. His kiss was all the response she needed and their kiss lasted a very long time.

'So you'll marry me,' he said at last into the stillness of the night, and she held him close and felt his heartbeat and wondered how he could ever ask that question.

'Of course I will. My heart.'

'Then I guess we should go back to the fire,' he told her.

She glanced along the beach, where their friends, the medics of Crocodile Creek, were clustered together on the warm sand.

'They're waiting,' Cal said.

'Waiting? For what?'

'To know whether you've said yes.'

'Did they know you were going to propose?' Gina demanded, prepared to be indignant, but Cal smiled and hugged her to him, and then chuckled out loud.

'Welcome to Crocodile Creek, Dr Lopez,' he told her. 'Welcome to our extended family. In this town—in this house—there is no such thing as a secret. There's life and laughter and loving and…' He tugged her hard against him and kissed her again, long and sweetly, with the promise of forever in his kiss.

'And the best is yet to come.'

THE DOCTOR'S
UNEXPECTED PROPOSAL

Alison
ROBERTS

Alison Roberts lives in Christchurch, New Zealand and has written over sixty Medical romances. As a qualified paramedic, she has personal experience of the drama and emotion to be found in the world of medical professionals and loves to weave stories with this rich background, especially when they can have a happy ending.

When Alison is not writing, you'll find her indulging her passion for dancing or spending time with her friends (including Molly the dog) and her daughter Becky, who has grown up to become a brilliant artist. She also loves to travel, hates housework and considers it a triumph when the flowers outnumber the weeds in her garden.

For Becky—who has provided all the research
material I could possibly need on just how strong
the bond can be between mother and child.

CHAPTER ONE

THE party on the beach would be in full swing by now.

If anyone had noticed that Emily Morgan, Crocodile Creek Base Hospital's anaesthetist and ICU/Emergency consultant, was late arriving, they might well have guessed that she'd gone back for another peep at a special patient in the hospital nursery.

Her colleagues would also not have been surprised to learn that she had sent the attending nurse off to make herself a cup of hot chocolate and a slice of toast while she herself watched over the baby for a few minutes.

Dr Morgan had, after all, been a key player in the drama that had gripped this hospital over the last three days. A drama that was attracting the attention of the whole community of the large coastal town in north Queensland, no less. A newborn baby had been left for dead in the Outback and, despite the best efforts of police and bush rangers, they were no closer to finding the mother of this infant boy.

Emily reached into the crib and straightened the soft woollen hat that covered the tiny head. She couldn't resist continuing the contact by tracing a very gentle fingertip across a silky cheek.

'They'll be talking about you, Lucky,' she murmured.

'Down there on the beach. They'll be stoking the fire with driftwood, which will smell lovely, and they'll be barbecuing sausages and prawns, which will smell even better. Everyone who isn't on duty will be having a drink and I should be there, too.' Emily swallowed the lump in her throat. 'Celebrating...'

A celebration was definitely called for, and not just because the tiny baby that hospital staff had named Lucky looked set to survive such a rocky start to life. The last few days had been tough on everybody. The poignant mix of tragedy and triumph that was a part of every medical community seemed somehow heightened here in Crocodile Creek.

And no wonder, with cases like Lucky's. The baby stirred a little and a hand came free of its wrapping. Emily watched the tiny boy's face twitch in exaggerated movements. Eyebrows rose over still closed eyes in comical surprise and then dropped into a fierce frown. Lips that were now a wonderfully healthy shade of pink puckered, and almost thoughtful sucking sounds could be heard amidst the soft beeps of the various monitors surrounding the incubator. Emily smiled. Competition amongst staff members to help with feeding this baby until they found his mother could well make life more interesting in the next few days.

Her hand was still inside the crib. It was too easy to move her forefinger within reach of that tiny hand but it was so good to feel the surprising strength with which Lucky gripped her fingertip. For just an instant Emily could recapture the joy she had felt only hours ago, when her finger had last been held just like this.

Joy that Lucky had been found at all after being abandoned on the outskirts of the Gunyamurra rodeo—an event that attracted hundreds of people to an area some three hundred miles west of Crocodile Creek every year. Joy that he'd come through an emergency procedure to correct his congen-

ital heart defect and that they'd found and could treat the inherited blood disorder that could have proved fatal.

Emily had had every intention of burying any personal
misery and joining the celebration on the beach when the
plan had been mooted that afternoon, but time on her own had
made it seem too daunting. She was tired. Physically and
emotionally exhausted, in fact. It would hardly add to the
spirit of the occasion if she couldn't control these stupid tears
and ended up crying on a friend's shoulder again or something. She couldn't face a party. Emily had never felt more
miserable in her entire life.

So she had slipped back to the nursery in the hope of recapturing and gaining strength from the joy they all felt concerning Lucky. And she had…for a moment. But suddenly that
tiny hand wasn't just touching her finger. It was touching
something so deep inside her the ache was simply unbearable.

And the tears were flowing again.

Not for the baby. History might be repeating itself for
Emily Morgan and, yes, she did have to accept the fact that
she'd been dumped by her fiancé and partner of nearly two
years for another woman, but the infant ghost that had haunted
her since she had first set eyes on Lucky was back where it
belonged.

Way back—in a past that had no bearing on the present.

This current pain was more selfish. It was about rejection.
Grief. The loss of something she had worked hard to try and
get right. There was anger in the miserable mix as well. Emily
Morgan had failed…again. And to top it off, there was a good
dollop of plain, simple loneliness.

Except she wasn't alone, was she? Not on the surface, anyway. Emily had a lot of friends. Good friends. And one of
them was approaching right now in the form of Lucky's nurse
for the evening, Grace.

Emily managed to ease her finger free from the tiny fist without disturbing the baby, who had drifted back to sleep, and she hastily scrubbed the tears from her cheeks with an embarrassed chuckle.

'Look at me, crying over Lucky. Professional, aren't I?'

'There's been more than one tear shed over this mite.' Grace smiled. 'I even caught our medical director blinking pretty hard not very long ago.' She leaned over the incubator. 'He's gorgeous, isn't he? They're not going to have any trouble finding him a foster-home, that's for sure.'

'We're going to find his real family,' Emily said firmly.

'You reckon? They haven't found any clues yet, have they?'

'No.'

'And there were hundreds of people at the rodeo. Bit hard to try and search the whole of north Queensland.'

'Somebody knows.' Emily stood up slowly. 'Maybe they haven't seen a newspaper yet or heard the news on the radio, and they don't know he's alive. When they do, they'll come and get him.' She took a last glance at the still sleeping baby. 'How could they not?'

Grace smiled again, nodding agreement. 'You going to the party on the beach now?'

'On my way.' Emily tried to sound convincing.

Lucky was going to survive. So was she. There was no good reason to avoid the celebration. None at all.

She hadn't sounded convincing enough, apparently. Grace's glance was sympathetic. 'I haven't had a chance to say anything, Em, but I'm sorry, you know? About Simon going off like that.'

'I'm practically over it,' Emily lied. 'As more than one person has said, Simon Kent was a rat.'

'He sure was. Charles is furious at the way he just walked out. It's hardly professional to leave a hospital this size with no cardiology cover. He's still muttering about suing for breach of contract. Personal concerns, my foot!'

'It was obviously fate.' Emily was keen to change the subject. 'We've got a new cardiologist now, by the look of things.'

'Mmm.' Grace nudged Emily. 'Go on, then. One of us should be down there, drinking a toast to the happy couple.'

Emily's feet dragged.

She was happy for Cal. Of course she was. The group of medics that lived in the rambling old house that had been the original hospital were a family, and Cal Jamieson the best of brothers.

So was Mike, a paramedic and rescue helicopter pilot— another of her male housemates. Charles was more of a father figure but that was probably due to his position as medical director rather than his age. And the fact that he'd been there longer than anyone else. There was also that uncanny ability he had to know just a little too much about whatever was going on in his hospital—thanks largely, Emily suspected, to his skill in travelling silently on those well-oiled wheels. The quick glance she threw over her shoulder was almost automatic. You just never knew whether Charles might be following or what he might see or hear.

There was no sign of their medical director, or the wheelchair he had been confined to since a shooting accident in his teens. Emily hoped that someone had managed to persuade Charles to go down to the beach despite the difficulties presented by sand. He took a keen interest in the lives—and loves—of the people living in the doctors' house. Not that he'd said anything to Emily about Simon yet, but when he did she knew it would be both comforting and wise.

Maybe Emily had been avoiding talking to Charles because she wouldn't receive the level of comfort she craved. They had both known that the relationship hadn't been strong enough to convince Emily to leave Crocodile Creek. And they had both known that Simon wasn't a 'stayer'.

Emily had been there for nearly six years now and was almost as good as Charles at picking the 'stayers'. Cal and Mike were. Simon had never come close but he wasn't alone in his reaction. The isolation was too much for some to handle. The closeness with which they all lived and worked together stifled others. As an air, sea and outback rescue base for all of far north Queensland, Crocodile Creek was a magnet to young doctors and other medical staff who wanted the drama of the Outback Flying Doctor Service or an escape from an ordinary career or life—for whatever reason.

Escape had brought Emily here but it had been the best move she had ever made. She loved her life. She loved her job and the community. She loved her friends. She just wasn't quite up to celebrating with them right now. Seeing Cal and Gina together, the way they would be looking and smiling at each other, witnessing that kind of love—it would rub salt into a wound that was surprisingly raw, given the edge of another emotion that Emily had not really admitted to feeling yet.

Relief.

But wasn't that simply due to the successful battle to save baby Lucky? The strength of that relief, coupled with her weariness, would inevitably lead to a bit of overlap when she thought of Simon, wouldn't it? So why did she have the nagging suspicion that it was more the shock of *how* Simon had dumped her than the ending of their relationship that was so upsetting? And, if she felt like that, did that mean she had been expecting it all along and had, therefore, not tried hard enough to make it work?

It was no wonder Emily felt so confused. No wonder that her feet dragged and her head turned, seeking distraction from the endless treadmill of thoughts about Simon Kent. The door to the radio room was enticingly ajar but when Emily stepped inside, there was no one to say hello to. Whoever was on duty for emergency calls had taken the hand-held receiver from its clip on the wall. They had probably gone down to the beach to join the party for a while.

As Emily should be doing.

With a heartfelt sigh, Emily sank onto a small couch that was positioned under a window on the other side of the room from the desk and bank of telecommunication equipment. Just a few minutes, she promised herself. Time to get her head together. A private moment to get rid of a few more of those stupid tears.

The sound of footsteps in the corridor forced the stopper back into that particular bottle, however. Emily blinked hard and warned her lip muscles that they would need to try and produce a cheerful smile for whoever was returning to the radio room. But they did not co-operate. They even went slack with surprise when a familiar, large figure appeared in the doorway.

'Why aren't you at the party?'

'I came to find out why *you* weren't at the party.'

Emily found a smile, albeit a rather wan attempt. She could feel her exhaustion ebbing away as it always did when she was in Mike's company. Mike could stand beside any patient with a slow heartbeat, she thought with amusement, as a cure—providing the patient was female, of course. Especially when he smiled like that.

Emily dropped her gaze. 'I'm just not in a very party mood, I guess.'

'Neither am I.'

Emily's smile gathered a few more watts. 'Oh, right. Michael Poulos not in the mood for a party.' She glanced towards the glowing lights on the radio equipment. 'Funny, I haven't heard any reports about them.'

Mike stepped into the room properly. 'Reports about what?'

'Those flying pigs.'

'Ah.' Mike grinned as he took another couple of steps. 'OK, I did *go* to the party. I thought it might be a good way to drown my sorrows.'

'Mmm.' The sound was sympathetic. It was, after all, entirely possible that Mike was feeling just as bad as she was. Unlikely, but possible. He had exactly the same reason to feel bad, didn't he?

'But I left as soon as I saw you weren't there,' Mike continued. 'We took a vote and decided you'd be in the nursery, cooing over Lucky.'

'I never coo. It would be unprofessional.'

Mike ignored the protest. 'Grace told me you'd just gone. She also told me she didn't think you were feeling up to partying. So I came looking for you.'

'Oh.' Emily fought to hold that bottle stopper in place.

Mike was so nice. The best kind of friend anyone could hope to have. She'd known he was an amazing person the first day she'd ever seen him—when he'd arrived back in his home town two years ago, with his gorgeous fiancée on his arm and a job waiting on Crocodile Creek's rescue helicopter.

When Marcella had abandoned both Crocodile Creek and Mike, Emily had been secretly delighted when he had decided to move into the doctors' house, and she cherished their friendship even though it still made her feel a little shy.

Friendship was as close as someone like Emily was ever going to get to a man in Mike's league but here he was, having left a whole group of people he was just as close to in order to look for *her*. The attention was unnerving enough to make her mouth feel suddenly dry.

'You didn't need to do that, Mike. I'd hate to think I was spoiling an opportunity to drown your sorrows.'

She expected a flippant response concerning the number of such opportunities that would be forthcoming, but any trace of amusement faded from Mike's features, leaving him looking uncharacteristically solemn. Not that it changed his unruly mop of black curls or the wide mouth that turned up at the corners even in repose, but a pair of eyes dark enough to appear black, and which normally danced with mischief, were suddenly serious and the flash of warmth and understanding Emily received was enough to make the stopper explode from the bottled-up tears.

The weight of Mike's arm settled around Emily's shoulders as he sat down on the couch beside her. Even in the midst of a wash of misery she was also aware that the size of the couch precluded any distance between them. The hard length of Mike's thigh was pressed firmly against Emily's leg. He was a rock. A warm, human rock, and Emily could think of nothing she wanted to do more than cling to it.

'Sucks, doesn't it?'

Emily could only nod. And sniff. Embarrassingly loudly.

'It's even worse when you have to front up to a party and see happy couples like Cal and Gina and you're supposed to be celebrating.' Mike's hand tightened on Emily's shoulder with an empathetic squeeze. 'It's just as well Simon bloody Kent's gone. I could quite happily deck him for doing this to you. He's worse than a rat. He's an idiot. And a bastard.'

Emily shook her head. 'If he'd been a real bastard I wouldn't have been with him for so long. He…he said he was very sorry.'

'Big of him,' Mike said scathingly. 'He was a charming bastard, I'll grant you that.' He snorted. 'Cardiologist, my eye. They're supposed to fix hearts, aren't they? Not go around breaking them.'

A sound somewhere between a laugh and sob escaped Emily. It was so comforting to have someone on her side like this. Someone who would defend her worth and assume anyone that left her would be the one missing out.

Maybe karma did exist after all, and this was payback time. Helping Mike pick up the pieces after failed relationships had been what had cemented their friendship over the last eighteen months. Emily decided she'd better make the most of this. It wouldn't be long before she would feel compelled to return the favour…again.

'I can't believe I got it so wrong,' she sighed. 'I'm angry as much as anything right now. I should have seen it coming and I didn't. OK, things haven't been that great for a while, but whenever I tried to talk about it Simon said he was just a bit stressed by work. And I *believed* him.'

'You loved him. Why wouldn't you believe him?'

'When I look back at the last few weeks, I just cringe. I made it so easy. I *helped* him.'

'You're a nice person, Em. The nicest person I know.' The words were like balm to the raw patch on Emily's heart and she was happy to let Mike's squeeze pull her a little closer. Close enough to rest her head comfortably on his shoulder. 'You can't help helping people. I heard about all the hours you spent with young Lucky when you were officially off duty. You can't tell me it was just because you didn't want to be around to see Simon bloody Kent pack his bags and move out. You were determined that baby was going to survive, weren't you?'

'It was helping me survive as well,' Emily admitted. 'I think any patients of mine would have got a fair bit of extra attention in the last few days.'

Like they had all those years ago, when throwing herself into her career had seemed the only way forward.

'It's not just patients that you help, though, is it?' The deep notes in Mike's voice rumbled against Emily's cheek. 'Look at all the times you've let me cry on your shoulder and tried to help.' He was silent for a few seconds and then sounded thoughtful. 'Wasn't it you that set me up with Kirsty? To take my mind off Trudi leaving?'

'Sorry.' Emily's tone was rueful. 'It seemed like a good idea at the time.'

Actually, it hadn't seemed like that great an idea. It had just seemed…inevitable. As ordained by fate as the fact that her relationship with Simon had just morphed into an unexciting engagement. The wild desire Emily had had of suggesting herself as a replacement for Trudi was still ridiculous enough to make her blush. And still just as easy to dismiss.

Mike grunted as though in agreement. 'Getting dumped doesn't do wonders for your ego, does it?'

'Trudi didn't dump you. She cried buckets when her visa ran out.'

'She didn't try applying for a new one.'

'She was going to.'

'Yeah. Until she met that guy in Switzerland and got married a few days later.'

'Maybe marriage was what she was looking for.'

'Obviously.'

'You were a bit slow off the mark, then.'

'What?' Emily could feel Mike stiffen. 'I didn't want to *marry* Trudi.'

'What about Kirsty?' Emily sat up and eyed Mike cautiously. 'Did you want to marry her?'

'Of course not.' Mike grinned disarmingly. 'She did have great legs, though.'

Emily rolled her eyes. Of course she did. So had Trudi. And Marcella. Great legs were just another item on a list that put her on a different planet from the women Mike Poulos chose.

'So you're not exactly devastated, then.'

'I guess not.' But Mike's grin had gone. For just a fraction of a second Emily had another glimpse into eyes that weren't shuttered by humour and realised she was seeing a part of Mike she had never been privy to before.

Maybe something good was going to come out of this whole mess. A bond of comfort in their friendship that was going both ways for the first time.

'I am upset,' Mike said slowly. 'And I'm starting to wonder what the hell's so wrong with me.'

'There's nothing wrong with you,' Emily assured him. 'You're a great guy, Mike. Kirsty's an idiot.'

'Yeah.' A familiar glint reappeared in those dark eyes. 'She is, isn't she? She and Simon bloody Kent should be a perfect match.'

'How did we not see it happening right under our noses?'

'Because it didn't. They took off to Brisbane when they found they couldn't keep their hands off each other.'

'Did you know what was going on?'

'I had my suspicions.'

'When?'

'The weekend before last. When you told me you were covering a night shift for Simon because he had to rush off to Brisbane.'

'When his mother mixed up her insulin dose and put herself into a coma. What was so suspicious about that?'

'Just that Kirsty had rung me ten minutes earlier to say she couldn't make it back to Crocodile Creek for a day or two because her father was having some sort of crisis with *his* insulin dosage.'

Emily huffed at the absurdity of it. 'Why on earth didn't they have the imagination to come up with different stories?'

'Because they're both idiots,' Mike reminded her promptly.

Her smile came much more easily this time. It wasn't even forced. Mike smiled back at her delightedly, clearly taking the credit for having cheered her up, at least a little, but Emily looked away quickly. She couldn't reveal just how much she was enjoying his company.

Neither could she put any real significance on some new connection she and Mike could be forging here. They were in the same boat right now, having had their respective partners run off with each other no less, but it was a very temporary thing. Michael Poulos never stayed lonely for long. It would be foolish to imagine that this almost intimate companionship would become a regular occurrence.

And right on cue, the radio on the desk opposite the couch crackled into life.

'Cooper's Crossing to Crocodile Creek Air Medical Service. Come in, please.'

Mike's attention was caught instantly and completely. He jumped to his feet. 'Where the hell is our radio operator?'

'Someone's got the hand-held,' Emily pointed out, following Mike's example and standing up.

'Yes. I have.'

'Oh!' Emily whirled so fast she almost fell over. 'Charles! I wish you wouldn't sneak up on people like that!'

'It's an advantage I have no intention of losing.' Charles Wetherby, medical director of Crocodile Creek Base Hospital, rolled his wheelchair towards the desk. 'The battery's low on the hand-held,' he said. 'That's why I was on my way back.'

'Cooper's Crossing station to AMS. Are you receiving me, over?'

Charles reached for the microphone on the desk. 'Crocodile Creek Base Hospital, receiving you loud and clear. Is that you, Jim?'

'Yes.' The voice sounded hesitant. 'Charles?'

'Speaking,' Charles confirmed. 'What's the problem, Jim?'

'It's my daughter, Megan. She's…she's not well.'

Emily knew that other people listening in could make it uncomfortable to give personal details, but Jim Cooper sounded more than hesitant now. He sounded desperate.

'What's happened, Jim?'

'She hasn't been well for a few days. She got out of bed and she's collapsed… I can't get any sense out of her.' A few words were broken by static. 'Fence down… Her mother's trying to round up the cattle… No way I can get her back into bed.'

'How old is Megan, Jim?'

'Nineteen.'

'And she's been sick for a few days?'

'I dunno what's going on. Flu, maybe. Stomach pains. She's just lying on the floor now… Her breathing sounds funny… I dunno what to do…'

Emily exchanged a horrified glance with Mike. This man was panicking. He sounded close to tears.

'Don't worry, Jim. We'll get some help out to you. Don't go too far from the radio. As soon as I've got things moving I'll talk to you again.'

Charles turned to Mike. 'Do you know if they've fixed that problem with the sticky needle on the fixed wing's altimeter?'

'They're working on it now.'

'It'll have to be the chopper, then.'

'How far is it?'

'Cooper's Crossing station is Wetherby Downs' closest neighbour.' Charles tipped his chair back and then swivelled to face the series of maps covering the wall. They were marked with a series of black, expanding circles that represented units of ten nautical miles. 'West. Here.'

Mike whistled silently. 'That's a long haul for the chopper, boss. We'd have to refuel.'

'Not a problem. We have a long-standing arrangement with Wetherby Downs to provide fuel for any AMS emergency if it's needed. I'll arrange it with the station manager. They'll be waiting for you.'

'What's the latest info from the weather bureau?'

Emily peered at the map as the two men engaged in a rapid-fire discussion about weather forecasts, GPS co-ordinates for navigation and flight times. Wetherby Downs station was where Charles had grown up. His brother Philip ran the vast station now. Why would Charles make it sound like ringing the station manager and not his brother to arrange a fuelling stop for the helicopter was the only option?

She cast a rather speculative glance at their medical director. How fair was it that he knew so much about all of them but managed to keep so much of his own life so private? Disconcertingly, Emily found herself receiving a stare from both men that spoke of an even more avid curiosity.

'So, how 'bout it, Em?'

'Sorry, I wasn't listening.'

'Christina's on emergency flight call but she's having a good time at the party.' Mike grinned at Emily. 'Charles and I thought you might like to cover for her.'

'Oh, no!' Emily took a step backwards. 'Sorry, but I don't do helicopters.'

'Why not?' Charles raised an eyebrow. 'You've been in the fixed-wing aircraft often enough.'

'That's different.'

'Why?' Mike sounded genuinely puzzled.

'A plane's safer.'

'Why?' Mike was sounding amused now.

'Because it's got wings,' Emily muttered. She could feel

her cheeks heating but continued doggedly when confronted by silence. 'If its engine conks out it can at least glide down. It's not going to drop like a stone.'

Mike and Charles exchanged a glance. They both grinned at Emily. She pressed her lips together stubbornly and glared back. She didn't like being laughed at.

Then, for the second time that evening, Emily felt the comforting weight of Mike's arm around her shoulders.

'I wouldn't let you drop like a stone, Em. Honest.'

The promise was as comforting as the physical touch. It offered protection. Never mind that Mike wouldn't want to plummet to the ground himself, he made it sound as though it would be Emily he'd be taking care of.

Right now she felt too bruised to remind herself that she was quite capable of looking after herself. Having someone else doing that, even temporarily, was attractive. It made her feel special. Safe.

Safe enough to actually consider confronting her fear of flying in something that didn't have wings?

'But it's dark.'

'Not a problem.' Mike squeezed her shoulder. 'There's a lovely bright moon out there and I'll turn the lights on when we need to land. I'll keep an eye out for the mountains, I promise.' The pressure he exerted on Emily's shoulder was enough to force her to turn and look at him. 'Hey,' he said softly. 'Neither of us really wants to go to that party right now. An escape is just what we need. Both of us.'

'Hmm.' Charles was looking at both Emily and Mike so thoughtfully she could almost hear wheels turning. 'I agree. What's more, you'll be an even more valuable member of staff around here if you can get past your helicopter phobia, Dr Morgan.'

Emily gulped. 'Are you ordering me to go, Charles?'

Mike's head tipped sideways as he chased eye contact with Emily. 'Ple-e-ease?'

It was the lopsided smile that did it. Made her think that Mike wanted her company rather than Christina's. Made her feel that she would be safe doing anything as long as she was doing it with Michael Poulos.

'Oh…all *right.*' The grudging agreement came out as almost a snap but Mike didn't seem to mind.

Neither did Charles. He was smiling benevolently as he waved them off. Then he reached for the microphone again.

'Crocodile Creek Base Hospital to Cooper's Crossing. You receiving me, Jim?'

By the time Emily was kitted out in the dark blue overalls, heavy black boots and the white helmet that contained the earphones and microphone for radio communication, Mike had done all his pre-flight checks and was waiting to help Emily into the cockpit of the bright red and yellow helicopter.

'Charles has been talking to the girl's father again. She's conscious and has got herself back to bed. Sounds like less of an emergency but he's decided she should still be evacuated.'

Emily nodded but knew she probably looked less than enthusiastic .Up close, this was even more daunting than she had feared. The machine was huge. Far too big for spinning strips of metal as flimsy-looking as those rotors to hold up. If her hand wasn't being firmly held by Mike at that point, Emily might have turned and fled.

'Step onto the skid here and then up into the front seat.'

'What? Isn't that where the crewman sits?'

'We're not taking anyone else. This should be a simple retrieval and I can help you with any stabilisation of the patient that needs to be done before we head back. Come on—in you get.'

Emily felt pale. She hesitated.

'It's as safe as houses,' Mike assured her. 'Statistically, you're safer doing this than crossing the road.'

'I know. It's just…'

'Look, I'll give you some extra protection. Watch.'

'*Mike!*' Emily was horrified. 'What *are* you doing?'

'Spitting,' he said unnecessarily.

'That's disgusting!'

'It's a Greek thing.' Mike didn't look at all perturbed by Emily's criticism. 'It's for luck. It wards off the evil eye.'

'Oh…for luck, huh?'

'Yep. Come on, it's time we took off.'

'Hang on.' Emily resisted the tug on her hand. 'Can I spit, too? For luck?'

Mike's face lit up as he grinned. 'Sure.'

Emily gave it her best shot. Luck was good. And spitting on the helicopter was so bizarre it was funny. She actually felt like laughing aloud and she hadn't felt like that for days and days. Expecting Mike to approve, Emily was surprised to find him shaking his head.

'You've got to do it three times,' he told her.

'But I don't have that much spit!'

'Well, actually…' Mike let go of Emily's hand, pulled the sleeves of his overalls down over his wrist and wiped the blob of saliva off the helicopter's paintwork. 'You don't have to make it *wet*.' His tone was injured. 'It's more of a token spit.' The glance was very stern. 'Especially when it's *my* helicopter you're spitting on.'

Emily was still grinning as she fastened her seat belt and watched the rotors lifting as their speed increased. She couldn't remember when she had last felt this alive.

Setting off for a medical evacuation always got the adrenaline going because you never knew quite what you were going to find at the other end. Meeting a personal challenge like facing a fear of helicopters at the same time made this experience well out of any comfort zone.

Emily would never have agreed to this if it wasn't Mike at the controls. Because it *was* him, and because she was doing this for the first time in her life and they were doing this with just the two of them, gave this mission an edge that could only boost Emily's adrenaline rush.

Every cell in her body was pumping. Fear kicked in far more feebly than she would have expected when the skids left the tarmac and the helicopter rose swiftly. They were still gaining height rapidly as Mike turned over the cove to head inland, and Emily welcomed the distraction of seeing the people gathered around the bonfire on the beach. A small person waved.

'There's CJ!' Emily shouted. 'Look—I can even see that weird-looking puppy beside him.'

'You don't need to shout, babe. We've got an internal intercom system and the earphones and mikes are inside our helmets.'

'Sorry.'

'Don't be. You weren't to know.' Mike looked down at the beach and then turned his head towards Emily. 'Who needs a party? This is much more fun, isn't it?'

And Emily had to nod.

Astonishingly, this suddenly promised to become the most enjoyable experience of her life.

CHAPTER TWO

HE WAS nothing short of a genius.

If he'd spent a week planning some way of bringing a smile back to Emily Morgan's face, Mike couldn't have done better than scooping her up and flying her off in his helicopter. And he hadn't had to plan it at all. It had just fallen into his lap.

OK, he'd had to do a bit of fast talking to cut the crew numbers for this rescue mission but he could be very persuasive when he wanted to be. He'd taken the line that he and Emily could manage perfectly well. He had advanced paramedic training to go with his considerable experience as a pilot, so they were a perfect team. Why pull anyone else away from the beach party when they deserved the time out after the wringer they'd all been through in the last few days, thanks to the shortage of medical staff and a surplus of major cases?

Charles had known what Mike was up to, of course. He could see that he wanted some time alone with Emily to try and cheer her up. Maybe he even knew some things that Mike had been confident he'd kept very well hidden. There wasn't much that went on in or around Crocodile Creek base hospital that Charles didn't know about.

Not that it mattered. Charles had approved, and convincing

Emily had been a cinch given that her fear of getting into the chopper outweighed any other concerns.

She'd done it, though, hadn't she? With a quick glance to his left, Mike stopped feeling proud of himself and felt proud of Emily instead. You'd never think it to look at her—she wouldn't look out of place behind an information desk in an academic library or some other such serious place—but she was gutsy all right.

Emily had seen him looking, so Mike did what came automatically and smiled at her.

'OK, babe?'

She nodded but bent her head again quickly to stare through the small Perspex panel near her feet. 'It's really different from being in a plane, isn't it? You can see so much more.'

'Bird's-eye view.' Mike was relieved that Emily had remembered not to shout this time. She was a quick learner as well as gutsy.

Moonlight bathed the outside world and visibility was great—with a ghostly but rather beautiful bleached effect. They were already past the sugar-cane plantations that surrounded the township of Crocodile Creek and over the foothills of rainforest-clad mountains now. The dense vegetation had been cleared in patches, and banana trees added to the tropical appearance of a landscape that Mike had grown up in and still loved with a passion.

Checking his instruments, he banked to follow the main road that snaked towards the pass leading to the arid cattle country on the other side of the mountains. Emily squeaked softly and Mike could see her fingers sinking into the upholstery of her seat as the aircraft banked.

'Don't worry,' he said cheerfully. 'I'm not planning any aerobatics.'

'Aren't we going over the mountains? Like the plane does?'

'Can if you want to, but the view's better this way.'

Grey-blue eyes were looking distinctly anxious again. 'This thing can go high enough to get over the mountains, can't it? If the weather gets bad or something?'

'This is an MBB-Kawasaki BK-117,' Mike informed her with an air of injured pride. 'State-of-the-art rescue chopper. We've got a ceiling of 10,000 feet, a range of 338 miles with standard tankage, maximum speed of 174 miles per hour and a maximum climb rate of over 1700 feet per minute.'

'Oh.' Emily looked as though she was trying to do several mathematical calculations simultaneously. Her face brightened. 'That's OK, then, isn't it?'

'Yep.' Mike couldn't resist teasing her just a little. 'We've got a thirty million candle-power nightsun, too. I can turn it on any time so you don't need to be scared of the dark.'

Emily snorted indignantly. 'You're the one who goes round spitting to ward off the evil eye, mate.' She watched Mike adjust a control on the panel that sat between them. 'Just out of idle curiosity, did you go round spitting on your helicopters when you were a member of that crack platoon or squadron or whatever you call them in the Special Air Services?'

'Sure did.'

'And what did your army buddies think about that?'

Mike kept a straight face. 'I suspect that anyone in the regiment that *doesn't* spit for luck now gets left on the ground.'

'Very unhygienic.'

'Didn't stop you doing it.'

'No.' He could hear the smile in her voice. 'Well, sometimes you need a bit of luck.' She was silent for a few seconds and then her tone became very wry. 'Maybe I should spit on the next man to ask me out on a date.'

'I wouldn't advise it.' It was hard to keep his own tone light. 'Unless he's Greek, of course.'

Dammit, Emily was thinking about Simon bloody Kent again. Mike's fingers curled more tightly around the control stick. The man had better not show his face in Crocodile Creek again, that was for sure. He'd never been good enough for Emily, anyone could have seen that, but she'd fallen for him and if the others had shared Mike's reservations, seeing the sparkle that emanated from the quiet young physician had been more than enough to stop them saying anything.

Mike decided he needed to distract Emily from her thoughts. 'Sounds like that young girl must be pretty sick to collapse like that.'

'She may have just had a spell of low blood pressure. If she's been unwell and lying in bed for a few days without adequate food or fluid intake, she could well have fainted by standing up too quickly.'

'Her father sounded pretty anxious.'

'Charles will have stayed in contact with him. He'll call us if there's any significant change.'

Emily fell silent as she watched the set of instruments on her side of the dashboard.

'What's that?'

'Airspeed. In knots.'

'And that one?'

'Artificial horizon. Gives us our position in relation to the real horizon.'

He kept answering the queries as Emily discovered the fuel gauge, engine temperature, altitude and vertical speed indicators.

Now Emily was leaning towards him to examine the rest of the dials. 'They're exactly the same as the others!'

'It's a twin-engined craft. It would be possible to fit a second set of controls and have two pilots so there's a duplicate set of instruments. Hey, maybe you should get your helicopter pilot's licence.'

Emily laughed. 'Not in this lifetime, mate.'

At least she wasn't thinking about Simon the rat any more.

It had lasted for months, that sparkle. If it hadn't still been there when Marcella had ended her engagement to Mike and stormed off back to her native Italy six months after their arrival in Crocodile Creek, he would have…

Would have what?

Told Emily just how special he thought she was? That her living in and loving his home town had made an appearance on the list of why he hadn't given in to Marcella's ultimatum and left Crocodile Creek for ever?

Not likely.

Not when his ego had actually been rather dented by Marcella having dumped of him. Or when he'd never had a hint of anything more than friendship being available from Emily. And especially not when she was obviously still in love with Simon the cardiologist, whom she couldn't see had no respect for hearts other than in their pumping capacity.

Not many people knew just how patient he was capable of being, however. Or how highly he prized his friendships. However hard it was right now, he was not going to jeopardise a friendship or risk something even bigger by moving too fast. Or by telling Emily just how much better off she was without Simon in her life.

And it was hard. As hard as it had been to watch that sparkle dimming and tendrils of unhappiness infiltrate Emily's life over the last twelve months. She'd tried so hard to make the relationship work and Mike had been sorely tempted on more than one occasion to take her in his arms and tell her that Simon simply wasn't worth the effort.

Thank goodness he had trusted his instincts and left things to travel naturally to their inevitable conclusion. Emily needed to work things out for herself. To see what was staring her in the face and decide whether or not she wanted it.

All Mike could do right now was to be there.

And to be patient.

The moonlight was even brighter as they neared their destination and it was quite light enough to appreciate the oasis that Wetherby Downs cattle station represented. The number of outbuildings and a cluster of what had to be staff accommodation made the hub of the station seem like a small village. A huge, majestic old homestead sat well to one side, isolated by a ring of irrigated lawns and gardens.

'Wow, look at that!' Emily breathed. 'Almost medieval, isn't it? The big manor-house and all the peasant cottages. This is where Charles grew up, isn't it?'

'Yeah.' Mike hovered for a moment, looking past the homestead. 'There's the airfield.'

'His younger brother runs the station now, doesn't he?'

'Philip,' Mike confirmed.

'And he's married?'

'To Lynley. Couple of teenage girls who go to boarding school down south.'

'Charles never talks about them.'

'No.' Mike clearly needed to concentrate as he brought the helicopter down close to a floodlit area where a rangy stockman was standing beside a series of fuel tanks.

Emily needed to distract herself from the landing process.

'Did it have something to do with his accident?' she wondered aloud. 'Was it a disappointment to his family that he couldn't take over running the station because he was in a wheelchair?'

'Dunno.' Mike reached overhead to ease the throttle control back and the engine noise abated as the rotors began to slow. 'I was just a kid when it happened. I do remember seeing old man Wetherby in town once or twice, though. He was pretty intimidating. He had a reputation for being pretty rough. On his family as well as the blokes who worked for him.' He unclipped his harness. 'I'll get on with the refuelling. Shouldn't take long.'

The helicopter felt strangely empty without Mike so Emily climbed out a minute later.

'This is Wayne,' Mike told her. 'He's the station manager for Wetherby Downs.'

'Gidday.' Wayne pushed the brim of his hat up and held out his hand. Emily winced inwardly at the firm grip. 'Long way for you guys to get hauled out in a chopper. How far have you still got to go?'

'We're headed for Cooper's Crossing,' Emily said. 'Next door, isn't it?'

'Been an accident?'

'No.' There was something weird about his tone, Emily thought. About the place in general, actually. This was Charles Wetherby's family station but he wanted nothing to do with it. The Coopers were neighbours in an area of country that was so vast people depended on their neighbours for support, but clearly they hadn't been in touch and Wayne sounded… disinterested.

'Be Jim, then,' the stockman decided. 'Can't say I'm surprised. Another heart attack, I s'pose?'

'No.' But Emily remembered how panicked the girl's father had sounded on the radio. If Jim Cooper had a heart condition they might find themselves with more than one patient to care for. Some more information could well be useful. 'Is he not well at the moment?'

'Almost didn't recognise him when I copped sight of him at the rodeo a few days ago. Looked like death warmed up.' Wayne was watching the gauges on the fuel tank. 'Thirsty beast, isn't it?'

'She'll be pretty empty,' Mike told him. 'Auxillary tank holds over 100 litres and the internal one takes 380.'

'Nice-looking bird.' Wayne's hat tipped further back as he admired the aircraft.

'Yeah.' Mike looked as proud as a new father and quite happy to embark on a conversation regarding the helicopter's attributes but Emily cleared her throat.

'When did Jim have the heart attack, Wayne?'

'Fair while back now. Maybe two or three years ago?' The hat had resumed its original position so Emily couldn't read the man's expression. She was startled when he turned his head and spat rather emphatically onto the dusty ground. 'He should have sold up years ago. Farm's been ruined now.'

'Has it?' Emily caught Mike's glance briefly and he raised an eyebrow. There was no evil eye to ward off here.

Or was there?

'We've lost some good stock because they won't do their share of the fencing.' Wetherby Downs' station manager sounded disgusted. 'And there was that trouble around Christmastime when one of the lads apparently took a shine to that Cooper girl. But never mind. The bank's going to sort it out before long, from what I've heard.'

A loud ding from the fuel tank seemed to signal a halt to

any gossip. Wayne spat into the dust again and then turned away to coil the fuel pipe and hang it up. 'That should do you,' he said dismissively.

'What did you make of all that?' Mike queried as soon as they were airborne again.

'There's some bad blood around here. I think we might need to check Jim out as well as his daughter.'

'You could be right.'

'I don't think Wayne's Greek either.' The instant smile from Mike was well worth the attempt at humour. 'That was no token spitting.'

'No…but look down there. He's got a point about the fences.'

They both fell silent as they flew over the Coopers' station. The moonlight could not conceal how rundown the property was. If anything, it accentuated an almost desperate atmosphere. Some fences were broken, the land looked as though it was suffering a permanent drought and the cattle they could see looked ill-nourished and lethargic.

The station homestead was only the size of one of Wetherby Downs' many staff dwellings. The roofing iron was rusty, the paint peeling and the only decoration in the immediate vicinity was a tired-looking chicken coop and a clothesline with several limp garments attached to it.

Mike turned on the powerful light beneath the helicopter as they came in to land and Emily could see a woman struggling to latch a gate behind several cattle. She was looking up at them, her expression a mixture of surprise and dread, and the tail end of the blast from the rotors whipped strands of hair across her face.

Inadequate-looking repairs had been made with rope and sheets of corrugated iron to a section of the fence beside the gate, and Mike didn't look happy.

'Let's just hope that lot holds until we can take off again.

I don't fancy getting stuck out here thanks to getting a cow tangled up in our rotors.'

Emily was thinking about the woman as the skids made gentle contact with the almost bare earth of the paddock.

'I don't think she was expecting us,' she said. 'She doesn't look very happy.'

'No.' Mike shut down the engine and pulled his helmet off. 'Why don't you grab the kit from the back and I'll go and talk to her?'

He had opened the clamshell door at the back of the chopper by the time the woman had run across the paddock.

'I'm Mike Poulos,' Emily heard him say. 'From the Air Medical Service.'

'But what are you doing here?'

'We got called a couple of hours ago now. Are you Mrs Cooper?'

'I'm Honey.' The woman was out of breath but wasn't going to be distracted by introductions. Her face creased into deep lines of anxiety and she shoved long strands of grey hair behind her ears. 'I've been out trying to move the cattle and fix the damned fences again.' The glance she cast over her shoulder towards the house was almost fearful. 'Why didn't she call *me*? It's Jim, isn't it? It's his heart. I should never have left them alone…'

'It was Jim who made the call, Mrs Cooper. It's Megan who's unwell, apparently.'

But Honey Cooper wasn't listening. She was running towards the house.

Emily caught Mike's hand as he reached to help her scramble from the back of the helicopter. He took the large pack containing their medical supplies in his other hand and then they were both running to catch up with the distressed Mrs Cooper. Mike hadn't let go of Emily's hand, though.

She liked that.

Honey stopped by the steps leading to a narrow veranda that wrapped around three sides of the house. The pause in her headlong flight was so abrupt that Mike and Emily narrowly missed cannoning into her.

Emily pulled her hand free from Mike's and touched Honey on the arm. 'Are you all right, Mrs Cooper?' She smiled. 'Can I call you Honey?'

She nodded, gulping in air and blinking hard. 'I'm…scared to go inside,' she admitted. 'What if Jim's…?'

'Jim sounded fine when he called us, Honey.' Mike's voice was calm. Reassuring. 'It was Megan he was worried about.'

But Honey did not seemed reassured by this information. If anything, she looked even more alarmed.

'What? *Megan?* What did he say? What's Megan told him?' She pulled away from Emily's touch and almost stumbled up the steps in her haste. 'But it's only flu. She said she was feeling better today. I told Jim that.' The words were tumbling out as Honey reached for the door. 'You'd better come in anyway, now that you're here, but Jim gets too worried about things.' She opened the door. 'It'll be the death of him one of these days.'

Emily glanced back at Mike as she climbed the steps but he looked just as puzzled. Why did Honey seem frightened? Just who was their patient going to be here, and was the situation anywhere near urgent enough to have summoned a rescue helicopter across hundreds of miles?

The furnishings of the small house were faded, the floors bare, and there was no sign of a television or music centre or anything else that might add comfort to an isolated lifestyle. That the house was so immaculately clean and tidy somehow added to the sad feeling it engendered.

Emily followed Mrs Cooper from the living area into a narrow hallway that led towards her daughter's bedroom. The struggle this family was having had undoubtedly been going on for a long time. The house seemed to have absorbed some of its inhabitants' weariness and it felt like they were only a very small step away from giving up.

They were clinging to something, however—this small family. Seeing the way Honey rushed to the side of the small, wiry man waiting near the last doorway in the hall and the way he reached out to take her hands, Emily could sense the bond between this couple. A belief that, no matter how bad things got, they would make it through simply because they still had each other.

'Jim! What on earth's happened?'

'It's all right, Hon, don't panic. I'm sorry—I thought you'd be back long before the medics got here. I went out to look for you but I ran out of puff.'

'I was right over by the creek. The cattle had broken through the fence there, too. They're desperate for feed, poor things. What's wrong with Megan?'

'I dunno. She doesn't seem so bad now.' Jim turned an apologetic gaze towards Mike. 'I'm sorry. I've probably called you out all this way for nothing.'

'We'd much rather get called out and find it's not serious than the other way round,' Mike assured him. 'But seeing as we're here now, how 'bout we check Megan out?'

And Jim, Emily thought as she moved after them. She wasn't surprised he'd 'run out of puff' if he'd gone looking for his wife. He looked as though he could well be in some degree of heart failure or respiratory distress from other causes. There was a nasty grey tinge to his skin and Emily did not need a stethoscope to hear the harsh sounds his breathing was making.

The girl in the bed looked even more taken aback to see

the AMS crew arrive than her mother had, and it seemed to be more than an unwelcome surprise. It verged on being a last straw. There was no sense of the strength her parents gained from each other. Megan looked as though she didn't have any desire to fight anything and Emily was struck by the air of hopelessness. She was, what, nineteen years old? It was far too young to have given up.

Megan turned her face away from the strangers invading her bedroom. 'I'm fine,' she said tonelessly. 'Go away. I told Dad not to call any doctors.'

'You weren't fine when I called,' Jim reminded her. 'You fainted, remember? And you've been shivering fit to bust on and off ever since, even in your sleep.'

Mike crouched beside the girl. He reached out and touched his fingers to her cheek.

'Hey.'

The tone was so gentle, and the following silence so patient, that Megan slowly turned her head inch by inch until she could see the man who had spoken. Then she received one of his most charming smiles.

'I'm Mike,' he introduced himself. 'You're Megan, right? And you're not feeling so flash at the moment, are you, sweetheart?'

Emily could see that Megan was caught by Mike's smile and the concerned expression that she would have to be seeing in those dark eyes. And who wouldn't respond to that? What female on earth wouldn't want to be made to feel special by having a man like Mike concerned about them?

Megan nodded reluctantly.

'Do you remember what happened when you got out of bed before?'

'I…got a bit dizzy, that's all.'

'She hasn't eaten anything for days,' Honey put in. 'I don't think she even ate a hot dog at the rodeo and that was last Thursday.' She was clutching Jim's hand and they were both staring anxiously at their daughter.

Mike laid his hand on Megan's forehead and Emily knew exactly why the young girl closed her eyes as though the touch was comforting.

'You're running a bit of a temperature. What else is going on for you, Megan?'

Emily unzipped the pack to locate a stethoscope and a blood-pressure cuff. 'Is it OK if I take your blood pressure, Megan?'

'I guess.' The assent was grudging.

Emily moved to the other side of the bed. She was happy to play a supporting role here. Mike was just as capable as she was of doing a patient assessment and he had already established far more rapport with Megan than she herself was likely to achieve. The teenager was still watching Mike as Emily wrapped the cuff around her upper arm.

Megan was overweight and the cuff didn't have much of an overlap so Emily had to hope the Velcro would stay fastened as she pumped up the pressure. Other impressions were also crowding in. The girl's breathing was faster than it should be and so was her heart rate. Not surprising given her fever and not unexpected if this was a viral illness, but something was triggering a faint alarm bell for Emily.

And for Mike, it appeared. He was frowning.

'What about these stomach pains your dad said you were getting?'

Emily could swear she heard a faint gasp from Honey but when she looked up her attention was caught by what she saw Jim holding in his free hand. A small red canister with a white pump nozzle on the top.

'Do you get angina?' she asked Jim. 'Have you needed your spray tonight?'

'I used it a while back.'

'Do you have any chest pain at the moment?'

'No. I'm fine. It's Megan you need to worry about.'

Emily turned back. 'BP's 95 on 50, Mike.'

'Mmm.' Mike had coaxed Megan into letting him exam-ine her abdomen. Emily could see that even gentle pressure was causing considerable pain. The glance she caught from Mike made that alarm bell ring more clearly.

'I'll set up an IV,' Emily said quietly. 'We don't want that blood pressure getting any lower.'

'Tell me about these stomach pains.' Mike encouraged Megan again. 'When did they start?'

'A few days ago.'

'And have you had anything like this before?'

'She's always had painful periods,' Honey offered quickly, with a swift, almost apologetic glance at her husband. 'But they don't usually make her sick. She's just caught a bug at a bad time of the month, hasn't she?'

Mike's attention was fixed on Megan. 'So you've got your period at the moment?'

A face that had already been flushed from fever seemed to lose colour and then go astonishingly red. Megan shot an ag-onised glance in her father's direction and it was only when Jim muttered something about putting the kettle on and left the bedroom that she finally nodded with extreme reluctance.

'Sorry, sweets, I know this is a bit personal but it could be important. Would you rather just talk to Emily?'

Megan shook her head emphatically but Emily wasn't of-fended. Given the choice, Mike would win as far as she was concerned as well.

'OK. Do you use tampons?'

Emily almost nodded at the line she could see Mike fol-lowing. Septic shock from ill-advised tampon use was a real possibility here. Appendicitis was also amongst a raft of conditions that could produce severe abdominal symptoms. A ruptured ectopic pregnancy was unlikely to cause the fever but Emily was running through every possibility she could think of. She had a strong impression that they were missing something important.

'Sharp scratch, Megan, I'm sorry.' The cannula slid into a vein on the back of the girl's hand and Emily secured the line and attached a bag of saline as Mike continued his examination and assessment.

Emily held the bag of saline towards Honey. 'Would you mind holding that for the moment, please?'

'She's really sick, isn't she?' They could all see that another shivering spell was gripping Megan. She had to stop answering Mike's questions because her teeth were chattering hard enough to make speech impossible.

'She's certainly going to need to go into hospital,' Emily said carefully. The anxiety levels around this place were quite high enough, without her adding too much. 'Would you like to come in with her?'

Honey opened her mouth, closed it again and then shook her head in distress. 'I can't! We can't afford to have the cattle loose again.' With a quick glance at her daughter she lowered her voice. 'Jim can't manage by himself and there's been enough trouble…'

Emily remembered Wetherby Downs' station manager's disgust at the state of the shared fence line between the properties. And she remembered something else. A comment about 'one of the lads'. She also threw a quick glance in Megan's direction. Wayne had implied that the 'trouble' had been some time ago. Around Christmas, which was eight months ago now. Too long for a ruptured ectopic pregnancy to cause the current symptoms. But what about a miscarriage? Maybe Megan's relationship was ongoing. The girl's weight was certainly enough to easily conceal a pregnancy for some time.

If her parents were unaware of the possibility then perhaps Megan had reason to want it kept confidential. Perhaps taking her to the hospital unaccompanied by any family members would actually be preferable.

Except that Jim clearly needed some kind of evaluation himself. Mike had had the same thought. He approached Megan's father after she was settled on the stretcher in the back of the helicopter, having been carried there, single-handedly and rather heroically in Emily's opinion, by Mike.

'When did you last see a doctor, Jim?' he queried casually.

'He won't.' Honey ignored the warning look from her husband. 'It's too far for us to try and get into town and the only clinic in the area is held at Gunyamurra.'

That was very close to Wetherby Downs and the station's population would provide the majority of any patients. The short silence spoke volumes about bad blood between neighbours. Emily broke the uncomfortable pause.

'Maybe you'll be able to get in to bring Megan home,' she suggested. 'It would be easy to set up an appointment to suit. We've got a really good cardiologist who's just joined the staff and I could help by—'

'We don't need your help,' Jim interrupted gruffly. 'I'm fine. We can manage by ourselves, thanks. Just look after Megan for us, eh?'

Monitoring the sick teenager kept Emily too occupied to worry about being airborne again in a craft that lacked wings. Her faith in Mike's ability to get them all back to base safely was absolute, and working with a patient in a helicopter was not so different to being in a fixed-wing aircraft. She still had to deal with engine noise while trying to talk to her patient or listen to breath sounds or get a blood-pressure reading, and to cope with unexpected fluctuations in her balance while reaching for equipment or trying to record observations on the patient record chart.

The first litre of fluid had run through with no improvement in blood pressure. Emily started another bag of normal saline and took another set of vital sign measurements. Megan's heart and respiration rates were way above normal and her temperature was 39.6 degrees Centigrade, which was worryingly high.

Conversation proved difficult and not just because of the engine noise. Megan seemed even more miserable and withdrawn, possibly because Mike was no longer there to coax or charm. Emily did her best to keep her comfortable and maintained a cheerful, reassuring manner, but trying to win the girl's confidence and talk to her properly might have to wait until she didn't have to shout. And when they had more diagnostic tools and tests for assistance.

Charles was waiting in the emergency department of Crocodile Creek Base Hospital as Mike and Emily rolled the stretcher through the doors. Jill Shaw, their director of nursing, stood beside his chair.

'I've set up the resuscitation area,' she told Emily. 'Charles offered to stay so I've held off calling any other staff in, but they're only over at the house.' She smiled. 'Apart from Cal and Gina, that is. I think they're still sitting on the beach somewhere.'

'I'll stick around,' Mike offered. 'I could be useful.'

Mike's strength was vital, in fact, as they transferred Megan from the stretcher to the bed. The girl's level of consciousness appeared to have dropped and she groaned loudly and rolled her head from side to side but said nothing in response to Jill's greeting as the nurse readjusted her oxygen mask and started to remove clothing to change her into a hospital gown.

Charles raised an eyebrow questioningly at Emily.

'I think we can rule out meningitis,' Emily told him, 'and her chest is clear. It's more than a viral illness, though. Something's going on abdominally and I'm worried about sepsis. We need to rule out peritonitis or maybe pyelonephritis or pancreatitis. Or possibly an incomplete miscarriage.'

Both of the rather bushy eyebrows that topped Charles's craggy features rose at the last suggestion.

'Plan of action?'

'I'll get bloods for chemistries. A complete count and coagulation studies from two separate sites. We'll get a catheter in, get an analysis, do a pregnancy test and start monitoring urine output. I'll do a pelvic exam and an ultrasound.' She glanced at the monitor above Megan's bed which was settling to give continuous readings of her ECG, blood pressure and pulse oximetry. 'I want to get her blood pressure up a bit as well. I'll start a dopamine infusion. And we'll get her on full antibiotic cover as soon as we've taken the first bloods.'

'I can take care of the samples,' Charles offered. 'I know my way round a few of those machines in the lab and I'm sure Alix won't mind if we don't haul her in at this time of night.'

Megan muttered incoherently and groaned frequently as Mike helped Emily collect the blood samples required. Jill was charting a new set of vital signs and looked up as the tympanic thermometer beeped.

'Temp's up to 40.2.'

Emily nodded. 'We'll need to cool her down.' The blood pressure showing on the monitor was also a concern, having dropped a little to 90 over 45. 'I'll get that dopamine infusion started.'

Within twenty minutes the medical care Megan was receiving seemed to be helping. Her level of consciousness improved with a drug-induced rise in blood pressure and reduction in her body temperature, and by the time Emily was ready to do a pelvic examination Megan was alert and orientated. She understood Emily's explanation of what she was about to do.

And she was not happy about it.

'Why do you want to do *that?*'

'I'm concerned about your bleeding,' Emily said carefully. 'It doesn't seem quite like a normal period.' Which was an understatement. The pad Jill removed in preparation for the necessary urinary catheter looked, and smelt, very abnormal.

Megan stared at her doctor. 'What if I refuse? I can refuse, can't I?'

'I'm only trying to help you, Megan.' Emily hesitated then took a steadying breath. She really needed some answers here. 'Is there something worrying you, Megan?' she asked gently. She took hold of her patient's hand. 'Are you—or have you been—pregnant?'

'*No!*'

Emily stayed still for a moment, maintaining eye contact. Offering what she hoped was a sympathetic and nonjudgmental ear. Jill was quietly busy, noting observations on the chart in a corner of the room. Mike had taken the blood samples to the lab where Charles was getting set up to do the analyses.

But Megan looked away. 'I'm not pregnant,' she told Emily. 'And I don't need any internal examination. I've just got the flu.'

'Having flu wouldn't be giving you such a sore tummy,' Emily said patiently. 'We need to find out what's making you this sick, Megan. If it's something like your appendix, then it's possible you may need an operation.'

'Is that what you think it is?' Megan sounded almost hopeful. 'My appendix?'

'We won't know unless you let me do what I need to do. I know it's not pleasant, Megan, but I'll be as quick and as gentle as I can be.'

This time Megan nodded and she stayed co-operative as Emily put gloves on and got Jill to assist in positioning Megan. The older nurse moved to hold Megan's hand reassuringly.

Emily was careful. And thorough. And very surprised. She caught Jill's gaze and the older nurse blinked. Megan stared at Jill. Then her gaze flicked to Emily who tried to keep both her face and tone very calm.

'Jill, can you take these swabs through to Charles and see what's happening with the blood samples?'

Jill eyed her curiously but nodded. 'Of course.'

'I'm feeling better now,' Megan announced as Jill left the room.

'That's great.' Emily smiled. 'We'll have to make sure you keep getting better.'

'I'm really thirsty.' Megan was staring at Emily with unnerving intensity. Had she guessed what Emily was thinking?

'We can't give you anything to drink just yet, I'm sorry—just in case you need to go to Theatre. Not until we're sure of our diagnosis.' Emily was sure now. All she needed was a minute to collect her thoughts and decide how to handle the new information she had.

'I need to go to the toilet.'

'I'll find you a bedpan.'

'Ew!' Megan looked disgusted. 'But I feel fine. Why can't I use a proper toilet?'

'You might not feel so good if you try standing up. And we need to do some tests on your urine in any case. Can't you wait just a minute or two? I don't want to leave you alone to go and get a pan.'

'No. I'm busting.'

Emily scanned the monitors. Everything was stable, and looking better than it had. She nodded reluctantly. 'OK. Just rest there, Megan,' she instructed. 'I'll be back in just a second.'

'Where are you going?'

'To the sluice room.' Emily hesitated. 'Do you want me to wait until Jill comes back? Or find another nurse to sit with you?'

'No, I told you—I'm *busting!*'

Emily's path back from the sluice room intersected with that of Mike as he came back into the department.

'Results will be through in another few minutes,' he told her. Then he peered at Emily's face. 'What's up, Em? Is it Megan?'

She nodded. 'I've just done a pelvic exam. I know what's wrong with her.'

Mike was still studying Emily's expression. 'She's had a miscarriage?'

'No.' Emily had used the last minute or so to assimilate the most recent information she had gathered on her patient. 'I think she's given birth. Very recently.'

Mike whistled silently. 'Like…in the last few days?'

Emily nodded again. Very slowly. 'She's got a perineal tear that's just starting to heal. The only likely explanation for that is giving birth—to at least a close to full-term baby.'

'And Megan was at the rodeo on Thursday. Her mother said she hadn't eaten any hot dogs.'

Emily's nod was excited this time.

'Which would make it entirely possible that Megan is—'

'Lucky's mother,' Emily breathed. 'Oh, Mike!' She held onto Mike's gaze. 'Do you know what this means?'

'That she might be septic from a fragment of retained placenta?'

'Yes, but…' It was almost too much to get her head around. Emily could so easily imagine what it would have been like if she'd been told *her* baby wasn't dead after all. Megan must think she'd lost her infant. Gina—the doctor who had discovered Lucky behind the bushes at the rodeo—had been convinced that the mother would have believed it to be a stillbirth.

'Should we tell her now?'

'Has she said anything about being pregnant?'

'She denied it.' Emily frowned. 'But, then, she would, wouldn't she? She might think she'd get into trouble for leaving it behind the bushes. I think she thinks I might know something now, though—after that examination.'

'Her family didn't seem to know anything about it.'

'No.' Emily's frown deepened. 'Maybe she doesn't want them to know.'

'Wouldn't be surprised. An extra mouth to feed around there might not be very welcome.'

Emily sighed. This wasn't going to be as simple as she'd thought. Maybe she wouldn't be producing a miracle. Maybe she was projecting too much of herself into this case. 'What should I do, Mike?'

'Talk to her. Carefully.'

'She might prefer to talk to you. She trusts you.'

'I'll come and say hello,' Mike suggested. 'And see where she's at. The number-one priority right now is to take care of Megan.' Mike eyed the bedpan. 'Does she need that?'

Emily nodded and started moving again. 'You're right, of course. Talking about Lucky can wait. If she's septic from postnatal complications, we need to get on top of things fast.'

Emily drew back the curtain screening the resuscitation area, though it had been an unnecessary precaution in the empty department tonight.

They both stared at Megan's bed. And at the end of the IV tubing that was dribbling a dopamine infusion onto the floor, drop by drop.

Emily turned to Mike in horror but he spoke first.

'Where the hell has she gone?'

CHAPTER THREE

'SHE won't be far away.'

Emily crushed a surge of panic. She shouldn't have left Megan on her own, even for a minute.

'She wanted to use a proper toilet.' Emily spun on her heel and moved towards the department's bathroom. 'That's where she'll be.'

But the cubicles were empty and Emily had known, deep down, that they would be.

Things were falling into place. The sense of hopelessness she had perceived in Megan when she had first seen the teenager. Not only was the poor girl physically unwell, she had to be suffering from grief and guilt and quite possibly postnatal depression.

And Emily knew a lot more than she had ever wanted to about all that.

Talking about something as personal as menstruation in front of her father hadn't been the real issue for Megan, had it? She had been terrified of the truth coming out.

Emily could still feel the intensity of that look Megan had given her after the last examination. Megan knew that Emily had discovered the truth.

Megan had fled.

'She's not in the department anywhere, as far as I can see.' Mike met Emily in front of the main desk. 'And her clothes seem to be gone.' Black curls bounced with incongruous gaiety as Mike shook his head. 'I just don't believe this!'

'I do,' Emily said grimly. 'She's panicked. She's trying to escape. Probably a rerun of what she did after she thought she'd given birth to a dead baby.'

Mike shook his head again. 'No, what I can't believe is *how* she's managed it. She was delirious when we were taking those blood samples. I wouldn't have thought she was capable of even getting off that bed, let alone climbing over the sides you put up.'

'She was feeling a lot better. Blood pressure was well up and her temperature was coming down. It won't last long, though. She's in shock and if it's septic, she's going to get a whole lot worse.'

'It's septic all right.' With his usual ability to surprise, Charles had glided silently into the department. He held a sheaf of laboratory printouts in one hand. 'White cell count is through the roof.'

Jill was following Charles. She stared at her colleagues. 'What's going on?'

'Megan's done a runner,' Mike said succinctly.

'I left her alone for a minute,' Emily confessed miserably. 'To get her a bedpan. This is all my fault.'

'But why would she have run?' Charles looked puzzled. 'Is she delirious?'

'There's a lot going on.' Emily managed to sound a lot calmer than she felt. 'My pelvic exam revealed that Megan's given birth rather recently. She has a perineal tear that's just starting to heal.'

'She was at the Gunyamurra rodeo,' Mike added. 'We think she might be Lucky's mother.'

Charles took the implications on board instantly. 'The von Willebrand's?' he queried. 'Could hypovolaemia be contributing to the level of shock she's in?'

'I hadn't thought of that.' Emily groaned, and tried to marshal her thoughts. Searching for Lucky's parents had been given medical as well as social urgency due to the inherited bleeding disorder the baby had. Like haemophilia, von Willebrand's could cause major problems if unrecognised and not treated. 'No, I don't think so,' she told Charles. 'That tear is healing well and I didn't notice anything unusual about bleeding from the puncture sites when we took those blood samples. Did you, Mike?'

'No.'

'Maybe she isn't Lucky's mother.'

'Or maybe it's the father he inherited the disorder from.'

Emily interrupted the others' conversation. 'Septic shock's quite serious enough on its own. We've got to find her…fast.'

'She could be anywhere.' Jill looked towards the automatic doors leading to the ambulance bay and loading platform.

Charles was looking at another set of doors that led into the hospital.

Emily glanced at the wall clock, registered that it was now midnight, and then caught Mike's gaze. 'Where will we start?' she asked helplessly.

'By getting help,' he answered promptly. 'You come with me, Em. We'll check at least some of the grounds on the way to the house and then see who we can wake up when we get there.'

'Jill and I will start looking inside,' Charles added. 'We'll get any staff on duty to check their own wards and any potential hiding places.' He swivelled his chair. 'Let's meet back here in fifteen minutes. If we haven't found her, we'll have to call the police.'

* * *

'It's only been about ten minutes since I last saw her.' Emily trotted to keep up with Mike's long stride as they headed for the ambulance bay. 'She *can't* have got far.'

'At least it's not cold.' Mike held out a hand to help Emily jump down from the loading platform.

'The wheelie bins!' Emily ran towards the orderly rows of the large rubbish containers that beckoned as a place to hide. 'I think I can see something.'

She held it up a moment later, her mouth too dry to say anything.

'It's her hospital gown,' Mike said heavily.

The voice Emily found sounded oddly unlike her own. 'And here's the bag that had her own clothing.' She picked up the large paper 'patient's property' bag. 'It's empty.'

'She's serious, then,' Mike said quietly. 'She's really trying to run away from us.'

'And it's my fault.'

'You contributed by providing the opportunity but you weren't to know. I wouldn't be surprised if Megan used the excuse of wanting to go to the toilet as part of a plan to escape. And there's absolutely no point in blaming yourself, Em.'

It was getting to be a habit, Mike putting his arm around her shoulders like this, but Emily didn't even try to remind herself not to feel too dependent on the support. Right now she needed it far too badly.

'Come on. We've got to hurry. Should we split up and meet at the house?'

'No. We should stay together.'

Emily wasn't going to argue with that. Being alone with her fears for Megan could be disastrous, given that she already felt too personally involved. Mike was so solid. So grounded. Being with him as they raced through the grounds between the new and old hospital buildings gave her the same feeling that flying in the helicopter had.

This time it was Megan in danger, not herself, but Mike still represented what felt like safety. A source of strength to cope at the very least.

The moonlight helped, but cast shadows that kept looking remarkably like a crouching person.

'There! What's that?' Emily pointed at a shape in the centre of the memorial garden.

'Just the shadow from the sundial.' Mike was moving fast, through the gap in the manicured hibiscus hedges that surrounded the old garden.

On the other side of the garden was the fenced area that contained a swimming pool. A series of steps beyond that led to the big veranda of the huge old two-storey building that was the doctors' quarters. Mike bounded up the steps, closely followed by Emily, and threw open the door that led into the large communal living and kitchen area of the house.

Their abrupt entrance startled the three people sitting at a long wooden table.

'What's the rush, guys? You've already missed the party.'

'We need some help, Hamish. We've got a patient missing.' Mike smiled at a member of the group—a young woman with brown hair caught back in a ponytail. 'Christina, you haven't gone home yet. That's great. We need everybody we can muster.'

Chairs scraped on the floor. The young woman beside Christina was Alix, their pathologist. She flipped a long dark braid over one shoulder and bent down to retrieve a pair of shoes. 'Who's missing?'

'A nineteen-year-old girl—Megan Cooper,' Emily told her. 'We brought her in by chopper not long ago.'

Christina had been eyeing the flight suit that Emily was still wearing. 'But I was on call for flight duty.'

'You were all having a good time on the beach when the call came in.' Mike was already moving back towards the door. 'Besides, Em really wanted to come with me.'

'I'll bet.' Alix was pulling the shoes on but looked up at Emily in astonishment. 'You went up in a *chopper?*'

'Yeah.' The brief flash of satisfaction was a welcome reprieve from Emily's anxiety, but it lasted no more than a heartbeat.

'Let's go,' Mike urged. 'Megan can't have got far yet and it's urgent that we find her.'

'I'll call Cal,' Christina offered. 'Gina will have to stay with CJ, I guess.'

'What's wrong with the lass?' Hamish queried as Christina sped off.

'Septic shock,' Emily responded. 'She hasn't crashed completely yet but it could happen any time. She was on a dopamine infusion.'

'What's the cause of the infection?'

'We think she's postnatal. Could be retained birth products.'

The group of young medics paused on the verandah as Cal joined them, hastily buttoning his shirt.

'We think she could be Lucky's mother,' Mike told them.

'Not that she's admitted even being pregnant,' Emily put into the astonished silence that followed Mike's announcement. 'She's frightened. She'll be trying to hide as well as escape.'

'Where should we start looking?'

'Let's get back to Emergency and see what Charles has organised. He and Jill are alerting night staff and checking inside the hospital.'

* * *

Charles had done more than alert staff. Sergeant Harry Blake, who manned the small police station on the hospital side of the creek, arrived as they gathered in an emergency department that was still, mercifully, free of any new arrivals in the way of patients.

'I've contacted town,' Harry told them. 'If she's trying to catch a ride she'll have to cross the bridge. They're getting someone down there to watch it.'

Crocodile Creek was named for the waterway that curved around the northern side of the hospital grounds, cutting off the hospital and its small cove from the main township. The bridge linked the two distinct areas and provided the only access to any main road.

'No sign of her anywhere inside so far,' Charles reported. 'Mike?'

'We found the hospital gown out by the wheelie bins. She's changed back into her own clothes.'

'Which were?' Harry flipped open a notebook.

'One of those over-sized T-shirts for sleeping in,' Emily told him. 'It was dark blue, with a pink teddy bear or something on the front. She put some track pants on for the trip because she felt so cold. They were dark blue as well. Or they might have been black.'

'Black,' Mike decided. 'And she didn't have any shoes.'

'Should be reasonably conspicuous, then.' Harry closed the notebook. 'Anyone checked the beach yet?'

'I'll do it,' Mike offered.

'Go with him, Emily,' Charles suggested. 'We'll split everybody else up and do a thorough search of the grounds. You'll all need to stay in touch. Make sure you've got either a radio or a mobile phone.'

* * *

They jogged the entire length of the small cove, checking the shadowed areas around the large boulders that marked the base of the grassy slope, then Emily was forced to stop and catch her breath.

Mike looked up at the house occupying the opposite and much higher bluff than the one where the doctors' quarters was situated. 'I should call my parents,' he said. 'You never know, Megan might have turned up asking for a room at the hotel.'

George and Sophia Poulos ran the Athina, a small hotel and restaurant. It was an inviting place for anybody who went past, and you had to go past if you were heading for the bridge, but Emily shook her head doubtfully.

'I don't think so. It's too close to the hospital and I doubt that she's thinking clearly enough to consider resting.'

'Could she have got much further away, though?'

'She might have. If she made it as far as the main road she could have hitched a ride. A lot of trucks do most of their travelling at night to avoid the heat and any tourist traffic.'

Mike called Charles to check in and they spoke for a couple of minutes.

'We're to head back,' he relayed to Emily. 'The search area is being widened. Everybody's hoping Megan might ask for help when she's feeling sick enough again, but they're discussing whether I should take the chopper up and use the nightsun.'

'Sounds like a good idea.'

'She'll be hard to spot at night with those dark clothes on. If she's lying under a tree or bush or something, it'll be impossible. We don't have any of those night-vision goggles the police can use in this type of search.' Emily could see the gleam of interest in Mike's eyes, despite the darkness. 'I know how to use them—we had them in the army. Maybe we should get some,' he added thoughtfully. 'Could be fun.'

'Do you miss the drama of the army, then?'

'Not really.' A sweep of Mike's arm took in the whole cove, the expanse of sea where a scattering of islands could be seen as black shapes in the moonlight, the gleam of pale sand and the buildings on top of the low bluffs that were now showing far more lights than normal and glowed against the night sky. 'I love this place. And I get my share of excitement.' His smile had a definite element of mischief. 'Waking up the whole of Crocodile Creek by shining thirty million candle-power through their windows won't be exactly boring.'

The remnants of the driftwood bonfire were still glowing as they retraced their path to the hospital. Emily eyed the embers and welcomed a brief distraction from her anxiety about Megan.

'Isn't it nice? About Cal and Gina?'

Cal Jamieson, a surgeon, had been working in Crocodile Creek for several years but nobody had met the woman he'd last had a relationship with. She had turned up only last week, with a small boy who looked just like Cal, and it had been Gina, in fact, who had found baby Lucky at the rodeo. It was clear to everybody that she wouldn't be leaving again in a hurry and celebrating the couple's reunion had been the pre-cipitating reason for the fire night.

'It's great.' Mike turned his head to smile at Emily and she almost stumbled as she tried to read his tone and expression. He sounded…wistful, she decided, which seemed odd, given that he hadn't had any hankering to marry either Kirsty or her predecessor, Trudi.

Maybe he still missed that gorgeous Italian woman which, of course, wouldn't be odd at all. But Marcella had loathed Mike's home town and had refused to contemplate staying. Mike had been just as stubborn in refusing to consider leaving, and the fights had escalated until the relationship was in tatters.

'You'll find the right woman one day, Mike.' Maybe it was already Emily's turn to offer familiar comfort but she couldn't resist adding a somewhat cynical rider. 'She'll love you, she'll love Crocodile Creek *and* she'll have great legs.'

'How will I know?'

'You mean, if she's wearing trousers or something?'

Mike gave Emily enough of a shove for it to take her a couple of steps to regain her balance.

'It was a serious question, Emily. Look at Cal and Gina. Or Kirsty and Simon bloody Kent, for that matter.'

'I'd rather not, thanks.'

Mike's only acknowledgment of Emily's interjection was a brief, sympathetic grunt. 'These people seem to know when they've discovered the love of their lives, though, don't they? What am I missing? Do people have a little badge that says "I'm the One" and it's only visible when the right other person gets close enough? Do women know something we don't?' His nudge was more gentle this time. 'Come on, Em. Help a bloke out and divulge some ancient woman-lore or something.'

'If I knew what it was, I'd be using it myself.' Emily sighed. 'I think there is a badge. Trouble is, you might see it on someone but if they don't spot one on you, then…' Emily had to pause in order to keep her tone very light. To make sure she didn't reveal anything she shouldn't. 'Then it can make everything a lot harder. You go hunting to find a badge somewhere else or you think you see it because you want to, and then it all turns to custard.'

'Did you think you saw a badge on Simon, then? And he pretended he saw one on you?'

'Kind of, I guess.' This was becoming way too personal. If Emily answered that question, maybe Mike would want to know if she'd been hunting because the person wearing the real badge was unavailable. Out of her league. Not even remotely interested in anything more than friendship.

To her surprise, Mike just echoed her sigh. 'I know exactly what you mean,' he said. 'It's not just a badge—I suspect they need to glow and they'll only do that if there's a reciprocal amount of electricity floating between the people in question. And they both have to feel the same way to generate that electricity, don't they?'

'I guess.' Emily wanted to change the subject. They needed to, anyway. They were entering the hospital grounds again now. 'You'll need someone to go with you if you take the helicopter up, won't you?'

'Would you like to come?'

'May as well. I'm still wearing these gorgeous overalls.'

'You don't sound too keen.'

'My confidence has slipped somewhat now that we've been on the ground for so long. Maybe it's like falling off a horse. I should do it again.'

'You didn't fall out of my helicopter.' Mike sounded offended. He turned and blocked Emily's path so she was forced to stop. 'I hope you also noticed that I didn't drop you like a stone either.'

'No. Thank you for that.' Emily smiled placatingly. 'Are you always that good at keeping your promises?'

She was standing very close to him. Close enough to feel his warmth. And to see an expression she couldn't remember ever seeing before in his eyes. Something so deep and so serious her heart actually skipped a beat.

'Always,' Mike said softly. 'Don't ever forget that, Em.'

'I won't.' Her heart thumped painfully as it made up for lost time. Or was it more that Emily could suddenly imagine what it would be like to hear other kinds of promises from this man?

Or maybe it was simply because they were standing so close that they were almost touching, and that had always done very funny things to Emily's equilibrium.

She had already held the eye contact for a heartbeat too long—stepping over the boundary of friendship into dangerous territory. But Mike wasn't breaking the contact either, and another heartbeat came and went.

He's going to guess, Emily thought desperately. Or maybe he had already, and was trying to work out how to handle an unwanted complication in his life at a point when he was fed up with women anyway.

The blaring notes of Mike's mobile phone cut the atmosphere like a cleaver and terminated the eye contact just as effectively.

'What?' Mike queried tersely a few seconds after he answered the call. 'Who was it…? Where…? How long ago…? No, we're almost back. We'll meet you out front.'

'Have they found Megan?' Emily touched Mike's arm in her eagerness.

'They've had a call from a trucker who was listening in on the emergency services frequency.'

'And?'

'And he picked Megan up by the bridge. Just after midnight.' Emily checked her watch. Nearly an hour ago now.

'She apparently told him she'd had a fight with her boyfriend and really needed help to get home.'

'Didn't he notice anything odd about the way she was dressed? Or how unwell she looked?'

'He thought she was upset and that was why she was acting a bit weird.' Mike had bypassed the quickest route back to the emergency department. He was heading for the main hospital entrance and Emily stretched her stride to keep up with him.

'So where is she now? *How* is she, more importantly?' The

second glance she took at her watch was an automatic double-check. 'Thank goodness we'll be in plenty of time for her next dose of antibiotics.'

'Hopefully.'

'What? She can't be that far away. Which way was the truck going? North or south?'

'West, so she chose the right direction for home but she's not in the truck any longer. She made the driver stop on a lay-by. Said she lived on a farm close by and her mother was on the way to collect her.'

'Oh, *no!*' Emily's spirits plummeted afresh. 'And he just left her there?'

'He's not feeling too good about it now, by the sound of it.'

Emily lapsed into silence. Of course he wasn't. The driver hadn't done anything worse than she had, had he? And Megan had been quite believable.

'At least she's still OK enough to have got that far. We'll get to her in time.'

'She may have got a bit further by now.' Mike didn't sound optimistic and that was so unlike him that Emily's very real fear for Megan returned in a rush.

'Why? Where exactly did he drop her off?'

'The lay-by was on the way into the mountains. Past the banana plantations. At the start of the rainforest.'

Emily stifled her groan of dismay as they rounded the corner of the building and she could see the convoy of waiting vehicles, headed by Harry's police car, with an ambulance next in line.

'Is that where we're going? To start searching the forest?'

'I am.' Mike nodded. 'I've got search and rescue experience and I know the mountains around here pretty well. I also have a first-class paramedic kit in a backpack. You don't have to come, Em. You shouldn't. You must be exhausted. Maybe you should wait here and rest. And be ready for when we bring Megan back.'

'No way! I've *got* to help search!'

Mike stopped abruptly and caught Emily, gripping both her upper arms. 'This isn't your fault, Em. You can't try and take the whole responsibility on board.'

'But…'

Emily couldn't begin to try and justify her vehemence. Nobody knew her history here and there was no reason for them to know. Maybe her involvement in this case *was* too personal to be professional but they all knew how hard she had worked to save Megan's baby, didn't they? Surely that was an acceptable motivation?

'She's Lucky's mother, Mike,' Emily said softly. 'She thinks she's lost her baby, and she hasn't. We saved him. I can't just sit around for hours waiting and wondering whether she's ever going to have the joy of knowing her baby actually survived. Or that Lucky could lose his mother…maybe for ever.'

She couldn't prevent her voice choking on that last word or her eyes filling with tears. But Mike seemed to understand. He pulled her closer, just for an instant, into a rough but comforting hug. His own voice was suspiciously gruff a moment later.

'Come on, then. We'll both go and find her. You'll have to stay with me, though.'

Emily pulled back far enough to see Mike's expression. 'Why?'

'Because…' Mike hesitated and seemed to change his mind about what he wanted to say. He also seemed to drag his gaze away from Emily's and he stepped away, ready to move. 'I might need your help,' he said briskly. 'You're the expert in emergency resuscitation after all.'

It was a perfectly valid reason to request her company. But it hadn't been the first thing to have sprung to mind, had it?

The look Emily had received had suggested that he had intended to say something very different.

Something far more personal.

She must be more tired than she'd realised, Emily decided as she followed Mike towards the vehicles. And the tension was doing her head in.

Why else would she be imagining that Mike would even think along personal lines like that?

Or be getting the impression that she had the potential to be as important to him as he already was to her?

She was tired all right. Part of her brain was already asleep. Emily knew that thoughts like that were just part of a familiar dream.

And always would be.

CHAPTER FOUR

THAT call had been way too close for comfort.

Mike sat on one of the stretchers in the back of the ambulance, his backpack kit wedged between his knees, as the convoy of vehicles raced west towards the mountains. His friends Hamish and Cal sat facing him on the opposite stretcher and Emily was sitting by his side. Every bump in the road—and there were plenty—jostled her against him, so that Mike was increasingly aware of the touch of her leg or shoulder.

Yes. He had come too close to saying something he shouldn't. When Emily had asked him why she had to stay with him if she joined the search party, he had nearly said because that was where she belonged. By his side. That he wanted her where he could see her—to protect her, if necessary.

Not just from an environment he knew could be unforgiving. Mike wanted to protect her from herself. Emily gave so much of herself to others and she blamed herself too much when things went wrong. They *had* to find young Megan Cooper before it was too late because if this ended in disaster, Emily would never forgive herself.

She was probably even finding a way to blame herself for the disaster of her relationship with Simon. Mike nearly snorted aloud at the thought. As if it could have been in any way Emily's fault. Simon had used her. Taken advantage of her sweet, loving nature and tried to turn her into something she could never be: a clone of himself—shallow and self-centred and overly ambitious. And then he'd found a far more suitable and willing model in Kirsty and had just wiped his feet all over Emily on his way out the door.

Thank goodness he was gone. Relief chased away any lingering anger on Emily's behalf. He even turned to smile at her.

'OK, babe?'

'Yeah, I'm good.' Emily smiled back but Mike could see the weariness and worry etched into her features in the flickering light.

'It'll be all right,' he said encouragingly. 'We'll find her. How far could she have got after all?'

'It's pretty thick forest up there, isn't it?' Hamish queried.

'Can be.' Mike nodded. 'I used to do a lot of bush walking around there as a teenager. It's easy enough if you stick to the tracks but once you get off them it's hard going.'

'Impossible in places,' Cal agreed. 'There are huge tree roots and dead branches and leaves everywhere, and some of those vines are as thick as tree trunks.'

'Strangler trees,' Mike told Hamish. 'They start off growing as air plants up in the canopy and they send their roots down to the soil. They can eventually kill the tree they're covering.'

'We'd better hope the lass has stayed on the track, then,' Hamish responded. 'Shame we haven't got a tracker dog or something.'

'Harry's been in touch with Brisbane police,' Mike said. 'They're sending a team with dogs but it'll be at least a couple of hours before they can get here.'

Cal turned to look out of the long window behind him where the headlights of vehicles behind them were lighting up vast fields of sugar cane. The track for the small train that carried the cane to the processing plant was running alongside the road. Then he looked at his watch.

'We must be about halfway there.'

Emily nodded. 'Maybe another fifteen minutes.'

The group lapsed into silence again and Mike heard Emily's determined, indrawn breath, like a reverse sigh. It sounded as though she was gathering her strength and focusing on the task ahead of them. Willing herself to succeed.

That quiet determination and strength had been the first thing Mike had ever noticed about Emily Morgan. It had set her apart because it seemed almost at odds with her pale colouring of fair skin and honey-blonde hair, her lack of height and a serious, almost shy demeanour on first acquaintance.

'Solid' had been the word that had occurred to Mike on that first glimpse. He remembered the occasion very well despite it having been over two years ago, and the clear memory was not just because it had been the welcome home/engagement party his parents had thrown for him and Marcella at the Athina.

Not physically solid, although Emily was nothing like the tall, leggy beauties Mike had always been drawn to, and the fact that she'd been standing beside Marcella at the time had accentuated just how different she was. Solid as in genuine. Trustworthy and honest. When they were finally introduced that night, Mike had nodded approval on hearing her name. It was perfect for someone who seemed to personify the kind of old-fashioned values Mike had never been lucky enough to find in combination with the great looks his girlfriends invariably possessed.

And Marcella had possessed them in abundance. The fiery Italian model he had met on holiday in Paris and brought home to Crocodile Creek as his fiancée less than a month later should have eclipsed Emily totally, but Mike had still noticed her.

More than noticed her. He had rapidly found himself watching out for her at work or on the beach, enjoying the start of what had promised to be a very genuine friendship once they'd got past Emily's shyness. Mike liked to think it had been Emily's idea that he move into the doctors' quarters after Marcella had stormed off and his mother had been was wringing her hands and loudly lamenting the impossibility of the gorgeous half Italian, half Greek grandchildren she'd hoped for, but he suspected he had planted the idea himself.

Not that it mattered because it had been the perfect solution to a minor family crisis back then. It hadn't even mattered that Emily had been in love with Simon. It had been friends that Mike had been in need of more than anything and the close living arrangements and camaraderie in the house were great.

A deepening friendship with Emily was the icing on the cake. Mike had never had this kind of closeness with a woman who hadn't been a lover. Hell, he hadn't even had it with women who *had* been lovers. Not like he had with Emily. Where you knew you could just be yourself completely and say or do anything and still be accepted and liked.

Bouncy Trudi had come closest to being a mate, but that had just been a bit of fun. And a smokescreen to stop Sophia hauling any more 'nice Greek girls' close enough to be subjected to a family dinner and significant introductions to her single son. Trudi had never touched Mike on the kind of level Emily did. The kind where he wanted to protect and nurture. To create happiness.

He loved her, dammit. How and when that interest and friendship had morphed into such intensity had slipped past without any lightning bolts, but the fact it was there and not about to go away had been undeniable for a long time. Catching Kirsty when she had thrown herself at him had been an attempt to discover whether distraction could work, whether those deeper feelings for Emily had been simply due to sexual frustration after Trudi had left.

They hadn't. And distraction would never work. An alternative would never be good enough because Emily was one of a kind.

Mike sneaked a sideways glance and was disconcerted to find that Emily's gaze swung to meet his virtually instantly. Coincidence…or some kind of subconscious connection?

Yeah…right! Mike winked at Emily to disguise any heavier signals he might be sending out. How appalled would she be to know what he was thinking? That he was ready to leap into a gap in her life that Simon had left only a matter of days ago and thereby take advantage of a woman who was in emotional distress?

He would be using an opportunity he had no right to exploit. And if it worked, he'd never know whether it had only worked because he had been in the right place at the right time and had caught her on the rebound. Mike wanted more than that. He wanted Emily to want him as much as he wanted her. Not as a substitute or an alternative, or anything else that wasn't as solid and genuine as he knew Emily would want long term.

How long would she need to get her heart and head into a clear space? Weeks? Months?

Would she even have the slightest interest in more than a friendship?

Fear that she might not gnawed at Mike's patience.

But he had sensed something tonight, he was sure of it. The way she had looked at him had been what had made that call so close earlier. He'd had the crazy idea she might have welcomed what he had really wanted to say about her staying close to him.

Maybe not *right* now, of course, when the anxiety and tension concerning their missing patient was building to crisis level, but what if they found her and she was OK, and Emily would be feeling much happier…?

If Mike was honest with himself, it wasn't fear that was wearing his resolve thinner by the minute.

It was hope.

There was a signposted track into the rainforest that started at the lay-by, and it was the most obvious route Megan would have taken if she had wanted to hide. The main track divided into three smaller branches within fifty metres of the entrance to the forest and Emily studied a board that had a map of the tracks and information about the forest.

Highlights for tourists were noted, such as a stand of giant kauri trees, various creeks and a small waterfall, and a boardwalk structure that had been built to allow visitors to climb into the canopy of the forest. She also spotted the warning not to eat any fruit or berries and that many of the species of flora and fauna were protected.

Equipment such as helmets with lights was being distributed and radios were being tuned to the same channel by members of the police and fire services who were called out for such purposes. Three groups were then formed to cover each of the tracks, and a doctor assigned to each group.

Emily found herself in a group with Harry, their local cop, another police officer and Mike.

'We went to school together,' Harry told Emily as they set off on their designated fork from the main track. 'Mike and I have done a fair bit of bush walking up here in our time.'

They moved very slowly, turning their heads to shine the lamps into what looked like impenetrable vegetation on either side of the track. It wasn't a complete barrier, however, for someone who was determined or frightened enough. You could push your way under and through the ferns and palm leaves and climb over fallen logs and root buttresses.

The dilemma of how much ground they should cover or how far from the track to search had been discussed in the initial briefing. For the next thirty minutes they would cover a fair distance and search two metres on either side of the track. If they failed to find any sign of Megan they would then divide the area into a grid and work methodically over each section.

There was a good chance they would simply find her on the track and, if so, the faster they could get her back to medical attention the better, but when thirty minutes had passed with no answer to their calls and no signs of the teenager, Emily began to think of other possibilities.

'What if she had just waited at the lay-by and hitched another ride?'

'We thought of that,' Harry answered. 'The trucker who dropped her off has been watching for any other traffic going west. He's going to flag down anyone he sees and ask if they've seen her.'

'What if she went the other way? Back into town?'

'She's sick. Somebody's going to notice something odd.'

'And if she ends up back at the hospital, we'll hear about it.' Mike was trying to sound reassuring. He cupped his hands to his mouth and called yet again. 'Me-gan!'

In the silence that followed, they could all hear the faint echo of the name as someone from one of the other search parties called. Then all they could hear was renewed croaking from frogs that had been disrupted by the human calls and vague rustlings that hinted of night creatures slipping into deeper hiding.

'She's here somewhere,' Harry said quietly. 'She has to be.'

'Yep.' The other police officer sounded even more confident. 'Those prints at the start of the track looked pretty fresh.'

'And how many people would set off bush walking with bare feet?'

'We could use a dog. It's going to be a long wait till the Brisbane crew gets here.'

'Maybe we should have brought Rudolph.'

Emily tried to smile at Mike's absurd suggestion, intended only for her ears. The funny-looking puppy that had been given to Gina's little boy, CJ, was about as far away from a trained search and rescue dog as it would be possible to get.

'He'd get lost himself,' Emily whispered back. 'Or trip over those ears.'

The notion was so silly it actually made her smile and lifted her spirits just a little. Or was it the fact that Mike was trying to make her smile that had lifted her spirits? Whatever. It had helped. Emily stepped off her side of the path again and lifted huge fern fronds to peer underneath. She jumped as something small scuttled away, making the deep covering of leaf litter ripple.

'This is the sort of place snakes like to hide, isn't it?'

'Most of them are harmless,' Mike told her. 'I wouldn't go poking or standing on them, though.'

'I won't,' Emily said fervently. 'Anything else I should be worried about? Like ticks?'

'You're well covered with that flight suit. And you've got gloves and boots on so you should be OK. It's all good protection against leeches as well.'

'Leeches! Oh, yuck!' Emily scrambled to get back onto the track and stumbled in her haste. Mike's hand shot out to help her catch her balance but Emily pulled away and dropped to a crouch.

'Look—what's that?'

'Where?'

'I thought I saw something white but I've lost it now.'

Mike raised his voice. 'Harry? Hold up a sec. Emily thinks she's spotted something.'

He crouched beside her and they both turned their heads, trying to systematically illuminate the ground around them.

'*There!* Don't move, Mike. Keep your light on it.' Emily crawled forward and reached up. The object was small but easily recognisable.

'What the hell is that?' Harry had come back to see what they'd found.

'A luer plug,' Emily told him. 'That scrunched-up stuff is the tape to hold it in place. It goes on the end of a cannula, which is what that little plastic tube is.'

'Like you have with a drip?'

'You got it,' Mike told Harry. 'And there's only one person who could have been wandering around here with an IV line still in their hand.'

Emily leaped to her feet. 'Come on,' she urged. 'Megan's got to be close.'

'Hang on.' Harry was unclipping his radio from his belt. 'Don't go off by yourselves. We need to call the other teams in and do this properly. We'll start from this point and work out slowly.'

Harry was right but having to wait even a few minutes was frustrating. Megan was close. Very close. They hadn't heard anything in response to their calls but that could mean she still didn't want to be found. Or it could mean that she was unconscious.

Or worse.

Emily paced back and forth, her head down, as she tried to cope with an almost crippling level of tension. She didn't realise that her pacing was taking her further and further away from her group until she turned and bumped into Mike.

'Stay close, babe,' he said softly. 'We don't want to lose you as well.'

Emily's head came up sharply and her eyes stung with unshed tears at his gentle tone.

'I'm scared, Mike,' she whispered. 'What if…if we're too late?'

His arms were around her in an instant. This friendly hugging business was becoming automatic but Emily wasn't about to complain. And this time his fingers were in her hair, cradling her head against the hollow beneath his shoulder.

Emily's helmet tipped back, the chin strap threatening to diminish her air supply, and a buckle on the strap of Mike's back pack pinched against her cheek rather viciously, but Emily barely registered the discomfort because she was listening too hard to the reassuring sounds Mike was making.

'We won't be too late,' he said. 'You'll see. I'm sure we're going to find her real soon.'

Emily straightened wearily, pulling out of the embrace so that she could see Mike's face. To see if he really was as confident as he sounded. She couldn't see his eyes, which were deeply shadowed thanks to the light from his helmet, clearly enough. It was easy to imagine she could see just what she wanted to see in them.

Hope.

A promise of success.

And something more…

Something much more personal.

It had to be a trick of the weird lighting from those helmets but Emily could have sworn that Mike's eyes were fastened on her lips. That his head was tipping, even. Agonisingly slowly, but with obvious intent.

'Hey, guys!' The shout came from further down the track, past the bend that screened the couple. 'Mike? Emily? Where are you?'

'Here.' Mike's clear response ended that fraction of time

in which he'd distracted Emily to such a degree that the intrusion of another voice was jarring. It flicked Mike back to the current situation just as cleanly—if he had, in fact, been as distracted as Emily had been. He reached to straighten her helmet. 'Let's go, Em. They need us.'

She nodded. 'I'm ready.' Then she took a deep breath. 'We are going to find her in time, aren't we?'

Mike's smile acknowledged that Emily was asking for a promise they both knew he couldn't make. It also offered understanding of how badly she wanted it.

'Spit for luck?'

And Emily found a smile she didn't know she had. 'Why not?'

They found Megan Cooper forty-five minutes later—at 3 a.m., well away from any track, lying unconscious beside a fallen log that was so covered by ferns it had provided an umbrella dense enough to screen the girl completely.

Emily and Mike were the closest medics to the middle section of the search line. Mike took a few seconds to pull the pack containing their medical supplies from his back so it was Emily who reached out to touch Megan first. To find out whether or not they had arrived in time.

Megan lay on her side, curled up in a foetal position. Emily brushed her hair aside and laid her fingers on the girl's neck over where the carotid artery lay.

Her voice was utterly flat a second later. 'I can't find a pulse.'

'Let's turn her over and check her airway,' Mike said calmly.

They rolled Megan onto her back and Mike held the girl's head and tipped it so that her chin rose and her neck was extended. Despite finding her unconscious, there was no indication that they had to worry about a neck injury. There was no evidence that she had fallen and every reason to believe that her unconsciousness was due to medical rather than traumatic causes.

'Try again,' Mike advised Emily.

Positioning Megan to open her airway had also smoothed out folds of flesh on a curled neck, and Emily's fingers pressed a little harder this time—desperately, perhaps—on one side of the trachea.

'Got it,' she breathed in relief on feeling the faint bounce against her fingertips. 'Low pulse pressure. She's tachy—maybe 120, 130.' Emily laid a hand on Megan's abdomen to feel for breathing movements as she tilted her head and put her cheek close to their patient's mouth. 'She's not moving much air.'

'There's a stethoscope in the pack.' Mike was pinching Megan's earlobe to see if there was any response to painful stimuli. 'Megan, can you hear me? Open your eyes, sweets.'

The only response was a very faint moan. Megan's Glasgow coma scale score could only be about 6 or 7. Any score lower than 8 was unconscious enough to be defined as a coma.

Emily looked up at the audience of fellow searchers as she unzipped the pack in a swift movement and flipped it open.

'We'll need the Stokes basket,' she told Harry. 'And oxygen and the life pack from the ambulance. As fast as you can.'

Two men set off a run to where the paramedics were waiting with a rescue basket on top of a stretcher and the extra, heavy equipment stowed inside. They had been positioned on the main track just before it forked into the three branches until it was known in what direction they needed to go.

Mike had a tiny oxygen cylinder in the pack but it was quickly apparent that just putting a mask and high flow on Megan would not be enough. Her breathing was laboured. Too fast and too shallow. Inadequate to the point of being life-threatening.

'You want to intubate?' Mike had a flat kit in his hand, instruments rolled up and tied with a bow of fabric tape.

Emily nodded briskly. Any overly emotional involvement in this case was now as neatly packaged as that intubation kit and had been put firmly into storage for the moment. She was faced with a critically ill patient and she knew precisely how to start fighting this battle.

'I'll get you to assist, please, Mike. As soon as Hamish or Cal gets here, we'll get some aggressive fluid resuscitation started. At least two wide-bore IV lines. How much saline have you got?'

'Two litres here. There's more in the basket.'

'My drug kit's coming as well. We'll get some dopamine on board again.' Emily was unrolling the kit that contained a laryngoscope and a selection of endotracheal tubes. 'Grab the bag mask, Mike, and the oxygen. Hyperventilate her for a minute while I get set up here.' She pulled the blade away from the handle of the laryngoscope and checked the light that came on.

The other doctors, Hamish and Cal, arrived at the scene just before the ambulance paramedics got there. Suddenly there was more expert assistance than Emily could have had in an emergency department, and a crowd of onlookers that she certainly wouldn't have had. With the less than perfect lighting and the difficulties in placing and handling equipment, thanks to the thick vegetation, however, the tension levels climbed again almost enough to wipe out the relief in having located Megan.

They climbed further as Emily found how difficult the teenager was to intubate, due mostly to her size. On her second attempt, Emily moved Megan's tongue to the left with the curved blade of the laryngoscope and eased it back even more carefully. She tilted the handle of the instrument to change the angle of the light but still couldn't locate the epiglottis.

'Can you give me some cricoid pressure, please, Mike?'

'Sure.' Mike pressed on the Adam's apple area of Megan's neck—a technique that helped prevent the aspiration of gastric contents but could also bring the structures Emily would prefer to see into clear view.

'Cool,' she murmured a moment later as she identified Megan's vocal cords. 'Got it. I'll have a size 8 tube, thanks.'

It took only seconds to slide the tube into place and inflate the cuff with air from a syringe to create a seal around it. Mike helped Emily to slip the tape around the back of Megan's head and then tie it to the mouth guard to ensure the tube didn't slip any further down her airway. He attached the bag mask to the end of the tube and started ventilating with high-flow oxygen.

Emily pulled the stethoscope from around her neck and listened to Megan's chest and abdomen as Mike squeezed air in to check that the tube was in the right place and sending oxygen to her lungs and not her stomach. Satisfied, she glanced up.

'How's that IV going, Hamish?'

'She's as flat as a pancake. I'll try again in the antecubital.' Hamish swabbed a potentially easier access point inside Megan's elbow.

Cal was using Megan's other elbow to try and get a blood-pressure reading.

'Systolic's under 60,' he reported grimly.

Emily nodded as she took the information on board. With a pressure that low, Megan was in danger of having inadequate perfusion to all her vital organs. It was not a situation compatible with life for very long.

'The sooner we get her back to hospital the better,' she announced. 'I want to get a central line in and I can't do that here.'

A central venous catheter would allow intensive monitoring of how well Megan's cardiovascular system was functioning but it was already quite clear that this teenager was going to need a lot of assistance to get into even a stable condition, let alone start to get better.

The team waited only until they had one patent IV line and a pressure bag to squeeze fluid in as quickly as possible. Then Megan was lifted into the basket. There was no shortage of willing men to ferry their patient back to the ambulance.

Emily, Mike and Hamish travelled in the back with Megan. Charles had remained in radio contact with Harry throughout the search and he and Jill now had the department ready and waiting. Extra staff who could well be needed, such as a radiologist and a CT technician, had been called in.

It was a rerun of what had been started hours ago, only this time the situation was far more serious. Megan was deeply shocked and in grave danger of developing multi-system organ failure. It would not be enough to attempt to keep her alive with life-support intervention while they tried to deal with the source of infection by aggressive antibiotic therapy until she was stable enough to consider surgery.

That source of infection had to be removed by a D and C. Now.

'Has someone called Georgie in yet?' Georgie Turner was the O and G consultant who had private rooms in town but covered emergencies as well as her part-time work at the hospital. 'She is back in town, isn't she?'

'Yes,' Jill responded, 'and I've called her. She's on her way.'

'Theatre staff?'

'Also coming. And I'll scrub.' Jill was their most senior theatre nurse and managed to make a regular appearance on duty on top of the administrative side of her position.

'I'll assist Georgie,' Cal offered. 'I'll go and check the setting-up now.'

'And I'll stay here and help Em,' Hamish said. 'Do you want to put that central line in now?'

Emily nodded. She would need to scrub up for the sterile and rather fiddly procedure of inserting the central venous line and a Swan-Ganz catheter into a vein just below Megan's collar-bone. The information it could give them would be vital in getting her through the added insult of an anaesthetic and surgery in her shocked state.

'We need to review the antibiotic regime, too.' Emily moved to the sink to scrub. 'What's going to be the most effective one to add in with the gentamycin to make sure we cover any anaerobic organisms, Charles? Clindamycin? Chloramphenicol?'

Staff numbers in the resuscitation area dropped as the next phase of Megan's care began. Mike had been helping the paramedics clean up the ambulance but he reappeared when it was time to transfer Megan to Theatre.

And he was still there when they emerged nearly an hour later and wheeled Megan's bed into the intensive care unit.

'How was it?' he asked.

'Touch and go.' Emily was still running on the adrenaline she'd produced during one of the hardest anaesthetics she had ever administered. 'And I thought that procedure on Lucky was tricky.' She stood back as the bed was eased carefully into position, so as not to get tangled in the spaghetti of leads attaching Megan to a bank of monitors. 'We came a bit too close to losing her, Mike. She arrested at one point.'

'You've got her this far.' Mike's quiet statement was almost a benediction. 'Maybe she's just as much of a fighter as you are, Em.'

'Let's hope so.'

'Who's staying with her now?'

'I am.' Emily's tone made it clear that she didn't need to be reminded of the rest she needed badly. There was no way she was relinquishing care of this patient to anyone else. Not yet.

It was Emily who inserted an arterial line so that serial and accurate measurements of circulating oxygen levels could be obtained. She checked the functioning of the urinary catheter and fussed over the dose of diuretic needed to boost urine output to an acceptable level. She worried about the rate of the dopamine infusion as Megan's blood pressure responded too slowly, and she studied the pressure settings on the ventilator, trying to ensure that the maximum level of oxygen that was so vital to cellular survival was being delivered. She checked and double-checked every reading.

Including the twelve-lead ECG. It was miraculous that Megan's heart had given up and then been restarted and was leaving no trace of any damage. Emily ran off another recording just to reassure herself and it wasn't until she looked up from scanning the printout that she noticed Mike sitting at the central desk in the unit.

Watching her.

'Why on earth aren't you getting some rest?' she exclaimed. 'I thought you'd gone back with Hamish and Cal. You've been up all night, Mike. You need some sleep.'

'So do you,' he responded promptly. 'I'll go when you do. You need it just as much as me.'

'But I'm supposed to be doing this. I'm an ICU consultant.'

'And I'm an ICU consultant's friend. I need to be here for when you fall over from exhaustion.'

'Day staff will be here soon. And Hamish is coming back when he's had a few hours' sleep. I'll get my head down for an hour or two then.'

'In that case, how 'bout a coffee?'

'Hmm.' The small staff kitchen and sitting room was only a few steps away. Another swift survey of all the monitors showed that nothing had changed in the last ten minutes, and Megan's nurse nodded encouragingly.

'Go on,' she said. 'I'll call you if anything changes.'

'OK.' Emily rubbed at her eyes, which felt as though they were full of grit, and then she gave Mike a weary smile. 'It's a good idea. Might even be essential.'

Mike made the coffee. Hot and strong and sweet. He put the steaming mug in front of Emily as she sat down at one end of a small Formica-topped table.

'I know you don't normally have sugar in your coffee but I thought you might need a bit of a boost.'

'Thanks, Mike.' Emily watched as he took the chair on the side of the table closest to her. 'You're wonderful, you know that?'

'You're pretty amazing yourself, Dr Morgan. I've been watching you work ever since we found Megan. If anybody's going to pull her through this, it'll be you.'

'I have to pull her through.' Emily sighed. 'There's a baby not very far from here that needs his mother.'

'Don't push yourself too hard. You're a human, not a machine.'

Emily pulled a face. 'I know. And I should apologise. I've made my weaknesses fairly obvious tonight, haven't I?'

'What *are* you talking about?'

'I've been a mess. I've lost count of the number of times I've been crying on your shoulder since you came to find out why I wasn't at the party.'

'Twice,' Mike said with a smile. 'But you were only really crying once.'

'You've hugged me more than twice.'

'Have I?' Mike sounded cautious. 'Is that a problem?'

Emily felt suddenly shy and dropped her gaze to her mug of coffee. 'No, of course not. You're the best friend I've got, Mike, and I really appreciate your support.'

'It's always there for you, Em.'

'Thanks. And ditto, you know? For when you might need it.' Emily raised her gaze and smiled. 'We should really have thrown some dice, shouldn't we? To see who went first in the "ego-boosting after being dumped" game.'

'I needed the practice,' Mike said. 'I get dumped a lot more than you do.'

'Only because you keep trying. I'm not brave enough to risk it very often.' Exhaustion was loosening Emily's tongue. 'I think I might be a once-in-a-decade kind of girl.'

'You mean it's been ten years since you were last in a serious relationship?'

'Yeah. How sad is that?'

'You would have still been in medical school. How old were you?'

'Twenty-two.'

'A baby,' Mike stated. 'That's only practising for the real thing.'

'It didn't feel like a practice run. We were engaged. I'd picked out my wedding dress and everything.'

'What happened?'

'Too much,' Emily said evasively. Her tongue hadn't been loosened to the extent of burdening Mike with all the sorry details. How galling would it be to have to admit that her planned marriage had simply been an obligation her fiancé had felt he couldn't dodge? 'Bottom line was that he left me for someone else.' She snorted wryly. 'And who says history doesn't repeat itself?'

'Who was he?'

'A house surgeon on one of the runs I was doing. Cameron, his name was.'

'He was another bloody idiot,' Mike said calmly. 'For God's sake, Em—you've got to learn to choose more carefully.'

'I don't want to,' Emily said decisively. 'I think I'll just accept my lack of ability in that department. I think I'll stay single.'

'What? *For ever?*' Mike sounded so horrified that Emily had to smile.

'It's not a curse, Mike. There are plenty of very happy, fulfilled women out there that are single by choice.'

'But…what if someone turns up who's wearing that badge? And it starts glowing?'

'I don't think that's likely to happen. Maybe I'm sick of looking. Maybe I'll just take *my* badge off and throw it up on top of my wardrobe.'

'You can't do that.' Mike shook his head firmly. 'Besides, it wouldn't make any difference.'

'Why not?' For some inexplicable reason, Emily felt her heart rate quicken. The extra oxygen in her system had to be responsible for that weird tingling in her feet and hands. Mike had that unshuttered look again. As though he wanted Emily to see something genuine. Or that he was about to say something very personal. And he did.

'Because I'd know it was there. *I'd* still be able to see it.'

There was no chance Emily could break the eye contact they had right now. No chance at all. It hadn't been her imagination that had conjured up the signals she'd received over the course of this long, tense night.

Given the emotional climate of both the events surrounding Megan and their current personal situations, could she put any faith in what she guessed Mike was about to tell her?

Mike was just as tired as she was and when you got this

exhausted it was a bit like being drunk. You could think things and even say things that would seem just plain ridiculous by the cold sober light of the next day. She could avoid any embarrassment for them both here. Pretend she hadn't picked up any signals and brush them away.

If Mike was serious, he'd try again.

But maybe he wouldn't. Maybe they had both needed to be pushed over the edge in an emotional arena to see what had been there all along. What was a little embarrassment to risk if that wasn't the case?

Emily barely moved her lips and she spoke very, very softly.

'Is it…glowing?'

Mike opened his mouth to answer. The door to the staffroom opened at precisely the same moment. The faint sound of an electronic alarm could be heard beeping from behind Megan's nurse.

'Emily? Sorry, but we need you.'

CHAPTER FIVE

MONDAY-ITIS struck with a vengeance.

Catching more than just a few hours' sleep would have helped but Emily knew there was no point trying. Her time as an ICU registrar in a big city hospital had given her the ability to switch off the instant her head hit the pillow, but she had also learned that if she woke up and was immediately focused completely on a particular patient, there was no way she could turn over and go back to sleep.

Not that Dr Morgan would have the chance for more than a flying visit to the intensive care unit, despite a delayed start time for the usual Monday morning theatre list. Her position as an anaesthetist meant juggling her duties in Theatre with those in the unit—a system that normally worked very well. But, then, Emily did not normally feel such an involvement with her patients. The case of Megan and the baby she didn't know she still had was pushing everything else well into the background and making the routine business of elective surgery seem almost a chore.

Not quite everything else was being pushed into the background, however. Emily was well aware, as she inhaled the wonderful scent from the frangipani on her way through the Agnes Wetherby memorial garden, that she would be feeling a great deal worse right now if she wasn't being energised by a rather delicious level of anticipation.

Mike had gone by the time the problem triggering one of Megan's alarms had been dealt with. Emily had heard the rescue helicopter taking off as she'd adjusted, yet again, the settings on the ventilator and had run off a new barrage of checks. She hadn't heard it return, presumably because she had been asleep by then.

Crocodile Creek Base Hospital's theatre suite was on the same level as the intensive care unit, so Emily made the theatre admissions area her first stop. A plump, fair woman in her mid-forties was the only patient present and a nurse was holding her hand. There was evidence of recent tears in the collection of scrunched-up tissues on the bed.

'Hey, Sonia.' Emily smiled at the patient. 'How are you feeling?'

'Scared stiff.'

'You're going to be fine.' Sonia was first on the list for the day and about to have her gall bladder removed after years of suffering the pain of chronic cholecystitis. 'We're going to take very good care of you.'

Emily caught the gaze of the senior theatre nurse on duty and moved to speak to her. 'Has Sonia had her pre-med?'

She checked the chart and nodded. 'Temazepam. Thirty milligrams.'

'How long ago?'

'Thirty minutes.'

'Should kick in pretty soon, then.' Emily had spent some time with Sonia the previous day, doing a pre-anaesthetic check and doling out a large amount of reassurance. 'She has been very anxious. Let me know if she's not a lot happier in the next fifteen minutes and I'll give her something more, IV. I'm just going to duck into ICU for a couple of minutes.'

The nurse nodded. 'How's the girl from last night doing?'

'That's what I want to find out.'

With another reassuring smile and word for Sonia, Emily moved briskly down the corridor. Her heart sank when she saw that Hamish was not alone. Cal was there as well. And Gina. The young doctors were all staring at a set of chest X-rays illuminated on the wall of the central station and they were all looking decidedly grim.

'What's up?'

But one glance at the X-rays told Emily exactly what the concern was. Widespread, diffuse opacification made the film look cloudy. Both Megan's lungs were filling with fluid. ARDS. Adult respiratory distress syndrome—'shock lung'. Whatever you called it, it was a disappointing if hardly unexpected development.

Emily raised her eyebrows at her colleagues. 'Pulmonary function parameters?'

'All deteriorating.'

'Damn.' Emily leaned over the desk and rapidly scanned printouts. She checked her patient swiftly, listening to the fine crackly noises over both lung fields, and she took another blood-gas sample to get an accurate current reading. Then she set about adjusting what she could to try and improve the situation in consultation with the other doctors.

'We'll increase the frusemide dose and try and get rid of some of that extravascular lung water.'

Cal charted the new dosage.

'Make sure you do frequent postural changes for Megan,' she reminded the nursing staff. 'And keep right on top of any suction required.'

'We'll need to start physiotherapy, too,' Hamish put in. 'For secretion management.'

Emily nodded but she was already concentrating on the

ventilator machine and wanted to discuss settings. 'We'll increase the tidal volume,' she decided eventually. 'And the PEEP level.'

'Do you want to increase the level of oxygen?'

'Not yet.' Emily shook her head warily. 'I really don't want to go over 60 per cent unless we have to. It would be good to avoid the complications of oxygen toxicity on top of everything else we have going on here.' She turned to Gina. 'Are you happy with her rhythm at the moment? She's throwing off the odd ectopic, isn't she?'

'I'm happy,' Gina said. 'But I'll be keeping a close eye on her today.'

'Great.'

Cal was signalling Emily. 'Time we got started next door, Em.'

'OK.' Emily scribbled some final orders on Megan's chart. 'I'll be back between patients,' she told the nursing staff.

'I'll be here,' Hamish said. 'Don't fret.'

'I'm not… It's just…' Emily turned back for one more look at Megan.

A white face against a white pillow, with the intrusion of tubes in her mouth and nose. Arms and hands that lay limp on a white sheet with more fine tubes *in situ*.

Could they win this battle?

They had to. And, as Mike had pointed out, they'd got her this far. As long as they—

'Emily!'

'Coming, Cal.' She skipped a step or two to catch up the surgeon. 'Sorry.'

'Bit full on today, isn't it?'

'Mmm. I'd like to clone myself at times like this. One of me could do the routine stuff in Theatre and the other one could stay in ICU.' Emily looked back over her shoulder and frowned as a new thought occurred to her. 'There's no new patients. Do you know what Mike flew off to in the middle of the night?'

Cal nodded. 'Hamish said he popped back up to ICU when he got back.' The look Cal gave Emily was almost amused. 'He thought you might still be up.'

'Oh?' Emily tried to sound casual but it was difficult. Had Mike come looking for her with the intention of continuing their interrupted conversation? She ignored the erratic thump of her pulse. 'That was nice of him.'

'Mmm.' Cal sounded curious but didn't pursue the topic. 'Anyway, the call turned out to be a false alarm. Someone had spotted a car upside down in the river down south a bit. Turned out that it was a wreck someone had dumped but they were searching for hours before they traced the owner and got the full story.'

'Poor Mike. He must have been annoyed about that.'

'I think he was too tired to be bothered. With the regulations on flying hours he has to stand down till about 6 p.m. so I imagine he'll be out for the count until then.'

A whole day to wait, then. Hours and hours. That odd prickle of anticipation was strong enough to be uncomfortable as well as exhilarating, so Emily was going to notice every passing minute of what promised to be a long day.

What if Mike regretted even starting that conversation? Maybe Emily had just been in the right place at the right time when Mike had been feeling the lack of significant female companionship and his ego had been a bit bruised. There she had been—available. And looking pathetically eager.

Emily cringed inwardly at the very thought as she pushed open the double doors into the theatre's anteroom, where her patient was waiting. She would have looked like that, wouldn't she, when she had asked if her 'badge' was glowing?

Thank goodness the next few hours would keep her far too busy to dwell on anything personal. That background buzz of nervous anticipation would just have to stay where it was and simmer quietly without being stirred. It was a shame she couldn't catch a little of her patient's now very relaxed demeanour.

The sedation had worked wonders for Sonia who smiled happily as Emily slipped a tourniquet onto her arm.

'I'm just going to pop a little needle into the back of your hand,' Emily said. 'For giving you the anaesthetic.'

Sonia was still smiling when the IV line was in place and Cal poked his head through the door to say hello before he scrubbed up. She actually giggled at her surgeon.

'Do you reckon you could take a bit of flab out at the same time as my gall bladder?'

Cal winked at Emily. 'Nice to see you keeping our patients so happy.' Then he smiled at Sonia. 'Sleep well.'

It was a routine protocol that went smoothly for Emily. She double-checked her equipment and the array of drugs, already drawn up into syringes and carefully labelled.

'Count down backwards from ten for me, Sonia,' she instructed as she began injecting the induction agent.

Sonia only got as far as six and Emily had already picked up the syringe full of muscle relaxant which would enable endotracheal intubation. Despite this being another overweight patient, the controlled environment of Theatre and the ability to position her patient perfectly made the procedure easy, and Emily spared only a brief thought to how fraught doing the same thing on Megan last night had been. And how difficult the later anaesthetic had proved.

Maintaining Sonia's anaesthesia was routine enough to be almost boring in comparison. Her ECG stayed steady, pulse oximeter readings were excellent, and the changes in her blood pressure simple to manage by adjusting the flow of IV fluids.

Cal was performing the surgery with a full laparotomy rather than keyhole surgery due to the very small possibility of a colorectal malignancy, which fortunately proved to be non-existent, but it was an hour or so before Emily could begin the reversal phase of the anaesthetic and another thirty minutes before she could leave her patient in the care of the recovery room staff.

Cal and others disappeared into a staffroom for a coffee-break before the next patient but Emily dashed back to Intensive Care to check on Megan.

The adjustments made to her ventilation had not led to any improvement in her status but the fact that she hadn't deteriorated further was some comfort. Emily eased up the level of oxygen being administered, reviewed a now extensive drug chart and ordered another set of chest films.

Then she returned to Theatre, still well before the scheduled surgery for Mr Gibbons, who was to undergo a partial gastrectomy for a benign tumour. She started her protocol to check all the machinery and draw up a fresh line of labelled syringes.

Marcia, one of the theatre nurses, was positioning another set of sterile trolleys.

'Have you had a coffee, Emily?'

'No, I'm good, thanks. You should go and grab one, though, while you've got the chance. We've got two minors after this so it's busy morning.'

'I hear you were up all night as well.'

'I got a bit of sleep.' Emily smiled at the young nurse. 'I'm used to it. I actually prefer to be really busy sometimes.'

'It's not good,' Marcia said doubtfully. 'Not if it goes on for too long. They're going to have to sort out the staff shortage problems we've got here.'

'Things will settle down. People leaving without working out any notice is bound to throw everyone for a while.'

'Mmm.' Marcia looked as though she wanted to offer some sympathetic comment about one of those people who had left but then she gave Emily a somewhat embarrassed smile, muttered something about being desperate for caffeine and took off.

Emily didn't mind. A minute or two by herself was exactly what she needed. Funnily enough, it wasn't until Marcia had disappeared through the double doors that she clicked about the reason for that embarrassment. The observation that Emily used her involvement in her career as a coping mechanism for personal problems must be more widespread than she'd realised.

And she hadn't even *thought* about Simon Kent since…since the first few minutes of that helicopter ride with Mike last night. The crisis of Megan going missing and then the search and rescue effort had driven Simon completely out of her head. And if that hadn't been enough to do it, those few minutes with Mike in the ICU staffroom certainly had been.

It probably always would have that effect, too, no matter what happened in her immediate future. The bubble of anticipation Emily had now was a very new sensation. Even the seed of a possibility that Mike could be interested was giving Emily more excitement—and trepidation—than any man's interest had ever produced before.

The sensation was as scary as it was exciting. Emily knew how she felt about Mike but she had never allowed herself more than the odd fantasy that the order of the universe might change enough for him to see her as more than a friend. This could be *it*. The one with all the bells and whistles on. The falling into love so deeply she would never be able—or want—to surface.

This was potentially *huge*.

It had never been huge with Simon. Or even Cameron, the fiancé of a decade ago. On both occasions she had been flattered by the avid initial interest of the men. With Cameron, she had still had the promise of time and a chance for real love to develop. With Simon, it had felt like time was running out and she would be stupid to miss the opportunity and not give it her best shot. If it was another ten years before she attracted a partner, she would be too old to fulfil her longing for a family of her own.

She had liked Simon. There had certainly been some physical chemistry present, which had been totally absent with the other single males living in the doctors' quarters at the time. Simon had been charming and very attentive, at least to start with, and Emily hadn't had to work too hard to convince herself that she had been in love.

She had been. But not with the person Simon really was. Emily had fallen in love with the person he'd presented in order to charm her into his bed and the effort had worn off within a few months. He'd been bored by then but gratified by Emily's efforts to keep him interested. He'd rewarded her compliance but Emily had made the mistake of abdicating any possibility of an equal partnership during their first disagreement.

Simon's temper had been frightening, and in retrospect Emily could see that his shouting at her had marked the beginning of the end. Her withdrawal had been self-protection. Simon had mirrored the withdrawal and it became increasingly evident to everyone that he was no longer interested. In her, or in working in an isolated hospital such as Crocodile Creek.

Why had they kept the relationship going as long as they had? Habit? The awkwardness of living and working so closely would have meant that one of them would have been obliged to move on if they'd broken up with each other. Simon had made no secret of the fact he had been looking for a better opportunity employment-wise elsewhere. Simon would have gone and Emily would have stayed and the break-up would have been perfectly civilised if a better opportunity in a personal arena hadn't arrived in the form of dark, vivacious Kirsty just a few months ago.

Emily wrote 'suxemethonium' on the label for the last syringe she had drawn up and laid it beside the row of others on the lip of the anaesthetic machine. It was time for her to go and talk to Mr Gibbons and make sure he was ready for his surgery, but she didn't move for another few moments because the thought of Kirsty had unearthed another cringe-making memory.

She *had* suggested to Mike that Kirsty was perfect for him, but her motivation had hardly been altruistic, had it?

Kirsty had been quite open about the fact she was on the hunt for male companionship from the moment she'd arrived in town, and Emily had seen the way her gaze had riveted itself to Mike when they had met for the first time out by the swimming pool.

And no wonder! Mike wore a traditional, small swimsuit rather than board shorts and the sheer, male presence was overpowering—even for people who were quite used to it by now. Like Emily.

Factor in the setting sun casting a bronze glow on already olive skin, wild black curls shaking a fountain of water free whenever he emerged from a dive and that contagious, mischievous grin, and they had all known it had only been a question of when, not if, Mike and Kirsty got it together.

So Emily had suggested it, after Kirsty had disappeared to get changed for her night shift in Emergency. She had done it because Simon had been there and he had been staring at Kirsty just as much as the other men, if not more. The motivation hadn't been to find the perfect partner for her friend, however. It hadn't even been to stop Simon's desire to stray. The suggestion had been prompted by the self-reproach Emily had felt her due for having the ridiculous thought that she herself wanted to be the one to fill that particular gap in Mike's life.

Perhaps it had been a test, set instinctively. Kirsty was so different to Emily. Tall, pretty, outgoing and dark. Greek-looking, in fact. Sophia would approve of any potential grandchildren. And if Mike was as keen as Emily feared he might be, then that would add weight to her certainty that someone like herself would never enter the picture on a romantic basis. That confirmation would force her to curtail any fantasies and get on with her own life. Alone, probably, if she and Simon couldn't recapture any of the closeness they had started their relationship with.

Mike wasn't in the least reluctant to follow up the suggestion either. That should be ringing a very loud alarm bell for Emily concerning the sincerity of what he might have been going to say last night. And it was. The problem was that that alarm was being drowned by that almost liquid sensation of excitement.

Or was it lust? Had those fantasies she'd added to bit by tiny, guilty bit over the last two years become some kind of addiction? One that was strong enough to lead her into taking any opportunity to fill even a tiny part of them, no matter what the consequences?

Emily shook the thought away and moved. The sooner she had company and couldn't agonise over this, the better. She would find out soon enough.

Mr Gibbons was looking quite relaxed as he waited patiently in the admissions area. He was more concerned about his wife.

'She hasn't said it directly but I know she thinks they might have made a mistake in saying the tumour was benign. She works herself up over something like this, Dr Morgan. Maybe you could have another word with her?'

'Is she in the hospital at the moment?'

'They've told her to wait in the relatives' room next to Recovery.'

Emily sped in that direction.

'All the tests have been conclusive so far,' she reminded a tearful Mrs Gibbons. 'And we'll be doing more during the operation. They'll send a good-sized piece of the tumour to our pathologist to look at under a microscope. It's very, very unlikely that they've missed anything.'

'But you'll let me know? As soon as you're sure?'

'Of course.'

Entering the corridor again, Emily glanced at her watch, hoping for a window of a couple of minutes so she could duck into Intensive Care again. She couldn't feel annoyed at the time Mrs Gibbons had stolen, however. Relatives were a part of every case, weren't they? Patients themselves in their own way.

How were Megan's relatives doing? The guilt that she hadn't found the time to call them herself yet took Emily by surprise. So did the voice behind her.

'Good morning, Dr Morgan.'

'Oh! Charles!' Emily swung around just as the doors to ICU came into view. 'Is it still morning? I'm losing track.'

'Almost lunchtime,' Charles admitted. 'How much sleep did you end up getting?'

'Enough.'

'Busy in Theatre?'

'Usual Monday stuff. It's busy because I keep going back to check on Megan.'

'I'm just about to go and review her case myself. How much time have you got?'

'None.' Emily grimaced as she checked her watch again. 'We've got a partial gastrectomy due to start in two minutes.'

'Come back after that. I'll be able to bring you up to speed by then.'

'Can you check that the last chest films have come through? We've got ARDS to deal with now.'

'Of course. Anything else pressing?'

'It's just occurred to me that I haven't contacted her parents. I know Jill rang last night when we admitted her to the unit but, as her primary physician, I should talk to them myself.'

'I spoke to Jim this morning,' Charles said. 'We go way back and I thought he might appreciate a personal touch.'

'Thanks, that was good of you. How much did you tell them?'

'I said that Megan is seriously unwell and that if there's any way they can get into town, they should.'

'Did you tell them why?'

'That there's a good possibility she's not going to survive? Yes.' Charles nodded grimly. 'I didn't say that the mortality rate for septic shock was at least fifty per cent but I made the gravity of her condition pretty clear.'

'No, I meant the cause of the septic shock.'

Charles shook his head and looked slightly uncomfortable. 'That's a minefield that will need careful handling. If it's at all possible, it should be Megan's choice over how it gets handled. I've told her parents that she has septicaemia. Blood poisoning. I did hint that it might have gynaecological connections and Honey picked up on that immediately. She's read about septic shock caused by tampons being left in too long and she's assuming that's the problem. I didn't try and change her mind. I'm ashamed to say I fudged.'

'You did the right thing,' Emily told him. 'And you've no doubt done a far better job than I would have. I'll leave you to it and get back to Theatre for a bit.' She grinned at Charles.

'I've got some haemorrhoids and an ingrown toenail to look forward to after lunch.'

A few steps down the corridor, Emily turned again. 'How's Lucky, do you know, Charles? Have you seen him this morning?'

'I held his bottle.' Charles didn't smile that often and when he did, the transformation of his face was worth seeing. 'I suspect he's going to grow up to be a member of the Wallabies rugby team.'

Emily took the image of that softening of Charles's craggy features back into Theatre with her like a talisman. Baby Lucky had touched all their hearts. His mother was going to get through this crisis. She *had* to. And she couldn't fail to fall in love with her baby when she did. The staff of the entire hospital loved the infant already.

Lunch was late for Emily because the analysis of the biopsies on Mr Gibbons's tumour had taken longer than expected, but the news was good and the visit to the intensive care unit to find Megan still stable buoyed Emily's mood even further.

When she ducked into a still crowded cafeteria to grab one of Dora Grubb's legendary chicken salad sandwiches, Emily found that the involvement with Baby Lucky's case was spreading rapidly into the community of Crocodile Creek as well. There seemed to be a baby shower happening, and it wasn't just hospital staff members forming the crowd.

Emily could see Cal talking animatedly to George Poulos, Mike's father. Harry, the local cop, was there, and even *his* father, whom Emily knew was involved in the running of the largest sugar mill in the district. He'd been a key figure in a large fundraising effort a couple of years ago to help purchase the new rescue helicopter.

'What's going on?'

Emily bypassed the sandwich cooler and stared at the array of items covering a table.

'Isn't this cool?' Christina was smiling happily. 'People read about Lucky in Saturday's paper and they've started bringing gifts. Look, there's even a pram, and Kylie knitted those bootees herself. Said she spent all day yesterday doing it.'

Emily grinned. The community on this side of the bridge was small but almost self-contained, thanks to the tiny shopping centre near the Athina hotel. Kylie ran Klipz, the hairdressing salon favoured by hospital staff, and the thought of the Dolly Parton look-alike, who was also the source of any juicy gossip to be had, sitting down for a day knitting bootees was incongruous enough to be delightful.

'And Sophia Poulos made this.' Christine picked up a small piece of embroidery that had blue beads sewn in a pretty pattern. 'Apparently it's for luck. We need to pin it somewhere near the bassinet and that will help us find Lucky's mother.'

'They haven't been spitting anywhere, have they?'

'What?' Christina looked startled but Emily just smiled, busy scanning the room. If Mike's parents were here, there was a good chance he would be here as well.

But Emily just knew he wasn't. She would have sensed his presence—as she always had. It was only just after 1 p.m. and he was probably still sound asleep. An image of what he would look like sprawled on his bed, with just a sheet carelessly scrunched over his lower body, actually brought a flush of heat that threatened to ambush Emily's cheeks. When Cal tapped loudly on the side of his coffee-cup with a spoon, Emily gladly gave him her attention.

'You've all heard me rabbiting on a bit in the last few days,' Cal said.

'About Gina?' someone with a suspiciously Hamish-like Scottish accent suggested from the back of the room. 'Noo!'

Everybody laughed and Cal went slightly pink, which did not suit the burnt red curls framing his face. He tried to look stern.

'I'm talking about the kids up at the Wygera Settlement. My idea of getting them a swimming pool as an incentive to keep them out of trouble and get them to go to school.'

A few heads were nodding. Most of the staff, including Emily, had at some time gone to one of the regular weekly clinics held at the Australian Aboriginal settlement. And it wasn't just Lucky who had caught the community's interest in the last few days. An awful car crash involving kids from the settlement and its aftermath had started a lot of people talking about the issues and whether something—anything—could be done that would really help. Cal's idea was great but dauntingly expensive.

'If we're going to get any serious support from politicians we're going to have to show them we mean business.' Cal smiled at two men standing nearby. 'Tony Blake wants a focus for a new fundraiser for the mill and George Poulos has just offered to host a dinner at the Athina on Saturday night. We'll invite every businessman in the area and see just how much support we can drum up.' Cal was smiling delightedly now. 'It'll be a great night. The best Greek food, music and probably a spot of plate-smashing as well.'

Sophia was making a beeline for her husband, her body language suggesting that her plates would be protected at all costs. George, however, was nodding and smiling benignly in response to the wave of encouraging and appreciative noises coming from the audience.

Emily edged her way towards Cal, collecting a chicken salad sandwich and a carton of juice on the way.

'You wouldn't be just trying to avoid those haemorrhoids, by any chance, Dr Jamieson?'

'Oh, Lord!' Cal's gaze went straight to the large clock on the wall. 'We *are* late. I got a bit carried away.'

'It's a brilliant idea,' Emily told him as they both hurried back towards Theatre. 'And well worth getting carried away by.'

'So you'll come to the dinner? Set price, and all profits are going to the pool fund.'

'If I can,' Emily agreed readily. 'It'll depend on rosters and how Megan is doing, of course.' It might also depend on the outcome of a conversation with the youngest member of the Poulos family still in town. Surely Mike would wake up soon. Emily would get back to the house by dinnertime. The opportunity to finish that conversation was getting closer.

'It's days away. We should know one way or the other about Megan by then.'

'Mmm.' Emily didn't want to consider the possibility of losing this battle.

'And the Athina is only ten minutes' walk away. Three minutes if you run fast. You can go there while you're on duty, no problem.'

'OK, I'm sold.' Emily chuckled. 'Did you have to be this persuasive with Gina?'

'More. That's why I'm getting so good at it.'

'But you guys are officially engaged now?'

'Oh, yes.'

'Will you stay on in the house?'

'Not for long. Having a small boy and a large puppy will be a bit much for shared living.'

'Not to mention that you want some space that's just your own. Are you going house-hunting?'

'As soon as things settle down a bit around here.'

'Don't go out of the cove,' Emily warned. 'Not if you want babysitters on tap.' Her smile was mischievous. 'You could move next door to the Grubbs. They've half adopted CJ by now.'

'And I'd be just down the road from the Black Cockatoo. I could go and prop up the bar with Mr Grubb every night.'

'Yeah, I can just see that.'

Emily smiled again and realised that any hint of Monday-itis was long gone. She was actually looking forward to the minor cases Cal had decided to squeeze in prior to his outpatient clinic that afternoon.

She enjoyed the challenge of providing adequate IV sedation and pain relief without administering a general anaesthetic. The good feeling engendered by both the stream of presents arriving for Lucky and the enthusiasm Cal was already generating for the swimming-pool project lifted everybody's spirits.

And while Megan was still not improving, she was holding her own. More time for her body to recover from the extra insult of surgery, and for the antibiotics to kick in and add real muscle to the supportive intervention.

'Any word about her parents coming in?'

'Doesn't sound likely, from what I've heard,' Megan's nurse relayed to Emily.' Her mother's going to try but it won't be before Wednesday.'

Megan was probably no more aware of the lack of any loved ones nearby than she was of the baby close by in the hospital nursery. How sad would it be if she died without ever knowing? Emily's last visit before she left the hospital for a dinner-break was to see Lucky, and she timed it perfectly because she got to help feed the baby.

Holding him was a mixed blessing, however. It stirred emotions that Emily had no desire to explore. She didn't *need* to. She clung to the present just as carefully as she was holding the tiny baby and she listened somewhat absently to Lucky's nurse, Grace, listing the gifts that had arrived so far.

'There's a cot and blankets and a whole carton of clothes.

And you should see all the soft toys! One little girl came into Reception and told them that this tiger was her "very favour-itest toy" but she wanted the lost baby to have it.'

It was part of the mix that kept medicine such a fascinating career. Joy amidst tragedy. Examples of human strength and caring. Emily was almost bemused by the overload of her day's impressions as she made her way slowly back to the old house.

She was too tired to try and sort it out. To see if she could use all the positive input to shine a light into the dark cloud still hanging over Megan Cooper.

She was so tired, in fact, that finding Mike sitting on the back steps of the house didn't even cause any resurgence of that nervous anticipation that had fuelled her for most of the day.

It was just so nice to see him.

And so easy to return the joyous smile of welcome she was receiving.

Dinner could wait. All the sustenance Emily needed was sitting right on that step.

CHAPTER SIX

'AT LAST!'

Mike patted the empty space on the step beside him. 'Come and take the weight off those pedals, babe.'

Emily's smile twitched. 'You calling me fat?'

'Hell, no!' Mike sucked in his breath audibly. 'Wouldn't risk that. You might spit on my helicopter again and corrode the paintwork.'

'Huh!' Emily snorted indignantly but sat down beside Mike, aware of a building disappointment.

It would be something a lot more than an anticlimax if they just slipped back into a long-standing friendship and that unfinished conversation from last night didn't rate even a mention.

But Mike was oddly silent now. They both gazed seawards, watching the light change and darken the silhouettes of the islands out to sea. Around them, they could hear the intermittent raucous cries from a troop of parakeets and the lazy heat of the day's end intensified the perfume of tropical flowers—especially the jasmine that frothed along the ironwork decorating the veranda roof. Splashing noises and laughter could also be heard from the direction of the swimming pool but the silence from the open doors of the house not far from the steps gave the impression that the living quarters were deserted.

Mike and Emily were alone.

The silence continued long enough for Emily to cast a sideways glance at Mike and she found herself the object of a steady regard. His dark eyes were fastened on her with serious intention but enough of a twinkle remained for Emily to know that Mike had no regrets about the conversation he'd started last night.

And he had every intention of continuing the topic.

Disappointment fled. There was no room for it because that excitement was back with renewed vigour. Emily's heart raced and she had to lick suddenly dry lips. The flare in the depths of Mike's eyes as he watched her mouth left Emily in no doubt at all about how serious he was concerning any proposed changes in their relationship.

'Fancy a walk on the beach?'

Emily could only nod. She was grateful for the offer of Mike's hand as she got to her feet. In fact, she was surprised to find herself so effortlessly upright. A second ago, Emily would have sworn that the supporting structure of her bones had vanished. Simply melted away. But they hadn't. Emily could walk perfectly well and she could feel every one of the bones in her hand as it continued to be held in a rather firm grip by Mike.

Nobody noticed them walking, hand in hand, past the swimming pool. Gina's little boy, CJ, was in there—crowing with delight as he rode on his father's shoulders. Rudolph, the weird-looking puppy, was barking and racing up and down the edge of the pool, either deeply concerned about CJ's safety or miffed that he was missing out on all the fun. Any second now and the dog would be in the pool as well, and both Christina and Alix were laughing helplessly as they waited for the inevitable development.

Emily and Mike kept walking. Past the pool. Through the

memorial garden. Down the rock-strewn slope that led to the
beach, on a path that wound through grass decorated with the
soft yellow blooms of moonflowers. They left their shoes at
the end of the path and let the warmth of sun-kissed sand bury
their toes.

'So...' Mike sounded amazingly cheerful. As though they
wandered off to redefine their relationship every day of the
week. 'How was your day?'

'Busy.' A normal kind of conversation was a good idea.
Emily found some of her nervousness retreating. 'But good.'

'How's Megan?'

'She's had a setback with developing ARDS but she hasn't
got any worse since this morning so I'm hopeful we'll get on
top of it.'

'Still on the ventilator, then?'

'Oh, yes. We won't attempt weaning her until we're getting some normal lung and renal function results.'

'How long will that take, do you think? Best-case scenario, that is.'

'If everything comes together and the antibiotics start
doing their job properly, it could be quick. We might have her
off the ventilator by the time her mother gets in to visit her
on Wednesday.'

And if it didn't, Megan could be on life support for much
longer. The possibility of having to switch it off with their patient still dependent on the machinery didn't need to be raised.
This was no time to be examining a worst-case scenario.

'And Lucky? How's he doing?'

'He's just wonderful.' Emily could hear the smile in her
voice. 'I fed him just before I left.'

'Yeah?' Mike was watching Emily's face and his lips curved
softly in response to her tone. 'You like babies, don't you?'

'Everyone likes babies,' Emily said lightly. Her own attitude to that topic was not something she wanted to get onto right now. One step at a time. '*This* baby, anyway. Have you heard about the truckload of presents that have started arriving for him?'

'Hamish told me. And Cal told me about the fundraising thing for the swimming pool and the dinner at the Athina. You going?'

'Are you?'

'I'll probably get roped in to wash dishes or something. I expect my mother will be cracking the whip. My sister's planning a visit this weekend so it could turn into a bit of a family gathering, what with her tribe of kids.'

'I should offer to help as well. It's a very generous gesture. All that work and no profit.'

'They do well enough. It's a boutique hotel. Costs the earth to stay there—especially that honeymoon suite that's got its own path to the beach.'

'They didn't charge me the earth when I stayed there.'

'Were you in the honeymoon suite?'

Emily laughed. 'Of course not. I had the little room at the back of the kitchen, but it was just perfect. I couldn't move into the house back then because they were doing some major renovations and there were no spare rooms. I lived at the Athina for nearly three months. Your parents were just wonderful to me. It really felt like home. I was very sad to leave.'

'I remember, vaguely. Something in a letter about a nice girl called Emily.' Mike chuckled. 'With the usual rider from my mother saying "but she's not Greek".'

Emily winced inwardly at the reminder of how different she was from the type of women Mike preferred. Perhaps she even winced outwardly because Mike gave her hand a reassuring kind of squeeze.

'She's always tried to steer me in the direction of some

"nice" Greek girl she's discovered somewhere, and I've always ignored her. She knows I'll pick who I want.'

But did he really want her? It was just too much of a fantasy to be at all believable.

'You've always picked girls that *look* Greek, though.' Emily tried to sound casual. 'Like Marcella.'

'Only Marcella.' Mike's smile was wry. 'And that could never have worked. Talk about a high-maintenance woman.'

'What about Trudi? And Kirsty?'

'They picked me.' Mike had the cheek to sound completely innocent. 'I wasn't even out looking, if you remember.'

'You didn't exactly run and hide.'

'Oi!' Mike sounded offended now. 'It was *you* that suggested Kirsty. I thought it might be because you'd guessed what I was thinking and were trying to warn me off.'

'Warn you off what?'

'Trying to steal you away from Simon bloody Kent, that's what.'

'Oh.' Emily was silent for a moment, hugging the thought that maybe Mike had been having fantasies about her for as long as she'd been indulging in them about *him*. 'So…why didn't you, then?'

Mike stopped walking suddenly and pulled Emily's hand so that she had to turn and face him.

'Because you never gave me the slightest indication that you were interested in being anything other than a friend. I'm still not sure that I believe you are.' Mike's gaze was searching. '*Are* you, Em?'

'I…I always thought the same thing.' Emily held the eye contact. 'That we could only ever be good friends.'

'Why?'

'Because…'

There were so many reasons. Mike was gorgeous and

clever and courageous, and his life, both personal and professional, would always be imbued with a kind of vitality and excitement Emily could never hope to provide. He could have his pick of any women that came into his orbit. Why on earth would he be interested in a quiet, somewhat serious, *ordinary*-looking doctor? How could she start trying to explain how inadequate she felt sometimes? But she had to say something so she picked the easiest example.

'Because I'm not Greek.'

A corner of Mike's mouth twitched. 'You can spit, babe. That's Greek enough for me.'

'And…and I'm so different from Mar—'

Mike's fingers on her lips stopped Emily making any comparisons to his former partners.

'It's *because* you're so different that I love you, Em.'

He loved her?

Whoa! This was going way too fast. Mike hadn't even kissed her, and he was telling her that he loved her? Or did he mean the kind of love that good friends had for each other?

'You still haven't answered my question,' Mike reminded her softly.

Emily just stared. Words had deserted her. Mike smiled patiently at her blank expression.

'Are you interested in more than friendship from me, Emily Morgan?'

Time hung, suspended, for a heartbeat and then Emily's head moved in a slow, sure nod.

'Thank God for that,' Mike murmured.

His hand seemed to be waiting to catch her head as soon as it rose from the nod. His fingers cupped her chin and his thumb stroked across her lips as lightly as the brush of a butterfly's wing.

Emily had that melting-bones sensation again, which only

intensified as she saw that Mike was about to kiss her. She needed to shut her eyes to concentrate on remaining upright.

And then she kept them shut and forgot about being upright or not. She forgot about Megan and Lucky and Simon and everything else that had been uppermost in her world in the last few days.

Everything except the man she was now kissing.

This was *Mike*.

Warm, strong, funny, gentle Mike. The best friend Emily had ever had. The man she had known she could love for ever but had never dreamed she would have the faintest hint of a chance with.

Maybe it was because of those fantasies that this now felt nothing like any first kiss Emily had ever had in her life before. It made every other kiss she had experienced seem a pretence of the real thing. Merely a meeting of mouths.

Emily could feel every cell attached to Mike's lips. The whole length of his solid body and the strength of his arms as he held her against him. The warmth of his breath and the controlled energy in the tiny movements of his fingers and mouth.

And more. With every variation in the pressure of his lips and every electric tingle from the slide of his tongue against hers, Emily could feel the sincerity of what he was doing. The desire to communicate how much he wanted this.

How much he wanted *her*.

Taking a breath was postponed long enough for it to become a gasp, and Mike drew back instantly. Emily's eyes flew open to meet the question in his gaze—the anxiety that she might not want this as much as he did.

She ran her tongue across her bottom lip, recapturing the taste and feel of Mike's mouth. And then she smiled and saw Mike's expression soften in relief. He pulled her back into his arms but this time he didn't kiss her lips. He drew her close enough for her head to be against his shoulder and then he pressed his lips to her hair and just held her in a wordless and wonderful hug.

The gesture was a confirmation that what they already had wasn't going to go away. That the bond between them was rock solid, and taking their relationship to a level so far beyond simple friendship was not going to change its foundations.

'Are you on call tonight?'

''Fraid so.' Emily swallowed, nervousness rearing its head again in the face of the obvious invitation underlying Mike's words. There was a curious relief to be found in the response she was obliged to give. Any more kisses like that would lead to more, just as inevitably as Rudolph would have fallen into that swimming pool by leaping so close to the edge, and the prospect of that kind of intimacy with Mike was still too much to be believable. Too much to trust that it could happen and not lead to heartbreak.

The only men she had shared a bed with in the past had become bored with her and moved on. Could she hope to offer him anything on a par with what the outgoing, vivacious and beautiful and therefore very experienced women he had known previously would have been able to?

A hint of that relief must have been evident because Mike said nothing for several seconds. They drew apart so that there was a space between their bodies and Emily felt that small amount of air like something solid and cool. She had to suppress a tiny shiver at the sudden perceived change in temperature.

Looking up, Emily met that unshuttered kind of gaze again. She was almost getting used to this invitation to step into a private part of Mike's world. She wanted to dive in head first, in fact, but it was scary.

And Mike seemed to understand.

'You can trust me, you know, Em.'

'I know.'

'You can trust how I feel about you. I'm serious here, babe.'

'I know,' Emily whispered. 'But…'

Mike waited patiently and Emily took a deep and rather shaky breath.

'We've both been in other relationships until only a few days ago. This is so…fast.'

'Maybe that's because it's always been there and we've got some catching up to do.'

Emily wanted to believe that. Desperately. But she needed something more in the way of reassurance before taking that leap of faith. She opened her mouth to say that maybe they shouldn't rush into anything but the words died as Mike reached up and touched a spot just above her left breast.

'I can see that badge we talked about,' he said very quietly.

His fingers moved as his hand flattened and then his palm was cupping her breast. 'I can feel it, too,' Mike continued, his head dipping as he brushed Emily's lips with his own. 'It's hot.' His lips moved against hers, the words a barely audible murmur. 'It must be glowing.'

Oh…Lord! Something was certainly glowing. The heat wasn't originating from any metaphorical accessory, however. A fire had been ignited deep within Emily's abdomen and tendrils of white-hot sensation were flickering through her veins to reach all sorts of strange places.

And then Mike took her hand and held it to his chest. 'Do you feel mine, Em? Do you want this as much as I do?'

Emily's hand pressed into the hard muscle over Mike's ribs. She wanted to slide it under the thin fabric of his shirt and feel that bare olive skin with her fingers. To taste it with her mouth. To…

'Yes,' she sighed.

Mike's hand closed over hers, stilling its movement. 'I can still hear a "but" in there somewhere.'

'I'm just not sure we should rush into anything.' There. She'd said it aloud now. 'I don't want to risk our friendship by maybe having some kind of fling that's just going to fizzle out.'

'You said you trusted me.'

'And I do.' Emily stepped back so that she could see Mike's face properly but she kept hold of his hand. 'Things aren't really normal right now, though, are they? There's been such a lot happening and we're all overworked and tired. And we've both just broken up with other people.' She caught her breath quickly. 'It could be that part of what we're feeling right now is a result of rejection. A…rebound thing.'

'You think I might want you just because there's a gap in my life that needs filling?'

'I…' Emily dropped her gaze. 'I hope not.'

Mike used his forefinger to tilt Emily's chin and he said nothing until their eyes met again.

'Is that what I am for you, Em?' The words carried a peculiar urgency. 'A replacement for Simon?'

'Of course not!' Emily was shocked. Simon and Mike were from such completely different planets that a comparison was ridiculous. Even at the very start of that relationship Emily had never felt anything like this. 'You're…you,' she added lamely.

'And you're you,' Mike echoed sternly. 'The place anyone else has had in my life is a place that doesn't need filling. And it's nowhere near where you fit in.' His voice softened but lost none of its conviction. 'It's you I want, Emily. It always has been.'

The silence that followed his words was filled with a sound Emily knew that only she could hear. The rustle of departing doubts, maybe. Or a song of pure joy.

Was this the moment she could tell Mike that she felt the same way? That she loved him? Judging by the look on his face, she might not need to. Perhaps her eyes were saying it for her.

And then the silence was broken by a sound they could both hear only too clearly. The insistent and intrusive beep of a pager.

Emily reached for the button of the device attached to her belt but pushing it did not silence the sound.

'It must be mine,' Mike groaned. 'Damn.' He read the message on his pager and then flipped open his cellphone. 'I need to ring the radio room and see what's happening.'

Emily stood beside Mike as he made the call, her breath escaping in a sigh as she accepted the break in atmosphere and the impossibility of continuing that very private conversation.

Maybe it was just as well. She needed a little space to think about it all. And it was just as well it *hadn't* been her pager sounding to call her to some crisis in the emergency department or the intensive care unit.

The last couple of minutes of her life had the potential to seriously undermine her ability to concentrate on her job. Mike really did seem to feel the same way Emily did and if that was the case, Emily's life was about to change so dramatically it was way too good to be true. A fairy-tale. It was like winning a lottery. Or being struck by lightning.

Both—at the same time. It blew anything else Emily might need to think about clean out of the water.

'I've got to go.' Mike's phone shut with a snap. 'There's a truck driver who's had to pull off the road because of severe chest pain. He's an hour's drive away and up in the mountains so there's nowhere for a plane to land.'

'Not a great spot to pick to have a heart attack.'

Mike was already moving swiftly back towards the path they had taken down to the beach. 'You on flight duty call?'

'No. It's Christina again, I think.'

'Just as well.'

'Why?'

Mike stopped abruptly, caught Emily's shoulders and planted a brief, firm kiss on her lips.

'That's why,' he said ruefully. 'I might have trouble thinking about anything else if I had you on board with me. I might be tempted to flag the job and fly you somewhere where we could be completely alone.' His hand caught hers and the look Emily received ignited the heat she had felt when Mike's hand had cupped her breast. 'For a long, long time,' he added.

'Mmm.' Emily tore her gaze away from that look and tugged his hand. 'Come on. I'd better make sure you get as far as the helipad, hadn't I?'

They had to pass between the hospital buildings and the doctors' quarters on their way to the ambulance station and helipad. Hamish McGregor was walking in the opposite direction, presumably taking a dinner break or finishing work for the day. Seeing Mike and Emily hurrying towards him hand in hand created an expression of concern rather than astonishment.

'Is everything all right?'

'Couldn't be better,' Mike responded firmly. 'Isn't that right, Em?'

'Mmm.' Emily's smile as they passed Hamish was shy. They were taking rather a large first step in their new relationship here, making their closeness so apparent to someone else. But this was Hamish, a close friend who cared for them both, and his own smile suggested that he was rather delighted with the vibes he was picking up.

'Of course,' she heard him mutter behind them. 'Perfect for each other.'

'That's torn it,' Emily told Mike. 'It'll be right through the house in two minutes. They'll probably have us beating Cal and Gina down an aisle.'

'Suits me.' They could see the gleam of Mike's helicopter ahead as it was pushed clear of the hangar by ground crew. With a final smile at Emily, Mike broke away into a jog. 'Catch you later, babe.'

Emily actually took another step or two in Mike's wake.

Why had she never felt the implications of how dangerous his job was before this?

Because this time he would be coming back to *her?*

Because he seemed to have no doubts that their future together was permanent enough to casually assume that they would be getting married sooner rather than later?

She wanted to follow him. To stay with him. Any fear of flying in helicopters was nothing compared to the flash of fear of what it would be like now if he took off on a mission and didn't come back. But what he did for a job was part of the man she loved and it was too closely tied in with the thirst for and enjoyment of life that was such a big part of his personality. Emily would never let her own fears have any kind of negative impact on the career he loved.

Her feet slowed. She managed to smile.

'Be careful,' she called, pleased with how casual she sounded. 'Don't forget to spit!'

As if he would forget! The superstitious gesture was simply part of an automatic pre-flight routine that kept Mike busy enough to distract him from any personal matters. Not that the distraction lasted, however. Once airborne, it became clear that Christina wasn't in the mood to chat and Mike was more than happy to let the part of his mind that wasn't needed for piloting duties return to where it most wanted to be.

Focused on Emily Morgan.

She *wanted* him. Maybe as much as he wanted her. It was unbelievable. Pure magic. Mike had never felt so happy in his entire life.

Banking to follow the curve of the road, he let just a little of that happiness escape in the form of whistling a few bars of a favourite song.

'You sound happy,' Christina commented.

'I am.'

'That's good. You weren't looking too happy last week.'

'No, I guess not.'

Mike had to make something of an effort to remember why he hadn't been looking happy. His relationship with Kirsty felt like ancient history already. Meaningless. Anything else was insignificant compared to how he felt about Emily. Especially now that her reciprocal interest gave him permission to give his attraction free rein. To let those feelings grow.

Hell, they weren't going to grow. They were in danger of exploding with enough of a blast to light up the entire horizon. Mike couldn't curb his grin at the notion but then he caught Christina's startled glance and gave a somewhat embarrassed shrug.

'Hey, life goes on, you know?'

'Hmm.' Christina sounded unconvinced. Or maybe she was unimpressed that Mike could bounce back so quickly from a failed romance. She retreated into the preoccupied silence with which she had begun this mission but then broke it a minute later. 'So, how have you managed it, then?'

'What?'

'Getting over a break-up so easily?'

'I realised that Kirsty did me a favour.' A huge favour, given that she'd removed Simon from Crocodile Creek at the same time. 'It was never serious for either of us. And now I know where I'm going. I can get my life onto the right track.'

'You sound awfully sure about that.'

'Oh, I am.' Mike smiled at Christina but he was thinking of blue eyes rather than brown. And honey-blonde hair rather than brunette. And just for a moment he let himself think about how it had felt to touch Emily properly for the first time. Really touch her. To kiss her. To let his hand shape the outline of her breast.

He covered the slightly strangled sound trying to escape by clearing his throat. 'I'm very sure.'

Christina was staring at him. 'Am I missing something here?'

Mike wanted to tell her. To explain that he'd found the love of his life and that by some miracle she seemed to feel the same way. And if Christina still wanted to know how he could be so sure, he could tell her about those badges.

No. That was too private to share now that it had provided an invitation for that touch he remembered with such agonising clarity. Some time, in the very near future, Mike intended to have his lips where his hand had been this evening. On top of that imaginary badge. Tracing a path down a breast that wasn't covered by any layers of silk or lace.

He gave himself a mental shake. No, he couldn't tell Christina any of that. Emily didn't want to rush things, did she? She had seemed a little embarrassed when Hamish had seen them holding hands. She was worried that either of them could be feeling the way they did because of a rebound phenomenon. Mike knew how wrong that was in his own case but hadn't he always been prepared to wait until Emily knew for sure that she felt the same way? He could be patient again now that he knew they were on the same path. Patient enough to let Emily dictate whatever pace would cement her trust.

But Christina still seemed to be waiting for a response.

'You just need to trust your gut feeling,' Mike said evasively. 'If you're on the right track, you can feel it. Just like you know if something's not working. Like me and Kirsty. That could never have worked.'

Christina looked away. She nodded agreement but her shoulders slumped in what looked like a sigh.

Mike frowned. 'You OK, mate?'

'I'm fine.'

There was no time to check whether that really was the case because they could see the flashing hazard lights of the truck waiting for them below and Mike needed to find a place to land.

Besides, Christina's relationship with Joe—the New Zealand doctor who flew into Crocodile Creek to fill any gaps for one week in every four—was solid. Anyone who'd seen them together over the last couple of years could see that.

They were crazy about each other.

Just like him and Emily.

CHAPTER SEVEN

FORTY-FIVE minutes was not a long time to wait.

The pleasure Emily gained from seeing Mike pushing one end of the helicopter's stretcher into the emergency department was definitely out of all proportion to their time apart.

'We're ready for you in Resus,' she called. 'And Gina's on her way.' They had called their new cardiologist in when a radio message from Mike had confirmed they had a cardiac patient on board. Emily was already busy with several patients in the department and she turned back quickly to the six-year-old girl on the bed.

'How's your breathing now, pet? Better?'

Her small patient nodded from behind wisps of vapour escaping the nebuliser mask. Emily turned to the child's mother.

'I think we have it under control. We'll let the rest of that salbutamol run through and then reassess Vanessa. I'll get a nurse to come and sit with you for a while.'

Emily hurried after the stretcher into Resus and arrived at the same time as Gina.

'Is this our cardiac patient?'

Christina nodded. 'Todd Baker,' she told her colleagues. 'He's fifty-two and has no previous cardiac history. He developed crushing central chest pain about an hour ago. Ten out of ten with radiation to his left arm.'

Classic symptoms for a heart attack and Mike was holding the strip of paper recording the three-lead ECG they had taken on scene with the portable monitor.

'ST elevation in leads II and III,' he told them calmly. 'Looks like it could be an inferior infarct.'

'Associated symptoms?' Gina was checking the flow of oxygen.

'Diaphoresis,' Christina said. 'And nausea but no vomiting.'

Emily pushed the twelve-lead ECG trolley closer to the bed and Mike reached to help her attach the new set of electrodes. Their hands brushed and the electric tingle made Emily glance up automatically. She was relieved to discover she could return Mike's smile briefly without distraction. It simply added to the pleasure of doing her job well. Had it been Simon present, the nervousness of waiting for the inevitable criticism about her performance would have removed a large proportion of that satisfaction.

'What's he had in the way of medication?' Emily asked Mike.

'GTN. Aspirin 300 milligrams. Ten milligrams morphine and Maxolon.'

'How's the pain, now, Todd?' Emily's pager sounded but she killed the beep without taking her eyes off their patient.

'About four out of ten, I guess. A lot better than it was.'

'We'll try and get that down a bit more for you,' Gina told him. 'We just need to check a couple of things first.' She hit the button to inflate the blood pressure cuff around Todd's upper arm.

'Try and keep nice and still for a moment,' Emily told him as she started the recording of the twelve-lead ECG. She glanced at her pager as she waited for the result to print out.

'ICU's calling me,' she said in dismay.

'Megan?' Mike paused as he was putting Todd's shoes into a patient property bag.

'She's the only patient in the unit at the moment.'

A nurse poked her head past the curtain screening the resuscitation area. 'Vanessa's nebuliser's finished and she's still pretty wheezy. What would you like me to do?'

Gina glanced up from her task of filling blood sample tubes ready for analysis of cardiac enzymes. 'We can manage here, Emily.'

'What's her oxygen saturation like now?' Emily asked the nurse.

'Only 93 per cent.'

'Start another nebuliser,' Emily instructed. 'We'll have to think about some oral steroids as well and admit Vanessa overnight. Could you give Hamish a call? She's one of his regular patients and I might need him to cover ED for a while anyway. I've got to dash up to ICU for a bit.'

She ripped off the twelve-lead ECG, having already noted the changes that could only be caused by a blockage in Todd's coronary arteries. He was watching Gina's face carefully as she looked at the test result and nodded.

'Am I having a heart attack, then?' he said in alarm. 'What's going to happen?'

'You're going to get the best possible treatment, mate, don't you worry.' Mike moved in to reassure their patient as Gina followed Emily for a few steps when she excused herself.

'What's the normal protocol for MIs here? Do you try and evacuate them for angioplasty?'

'We start a streptokinase or TPA infusion. If pain and ECG changes don't settle or the bloods indicate a major infarct then we look at emergent angiography and-or try and arrange urgent transfer.'

'Where do you monitor the streptokinase infusions? We don't have a coronary care unit here, do we?'

'It's incorporated into Intensive Care. We've got continuous monitoring facilities and well-trained, one-on-one nursing care.' Emily smiled as she left Gina behind and sped towards the doors to the main hospital corridor. 'I'll get them to set up an infusion and see you up there.'

Emily ran up the stairs rather than using the lift and raced into the unit with a sinking heart. Another complication on top of ARDS could well mean disaster for Megan. Was she showing signs of irreversible renal failure now? Or was her heart giving up the struggle of trying to cope with such a severe strain on her body?

'What's happened?'

Megan's nurse was beside her bed and there was no evidence of a dire emergency. No alarms were sounding on any of the monitoring equipment, the suction gear lay unused and there were no other staff members or trolleys nearby that could have advertised a cardiac-arrest scenario.

In fact, Megan's colour was good and a swift perusal of the monitor readings showed, at first glance, an improvement rather than any deterioration.

'She's fighting the tube,' the nurse informed Emily. 'She was gagging a bit and groaning and she's trying to breathe against the ventilator at times. She's not due for more sedation for quite a while so I thought you might want to review the dose.'

Emily nodded. 'Thanks. I'll give her a thorough check first.' Her breath escaped in a sigh of relief as she smiled. 'It actually looks as if things are on the up and if that's the case we might start weaning her from the ventilator. Can you call the radiologist in, please? I'd like to get another chest X-ray.'

Todd Baker was wheeled into the unit and transferred to the bed opposite Megan as Emily was drawing off a sample of arterial blood to check oxygen levels.

Waiting for the results on all the tests gave Emily a few minutes to join Gina and the staff assisting with Todd's admission. Mike didn't need to still be present but he seemed to be completing his own paperwork while taking an interest in the continuing treatment of his patient and nobody was going to suggest that he leave the unit.

Especially Emily.

'No contra-indications for administering streptokinase,' Gina informed Emily. 'We're infusing 1.5 million units over thirty minutes.'

'Blood pressure's dropped a bit,' Todd's nurse advised.

Gina checked the monitor. 'Right.' She pressed some buttons on the unit controlling the IV infusion. 'We'll slow this down.'

'Let's take one of those pillows away, too,' Emily suggested. 'Being a bit flatter might help maintain blood pressure.'

'Rate's slowing as well.' Gina's gaze was on the drift of ECG spikes across the screen of the beside monitor. 'If it drops any further we'll give some atropine.'

Mike picked up his paperwork and clipped his pen back into his pocket. 'How're you feeling, Todd?'

'Not bad.' Their patient actually managed a quite cheerful smile. 'Who wouldn't with a bunch of gorgeous women looking after them?'

Mike grinned. 'I hear you, buddy.'

'I'd rather be standing in your shoes, though.'

Mike was standing right beside Emily and he caught her gaze as he responded to Todd. 'Me, too,' he murmured. Then he raised his voice. 'I'll come back and see you a bit later, mate. I'll bet you'll be feeling a whole lot happier by then.'

He came back an hour later. Todd's infusion of clot-busting medication had been completed without major complications and results from the blood tests suggested a relatively minor heart attack. The truck driver was now pain-free and resting comfortably.

Gina had gone back to the doctors' house but Emily was showing no signs of resting. Neither was Hamish. After admitting Vanessa to the paediatric ward for overnight observation following her asthma attack, he'd come to the intensive care unit to see if Emily needed any assistance. She was only too happy to discuss Megan's condition and had a whole sheaf of new test results to share with her colleague.

'Tidal volume with spontaneous breathing is not looking too bad, is it?'

'There's not much of a drop in arterial oxygen levels either.' Hamish observed with obvious satisfaction. 'And the white-cell count is well down. We might have got round the corner here.'

'I don't want to take her off the ventilator and then have to put her back on, though. Her lungs aren't completely clear yet.'

'Let's watch her overnight on spontaneous resps. Half-hourly observations if necessary on blood-gas levels.'

'I'll shift ventilation from PEEP to triggering,' Emily decided. That way Megan could breathe for herself but the machine would kick in if spontaneous respiration ceased. 'And I'll stay in the unit overnight. Hopefully I won't be needed in Emergency again.'

'Get them to call me if you're busy,' Hamish said. 'But right now I'm ready to go home. Coming, Mike?'

Mike's smile at Emily, as he left with Hamish, was sympathetic. There was no hint of disappointment that he would have no further time alone with Emily just yet and, if anything, that lack of disappointment added to an air of supreme confidence his departing glance bestowed on her.

Someone else needs you more than me right now, the look

suggested, but that doesn't matter because we'll be together soon enough.

Really together.

Very soon.

It was remarkable how well young people could sometimes bounce back from even critical medical situations. By the following morning, Emily was happy to remove Megan's breathing tube and allow any sedation to wear off completely. The teenager would be kept in Intensive Care, however, on both oxygen and antibiotic therapy, and close monitoring would continue for as long as necessary.

At 7.30 a.m. Emily dashed back to the house for a shower and a change of clothes. She also had a mouthful of the coffee Mike had brewed and buttered a piece of toast to eat on the run. Tuesday morning was an obstetric and gynaecological session for Theatre and Emily would be responsible for anaesthetics for Dr Georgie Turner. Their 8:00 a.m. start time was only minutes away.

Mike shook his head as Emily headed for the door, her un-bitten toast in her hand.

'You need to slow down, babe.'

'I'm fine,' Emily assured him. 'Everything's good. And I've got a night off tonight. I'll rest then.'

'Hey…' Mike's voice floated after her as she reached the veranda. 'I'm not on call tonight either. Let's rest together.'

Emily had to throw her piece of toast to the resident para-keets a few seconds later, her appetite gone. The shaft of sen-sation that had encompassed any space in her stomach felt like pure excitement. Or lust. Or possibly nerves.

Whatever it was, she was fairly certain that if she spent time with Mike that evening, the time would not be in any way restful.

Being too busy to give the evening's potential agenda any further thought was a blessing. Emily knew she was quite capable of over-thinking to the point where she could undermine what could possibly be the most important night of her life.

She wasn't going to spoil the opportunity she had here. No way! No seeds of doubt were going to be strewn in their path by her hand. Emily was going to trust that this happiness would not just continue—it would grow. And what did it matter if they caused raised eyebrows by allowing things to happen fast? Mike was right. If they'd both wanted this for so long and it was meant to be, then they had a lot of catching up to do.

Everything seemed so much more positive today. Megan was going to survive and the morning cases in Theatre went so smoothly they were fun. Georgie dealt with a hysterectomy on a woman with fibroid problems and then they had an elective Caesarean on a second-time mother who'd had huge difficulties with her first labour.

The anaesthetic for the Caesar was an epidural and Emily enjoyed having a conscious patient to talk to during the procedure. And she always got a real thrill from witnessing the delivery of a new life. Today that special kick was enhanced by all the other positive things happening in her life.

With the first cry of the newborn baby late that morning, Emily found the tears of joy from its parents contagious. She was not only sharing their happiness at a new life, however. She was *living* it.

She spared just a moment or two to feel thankful that she *had* been found wanting in the past and that she'd been dumped, first by Cameron and then by Simon. Fate must have decreed that she felt the pain of rejection and that she'd had to wait this long because now she could recognise the one that really mattered.

Mike could very well be *it*.

The love of her life.

And this time it was going to work because fairy-tales could sometimes come true for the very lucky.

Megan was going to be one of the lucky ones as well.

Emily went back to the intensive care unit after the Theatre session finished and found that Megan was not only continuing to breathe adequately on her own but that she was awake and aware of her surroundings. Once again, she was the only patient in the unit as Todd had been moved to a ward earlier that morning.

'She won't talk.' Megan's nurse had signalled Emily over to the central desk before she'd approached her patient and she was looking concerned. 'She shuts her eyes and pretends to be asleep whenever I'm near her and then she opens them and just stares at nothing when she's by herself.'

Emily's nod was thoughtful. She could see from where she was that while Megan's eyes were open, she was simply staring at the ceiling and ignoring the movement of any staff members around her. 'I'll stay with her for a bit. Why don't you take your lunch-break now?'

She approached her patient with a smile a short time later, having reviewed her chart. 'Hi, Megan. How are you feeling?'

There was no flicker of response. Wanting to establish contact, Emily reached for Megan's wrist rather than looking at the monitors for a heart rate.

'I'm Dr Morgan,' she said. 'Emily. I came to see you at home, remember? When you first got sick?'

Megan pulled her wrist free from Emily's touch and made a noncommittal sound as she continued to look at the ceiling.

'You've been in Intensive Care for a couple of days now,' Emily continued. 'And you've been very ill. You had a nasty infection and we needed to keep you on a breathing machine for a little while. I imagine you've got a sore throat right now from the tube and you're probably still not feeling too flash, but you've going to be fine, Megan. We'll get you back on your feet in no time.'

'I don't want to be here.'

'No, of course not.' Relief at hearing Megan speak made Emily smile again but this time it was with empathy. She caught and squeezed the girl's hand gently. 'Nobody wants to be here, but it's not for long, pet. We'll be able to move you to the ward in another day or two. There'll be a lot more happening there and you'll be able to start having visitors.'

'No.' Megan's voice was scratchy and muffled by the oxygen mask but its toneless quality was not completely disguised. She rolled her head on her pillow in a negative motion. 'You don't understand.'

'Tell me, then,' Emily encouraged her softly. 'What can I do to help?'

'It's too late.' Tears welled and then trickled down Megan's face. 'You should have just let me die.'

'Oh…' For a horrible moment Emily was taken back to the darkest moment in her own life. She knew exactly how Megan was feeling. And why. Nobody in her own case had had the kind of power Emily now had to put things right, however. Just how she could start was the tricky bit.

'Nothing's ever quite as bad as it seems, Megan,' she said carefully.

'You don't know anything,' the teenager said flatly. 'I wish you'd just go away and leave me alone.'

'I can't do that.' Emily picked up a box of tissues and then pulled a chair closer and sat down beside Megan's bed.

'I know more than you might think, Megan.' She pressed a wad of tissues into the girl's hand. 'And I'm here to help you. I *can* help.'

'You can't. Nobody can.' Megan sniffed but didn't raise the tissues to her face.

'I think I can.'

The quiet conviction in Emily's tone seemed to hang in the silence that followed. Finally—slowly—Megan turned her head just far enough for her to actually look at Emily.

'How?'

'I can look after you and help you to get better physically,' Emily said. 'And I can help with…with the baby.'

Megan's eyes widened in a flash of fear and Emily could hear the beeping of the monitors recording her heart and respiration rates speeding up.

'What baby?'

'Your baby, Megan,' Emily said gently. 'It's OK. I know you've just had a baby. Was it when you were at the rodeo?'

Megan was still staring at Emily. She looked as though she was set to deny having given birth again until she saw the truth in her doctor's face. Then she turned her gaze back towards the ceiling and just nodded miserably—the picture of defeat.

'That's why you got sick,' Emily explained. 'A little bit of the baby's placenta got left behind in your uterus and caused the infection.'

'No.' Megan closed her eyes. 'I got sick because I wanted to die. Same as the baby.'

Emily took a deep breath. 'Is that what's upsetting you so much, Megan? That you think your baby died?'

The headshake was tired. Uncaring. 'It was the only way out. For both of us.'

The utter misery the statement encapsulated was shocking and Emily's voice was no more than a whisper.

'Why?'

'Because I could never have kept it.' Megan lapsed into silence and took several short breaths but Emily just waited, hoping that she would tell her more. The strategy worked.

'Things are bad enough at home already. It would kill Dad if he knew.' Megan opened her eyes again and she stared at Emily, looking even more frightened than she had a minute ago. 'You can't tell him.' Her voice finally lost its toneless quality. 'You can't tell my parents about this.'

'I won't tell them anything you don't want me to,' Emily promised. 'But there is something I need to tell you, Megan.'

'What?' Megan's eyes drifted shut again and she looked exhausted. The conversation and emotional upset was too much for her right now and Emily knew she needed to let her patient rest. But she couldn't leave her like this, could she? So down that she wished she had died? Thinking that it was 'the only way out'?

'There are lots of ways we can help you,' Emily said first. 'You're going to be all right, Megan.' She took a deep breath. 'You and your baby.'

'There's no baby.' Megan shook her head. 'It was dead.'

'No.' Emily was watching Megan's face carefully to gauge her reaction to her news. 'Your baby didn't die, love.'

'Yes it did.' Megan's inward breath was a gasp. 'You can't say that! I *saw* it.'

'Someone found him.' Emily stood up and used her fingers to wipe some of the tears from Megan's face. 'It's OK, Megan. He's alive. He's going to be fine. So are you.' She stroked the girl's hair. 'Try and slow your breathing down, pet. Everything's going to be all right.'

'No-o-o…'

But Megan's eyes closed as she gave in to both her exhaustion and the comforting patter of Emily's words. Within seconds she had escaped into sleep, but Emily stayed until she could see all the readings on the monitors return to more normal levels.

Had she done the right thing by breaking the news so soon?
Had Megan actually believed what she'd been told?

Would it have been better to wait until she was well enough
and then have taken Megan to the nursery to see for herself?

The promise not to tell her parents was a concern as well.
Emily had no idea how to handle the next step in this case. She
needed help and Megan needed counselling from someone far
more expert than herself. The problem there was that Crocodile
Creek Hospital's physician, who also had an interest in psy-
chiatry and handled cases like this, was away on leave.

Megan was Emily's patient right now and she desperately
wanted to help on all the aspects this case was presenting.
Tackling the physical challenges might be the easiest part.
Megan's mental state and the social aspects that were clearly
looming might be a lot more difficult. Simply understanding
what the teenager was going through was not enough of a base
to feel confident in giving psychological assistance.

And Megan could well be in a completely different space
anyway. The timing of Emily's own baby might have been a
disaster in terms of her career at medical school and the relationship she'd been in with Cameron, but she had wanted that
child very badly by the end of her pregnancy. She would have
given anything not to have lost it at birth.

What if she was projecting too many personal feelings
into dealing with Megan? What if the sex hadn't even been
consensual or a child was the last thing the teenager wanted,
even without the stress it could cause her family? Emily didn't
know the Coopers at all.

She did, however, know someone who did. Someone
whose opinion and advice she would respect, both as a physician and a friend.

Emily left the unit as soon as Megan's nurse returned, having charted medication that would help the teenager get the

rest she needed for the next few hours. She moved purpose-
fully through the hospital, sparing only a moment to greet Mrs
Grubb, who was pushing one of the large stainless-steel meal
trolleys back to the kitchens.

Emily knocked on a door that was a little wider than most.
It had a plaque that advertised the office as belonging to the
hospital's medical director. She opened the door and poked
her head through the gap.

'Charles? Can you spare a minute? Oh, sorry!' Finding Jill
in the office wasn't surprising, but seeing their somewhat
dour nursing director with a broad smile on her face was.
Emily had the distinct impression she could be interrupting
something. 'I'll come back later, shall I?'

'Not on my account.' Jill stood up swiftly, her smile fading as she smoothed the tunic of her uniform. 'I've had my
roster problems sorted and it's high time I was back on duty.'

'Come in, Emily.' Behind a desk, it was easy to forget that
Charles was in a wheelchair. Just like it was easy to forget that
Charles might well be frustrated by not being able to use his
medical degree in a more hands-on capacity because he ran the
empire this hospital represented so well from behind this desk.

Emily had also forgotten, momentarily, that Charles had
his finger on the pulse of what went on around him with uncanny precision. He was smiling at Emily as she entered his
office properly.

'You want to talk to me about Megan Cooper, don't you?
Sit down, Em. How can I help?'

'So what did Charles have to say?'

'He was a bit shocked, I think.'

'About Megan getting pregnant?'

'More about how sad the whole family is. About Jim's
health and what terrible condition the farm is in. He and Jim

grew up as best mates. Charles said that Cooper's Crossing was thriving back then. They had prize-winning cattle and Jim was determined to keep things going after his father died. Charles went to the wedding when Jim married Honey about twenty years ago and they were talking about the wonderful new house they were going to build before they started a family.'

'So what happened?'

Emily shook her head, pushing her empty cup away. It was late and the rest of her day had been busy, what with an out-patient pain-management clinic and frequent visits back to Intensive Care to check on Megan. A visit to the nursery had been slotted in, of course, after Emily had gone for a late dinner and found that Mike was also having a long day and hadn't returned from a patient transfer to Cairns. The others had all gone to bed by the time Mike returned to the house but Emily had been waiting, with hot chocolate and toast ready for them both.

'He doesn't know. The wedding was a one-off by the sound of it. They'd grown apart because Charles was in the city for ten years after his accident.' Emily paused, letting Mike lean over the corner of the table to weave his fingers through hers, and she smiled as he traced circles on her palm with his thumb. Then she sighed lightly.

'Actually, I got the impression that Charles was really hurt. That the friendship died because Jim couldn't cope with his disability. That radio call the other night was the first time they'd spoken for years.'

'That's a bit sad. What else did he say?'

'Nothing about Jim. We talked about Megan. All the stuff I've already told you about her state of mind. She could be clinically depressed, which isn't going to help her recovery or trying to sort out what she wants to do about Lucky. Her mum's still going to try and come in to see her tomorrow and

I can't break patient confidentiality, but I'm sure her mother would want to support her. I don't know what the best thing to do is.'

'Are you supposed to be telling me all about this?'

'You're a colleague,' Emily reminded him. 'And you've been involved in this case from the word go. Besides…' Emily smiled at her companion.

'Besides, what?'

'You're trustworthy,' Emily added softly. 'And I needed to talk to you. I feel bad.'

Mike's eyebrows rose sharply. 'Why?'

'It was too soon to try and talk to Megan about the baby. I thought it would help. I thought that thinking she'd lost him could be causing her depression, but I may have made things worse. A baby might be the *last* thing she wants.'

'Are you surprised?' Mike was giving Emily a curious glance. 'She's only nineteen and she's not in any obvious relationship with the father of the baby.'

'But…' Emily fought back a wave of longing so strong it was painful. She hadn't been much older than Megan when she had become pregnant. Only twenty-two. A student at medical school. Motherhood would have been totally disruptive to her life and career but she was only too well able to remember the way she'd felt the first time she'd felt that baby move within her. She couldn't hide the tears in her eyes as she held Mike's gaze.

'But it's her *baby*.'

'Oh, babe,' Mike whispered. He got to his feet. 'Come here.'

He pulled Emily's chair back and took her hand. As he helped her stand up, he drew her into his arms.

'I love that you don't understand,' he told her softly. 'You are the sweetest and most loving person I know, Em.' A comforting kiss was pressed into her hair. 'And one day you are going to make the most wonderful mother.'

That longing changed. Developed sharp edges and became something close to panic. Emily had already been there, hadn't she? Been there, tried that and failed miserably enough to make another attempt a terrifying prospect.

She needed to tell Mike. He already knew about her failures in the relationship stakes. Would knowing that she had failed in her attempt to become a mother make him think any less of her?

It might. Mike was Greek. Family was important enough to have contributed to bringing him back to settle in the small town of his childhood. His siblings were scattered and his mother desperate for a tribe of grandchildren living nearby. Emily could almost hear Sophia right now. 'Such a nice girl, Michael, but she's not Greek. And what if it happened again? What if she can't produce a healthy child? No children…no *grandchildren.*'

Mike hadn't noticed Emily's silence. He kissed her hair again. 'You smell nice, too. Good enough to eat.'

It was too easy to turn her face to look up. To smile, knowing that it would be taken as an invitation to kiss her. And it was even easier to accept the kiss. To return it and know that within a very short space of time she would lose herself so completely that she could bury those fears.

She had promised herself she wouldn't cast doubts. 'It' wouldn't happen again. They had told her that at the time. The fact that the cord had been wound around her baby's neck and strangled him during labour had simply been a tragic accident. She would tell Mike all about it, of course. But not just yet.

Not while what they had between them was itself a newborn and taking its first breaths. She had made one mistake already today in trying to talk to Megan while she was still weak. She wouldn't make that mistake with Mike. Or with their relationship. Her past had been buried for ten years. It could stay that way just a little longer. Until she was confident the strength was there to handle any stress the revelation could provoke.

All they needed was a little time. Hopefully, it was all Megan needed as well. Lucky needed his mother. Emily knew she was too personally involved with this case. She also knew it was ridiculous to feel that if she could put that baby into his mother's arms and see him accepted and loved, it would somehow exorcise a ghost from her own past.

Ridiculous it might be, but it was undeniably there. Like a powerful omen. If—no, *when*—Megan accepted Lucky, then Emily would know that somewhere in her future was another baby of her own.

Mike's baby.

And when he knew about her past he would understand and be patient. He wouldn't rush her into something she was afraid of. Just like he wasn't rushing her into bed with him. He would win her trust as he had done before she'd climbed into his helicopter, and then he would be there to support her and keep her safe while she pushed those personal boundaries.

The gentle kisses that were spiralling so easily into passion made Mike's embrace a haven that Emily did not want to lose. She didn't need to think about anything else while she was in Mike's arms. She couldn't think of anything else with any coherency anyway.

She felt absolutely safe for the moment and with the feeling of safety came a sense of urgency. Emily wanted to cement this bond. To take the fairy-tale her life had suddenly turned into a little further. To find out whether the fantasies she had been harbouring for too long had any basis in reality.

Besides, they were standing in the kitchen of the doctors' house and it was hardly the place for passion like this. Emily pulled away from Mike's kiss just far enough to allow her lips to move and for speech to be audible.

Mike groaned softly. 'You're not thinking of going to bed already, are you? And leaving me here alone?'

'Yes.' Emily smiled. 'And no.'

CHAPTER EIGHT

EIGHT years.

Emily counted them off on her fingers as she sat on the edge of her bed the following morning, wrapped in a towel, with tendrils of hair still wet from its wash dripping over her shoulders.

Including her last year at medical school, she had spent eight years in full-time clinical practice. How many nights would that represent? And how many of them had been virtually sleepless?

So many.

And never, ever had any of those sleepless nights left her feeling like she did right now. It had been even harder to drag herself out of bed than it had ever been before, of course, but lack of sleep hadn't contributed to the difficulty, had it? The magnet that held her there was the man whose bed it was. The man who had proved himself to be the most glorious, generous lover imaginable. Far more exciting than Emily had ever dreamed and embarrassingly attentive to her own pleasure.

Her fantasies had never included any of that. Had never had him ask where she most liked to be touched or what she wanted him to do for her. Emily hadn't been able to think of a single thing to say and Mike had been supremely unfazed.

'That's cool,' he'd murmured. 'I'm going to touch you everywhere, then. And try everything—until you tell me you *don't* like it.'

They never reached that point, despite Emily learning things she had never known. If she stopped now to think of the magic Mike had wrought with his hands and fingers…and tongue…Emily would quite likely blush for the rest of the day and people might well guess why, which would mean the effort of returning discreetly to her own room early enough to remain unnoticed would have been wasted.

Mind you, at the rate she was moving at present, she might not even make it as far as interacting with her colleagues. Emily made a new effort and stood up, moving to her chest of drawers to select some clean underwear.

The lace of her bra prickled against nipples that still felt overly sensitive. The soft elastic on her knickers brushed her inner thighs and reminded her instantly of the touch of Mike's lips. Emily stood in front of her wardrobe and couldn't, for the life of her, make a decision about what she wanted to wear for the day.

How on earth was she *not* going to make it patently obvious to everyone that something momentous had occurred in her life?

A skirt, she decided in desperation, even if it was impractical when there was always the possibility of being sent on a rescue mission. If she went by helicopter, she'd have to change into overalls anyway, and she had every intention of making sure she was included on the helicopter staff roster from now on. She was perfectly happy to fly without wings as long as Mike was her pilot.

A very private smile stretched almost to a grin as Emily chose a camisole top and a soft shirt to wear as a light jacket. Michael Poulos could make her fly with no aircraft anywhere in the vicinity!

Cloud nine. That was the expression that pretty much summed up her mood this morning. Amazingly, Emily felt more refreshed than a solid night's sleep could have achieved. More than refreshed, actually.

Reborn.

Of course she could cope with the day ahead. With any interaction with her colleagues and patients. With…anything. Emily grabbed a comb to pull through her nearly dry hair. All she needed now was some brief attention to her make-up and she would be ready to go out for breakfast.

And Mike would probably be in the kitchen.

He'd look at her and then she would know it hadn't all been a dream. That Mike had done and said everything he could think of to show her how much he loved her.

That she had done the same.

That she had, in fact, accepted the proposal whispered into her ear in the euphoric, drifting doze in which Mike's arms had had her cradled at some point during the night.

Surely she *had* imagined that part of it all?

Emily couldn't really have agreed to marry Mike so soon, could she?

But would it matter if she had? It was what she wanted. What she had wanted for ever. If Mike felt the same way, why *should* they waste any more of their lives?

Emily couldn't wait to get to breakfast now and she shoved her feet into her shoes, cursing the time she had spent just sitting on her bed. She had to see Mike and find out whether he could confirm the reality of their new relationship with just a look.

Or had he gone back to sleep? Mike had a day off today, lucky thing. Due to the current staff shortages, Emily would not be getting any time off before Saturday and even then she might need to be on call for emergency anaesthetics.

Maybe she should just peep into his room on her way to the kitchen. If he was still there, she could say good morning properly and start her day the way she wanted to start every day from now on.

And maybe Mike had had the same thought. The ringing of the phone in her room sent Emily back inside just as she was about to close the door behind her. She was smiling as she picked up the receiver.

'Dr Morgan?'

'Speaking.' Disappointingly, it wasn't Mike. Emily recognised the voice of one of the hospital's switchboard operators.

'I'm sorry, I know it's awfully early but I've got an outside call for you. A Honey Cooper. Do you mind taking the call?'

'Of course not. Put her through.' Emily sat on the edge of her bed again and barely repressed a sigh. Her day had started already, it seemed, and any intimate thoughts about Mike simply had to be banished for the time being.

'Dr Morgan?'

'Call me Emily. Is that Honey?'

'Yes. Look, I'm terribly sorry, but I won't be able to get in to see Megan today like I said. I tried to tell her myself but she's asleep and the nurse suggested I talked to you...'

'Don't worry,' Emily said.

Honey was talking very quickly and sounded as upset as she'd been the other night when Mike and Emily had arrived at the rundown station. She could imagine that the expression on the older woman's face was just as anxious as well. Megan's mother must have been very pretty in past years but the impression Emily had kept was one of a woman exhausted by hardship.

'I'll explain to Megan later on, when she's awake, Honey.'

'I missed the bus.' Emily's words did not seem to have been any comfort. Honey sounded as though she was struggling not to cry. 'The truck had a flat tyre and by the time I got to Gunyamurra, the bus had gone already. I'm using the phone in the general store. I thought if I couldn't see Megan, at least I might be able to talk to her, but…but the nurse said she's sedated so even if she tried to wake her up she might not be able to talk to me.'

'Yes.' Emily's mind focused more sharply at the reminder of Megan's sedation and the reason for it. Talking to her mother might be just what Emily needed to find a way to achieve real communication with her teenage patient. 'It's nothing to worry about, Honey. Megan's on the mend now. She just needs a period of rest to help her recuperate.'

'But she's still in Intensive Care!'

'It's a precaution. She *has* been seriously ill and we want to keep a very close eye on her for another day or two. She's off the ventilator now and breathing well on her own, so that's very good news, isn't it?'

'Oh, yes! Oh, I'm so relieved. I've been worried sick and I couldn't tell Jim why.'

'How do you mean, Honey?' Did Megan's mother know about the baby after all? If she did, then Emily wouldn't be breaking her promise to Megan by discussing the issue, would she?

'I know about it.' Honey's voice became muffled, as though she was cupping her hand close to her mouth. She also lowered her voice so that Emily had to strain to hear her. 'About the…miscarriage.' There was a tiny pause and then Honey's voice became clear again. 'Isn't that what made her so sick?'

'It…um…could have contributed,' Emily said cautiously. Damn. Honey had no idea she had a live grandchild and that meant that Emily couldn't try and assess what level of support might be forthcoming from Megan's family. 'Right now,

I think getting Megan back on her feet is more important than worrying about the cause of the infection.'

'So she'll still be able to have a baby one day? It hasn't done any permanent damage?'

'Not as far as we can tell.'

'And I won't have to tell Jim?'

'Not if you don't want to, Honey. Or if Megan doesn't want him to know.'

'Oh, she doesn't. Of course she doesn't. We couldn't…' Honey was definitely crying now. 'I was so scared about what I could say without making him sick. His blood pressure, you know. It's…'

Emily let Honey talk on, making encouraging noises as she realised that being able to air her concerns was calming the woman. She heard about Jim's heart attack and the problems ever since. The drought and the broken fences. The sick cattle and the veterinary bills that couldn't be paid.

A soft knock at Emily's door distracted her for a moment and when Mike's head appeared, she completely missed something Honey was saying about how their phone had been cut off so they only had a radio for emergencies.

Emily covered the mouthpiece of the phone for a second as Mike leaned down and kissed the top of her head.

'It's Honey Cooper,' she whispered. 'I want to see what I can find out that might help with Megan.'

Mike nodded. 'Breakfast?'

Emily shook her head, her expression calculated to let him know that she regretted having to forgo that time with him. 'It sounds very difficult for you all, Honey,' she said into the phone. 'You must be missing having Megan around to help at the moment.'

Mike blew her another kiss as he stole away. 'Later, babe,' he said softly. 'Good luck.'

'We can't really manage without her,' Honey was saying at the same time. 'Such a shame she hasn't been able to go away to university. She's so bright. She topped her year with the School of the Air.' Honey sighed heavily. 'But that's just the way things are…until the rains come, anyway.'

'Is Megan happy at home?'

There was a short silence, as though the question was puzzling, and Emily hoped she hadn't been too blunt. It seemed obvious to her that the kind of workload and pressure Honey had been describing on a nineteen-year-old girl who would rather be away at university could well be a major factor in Megan's depression. If so, it was another area in which her patient needed assistance.

'I just wondered what she was normally like,' Emily added. 'It would be good to know—in terms of assessing her recovery. Is she a talkative girl? Cheerful?'

'She used to be.' Honey sounded sad rather than anxious now. 'This last year's been tough on all of us. I know Megan was terribly disappointed about not being able to go away but she understands. She knows we can't afford it and she knows how much her dad relies on her. She *wanted* to stay to help. She loves her dad, Dr Morgan. And the farm. She says she can always go away later. When things are right again.'

Had they ever been right? Emily wondered. Another thought occurred to her as she ran through a mental list of the signs and symptoms of chronic depression.

'Has Megan always had a problem with her weight?'

'No. But I've always been a bit on the plump side so maybe she's inherited the tendency. It's probably my fault. I do tend to make a lot of food. We haven't got much here but at least there's always food on the table, even if it is mostly roast beef and potatoes.'

The sound of another voice interfered with Honey's last words and then Honey sounded anxious again.

'Mrs Considine's just warning me how much this call is going to cost. She doesn't look too happy about putting it on our account.'

'The hospital will cover the cost, Honey, don't worry.' Emily was sure Charles would be able to swing that somehow and if he couldn't then Emily would have it deducted from her own salary.

'I'd better go anyway. I need to get home. Goodness knows what Jim will be thinking he has to try and do, seeing as he doesn't think I'll be home before tonight.'

Emily's pager sounded as Honey was speaking and Emily nodded. 'Looks like I need to start work, too, Honey. It's been good to talk to you.'

'I feel ever so much better, Dr Morgan.'

'Call me Emily,' she reminded Honey.

'Look after our girl for us, won't you?'

'Of course.' In fact, ICU was where Emily needed to go now. With a bit of luck Megan might be awake and in a better state to talk to her. Having her mother's conversation to relay and break any ice would be a great help. 'I'll tell Megan that you rang.'

'Give her my love. And from her dad, too.' Honey was crying again. 'We do love her, you know.'

'I know. I'll tell her.'

'You'll call, won't you? If she gets worse again?'

'Of course. Try not to worry, Honey. You take care of yourself.'

Ten minutes later, Emily wondered if she'd done the right thing in telling Honey not to worry.

She was more than a little worried herself.

Standing beside Hamish at the central desk in the unit, she examined the strip of paper that Megan's cardiac monitor had printed out automatically when the alarm had been triggered.

The long burst of QRS spikes were far too close together, indicating a dangerously rapid rate. They were regular but that wasn't reassuring.

'It could be supraventricular.'

'Let's hope so,' Emily agreed. If it was the largest chamber of Megan's heart producing this rhythm they could be in trouble again. A ventricular tachycardia could easily degenerate into fibrillation and cardiac arrest.

Gina was called in for an expert opinion.

'We can find out whether it's ventricular easily enough,' she told them.

'How?'

'We'll give her a dose of adenosine. It knocks out the AV node so we'll see flutter waves but no QRS. Half-life is only twelve seconds, so normal activity resumes soon enough.'

'And if it is SVT?'

'We can give her adenosine every time it happens until it settles down. We'll start with a 6 milligram dose and titrate to no more than 24 milligrams if necessary.' Gina looked across to where Megan lay, her eyes closed. 'Is she awake properly yet?'

'She's pretty drowsy,' Emily said. 'I kept her lightly sedated overnight. She got rather distressed yesterday when I tried to talk to her about the baby.'

Gina's eyes widened. ' So she really is the mother?'

Emily nodded. 'She's not ready to accept that the baby's survived, though.'

'Hmm.' Gina's attention returned to the ECG. 'I was going to suggest keeping her sedated for a while anyway. The problem with using adenosine is that, if the patient's awake, it makes them feel pretty awful.'

The option seemed a good idea all round. With Megan kept drowsy enough, they could watch and treat the arrhythmia without distressing her too much. With every passing hour the antibiotic and other therapies she was still receiving were improving her physical condition. The more physical strength she gained over the next day or so, the better she would feel, and with a noticeable improvement after a long period of rest, Megan might see everything in a more positive light.

Including the fact that both she and her baby had survived.

The arrhythmia gradually settled until, twenty-four hours later, the intensive cardiac monitoring and additional medication could be discontinued. By Thursday afternoon the consultants were all happy to remove any sedation from Megan's drug regime and allow her to wake up fully.

A chest X-ray had shown her lungs to be clear again and her oxygen levels remained steady even on room air. All the other tests on vital organs came back with results that were reassuringly closer to normal, and by that evening Megan was sitting up for the first time since Sunday and she had eaten a small meal of shredded roast chicken with mashed potatoes and gravy which Mrs Grubb had prepared specially.

'Was that good?' Emily was delighted to see the empty plate on Megan's locker.

'It was OK, I guess.'

'We're going to shift you down to the ward soon,' Emily told her. 'You're going to have a lovely room to yourself, and a sea view. How cool is that?'

'I just want to go home.'

'I know you do, pet. Not just yet.'

'When?'

'When you can walk around and take care of yourself with things like having a shower. You'll be pretty weak for a day

or two yet. And from what your mum told me, you're expected
to do a lot around home. We don't want you trying too much,
too soon.'

'When did you talk to my mum?'

'Yesterday morning. You've been pretty sleepy since then
so you probably don't remember me telling you about it.'

'What did she say?'

'That she was worried about you and missing having you
around. She sent her love. So did your dad.'

'Did she say if things were OK at home?'

'In what way?' Megan didn't need to hear about the litany
of worries Honey had shared with Emily.

'Like the cattle and stuff.'

Emily shook her head. 'Tomorrow we could get you up in
a wheelchair. If we take you down to the radio room, you'll
be able to talk to them yourself.'

'Did she say anything else?' Megan looked past Emily as
though checking whether anyone else was within earshot.

'What about?' Emily knew that Megan's nurse was safely
away, writing up notes at the central desk.

'You know.'

'Your mum thinks you had a miscarriage,' Emily said quietly. 'Is that what you told her?'

Megan was silent.

'We need to talk about this, sweetheart.'

Megan shook her head. 'I'm tired. I just want to go to
sleep again.'

The orderlies would be here to transfer her to the ward any
moment, in any case, and it was not a conversation that should
be interrupted. By the time Megan was settled into her new
room, she really would be too tired and it would be unpro-
ductive to force the issue.

'Will you talk to me about it tomorrow, then?'

Megan's grunt was noncommittal.

'Is there anybody else you'd rather talk to?'

'Like who?' The look Emily received, suggesting that she was a prize idiot, if not certifiably insane, was such a normal teenage reaction it was a relief.

'Have you got any family or friends in town?'

'No.'

'Any of the other doctors or nurses maybe?'

Megan's glance suggested just a flicker of interest. 'Where's that doctor I saw when I was first sick?'

'You mean Hamish,—Dr McGregor? Or Dr Jamieson?'

'No. I mean at home. The one who came with you.'

'Oh…' Emily's smile just happened. For the last two days she hadn't been able to think about Mike without that smile happening. 'You mean Mike. He's a paramedic, not a doctor—but that doesn't mean he can't come and talk to you,' she added hastily.

Emily's smile had not gone unnoticed.

'Is he your boyfriend?'

'Ah…yeah.' Sharing personal information might be a little unprofessional but if it could make a difference in her rapport with this particular patient it would be well worth bending the rules of accepted practice. Emily smiled again. 'Yes,' she said more firmly. 'He is.'

Megan just nodded wearily before resting her head back on her pillows and closing her eyes.

'I guess you can come, too, then.'

'Are you sure you don't mind?'

'Hell, no! Why would I?' Mike's smile almost brought tears to Emily's eyes. It was *so* gorgeous. So caring. 'If there's going to be a happy ending here, I'm in, babe. I'm your man.'

'Mmm.' Emily snuggled closer on the old settee on the veranda. 'So you are. We'll go and talk to Megan together, then. Tomorrow morning?'

'Whenever you like. I've got to meet my sister at the airport in the afternoon but apart from that I'm free. Barring callouts, of course.'

'I'll see what the theatre lists are looking like. Late morning might be the best plan. Then we could have lunch together.'

'I'm thinking of other things we could have together.' Mike's hand trailed upwards from Emily's knee. 'Feeling tired yet, babe?'

Emily straightened and Mike took his hand off her leg as the sound of voices warned of an interruption to their privacy. The sight of the visitors was a surprise. Flight doctor Christina Farrelly was not a rare visitor to the house but the man with her was. Brian Simmons, the hospital administrator.

'Emily! How nice to see you. Are you well?'

'Never better, thanks, Brian.' Emily might have straightened up but she hadn't moved far enough to create a gap between herself and Mike, and their closeness hadn't escaped Brian's sharp glance.

'Mike.' The tone was clipped now. 'How are you?'

'Never better,' Mike echoed mischievously. 'Must be contagious.'

Emily smiled at Christina to disguise her amusement. Mike knew, along with everybody else in the house, that Brian Simmons's attempts to date Emily, so soon after his wife had left him, in the pre-Simon days, had been less than welcome. Mike might be using humour but he was advertising his right to be so close to Emily right now.

He was not just her man. He was letting it be known that Emily was his woman. She liked that.

Christina didn't appear to have noticed the undercurrents. She returned Emily's smile then followed Brian into the house. The hospital administrator's voice floated back through the doorway.

'The room's this way. I'm sure he'll find it most acceptable.'

'What's that all about?' Emily wondered aloud.

'Dunno.' Mike frowned. 'Christina wasn't looking so happy the other night, come to think of it. I kind of got the impression that maybe things aren't so rosy between her and Joe.'

'Oh, no! What did she say?'

'Nothing really. I don't think she wanted to talk about it.' Mike's arm came around Emily's shoulders. 'Don't worry. I'm sure they'll sort it out, whatever it is.'

'I hope so.'

Even a hint of relationship problems among their friends was unsettling. It happened, though, didn't it? Even with couples who appeared to be as much in love as Christina and Joe.

Or as much in love as she and Mike were.

And when it did happen, it could have devastating results. Emily tried to push the fear away but it had sticky edges. She could never stay here if things didn't work out between her and Mike. She wouldn't be able to bear living in the same small town with this man who had claimed her heart and soul so completely if history repeated itself yet again and Mike wanted out.

She would lose both the man she loved and the life she had worked so hard to create. A home and career she also loved. The prospect of losing everything was terrifying. Not that it was going to happen, but the risk was there, wasn't it?

The risk that Mike might get bored as others had done before him. That he might realise that his attraction to her 'differentness' was just a reaction to emotional stress caused by the abrupt ending of another relationship and that, long term, he really wanted a woman true to his preferred type.

He didn't think so now, of course. He'd be insulted if Emily suggested it. Or it might come across as her being pathetically needy and craving reassurance.

She had another night in Mike's arms ahead of her right now. What more reassurance could she possibly want?

CHAPTER NINE

THE face in the mirror was scowling.

Mike dragged the razor down his cheek and then swished it clean in the basin of warm water.

Damn it! *Why* didn't Emily want to go public? There was going to be a crowd in party mood tomorrow night at the fund-raising dinner and it was being held in Mike's childhood home. The majority of their friends and colleagues would be there, not to mention a few extra members of Mike's family. It was the perfect opportunity to announce their engagement.

To tell the world just how much they loved each other.

It would make his mother so happy. She would be so excited planning for a wedding that she would forgive him for snapping at her on the phone last night when she'd rung to tell him that his sister, Maria, was bringing a friend with her from Melbourne for the weekend.

'She's a nurse, Michael. Sounds like *such* a nice girl. And she's *Greek!*'

He'd been so frustrated by his promise to wait until Emily was ready to announce their news that he'd taken it out on his mother.

'For God's sake!' he'd exclaimed crossly. 'Will you just give up trying to arrange a marriage for me? It's not going to work. And anyway, I...'

The frantic eye-widening and head-shaking coming from Emily's direction had stifled the words he'd wanted to utter.

'I'm sick of it,' he'd finished curtly.

Sophia had been hurt, and no wonder. She only interfered in his life because she loved him and wanted him to be happy. More than anything, she wanted him to find the kind of life partner she'd been lucky enough to have with his father.

And he had.

So *why* couldn't they tell everybody?

Mike had to change his expression to facilitate shaving his chin but the scowl continued inwardly. If Emily felt the same way he did, she wouldn't have any qualms about making an announcement. To be even slightly reluctant mean that she had doubts.

Not about whether she loved him or not. Nobody could make love the way they had the last few nights and not reveal any lack of sincerity. By the same token, Emily had to know how deeply Mike felt. She appeared to feel the same way.

If her doubts were not about the depth of feeling, then they had to be about the future. Whether it would last. You couldn't know that until you tried, though, could you? Emily just needed to be brave enough to take that first step. He'd tried his best to help. Surely, letting her know how badly he wanted to get married and plan a family and future together should be all that was needed to reassure her?

Mike didn't know what else he *could* do.

OK, it had only been a few days and maybe he was expecting too much too soon, but the way Mike saw things, the time frame meant nothing in the face of the strength of their love. So what difference would waiting make? Apart from giving him a niggling sense of anxiety?

He wanted the reassurance of a public affirmation. His heart was on the line here. He'd waited a long time for this and he knew he'd never find it again with anyone else. If it fell apart, having reached this stage, it could shatter his whole life.

Staying in Crocodile Creek wouldn't be an option. If Mike couldn't settle down with Emily, he'd never settle down at all. He'd rejoin the military service and have himself posted to every hotspot that flared anywhere in the world.

It would break his mother's heart, that would.

Twisting the mixer, Mike waited a few seconds for the water in his shower to get to the right temperature. Then he stepped in and raised his face to rinse off the last of the shaving foam. Some of his anxiety seemed to disperse along with the suds.

He'd been very patient up till now as far as Emily was concerned. Where was this urgency coming from? He needed to be patient just a little longer. To win whatever final piece of trust Emily was holding back. He could do that.

He had no choice, did he?

Megan had had a shower and washed her hair. She had discarded her hospital gown in favour of the sloppy dark blue T-shirt with the teddy bear emblem that had been laundered through the hospital system the night she'd been admitted. Was she feeling that much better or had she made a huge effort because of Mike's impending visit?

Probably for Mike's benefit, Emily decided when they arrived in Megan's room just before lunchtime. It was the first time she had seen the girl smile, she realised—and it made such a difference. A hint of happiness was there and Megan, when she was well and happy, would be a very attractive young woman.

'So, how's it going?' Mike pulled up a chair and sat close to Megan's pillows while Emily perched herself on the end of the bed.

'OK, I guess.'

'I haven't seen you awake for a few days. Not since you had that ride in my chopper.'

'Will you take me home in the helicopter, then?'

'We'll arrange for you to get home, Megan.' Emily answered to save Mike having to turn down an impossible request for the use of a rescue aircraft. 'It's quite likely they'll take you out with the plane when it goes to the next clinic at Gunyamurra.'

An awkward silence fell. They all knew what they were there to discuss but it was difficult to know where to start.

Mike solved the problem. He smiled winningly at Megan.

'You're looking a hell of a lot better than the last time I saw you,' he said easily. 'I can understand now how you managed to produce such a beautiful baby.'

Megan's jaw dropped but Mike kept smiling. 'Would you like to see him?'

Megan screwed her eyes shut and shook her head violently. 'No way!'

'Why not, love?' Mike's query was gentle.

'Because it's easier this way.' Megan opened her eyes in the pause that followed and shot a quick glance in Mike's direction.

'Is…is he really beautiful?'

'Yep.' Mike looked at Emily who nodded agreement.

'Everybody loves him,' she said.

'So it won't be hard to find someone who wants to adopt him, then?'

'You don't need to make any decisions like that yet,' Emily said. 'You need time to get used to all this, Megan. To talk to lots of people and think about it all carefully. There *are* other options.'

'Like what?' The tone was scathing.

'There would be help available if you wanted to keep the baby. I'm sure your mum—'

'No! She's not to know about this.'

'But—'

'*No!*' The word was a sob this time. 'I don't want my parents to know. I won't let you tell them.'

'They love you, chicken.' Mike leaned in and took hold of Megan's hand. 'They'd want to help.'

'There's no way. We barely manage as it is. We couldn't afford a baby.'

'There's help available.'

'Oh, *God!*' Megan pulled her hand away from Mike's and covered her face. 'You don't know what you're saying. My dad would die of shame. No matter how bad things have been, he's always said he'd die rather than go on welfare.'

'It doesn't necessarily need to be government assistance,' Emily said. 'You're going to be amazed at the presents that have been arriving for Lucky.'

'Who?'

'He needed a name,' Mike explained. 'The staff named him Lucky on the first night he was here.'

'Why?'

'Because he was so lucky that Gina found him in time. And that she was there so he could have the operation he needed.'

'What operation?'

'He was a very sick little baby,' Emily said quietly. 'He had a problem with one of the valves in his heart, but it's been fixed now.'

'I didn't know he was sick.' Megan sounded defensive.

'Of course you didn't. And it's no wonder you thought he was dead. That's what Gina thought when she first saw him, and she's a doctor.'

Emily paused for a second. Talking about Lucky's medical problems was inevitably leading to the opening of another can of worms. Megan wasn't openly hostile yet, though, so maybe it was a good time to get everything discussed.

'There was another medical problem we found,' she told the young mother. 'Lucky's got a blood disorder. Something called von Willebrand's disease.'

Megan shrugged. 'So he's going to die anyway, then.'

Emily shook her head. 'It's treatable. It means that he might have a tendency to bleed more badly if he ever gets injured, but as long as it's known about it shouldn't present problems. It's when you don't know about it that it can be dangerous. We needed to test you before you had surgery.'

'Why?'

'It's an inherited disorder.'

'So, have I got it as well?'

'No.'

'Which means,' Mike said casually, 'that the baby's father might have von Willebrand's.'

The silence stretched on this time. Emily cleared her throat.

'Do you know whether that's the case?' she asked.

Megan shook her head and looked down at her hands.

'Are you in any contact with him?'

Her head dipped lower as she shook it again. Emily could see fresh tears collecting on dark lashes.

'Do you know where he is?'

Megan's breath escaped in a harsh sob. 'No.' She pulled her knees up and rested her head on her arms, giving way to her misery. 'And it doesn't matter,' she choked out, 'whether he's got a disease that's going to kill him. I'll never see him again so he might as well be dead.'

Mike and Emily both did their best to comfort Megan. To persuade her that she would get through this and that they were there to help her. That she needed time and plenty of rest and that nobody was going to rush her into making any decisions in a hurry. They all wanted what was going to be best for her.

Megan finally stopped sobbing and looked up. 'What's best is if you just make it all go away,' she said forlornly. Huge eyes in a tear-stained face made her look a lot younger than her nineteen years. Too young to be faced with the prospect of single parenthood. 'Give my baby to someone who can take care of him.' Megan sniffed and scrubbed at her face with a fist. 'Someone who really wants him. Make things go back to the way they were before.'

Mike met Emily's gaze over the top of the teenager's head. 'My baby', she'd said. If they'd achieved nothing else this morning, at least Megan had accepted the fact that she was a mother.

Leaving her to rest, Mike and Emily walked quietly through the hospital corridors. By tactic consent they made their way towards the nursery.

'Do you think we upset her too much?'

'No.' Mike's tone was very sombre. 'It's hard, but there are decisions that only Megan can make. She's got to think about it. We've started the ball rolling.'

Lucky was asleep but they stood for a minute and admired the infant.

'She wouldn't have been that upset if giving up her baby and forgetting she'd given birth was really what she wants.'

'No.' Mike was smiling at Lucky. 'And I think she's refusing to see him because she knows how much harder it would be once she did. She'd have to face the reality of giving up her child.'

'She's going to have to do that at some point. Nobody's going to let her sign adoption papers until they're absolutely sure it's what she wants.' Emily touched Lucky's cheek softly enough to leave him undisturbed. 'So maybe that's the next step. We get her to see him. Hold him, even, and then see where we go.'

She'd never let him go. Emily certainly wouldn't if Lucky were her baby. And when he was cradled in Megan's arms, Emily would be able to let go of that small black cloud hanging over her future with Mike.

'Hmm.' Mike sounded as thoughtful as Emily felt. 'If we force him on her, it might make her even more determined. We all need a little patience here, babe. ' He smiled at her. 'I have a feeling it's all going to work out just fine.' He lowered his voice. 'I'd do a bit of spitting for luck but Grace would have me out of here before you could say "unhygienic", and I might never be allowed back in.'

The smile didn't last.

The rest of Friday was quiet for Emily and gave her too much time to think. To worry about Megan and Lucky, and to rack her brains, trying to think of a way to bring them together.

She had nothing against adoption and, indeed, it could be the best option in this case. There would be any number of loving families ready to take this tiny boy into their homes and hearts.

But that would haunt Megan for the rest of her life.

The birth date of that child would stand out every year. Megan might try and brush it off as just another day. She might even think it was forgotten after years had passed but Emily knew differently. She'd see someone with a baby or a toddler or a small child and it would sneak up and hit her like a brick. She'd think, Yes, he would be about that age now. Would he be smiling like that? Have so many teeth? Be learning to point or wave or say 'No!'?

Would he be off to school with lovingly made sandwiches tucked into his backpack and a plastic dinosaur in his pocket?

Learning to ride a bike or climb trees and have scraped knees and elbows that needed a sticky plaster and a kiss to make it better?

The ghosts would be so much worse for Megan because when she saw those children, she would not only wonder if Lucky would be like that. She would have to wonder whether that actually was her own child.

Never mind about any omens. This had nothing to do with the future she, Emily, could have with Mike.

That she *would* have with Mike.

It had nothing to do with her own past either, or any ghosts that were never going to go away. Emily simply had a unique perspective on this case, and what it had everything to do with was the young mother lying alone in her room. And grandparents, hundreds of miles away, who were oblivious to how their futures might be changing.

The potential ripples kept expanding as Emily ignored her paperwork, too absorbed by thoughts about Megan and Lucky. So many people were going to be affected by the decisions made in the next few days or weeks. What about the young man out there somewhere who might have no knowledge that he had become a father? Who might not even know that he had a potentially life-threatening blood disorder? There was another set of grandparents as well. And maybe aunts, uncles and cousins.

Emily could see those ripples fading into a murky future, only to gather strength like an embryonic tidal wave and cause more heartache twenty years down the track when Lucky might set out to discover his birth family.

She couldn't be entirely sure that Megan would be able to have any more children easily either, despite her reassurance to Honey. An infection like that was bound to have left scarring. They couldn't know what long-term effects it could have

on Megan's Fallopian tubes or fertility without further tests
once she had healed completely.

What if Lucky was the only child she would ever bear?

Mike phoned late that afternoon to find Emily still in her office.

'I'm at the Athina,' he told her. 'I've collected the tribe from
the airport and we've got a bit of a family party going here.
How 'bout joining us?'

'I'm on call,' Emily reminded him.

'You wouldn't be trying to get out of dish-washing duties,
would you? There's a riot in the kitchen with all the preparation for the fundraiser dinner tomorrow night.'

'I'll try and get up later,' Emily promised. 'I want to visit
Megan again after dinner and follow up on this morning, now
that she's had a bit of time to think about things.'

'Oh, right.' Mike didn't sound particularly interested in discussing a patient case, but that was hardly surprising. Emily
could hear the shrieks of small excited children in the background, interspersed with adult laughter and a commanding
voice she recognised as that of Sophia.

'I'd better go,' Mike said apologetically. Then he laughed.
'If someone doesn't restore some law and order around here,
I suspect there'll be a fatality.'

'Good luck! Sounds like you'll need it.'

'Yeah. Oh, I'll probably stay here tonight. Looks like it
could be a late one. Come as soon as you can. Love you, babe.'

'Love you, too,' Emily said softly. But Mike had already
gone.

The background accompaniment to the call stayed with her
long after she hung up and made a concerted effort to deal
with the paperwork. It had been such a happy noise. Probably
quite typical of any gathering involving Mike's family, but totally outside the realm of Emily's existence so far.

As an only child, raised by busy, professional parents, Emily had always hungered to belong amidst such family chaos. It would be the perfect antidote to the tension that had been building all day as well. But it would also be an escape. Shirking a responsibility that was weighing more and more heavily on Emily's shoulders.

If she didn't do her utmost to help Megan right now, she would be a failure as the teenager's primary physician. She felt she had failed too often in important areas of her life to allow anything to set her up for a repeat performance if she could help it. Taking selfish time to enjoy the company of Mike and his family instead of talking to Megan was precisely the kind of situation that could lead to missing some vital step and to failure.

Emily got to the small coffee and gift shop in the hospital's atrium just before it closed. She stood in front of the magazine rack, pulling out everything that looked of potential interest to a teenager. The front cover of the *Australian Women's Weekly* had a picture of a young television star with her new baby and Emily hesitated for a long moment.

The photographer had captured the joy of new motherhood beautifully. Emily snorted softly as she realised she was viewing the picture as another omen. Maybe she did have a drop or two of Greek blood somewhere in her veins. She'd be spitting surreptitiously in corners soon if she wasn't careful!

She did, however, pick up and purchase the magazine. She put it at the bottom of the pile, hoping that Megan would come across it in her own time. There had to be a key to solving this issue and it could be anything. Maybe seeing that picture could provide something that no amount of talking could.

The pile of magazines was exactly where Emily had left it when she returned to Megan's room late on Saturday morning.

'How are you feeling, pet?'

'Better. The same. I want to get out of here and go home.'

'Soon.'

Megan was avoiding eye contact. She stared at her locker. 'Did you bring those magazines?'

'Yes. I came to visit you last night but you were asleep.' Emily had waited well over an hour in the hope that Megan would wake up and want to talk, but she had been disappointed.

'Thanks.' The appreciation was grudging. 'Maybe I'll look at them later.'

'It's a gorgeous day. You might like to go and sit in the sun for a bit. Or would you like to call home on the radio again?'

'Nah.' Megan shook her head. 'I'm tired. I think I'll go back to sleep for a while.'

Emily just nodded. She was tired, too. Weary in spirit as well as body. Last night had been her first night apart from Mike since they had first made love. After the frustration of not being able to talk to Megan, the hours had been long and lonely.

Called in for emergency surgery this morning on an elderly woman with severe abdominal pain from the nursing-home adjacent to the hospital, Emily and Cal had had to face their inability to rescue her from the effects of an aortic dissection. She had come straight from Theatre to get another kick in the gut by discovering that Megan hadn't even glanced at that magazine cover.

Nothing was helping.

Difficult cases for the afternoon which would normally have provided a satisfying challenge for Emily had the opposite effect today. Trying to anaesthetise a screaming toddler who needed a fractured radius reduced was an ordeal.

Intubating a middle-aged woman who was brought in having suffered a catastrophic brain haemorrhage was even more distressing. The only point to putting this patient on life support was to give the family some time to say goodbye and to keep the woman's organs viable in case they agreed to donation.

Settling this patient into Intensive Care, and coping with distraught relatives including the woman's fourteen-year-old son, kept Emily occupied until 8 p.m., at which point she realised she was extremely late for the fundraising dinner at the Athina.

She almost didn't go. But then she thought of the fourteen-year-old she had just seen, who was struggling to make sense of the blow life had just dealt his family. She thought of the patient they had lost on the table that morning and remembered another such loss, only last week, during surgery on one of the survivors from the terrible car crash when those kids from Wygera had been playing chicken with their cars.

That was what this fundraiser was all about. Trying to do something that could prevent another such tragedy. Besides, Mike would be there, and Emily was sadly in need of being close to someone who loved her.

She had a quick shower and changed her clothes, choosing a gypsy-style skirt with ruffles and a pretty puffed-sleeve top. She clipped a pager to the waistband of her skirt and let the staff in both Intensive Care and the emergency department know where she would be. And she took her car so that she could be back within minutes if she was needed.

Fairy-lights adorned the exterior of the classically Greek-looking roughcast building that housed the restaurant and hotel, and Emily could hear the music and buzz of humanity before she even stepped out of her car. Edging inside through a crowded foyer, she took in the rich smell of foods like roast lamb and olives, garlic and eggplant. She caught the distinctive aroma of ouzo amongst the more familiar odours of beer and wine and felt faintly unwell.

To step into the middle of well-established gaiety was too much after the stressful day she'd had. Or maybe there had been too much to disappoint her and it had accumulated into a knot that was creating a distinctly sinking sensation in the pit of her stomach.

She moved further into the restaurant, which was clearly the hub of the evening's entertainment. A traditional Greek band was playing and the dance floor was alive with movement. Charles was parked near the doorway and he smiled at Emily, but she was prevented from moving towards him by Sophia, who sailed out from the crowd and gripped Emily's shoulder firmly.

'Emily! Darling!' One cheek was kissed and then the other. 'Have you met my daughter, Maria?'

'No. Hi.' Emily smiled at a much younger, feminine version of Mike who appeared beside Sophia and was holding a baby in her arms.

'Have a baby,' Maria instructed, thrusting the infant into Emily's arms. 'I have to find out what my other little monsters are up to.'

'She has four boys,' Sophia said happily. 'All under five.'

Maria was scanning the room. 'I can't see any of them,' she said. 'This isn't good.'

'I keep telling you, Maria—you should move home.' Sophia seemed to have forgotten Emily was there. 'We'll convert the bridal suite and make it self-contained. I can help with the children.' She followed Maria towards the dance floor. 'You could go back nursing whenever you wanted. The hospital's only a step away. I keep telling you this! Why won't you listen to your mother?'

George, dressed in traditional clothing of a pleated white skirt, colourful garters on white leggings and a matching waistcoat over the top of the tunic, came past, carrying a stack of plain white dinner plates. He winked at Emily. 'For later,' he said in a stage whisper. 'Don't tell Sophia!'

Emily shook her head. Separated from Charles by a group of people, including Kylie the hairdresser, who were having an animated conversation, Emily felt like a sombre island in a sea of happy people. She also felt firmly anchored by the surprisingly heavy baby she was holding.

She caught a glimpse of Sophia near a queue of children, headed by Max, the seven-year-old son of O and G surgeon Georgie Turner, who had the shadow of CJ close behind. The small boys were eyeing a trestle table laden with delicious-looking desserts that were obviously on the agenda for later.

Emily watched as Sophia flapped her hands at the children and then swooped to catch what had to be one of her grand-sons. The child shrieked with enough glee to be heard over the music and then wrapped his arms around his grand-mother's neck and kissed her soundly on the lips.

The conversation beside her was only a buzz because Emily was still thinking of what Sophia had been saying to Maria. She was desperate to have her grandchildren close by. Enough to offer a make-over of the hotel's highlight suite. Would she make the same offer to Mike? How perfect would that be? A home of their own with the most beautiful outlook imaginable and a private path to the beach.

Support—encouragement, even—for them both to con-tinue their careers to whatever level they desired after the children came along. The more time Sophia had with them the better. The more children the better.

As if to echo her thoughts, Emily spotted the now mobile train of small boys weaving their way through the dance floor and creating a hazard people seemed happy to accommo-date. They made way and then Emily could see one side of the area clearly, where a traditional Greek dance was taking place with a line of people who were linked by holding each other's arms.

In the midst of them was the most gorgeous woman Emily had ever seen. Tall and incredibly slender, she had dark, very curly hair that spiralled down to her waist. Tiny silver star clips glittered on her scalp. She clearly didn't know the steps to the dance and was laughing, but her ineptitude didn't matter because the men on either side of her were keeping the dance going.

And one of those men was Mike.

Emily had to look away. She found herself looking directly at Charles, and did her best to summon a smile. She jiggled the baby in her arms as he whimpered. And then Cal was nearby and it was easy to smile because he was looking happier than she had ever seen him look.

'You've missed most of the food,' he said in dismay. 'But don't worry—we haven't had dessert yet. And look at this!' He was clutching a fistful of cheques. 'We've raised at least five thousand dollars, and this is just the beginning. We'll have a swimming pool for the settlement in no time.'

Cal had his arm around Gina, who was alternately looking happy and proud and then sporting a slightly more anxious expression as she scanned the room to see where CJ had got to.

'He'll be into that Pavlova,' she warned Cal. 'And I wouldn't be surprised if he brings Rudolph in from the back. I'd better go and find him.'

'I'll come with you.'

Emily smiled at Charles again and Hamish who was beside him, fully intending to move closer and speak to them, but Mike had finally spotted her arrival. He broke away from the dancers and moved with purpose.

'Save me,' he implored as soon as he was close enough. 'I'm exhausted.'

'I'm not surprised. This is one hell of a party.'

'It's a Poulos party.' Mike grinned. 'You'd better get used to it.' He reached to take Maria's child from her arms. 'And this is a Poulos baby. Beware—it spits!'

Emily laughed. She turned to shake her head as George stopped to offer her a glass of ouzo. Then her attention was caught again for a moment by the sight of the gorgeous dark-haired woman on the dance floor. She was much easier to see now because someone had lifted her onto a table and she was dancing alone, to the accompaniment of hands clapping and feet stomping all around her.

And then she turned back to Mike and her heart stopped.

He was nuzzling his nephew. Dropping kisses onto the downy head and making the kind of cooing noises generic to besotted parents. He would look exactly like that holding his own child.

If the child was alive.

The horrible knowledge, burned into Emily's memory banks, of what it was like to hold a child that was no longer alive was way too easy to access today. Impossible to hold back, however hard she tried. And as that memory surfaced, Emily knew she could never go through that again.

Never.

Pregnancy just wasn't an option any more. Nine months of waiting to see if one's worst fears were going to be realised, and knowing the horror that awaited if they were, was an ordeal Emily couldn't face.

But she couldn't take the prospect of a family away from Mike. Or his family. The ripples would spread—just as they could do in Lucky's case.

Maybe they could adopt, she thought wildly. Maybe, if Megan didn't change her mind, they could adopt Lucky.

Mike was staring at her with the strangest look. 'What's up?'

As if Emily could have told him right then!

Not that she had the chance to say anything. George was back, determined that Emily should accept his hospitality— and his ouzo.

'I can't, George, but thank you. I'm on call.'

'Always she's on call!' Sophie steamed towards them and received a noisy kiss on the cheek from her husband. 'You work too hard, Emily.' She didn't wait for Emily to demur. She was gently tickling the baby Mike still held. 'Isn't he the most beautiful baby? Your babies will look just like this, Michael. If you ever get around to becoming a father!'

'I will, Ma.' Mike winked at Emily. 'I promise.'

Sophia sniffed loudly. 'We'll see.' She waved towards the dance floor. 'What's wrong with Anna, then? Beautiful girl. She's a nurse, Michael.'

Anna had to be the gorgeous creature with the stars in her hair who was still dancing on the table. Emily swallowed hard, her gaze riveted on Mike.

'Yes, you told me,' he was saying.

'She's come all the way from Melbourne.'

'Not just to meet me, I hope.'

'And she's *Greek,* Michael! What more could you want?'

Mike was making urgent signals to Emily with his eyebrows. Let me tell them, the eyebrows pleaded, and save me from being pushed into Anna's arms.

Emily just stared back, aware that that sinking sensation in her stomach had intensified to the point of pain. Maybe that was where Mike should be pushed. Towards a gorgeous Greek girl who could produce enough healthy babies to start her own kindergarten.

'I know exactly what I want, Ma,' Mike said firmly. 'And what's more, I've found it. Isn't that right, Emily?'

Heads swivelled in unison to stare at her and Emily, to her horror, had a sudden, irresistible urge to shake her head violently and deny everything. She wasn't ready for this. She couldn't set herself up for what could be the most devastating failure in her life by confirming Mike's statement.

She just *couldn't.*

'I don't understand,' Sophia said.

'*There* he is.' Maria swooped in from behind Emily and held out her arms. 'Give him back,' she ordered her brother. 'You get your own babies, Mickey. This one's mine.'

Mike relinquished the baby but ignored his sister. His expression, as he kept his gaze fixed on Emily, had gone from one of joyous confidence to puzzlement.

'What *did* you mean, Michael?' Sophia was tugging on her son's sleeve. '*Tell* me!'

'*Opa!*' Someone jostled Emily as they reached past to claim a glass of ouzo from George's tray.

'Come, Sophia.' George held his tray high. 'We have guests to look after. Talk to your son later.'

With a despairing headshake Sophia gave up and followed George.

Mike stared at Emily. 'What's going on?'

'I can't do this, Mike.'

'Can't do what? I wasn't making a public announcement here. I just wanted to tell my *family,* for God's sake.'

'Tell them what? That we're going to get married? That I'm going to provide the next set of Poulos grandchildren?' Emily felt like she was suffocating. She had to get out of here. 'It's not going to happen, Mike.'

'*What?*'

Emily didn't know what to say. He was already hurt that she hadn't come out and made their relationship known at least to his family. He had every right to be angry. He *would* be very angry when he realised she was talking about the whole relationship and not just telling anybody about it.

Unexpectedly, the need to find something to say vanished. Charles had arrived beside them as silently as he always did. A cellphone lay on his lap, as though it had been in very recent use.

'How much ouzo have you had, Mike?'

'None…yet.' Mike's tone was as heavy as the gaze that had Emily pinned. 'I think I might be about to start, though.'

'No. I need you.' Charles flicked his gaze towards Emily. 'And you.'

'What's happened?'

'Someone's collapsed. At the resort on Wallaby Island.'

'They've got an airfield.' Being unhelpful was very unlike Mike. 'Send the plane.'

'It's already out. That's why Christina isn't here.'

'I'm on call,' Emily told Charles. 'And I've got a new patient in ICU. I should really be back there now.'

'I'll go,' Charles said. 'I can monitor your patient. What I can't do is get in the helicopter and go and save a life. What are you two waiting for?'

Mike nodded curtly and headed for the door.

Emily looked at Charles, begging him silently not to send her on this mission. She couldn't claim that she didn't 'do' helicopters any more, though, could she?

It was how this whole thing had started—being sent on a mission with Mike.

So maybe it was fate decreeing that it turn a full circle. It was time to be honest and if that was enough to finish things, then so be it.

In the end, Emily just mirrored Mike's nod of acquiescence and followed him out the door.

CHAPTER TEN

'CROCODILE CREEK BASE HOSPITAL to Air Rescue 711. How do you read?'

Mike squeezed the radio mike button on the central stick control. 'Loud and clear. Go ahead.'

'Your call has been cancelled.'

'Say again?'

'Cancel, cancel. You are no longer required. Return to base.'

'Roger.'

The sound of a chuckle came through their headsets. 'Actually, my name's Craig.'

'Roger, Craig.' But the familiar humour didn't rate more than a wan smile and Mike cursed softly as he banked the helicopter to abort the mission. 'Waste of bloody time,' he muttered. 'What was that all about?'

'False alarm, I guess.' Emily was no happier than Mike.

Here they were shut in a box, without any wings, above a vast and probably very cold ocean, halfway between the mainland and Wallaby Island. They were alone—again—and they didn't need to be here at all.

Emily let the now established and rather grim silence continue as she dealt with a sneaking suspicion that Charles had somehow engineered precisely this situation.

Surely not!

'So…' Mike was now making an attempt to sound cheerful. 'You going to tell me what's going on in your head, then?'

'What do you mean?'

'I mean that I get the distinct impression that something's changed and I'm not going to like it, which is why you're avoiding talking to me.'

Upsetting someone who was responsible for keeping this box well above sea level did not seem like a sensible idea.

'I'm not avoiding talking to you,' Emily said. 'I've just had a bad day.' Oh, God! She sounded like Simon—telling her he was stressed at work when she knew perfectly well their relationship was all over bar the shouting.

'Hmm.' Mike was unimpressed. 'Funny, I thought that having someone who cares to talk to about "bad days" was part of what a relationship was all about.'

'It is,' Emily agreed uneasily.

'I also thought that you felt the same way about me as I do about you.'

'I *do*.'

'Doesn't feel like it. I get the impression that you'd rather make it all go away. You don't want to tell anybody because you think that's exactly what's going to happen.'

Emily was silent.

'I've got news for you, babe,' Mike said heavily. 'I'm not going away and I'm not going to take you back to base until you tell me what's going on.'

'You can't just fly round and round!'

'Why not?'

'Because I don't like it. I don't feel safe…especially when we're over the sea like this.'

'You mean you're not going to talk to me because you're nervous of being in the helicopter?'

Emily made a strangled noise that could have been taken either way. She wasn't really nervous of the helicopter any more but she was scared stiff of how Mike was going to react when she told him the truth about her failings. No way could she do that hundreds of feet up in the air!

'Right.' Mike seemed to have taken the sound for assent. With his mouth set in a grim line, he made a movement with his hands and feet and suddenly the helicopter was dropping.

Like a stone.

Emily barely repressed a scream of pure terror. '*Mike!* Oh, my God, what's *happening?*'

'Chill out,' he ordered briskly. 'I'm not about to kill you.'

It *felt* like they were both going to die.

The helicopter plummeted for what seemed for ever and then it levelled off with its skids so close to the sea Emily found she was holding her breath, waiting to plunge below the surface.

She screwed her eyes shut and waited for the impact.

And then she opened them again because she could feel the lack of forward momentum. They were hovering. Not over the water. In the pale moonlight outside, Emily could see the outlines of a tiny cove with high bluffs and a tumble of black rocks at their base. She could also see a small crescent of white sand, and by the time she realised what was happening Mike had touched down on the beach. He reached up and pushed the throttle closed and the rotors started to slow.

'What's wrong?' For a moment the relief at a successful emergency landing outweighed anything else.

'With the helicopter? Nothing.' Mike pulled off his helmet. 'Come on, out you get.'

'What? Why?'

'I want to talk to you.' Mike climbed out of his side of the helicopter, ducked under the slowly rotating blades, and came round to Emily's side. He pulled open the door. 'You didn't want to talk in the air,' he reminded her. 'So here we are. On the ground.'

Emily unclipped her harness. She pulled her helmet off and pushed past Mike to jump to the ground unaided. She stalked several metres away. Then she turned.

'You mean you scared the hell out of me for *nothing?*' Anger sparked and then exploded into white-hot fury. 'You *bastard!*'

'I want to talk to you,' Mike said calmly. 'That's hardly "nothing".'

'How *could* you?' Emily shouted. 'Today, of *all* days!'

'What's so special about today?' Mike wasn't as calm as he was trying to sound. There was a dangerous quality about him right now as though he, too, was capable of the kind of fury Emily was exhibiting. 'Is it the day we're *not* going to let people know we're in love? That we're *not* going to announce our intention to spend the rest of our lives together?'

Emily's fury evaporated into the night like a reverse tornado. This was it. The moment she had to tell Mike the truth and take whatever consequences it might bring.

'You've changed your mind, haven't you? You don't want to marry me.'

'It's not that, Mike. I want that more than anything.' The gap between them seemed to have stretched into a canyon. '*You* might want to change your mind.'

'And why would I want to do that?'

'Because I don't think I can be what you want me to be.'

'What?' Mike took a step closer to Emily then stopped. He shook his head, bewildered. 'I don't understand. How can you *not* be what you already *are?*'

'I'm talking about your expectations. Your family's expectations. For me to be your wife and the—'

'You have a hang-up about marriage?' Mike interrupted. 'Fine. We'll live in sin till death us do part.'

'And the mother of your children.'

Mike frowned. 'I'd be upset if you wanted to be the mother of someone *else's* children, sure, but—'

Emily could feel a kind of vice closing around her. Imprisoning her. 'But that's why it can never work. I'm sorry, Mike. I didn't realise I'd feel like this and maybe it's just because of today but—'

'Hold it!' Mike held up a hand. 'That's at least the second time you've made a reference to today. What's been so bad about it? That patient you mentioned to Charles who's in ICU?'

Emily shook her head.

'Something else? You're still worried about Megan?'

A nod and then a shake. 'Yes, but that's not what I meant.'

Mike took another step closer. 'What do you mean, babe?'

'I mean the day. The date. I'd forgotten until I started filling in charts this morning. I don't know *how* I forgot because I've been thinking about it a lot ever since Lucky was found.'

Mike ran stiff fingers through his hair in a gesture of frustration, tousling the curls even more than they had been naturally. 'You've lost me.'

'It's ten years ago. Today.' Emily took a long and shaky inward breath. 'It would have been my son's tenth birthday today...if he'd lived.'

Mike could have been turned to stone. His face—his whole body—went utterly still. 'You had a *baby?*'

'Ten years ago.'

'With that guy you were engaged to?'

'It was the only reason he was going to marry me. When it turned out to be a stillbirth, he was off like a shot.'

Mike was silent for a long, long moment.

'What was his name?'

'Cameron. I told you about him.'

'I'm not talking about the bastard that got you pregnant, babe. What was your baby's name?'

A nasty, prickling sensation ran through Emily's limbs to settle in her chest. The question was shockingly callous.

'He didn't have a name. Why would he?'

'Why wouldn't he?'

The shock had worn off. Emily was angry again. Mike was supposed to love her. Why was he making something worse when it was already more than painful enough?

'Because no one wanted him,' she said bitterly.

'You did,' Mike suggested quietly.

'No.' Emily folded her arms tightly around her body. 'I didn't want to be a single mother. I didn't want a baby that wasn't going to have a father or…or a family.' She turned away from Mike and walked a couple of steps. 'I didn't have a family any more. I would have had no money. No career. *Nothing.*'

'You would have had your baby.'

Emily whirled to face Mike again. 'Why are you doing this to me? It's not fair. You said you *loved* me!'

'Oh, I do, babe.' Mike walked towards Emily. 'I'm doing this because I think you're letting it put up a wall to your future. *Our* future. Whether or not we end up having kids doesn't matter a damn. But your happiness matters a lot more to me than mine does right now. What happened in the past shouldn't be allowed to destroy a future. I don't think you've ever been able to let go of your past because I don't think anybody helped you grieve when you should have.'

He was close enough to touch her now. And he did. The softest touch that gave just a promise of the comfort available.

'Did he have a funeral?'

Emily's head jerked in a negative movement. Her throat felt

tight. 'Cameron took care of all that. They took him away after I held him for a while and I never saw him again.'

'It's haunted you ever since, though, hasn't it? You think of him on his birthday. And when you see other children, I bet. Especially babies. No wonder you feel so strongly about getting Megan to accept Lucky. I understand, Emily. I love you. For what you are right now—not what you've been in the past or even what you will be in the future. None of that matters because you always have been and always will be *you*…and that's who I love.'

The tightness was threatening to suffocate Emily. The love and acceptance she was being offered was too huge to accept.

Mike stepped even closer and his arms came around Emily. He bent his head so that his lips were against her hair, and when he spoke, the words were as gentle as summer rain.

'*You* gave him a name, didn't you?'

Emily finally nodded because Mike had been patient enough to wait. The tightness had become pain now—spreading through her entire body.

His arms tightened, too. 'What was it?'

The word came out as a hoarse cry that Emily didn't recognise as her own voice. '*Ben…*'

It hit her then, like it never had before. The name had never been spoken aloud.

Never bestowed.

Doing so now, even after so many years, gave that lost baby an identity. Made it somehow far more real. Fresh again and so, *so* painful. Sobs were torn from Emily's soul and her knees buckled with the weight of her grief.

But she didn't fall. Mike's arms held her as she crumpled and he came with her, kneeling on the sand and holding her tightly. Rocking her and holding her like an anchor as the storm hit.

And as her sobs finally diminished and the shaking ceased, Emily realised that something fundamental had changed for ever. What had always been a private ghost was now something shared. And that made it real again. But this time her baby had a name. And she had, finally, been given permission to mourn his loss.

Nothing could have touched her more deeply. Could have welded her so permanently, heart and soul, to the person who had understood... She had to move so that she could see Mike's face, touch it as she spoke to him.

'I love you,' she said. 'I can't even begin to tell you how much.'

'That's exactly how I feel.' Mike's gaze searched her face. 'Are you OK, babe?'

'I'm exhausted,' Emily admitted. 'I don't think I've ever felt so drained in my life.' Then her lips curved in a soft smile. 'But I don't think I've ever felt so good either. You've given me something I never thought I would ever have, Mike.'

'What's that?'

'I'm not sure yet. Acceptance, I think. For wiping out what I've always seen as an ultimate failure. I feel like something's been torn out of me. Something dark that shouldn't have been there.'

Mike simply nodded and tilted Emily's face so that he could kiss her. 'I've given you something else, too,' he murmured. 'If you still want it.'

'What's that?'

'Me.'

Emily smiled properly this time. 'Oh, I want it. In fact, I think I'm ready to tell the whole world just how much I want it.'

'Cool. Maybe we could start with a radio message to base. I'd hate them to think we've gone down in the drink.'

'We did go down.' Emily shuddered at the memory. 'We

dropped like a stone and you promised you'd never let that happen.'

'It was an emergency,' Mike said gravely. 'Called for desperate measures.' He helped Emily to her feet. 'Shall we?'

It was only a short journey back up the coast to Crocodile Creek but it created a sense of distance and gave Emily time to recover from the emotional wringer she'd just been through.

What an incredible roller-coaster of a week it had been, thanks largely to the man now guiding his aircraft back into its hangar, hopefully for the rest of the night. She would never doubt the strength of Mike's love ever again. And she would never doubt herself as long as she was near him.

He was smiling as the huge door to the hangar rolled shut. 'They'll still be partying at the Athina. Do you feel up to popping in just for a few minutes?'

'I'd like that. We've got something to tell everybody, haven't we?'

'Only if you want to. I'm happy to keep it a secret for a while if you want some more time.'

Emily shook her head firmly. 'I want everybody to know. Especially your mother.' She looked down at the flight suit she was wearing. 'I suppose we should get changed again.'

'Nah. Let's go as we are. A matched pair.'

'Can we do something else first? It won't take very long.'

Mike's eyes gleamed. 'Sure, babe. What—here? Shall I open the hangar again?'

'No!' Emily intended to give him a shove but found herself swept into his arms and kissed very thoroughly instead. As soon as she was released in order to let her breathe, she took the opportunity to whisper in Mike's ear.

He smiled. 'Good idea. Let's do it.'

Hand in hand they walked into Crocodile Creek Base

Hospital. Somehow, Emily was not surprised to see Charles gliding towards them along the first corridor they entered. He was at eye level with their linked hands and he was smiling as he raised his gaze.

'Successful mission, then?'

Mike blinked. 'You don't mean you—'

'Don't ask,' Emily advised. She grinned at their medical director. 'Very successful mission, thank you, sir.'

'You're both officially off duty, by the way,' Charles told them. 'Just in case you were thinking of going back to the Athina to celebrate anything.'

'He worries me sometimes,' Mike murmured as he and Emily continued their journey.

'How come?'

'He sees too much. Sometimes I get the feeling he might know more about us than we do.'

'He cares about us, that's all. When you care enough, you can see things other people can't.'

'And he can sneak around and eavesdrop. That's got to help.'

'He's a lovely man,' Emily said stoutly. 'And I think I'll ask him to give me away at our wedding.'

They tiptoed into the hospital's nursery. The lights were dimmed and Grace sat at her desk, reading a romance novel. She glanced up, smiled and dropped her gaze again.

'Be with you in a minute,' she whispered. 'I've *got* to find out how this ends.'

Mike and Emily went to Lucky's crib. Some of the soft toy gifts had found their way into the nursery and a toy tiger sat on one end of the crib.

The other end was empty.

Emily's mouth fell open in a silent cry of consternation. She looked back at Grace. Had Lucky's nurse been so caught up in her book she had been unaware of an abduction taking place?

Then Mike's grip on her hand tightened. She turned and there, in the soft glow of a floor-level nightlight, she saw the figure in the armchair. Someone cradling Lucky as she held his bottle.

'*Megan,*' Emily gasped. 'Oh…'

Megan looked up but only for a split second before her gaze dropped again to the infant in her arms.

'He *is* beautiful, isn't he?'

'Yes,' Mike said softly. 'He sure is.'

Megan glanced up again. 'And he really is *mine?*'

Emily had to swallow the lump in her throat. 'He really is.'

'And I can keep him if I want to?' Megan saw her answer in the faces watching her and she sighed.

'I had a dream,' she told them quietly. 'That night I got really sick and you guys came to get me. I dreamt that I was holding my baby and he was alive. I could feel how warm he was. I could even *smell* him, and…' Megan's voice cracked. 'And I wanted to die, you know? Because I thought that was the only way I *would* ever get to hold him.'

'You're holding him now.' Mike's voice was oddly gruff. 'He's your son, Megan.'

'I can't give him away. I know it's not going to be easy but I want to try and be a good mother.'

'You won't have to do it by yourself,' Emily said with conviction. 'We'll help you.'

'Have you thought of a name for him?' Mike asked.

Megan nodded shyly. 'Jackson.'

Emily tried it out. 'Jackson Cooper. I like that.' She gave Megan a curious glance. 'What made you change your mind about seeing him?'

'Dunno. I'd been reading those magazines you gave me and I couldn't get to sleep. I kept thinking about that picture of the girl from that TV show and her baby. She looked so happy.'

'Things will get happier for you, too, Megan.'

'Shh…' Megan adjusted the hold she had on the tiny baby. 'He's nearly asleep.'

Emily shushed. There was really nothing more to say just now, was there? She stood there, clutching Mike's hand, gazing at the young mother and child and that raw patch on her soul— the hole from which the name of her baby had been torn—was suddenly filled with something warm. And wonderful.

And Emily knew she'd been right about that omen. She would have another child of her own one day.

Mike's baby.

It was a gift that might, to some degree, show the depth of the love she had for this man. There was nothing she couldn't face now.

Now that she was finally whole.

They stole away from the nursery a short time later.

'Mike?'

'Yeah, babe?'

'I love you.'

'I love you, too.'

'I do want to marry you.'

'I should hope so.'

'And…and I want to have a baby. *Your* baby.'

Joy added an extra glitter to those dark eyes. Or was it due to unshed tears? 'Are you sure, Em?'

'Absolutely. I know it'll be all right this time.'

'Of course it will.' Mike shot a sideways glance down at Emily. 'Want to spit for luck anyway?'

Emily shook her head. 'I've given up spitting. It's unhygienic. And besides…' She stood on tiptoe and put her arms around Mike's neck, offering a kiss that he accepted very willingly.

'Besides what?' he queried after so much time had passed that Emily had to make an effort to remember what she had intended to say.

'We don't need luck any more,' she told him firmly.

'We don't?'

'We've got each other. How much luckier could we get?'

Mike smiled and then kissed her again. 'So true. Maybe we had better leave some of that luck out there for everybody else. I think I've had more than my fair share in the last week or so.'

'You and me both.'

'And now…' Mike bent and swept Emily into his arms, carrying her away from the hospital and up the hill towards the Athina.

Towards her future.

Their future.

PREGNANT WITH
HIS CHILD

Lilian
DARCY

Lilian Darcy has written nearly eighty books. Happily married with four active children and a very patient cat, she enjoys keeping busy and could probably fill several more lifetimes with the things she likes to do—including cooking, gardening, quilting, drawing and travelling. She currently lives in Australia but travels to the United States as often as possible to visit family. Lilian loves to hear from readers. You can write to her at: PO Box 532, Jamison PO, Macquarie, ACT 2614, Australia, or email her at: lilian@ liliandarcy.com.

CHAPTER ONE

DR CHRISTINA FARRELLY had only one significant item left on her 'to do' list for today. She hadn't written it down. It wasn't something she was likely to overlook.

Dump Joe.

Driving to the airport to pick him up in the sweet, warm darkness of a typical North Queensland autumn night, she felt sick about it.

Heartsick.

Sick to her stomach.

She didn't want to do this.

And even this early in the piece it wasn't working out according to plan, anyhow.

His flight from Cairns had been delayed and he was getting in six hours late, which meant that the almost bearable scenario of having a private late-afternoon coffee at her place while they talked about it had morphed into the utterly non-bearable scenario of delivering him direct to the doctors' residence at eleven o'clock on a Sunday night, gabbling at him, 'Dumping you, sorry, but fixed you up a room here,' and laying rubber all the way down the hospital driveway as she screeched her car off into the night.

No.

She really could not do *Dump Joe* that way.

Not when she didn't want to end their relationship at all.

Maybe the flight delay was an acceptable reason to put it off.

The airport was only a few kilometres from her house, an old-fashioned Queenslander a couple of streets back from the commercial heart of Crocodile Creek, which she'd inherited from her grandmother several years ago. The big creek itself flowed in a slow, lazy curve between the town and the airport, while a smaller tributary curved with equal laziness between the airport and the hospital before joining forces with Crocodile Creek just a hundred metres before it spilled into the ocean.

The main road crossed Crocodile Creek's wide stream-bed over a bridge that was slated to be replaced very soon. Construction on the new one, a hundred metres upstream, had recently begun. Christina would be sad to see the old bridge go, but, then, maybe she had a tendency to hold onto things…hopes…relationships…for longer than she should.

Dump Joe.

Yes, no excuses, no delaying tactics, just do it.

To get to the modest-sized passenger terminal, she had to skirt around the emergency services headquarters and the runway for fixed-wing aircraft, with its rows of night-time guidance lights staring at her balefully the entire way.

The whole place was close to deserted at this hour. Joe's flight would have been the last one in tonight. She saw it still taxiing towards the terminal, bringing Joe ever closer to an emotional crisis—or merely an incomprehensible, irritating disappointment?—that he had no inkling of as yet.

Other people did have an inkling. Mike Poulos had guessed that something was wrong last week when he and Christina had flown together in the Remote Rescue chopper to bring in a heart-attack patient from an isolated location, but he wouldn't have said much to anyone else, both because he was a decent, non-gossipy kind of guy and because—well—he had much better things to think about right now.

He and Emily Morgan, after knowing each other for a good eighteen months without a ripple to ruffle the surface, had suddenly discovered they were madly, ocean-churningly in love, *marriage-mindedly* in love.

And, oh, lord, she shouldn't think about it in such a bitchy way, she liked both of them a lot, but…how come everyone else could connect the dots and come up with the obvious answer when Joe Barrett wouldn't even admit to the existence of dots in the first place?

Turning into the car park, Christina felt the tears starting and blinked them back. Shoot, if she was crying about this now, before she'd even done it, said it—how bad was the actual conversation going to be?

And how bad was it going to be when the news had travelled all around the hospital?

Or had it done so already?

In a foolish attempt to distance herself from the reality of what she was doing, she'd involved Brian Simmons in his role as hospital administrator, asking him to organise the room for Joe at the doctors' residence. This was the original bush nursing hospital, over a hundred years old, and it was situated on the grounds of the current, much more modern set of hospital buildings that provided the nexus for Crocodile Creek's outback air medical service.

Most of the single doctors lived there, but Christina never had, since she had her grandmother's house, with its lush jungle of garden screening the cool privacy of a wraparound veranda, its antique-filled rooms, its peace and tranquillity. And because she had a spare room in that house, and because Joe was only in Crocodile Creek for one week in four, he'd become her part-time boarder two years ago.

He hadn't stayed in that limited role for very long.

The doctors' residence was a noisy, welcoming and very pleasant place, and Christina dropped in there quite often. She liked most of the medical staff currently living there, but she didn't want them asking questions behind her back, worrying about her, telling each other that they didn't understand what was going on because Christina and Joe had always seemed so *good* together.

They would do and say all of that, of course.

There was only one factor that might dilute it a little. The past couple of weeks at Crocodile Creek had been pretty dramatic ones, starting with Simon-the-cardiologist and Kirsty-the-intern sneaking off into the sunset together, followed by the far more serious discovery of a critically ill newborn left for dead after an outback rodeo, and a head-on collision in the outlying settlement of Wygera which had left four young aboriginal kids dead and others still hospitalised down south.

'People do have other things to think about, Christina Farrelly,' she scolded herself, punctuating the statement with a wrenching pull on the handbrake of the car.

The newborn was doing well now. He had a mother, Megan Cooper, who'd almost died herself following serious post-partum complications on top of the traumatic belief that her baby had been born dead. Over the past few days, Megan had slowly begun to recover. And he had a name.

Jackson.

He didn't yet have a known father—Megan wasn't saying anything on that subject—or grandparents who'd been told of his existence. Meanwhile, the community at Wygera would take months to find its feet again...

Yes, everyone in Crocodile Creek most definitely had other things to think about.

But right now all Christina could think about was that mental 'to do' list, and the item right at the top of it.

Dump Joe.

When she reached the arrivals area of the almost-empty terminal, passengers were just starting to come through the gate. There were no fancy jetways at this air-port. Joe would be walking across the open tarmac with the other tired arrivals, while the luggage-cart swung in an arc around them through the humid press of diesel fumes, beating them to the baggage claim area by a scant minute.

With the flight only half-full, Christina had no trouble spotting him. He stood half a head above the tallest of the other passengers, and he was broader and stronger, with darker skin, a wider smile... He had always seemed to her to have so much more than anyone else she'd ever met.

More heart.

More energy.

More strategies for keeping their part-time relationship in exactly the place he wanted it.

Which had slowly and inexorably become a place she just couldn't bear for it to stay.

Dump Joe.

'Hi,' she said, her voice wobbly.

'Tink.' He buried his face in her neck, inhaling the scent of her hair in open appreciation. 'Oh, Tink!' He was the only person who ever called her Tink. Tunk, really, with his strong New Zealand accent. 'Hell, I've missed you.

Mmm, you smell so good!' And he was the only person who ever made her feel this way when he hugged her.

Tingling.

Exultant.

Weak with need.

Where she belonged.

And, tonight, utterly miserable.

She felt his mouth press hard against her hair, her cheekbone, the corners of her lips. Hungry kisses, but they promised nothing.

'I am wiped!' he said. 'Seven hours in the transit lounge in Cairns.'

'Do you have a bag?'

'Nope. Everything's here.' He patted the heavily packed overnight bag that swung on his shoulder. Beneath the white band of his T-shirt sleeve, the smooth skin of his upper arm bulged with muscle, and the thin, braided shape of his blue-black tattoo was visible. It looked like a bracelet, and made a clearer statement about his part-Maori ancestry than did the honey colour of his skin. 'Let's go. Are you on flight duty tomorrow?'

'Yes, I'm due back here at seven, for a clinic run.' On the opposite side of the runway, really, but it counted as the same place.

'And I'm rostered on from eight. Still, we can grab a bit of time tonight, eh?' His dark eyes flicked down at her, with that familiar sense of a shared secret in their depths, and the total confidence that she wanted exactly what he did. Her body stirred and her heart fell.

'Yes, we need some time.' The words were neutral. Far too neutral. He should have noticed. Or was he simply too tired to hear them as significant?

Dump Joe.

She really, really had not wanted to have to do it like this. For his sake, or for hers. They would have to talk at her place. She wasn't going to say everything here in the airport car park, or with the car engine idling outside the doctors' residence.

As they drove past the hospital, he commented, 'Quite a few lights on there tonight, in the house and in the main building.'

'We've had a busy couple of weeks.' She filled in some of the details. The personal as well as the medical.

There was Cal's engagement to Dr Gina Lopez, the American cardiologist he'd known in Townsville five years ago, and who'd turned out to have given birth to his son, CJ, now four years old. There were Kirsty and Simon, Emily and Mike, the car accident at the Wygera settlement, and darling, heroic baby Jackson and his mother.

'He has von Willebrand's disease, on top of everything else, brave little sweetheart,' she finished. The rare blood disorder had been diagnosed after Dr Lopez had been alerted by the unusual amount of bleeding from the baby's cord stump. It was treatable and shouldn't cause ongoing problems now that they knew about it.

'So the mother has it, too?' Joe asked.

'No, she doesn't, and neither do the mother's parents— although her dad's health is pretty iffy in other areas, apparently—which means the carrier must be the father. But so far Megan isn't telling us who or where he is. Dr Wetherby's father had von Willebrand's, apparently, but if there's a family connection he knows about, he's not saying. It could be a coincidence.'

'Whew!'

'That pretty much sums it up.'

She hated having so much news to dump...*dump*...on

him all in one big, stodgy mass. It always happened, even when events in Crocodile Creek weren't nearly as fast-moving as they'd been this time around. Joe spent three weeks out of four at home in New Zealand.

Or possibly, for all she knew, on the far side of a worm-hole leading to a distant galaxy.

No, OK, that was a slight exaggeration.

Over the two years they'd been a part-time couple, he had let slip a few salient facts. He lived in Auckland. He'd done his medical degree at Auckland University. He worked in a group general practice. He wasn't married. (But he could be lying. Was he lying? Would she know?) He had a mother, a younger half-sister, a stepdad.

But he made it painfully clear how much he hated talking about his life at home. He never phoned her from New Zealand. He'd given her both his home and work numbers there 'for an emergency' but the handful of times she'd eagerly dialled those, early on in their relationship, he'd again made it clear that the calls weren't wanted.

He didn't do it nastily. Christina wasn't convinced he had a nasty bone in his body.

He did it with an upbeat, warm-voiced energy. 'Listen, Tink, I can't talk, OK?' Didn't suggest a better time. Didn't phone her back. Didn't mention the phone calls the next time she saw him.

She'd begun to feel that she was the equivalent of a sailor's girl in every port. True, Joe kept coming back to the same port, and it was apparently a port he really, really enjoyed, but that didn't change the basic fact about their relationship. Christina's life was an open book to him. She'd told him an-ecdotes about her childhood, dreams she had for the future, beliefs about what mattered in life. But in return she was his 'rest and recreation', his R&R, as the American navy seamen who occasionally berthed to the south in Townsville phrased it, and that was very plainly all he wanted from her.

Which did suggest that he might be married.

No! No...

She'd never caught him out in a lie, and didn't want to launch into a paranoid confrontation. It wasn't her style.

And it almost didn't matter if he *was* married. The point was, for whatever reason—and the fact that she had no real idea of the reason was a problem in itself—this relationship was going nowhere, while her biological clock had hitched a ride on a racehorse some time last year and was contemplating the imminent switch to a faster mode of transportation.

Christina was thirty-three. She had a sensible head on her shoulders. She wanted marriage and a family with a decent, honourable man. She didn't want to stay perpetually at the 'young, in love and having fun' stage with a man she only saw for a handful of hours each month, no matter how nice that was while it was happening. Joe knew that. She hadn't said it straight out, or put on any pressure on him, but he had to know it from the way she talked about her brother's kids in Brisbane, her admiration for her parents' marriage.

If there had been any sign of a deepening in Joe's commitment, if he'd started sharing more of his life in New Zealand with her, if she knew why he kept the boundaries so firmly in place, she would have been prepared to wait a lot longer, but there was none of that. He was a couple of years younger than her, but that was no excuse.

She was also the faithful type, and if she was ever going to find a man who wanted what she wanted, she was going to have to get Joe Barrett well and truly out of her system before she started looking.

Which didn't give her the luxury of putting things off and had thus led her to where she was right now, at eleven o'clock on a Sunday evening, approaching the past-its-use-by-date bridge over Crocodile Creek with a gorgeous man beside her in the car.

A man who was also past his use-by date.

A man she was about to dump.

Even though she really, really didn't want to do it.

There was a grey humped shape lying in the road, just a metre before the bridge.

'Kangaroo,' Joe said, sitting up higher in the passenger seat. He craned to look at it as Christina slowed the car. 'Was that there ten minutes ago when you came across?'

'I don't think so.' She skirted it and the tarred planks of the two-lane bridge went thunkety-thunkety-thunk as she drove across. 'No,' she added, more certain about it now. 'No, it wasn't.' Because she'd been thinking about the bridge, about not wanting to see it go. She'd have noticed.

'It's dangerous, anyhow. We should stop and get it off the road.'

She slowed further and looked for a place to turn, which was easy to find at this time of night when there was so little traffic. The kangaroo had been unlucky, in the wrong place at the wrong time. Back on the far side of the bridge, she parked safely on the shoulder and walked across to the still, silent shape in Joe's wake.

'Yep, it's still warm,' he said. He felt its neck. 'But it's dead, all right, poor thing.'

Except that just then it moved.

No, not the mother, Christina realised, the joey in her pouch.

'Crikey!' Joe said. 'There's a little fella in there!'

'Don't start doing your crocodile hunter imitation, Joe Barrett!'

She couldn't help laughing. For a man who'd just spent around eleven hours in transit, on top of a solid week of general practice, he'd summoned up his energy and his good humour pretty fast. He was always like this. Loved the chance to get a laugh out of a situation. Never complained for long, just got on with things.

The way she had to do, as soon as they got home…

'I could do my British wildlife documentary presenter instead,' he offered.

She summoned another smile. 'No, because you're terrible at him, too. Just be nice and male and masterful for me and tell me what we're going to do.'

Because I'm tired and stressed and I wanted an excuse to put off the dumping-you conversation, but not this kind of an excuse.

'Well, we can't leave it, Tink.' He was working as he spoke, carefully dragging the warm, soft body of the mother safely off the road and turning her so that they could gain access to the pouch.

'I know that. I wouldn't want to.' She gathered herself, focused on the right priorities. 'There's the park, up towards the mountains—would that be best? They have a sanctuary and an animal nursery enclosure. We'd have to wake up the ranger.'

'He'll handle it.' From the size of the movement they'd seen, this joey should be big enough to survive the loss of its mother, as long as it hadn't been injured itself.

A ute rumbled across the bridge with a load of bulging garbage bags bouncing in the open tray at the back. It slowed.

'You right there, mate?'

Christina recognised Bill Doyle, owner of the Black Cockatoo Hotel.

'Dead mother, living joey,' Christina summarised quickly. 'Hi, Bill. It's me, Christina Farrelly.'

'Oh, hello, Doc. You're branching out into the vet business now?'

'Something like that. We thought we'd take it up to Atherton National Park, to the ranger.'

'Right you are, then.' He nodded, and drove off, happy to leave them to it. He was obviously heading to the town rubbish tip.

Christina and Joe shared the task of examining the joey, which was half-grown and should have been thrashing its gangly, growing legs around in terror, but wasn't. Huddled in the pouch, it had its eyes open and it was breathing fast, but there was no obvious sign of injury.

'We do need to get it to the ranger,' Christina said. 'We can't feed it or take care of it ourselves.'

'I'll grab my sweatshirt from the car,' Joe said. 'We'll wrap it in that.'

It was awkward and both of them narrowly escaped getting scratched by the sharp toenails at the end of those long legs, but once Joe had the animal on his lap in the car, all bundled up tight, it seemed to settle again.

Christina got behind the wheel and drove.

The highway leading to the south-west was dark and empty, apart from one lone long-haul truck that roared past at one point, making her wonder about the driver's schedule and the chemical means he might use to keep himself going. On a couple of the main highways down south, cameras captured licence plate details at certain points on the route and truckers were fined for making the journey in too short a time, but out here that wasn't practical. The accident rate was higher than it should have been.

'How's he doing?' she asked Joe.

'He's good. Quiet. Breathing.'

She risked a glance across.

Joe and a joey, both good, quiet and breathing.

Her stomach sank as she thought again about rocking the boat.

The truck slowed. Was it stopping for him? It had to be.

Yes! Yes!

The big rig ground to a laborious halt and he ran after it, eager to seize on the first piece of good luck he'd had all day. Make that all year. His whole life, it felt like.

This was an omen.

'Looking for a ride somewhere, mate?' the driver said.

'Yes.' Anywhere. 'Over the ranges.'

'Hop in, then.'

It felt so good. To be off his feet. To be moving. He'd been standing there for hours and no one had even thought about picking him up. Did he look that much like a dead-beat or a criminal?

Evidently.

Other people had thought so. Her father, for example.

Her.

His love.

The reason for this journey.

His mates would laugh if they knew he thought this way about her. Like some soppy male lead in a soppy film who can get any girl he wants but can't forget The One.

Not that you can get any girl you want, you drop-kick. How many do you even meet?

But he didn't care. He was the soppiest of the lot. He just wanted her.

He'd been turfed off her parents' property in a blast of anger so intense it had driven him five hundred kilometres north, and he'd really believed the old man might kill him if he went back.

But the loss of her from his life had taken the heart out of him. He should have fought harder for her, he should have stood up to her father's anger. Why had it taken him so long to get it right? Why had he let other people make his decisions for him?

He couldn't understand the person he'd been back then. He'd toughened up since, a lot, because it had been months ago, and you'd never know now that he'd grown up pampered in Sydney—private school, bloody violin lessons, of course you can learn to ride if you want, darling, which had meant tutoring in dressage, not the bush horsemanship that he knew was in his blood.

So if the drought-crazed old man killed him, or tried to, so be it. He'd fight back a lot harder than he could have done six months ago. He'd had his twenty-second birthday last week. He'd shaken off a lifetime of parental mollycoddling. He could show her, now, how much his love was worth and maybe she'd leave with him this time, leave her father and her mum, and it'd all be OK.

Yes, sitting here high in the cabin of the big rig he could see it, how it would all work out, as long as he could get to her, see her and talk to her and be with her even just for a few precious hours, show her what he was made of, before he had to turn around again and head back north tomorrow, noon at the latest, or lose his job and the three months of precious back pay that was owing to him.

His boss hadn't wanted to let him go at all, but he'd managed to squeeze just these few days before the big cattle drive began. They were moving the beasts hundreds of kilometres between properties, starting next week, and taking a route through rough country that stirred something deep in his spirit. If he could hear from her own mouth that she still loved him, he'd go droving with the feeling that he owned the whole world.

'As far as the turn-off to Mount Evelyn. Is that far enough for you?' he heard.

'Sorry?'

'I said I'm only going as far as the turn-off to Mount Evelyn.'

'Right. OK.' His heart dropped like a spent firework.

Talk about omens!

This guy was going a tenth of the distance he needed. Less. He'd never get there before morning. His stomach rumbled. He should have stopped for a hamburger and chips in Crocodile Creek, but he hadn't wanted to lose the precious time. That seemed stupid now. He wasn't going to get to her tonight. He'd have to go back, leave it for weeks more. He hadn't thought this through.

Talk about omens.

This one, he'd listen to.

He couldn't see that he had a choice.

It was almost midnight by the time Joe and Christina reached the park entrance. The boom gate was closed and locked, but a four-wheel-drive such as the light one she drove could skirt around it if she moved a couple of half-rotted logs.

Joe had reached the same conclusion. 'If you take Junior here…'

'No, I'll do it. He's quiet, don't disturb him.' She jumped out while she was still speaking, and the job was easy in her sensible jeans, T-shirt and running shoes. The T-shirt wasn't quite adequate warmth-wise. They'd climbed around six hundred metres from the coastal plain, and at this hour on a May night, it was chilly.

'You're an Amazon,' Joe teased her when she got back in the car.

I'm going to have to be, she thought. And she wasn't thinking physically.

They knocked at the front door of the ranger's house five minutes later, and roused his wife. 'Don't worry, I was up with the baby anyway. Oh, look at him, he's a gorgeous little fella, isn't he? Yes, we can take care of him, he's big enough, and we have a couple of others so he won't be lonely.'

She offered a cup of tea, and her sleepy husband appeared, but Joe and Christina looked at each other and wordlessly reached the same conclusion—which happened quite often. They didn't want to keep these two up in the middle of the night, or themselves out, driving on an inadequate rural road, any later than necessary.

'We should get back,' Joe said. 'Shouldn't we, Tink? We're both working full days tomorrow.'

This time he drove, which gave Christina too much time to think.

I can't do it tonight. But I won't sleep if I don't. Oh, I won't sleep anyhow. It'll be impossible in the morning, we'll both be scrambling to get out the door and get to the hospital and the base. I can't leave it, though, not if I'm really going to say it. That room is waiting for him, and people will be wondering what on earth is going on. Maybe now, while we're driving?

She got ready. Tried to. Took a deep breath and prepared herself to say his name. *Joe, we have to talk.* But then she let the moment pass. She was a coward!

They came to a bend and he veered around it, seeming not fully in control. His breath hissed out sharply between his teeth. 'That's not right,' he said.

'What, Joe?' She touched his shoulder instinctively, her open hand dwarfed by its warm bulk.

'Think we've got a flat tyre.' He slowed the vehicle carefully and pulled onto the verge.

She erupted into silent, stress-filled laughter. 'You are joking! Just tell me you're joking, Joe Barrett!'

'Uh, no. That's just slightly the last straw, isn't it?' Joe said.

'You got that right!' *More than you know, Joe.*

If she believed in omens, she would have taken good notice of this one, and decided that somebody up there really didn't want her to dump Joe tonight. But she didn't believe in omens—didn't believe her personal life warranted quite that much cosmic attention—so she just gritted her teeth and thought, *Maybe while we're changing the tyre?*

Which was indeed impressively flat. It was the front left one, while the bend Joe had taken curved to the right. No wonder he had struggled to keep control of the vehicle.

As they'd done when they'd examined the joey, they worked together in silent harmony. Joe set the hazard lights flashing. Christina got out the jack. Joe positioned it and wound it up till it was in the right position to take the vehicle's weight. Joe stomped his foot on the wrench to loosen the nuts while Christina detached the spare from its big bracket on the rear door.

He was so strong! She felt a crippling wave of longing

wash over her as she looked at him, and it was hard to drag her eyes away. *I won't be able to look at him this way after tonight. I won't have the right to. And it'll hurt too much.*

Together, they took off the damaged wheel and manoeuvred the spare into position, then took turns tightening the nuts.

Joe grinned at her when they were done. 'Love a woman with axle grease on her nose,' he said. 'Ver-r-ah sexy.'

'Joe, we have to—'

Talk.

Too late. He kissed her, a raunchy, confident, full-bodied, sweet-tasting smooch on the mouth, anchored in place with his hand, which was no doubt leaving more grease on her jaw… Oh, and probably a smudgy handprint on her backside as well. When he pulled away, he was still grinning, and he was so gorgeous, big and full of life and gorgeous. She couldn't utter any fateful words to him right now.

She couldn't have uttered them anyhow. They weren't alone.

'Hey!'

'What the heck—?'

'Hey, wait! Wait!' A figure came jogging towards them, out of breath and frantic for their attention.

Joe waved and nodded, then muttered, 'Not our night, is it?' He put the jack away and closed the back door of the four-wheel-drive. He and Christina both stood waiting and watching as the figure approached. It was a man, a young man, not nearly as big and tall as Joe but well built and strong all the same.

He came to a halt, panting, and Joe asked sharply, 'What's wrong?'

Christina knew he'd be thinking about an accident, some kind of emergency. It happened out here. As doctors, they'd seen more than their share of the unexpected, and there weren't many ordinary, innocuous reasons why someone would be running along a deserted highway like this one in the middle of the night.

Not many ordinary reasons, but this was one of them. 'Can I hitch a ride?' He looked as if he wasn't that long out of his teens. Twenty-one or twenty-two.

'Into town? Home? You from around here?' Joe asked.

'No, but, yeah, I'm heading into town.' He didn't offer an explanation as to what he'd do when he got there, and the admission that he wasn't local had been hurried and edgy.

Christina and Joe looked at each other again. They really had to take him. He didn't look dangerous. But what was he doing here?

'Hop in the back,' Joe said, then added casually to Christina, 'You OK to drive again?'

She nodded, understanding the direction of his thoughts as she so often did. If this guy did turn out to be trouble, it made sense for big, strong Joe to be the one with his hands free.

'What's your name?' Joe asked, as Christina sped up along the road.

'Uh, Jack.'

Joe and a joey. Wheel jack to prop up the car, strange Jack appearing in the night, hopefully not planning to carjack Christina's four-wheel-drive. It was too far past her bedtime for any of this.

'You look like you were a bit stranded back there,' Joe said. 'We had an errand up at the park headquarters, but we didn't pass you on the way up, did we?'

'Think I passed you,' Jack said. 'In a truck. But the driver turned off to Mount Evelyn. He reckoned someone else might still come through, but I got cold and no one did, and—yeah.'

'So you turned round?'

'Yeah, and you passed me—I was off to the side—and then I saw your hazard lights flashing through the trees, and so I ran.'

'Where were you headed?'

'Ah…just one of the stations out west. To see a friend. I'm on a station further up. I'm a stockman, and I had a couple of days off. Thought I could make it, but I just didn't get the rides.'

For someone who'd been reticent, not to say cagey, at the start, after five minutes they couldn't shut him up. He discoursed on the pitfalls of hitching, the need for rain. It must have been the relief at getting picked up when he'd resigned himself to a cold, lonely night of walking back towards the coast.

He wouldn't have let Christina get a word in edge-ways, even if she had been happy to dump Joe in front of a total stranger. He seemed quite bright, articulate. And there was something about the way he talked, a sugges-tion that he was deliberately lowering the pitch of his voice by a couple of notes, roughening the edges of his accent.

If he was working as a jackeroo, that made sense. City lads with cowboy fantasies could get given a rough time up here if they didn't fight back. This one looked strong enough and intelligent enough to make his way—although not, perhaps, when he was hitching.

'Should have known I couldn't do it in two days.' He sounded defeated suddenly, as the lights of the base and the town came into view. 'My…my mate would probably have been…' He paused again. 'Yeah, busy anyhow.'

They reached the T-junction a couple of hundred metres south of the hospital and air rescue base, where the highway to the west joined the coast road. 'Where should we drop you?' Joe asked their passenger.

'Oh. Here? Right here is fine.' The reticence was back in place.

'You've got somewhere to go?'

'Yep. No worries.'

'If you're sure,' Joe said. 'Because we can take you into town.'

'Nope. It's fine.'

OK, he'd had his chance. If he was sleeping rough, it wouldn't matter. Down here at sea level, the temperature was several degrees warmer, and there was no rain forecast. They let him off at the junction, and Christina glanced at him a couple of times in the rear-view mirror. He hadn't moved by the time the dip of the road towards Crocodile Creek took him out of sight.

'Was he real?' she asked Joe.

Or had he been sent by a meddling cosmos to prevent her from biting the bullet on the big break-up talk?

All her tired, repetitive thoughts came crashing back into place. *I don't want to do this. I'll leave it until tomorrow. But we're both working all day. If someone at the hospital—bloody Brian—mentions the room at the house…*

They crossed the bridge and reached the overhead lights in the main street. Joe looked at his watch. 'Sheesh, it's a quarter past one!'

'I'm wide awake, though.'

'Yeah, me, too. Buzzing. And filthy. Remind me, Tink.' He grinned across at her, and her heart did its ninety-seventh lurch of the evening. 'Where were we, before we were so rudely interrupted?'

On the edge of a precipice, Joe. That's where we were. But she didn't say it.

CHAPTER TWO

THEY GOT OUT of the car and went inside. Joe put his overnight bag down in the middle of the living-room rug and hugged her again. Blissfully. His arms were hard and warm and familiar, he made a hungry, appreciative *mmm* sound deep in his chest, he rubbed his strong, smooth jaw against her cheek like a cat.

Christina felt the familiar stirring of desire. It began low in her stomach and radiated outwards like the heat from a glowing coal, and it hadn't lessened or lost its dizzying sense of importance in two years. In fact, it had only grown stronger. Because she had always been so unsure of how long Joe Barrett would stay in her life?

He kissed her.

And, oh, she shouldn't let him do this, but if it was for the last time…

At some level, had she wondered if every kiss would be their last?

She couldn't hold the question long enough to really consider it. It was too abstract. All she could think about was now, because there was no 'maybe the last' about this kiss. This time she knew for certain.

His mouth teased her, clinging and tasting, lavishing her

generously with hot sensation. He was never a man who did things by halves. (Except that this didn't gel, did it? Their relationship was only a half, or even less. A lopped-off, uncompleted thing.) He was never a man who did things by halves *in the present moment,* she revised fuzzily. He kissed her with his whole soul, his hard-packed male energy, his astonishing heart, and she kissed him back.

For the last time.

She ran her hands up the back of his head, releasing the scent of his shampoo into the air. She drank in the taste and feel of his warm mouth and pushed deeper, wanting more, wanting to get still closer, never wanting this to end. Time was standing still right now, but it couldn't stand still for much longer.

Joe was the one who broke the moment. 'I need a shower,' he muttered, still holding her. 'Smell like a plane. And probably kangaroo. I'm amazed you're letting me do this.'

So was she.

She was appalled that she was letting him do this, appalled that she couldn't even smell plane or kangaroo, she could only smell him.

'I need a shower just as much,' she said out loud.

'Wanna share?' That teasing sideways grin came at her, that sexy, dark-eyed look from beneath deliberately lowered lashes. He rubbed his jaw against her cheek and her head turned all on its own, her mouth once more in search of his.

Christina Farrelly, you have to be stronger than this, she coached herself.

'No, you go ahead and have it to yourself,' she told him. So hard to say it. Even harder to let him go. 'I—I'll just wash up in the laundry sink. I don't have the Cairns transit lounge to wash off.'

'I'd still like to share,' he said. He pulled her back against his chest, teasing her, so confident about how she'd respond. He had no idea.

'Joe, we have to talk,' she blurted out. Her heart started to pound as soon as the words were spoken.

Crunch time.

Moment of truth.

'Yeah?'

His big dark eyes were puzzled but untroubled. He still didn't see it coming. Why should he? She hadn't given any hints or warnings. She hadn't known until a week or two ago that she'd reached ultimatum time.

Make this easier. Make it civilised.

If that was possible.

'Are you hungry or anything?' she offered vaguely, waving her hand in the direction of the kitchen. Then she caught sight of the clock. Almost one-thirty. If she was really going to do this tonight, it was way past time.

She was going to do it. She'd said that first fateful line about talking. She had to go through with it now. Bringing her hand to his shoulder she felt another sudden, sick-making lurch in her guts.

'Hungry? No,' he said. 'We got a fistful of meal and drink vouchers in Cairns to make up for the delay.' He studied her face more closely, his own softening. He bumped his nose lightly against hers. 'Hey, what's up? Something else has happened? You didn't tell me everything in the car? What were you waiting for?'

His tone had dropped to the intimate pitch that she loved. It was the voice he used in bed, the voice he'd used last month when a gastric upset picked up from a patient had laid her low for the last two days of his visit. 'Still feeling crook, Tink?' he'd said several times.

He'd had to fly home while she'd still been spending a miserable amount of time in the bathroom and maybe that was when she'd begun to understand once and for all that she needed more—more than a man she only saw once a month, in the snatches of time where their long working hours didn't clash.

Should she tell him to sit down? She was the one with the shaky knees, because she didn't know where to start. 'This isn't going anywhere, is it?' she blurted out. 'Us, I mean.'

'Going anywhere?'

'Joe, don't be thick about it.' Shaky knees and a shaky voice. 'Don't make it harder. Please. Take a second to think about it and then try and tell me you don't know what I mean.'

She tore herself from his touch and began to pace around the room, wishing it was bigger, wishing he'd trap her and pull her back into his arms. She felt claustrophobic, and desperate for him to pre-empt this and tell her she didn't have to say it.

So far, he wasn't doing so. He'd stilled, retreated to lean his broad shoulder against the open archway that led between this room and the dining area. He looked as if he wanted to touch her and hold her again but had decided that he shouldn't.

'I want you to move out,' she said. 'Tomorrow, if you can. I can't bear to drag this out, and I can't imagine you'd want that either. I've arranged a room for you at the house.'

There was only one house, the doctors' residence at the hospital. It should be spelt with a capital H.

'I can't keep going with this,' she went on. 'We've been together—a quarter together—for two years. More. And I want…more. More, Joe. Some idea of a direction. Commitment. Some indication that…that this isn't just time out for you. You know, the Christina Farrelly full-service day spa. I—I—' *Oh, hell, I'm going to say the L word.* '—love you. You have to know that by now, surely, and what we have just isn't good enough any more.'

Silence.

Around three seconds' worth.

'I love you, too,' he said slowly. 'Is that what this is about? That I haven't said it? I love you, Tink.'

But he was floundering, and the way he said it told her that the other shoe was about to drop.

He swore. Which was unusual. Especially with such force.

'I'm sorry you're not happy.' He took a breath. 'I'm a bit, um, stunned that you're not happy. It's one-thirty in the morning. We've had a hell of a night. And you're suddenly saying all this.'

'You thought this was what I wanted? All I wanted? For it to go on like this forever? It's not sudden, Joe.'

'We have such a great time together.'

'You think that's all I want? A great time?'

'Better than a miserable time.'

'Don't joke about this. Don't.'

'I'm not belittling—I care about you. I love you. I'm—yeah—stunned.'

She closed her eyes, then opened them again. He'd said the L word, too. Three times. But it was just a word. Some men could splash it around like wet paint. *Yeah, 'course I love ya, babe.* She hadn't picked Joe as being one of them. 'Sorry, I'm being a bit slow here, Joe.' Her voice came out slow and rusty. 'Are you fighting this?'

Please, please, fight it!

'No. I wouldn't. Fight it. How could I? If that's what you're saying you want. If you've…' He swore again, and for the first time he sounded angry. '…arranged a room.'

It's not what I want! It's not!

'I've got no grounds to fight it on,' he said. 'If it's how you feel. But, hell, Christina, you couldn't have given me a bit more of a warning? Told me at the airport, or—?'

'I didn't think we'd get sidetracked on the way home.'

'You could have phoned me in Auckland.'

'You hate me phoning. You *never* phone me.'

He didn't deny it. He was too angry. 'You've arranged a room!'

'That was the best thing to do, wasn't it? Make it easier, on both of us?'

'Guess you can look at it that way.'

'But...' OK, time to lose all pride here, and give him a hint.

Oh, this was miserable! She hadn't realised quite how much she'd been hoping the room at the doctors' house would stand empty after all, throughout her process of decision-making, when she'd arranged the room with Brian Simmons, all through the sad and farcical delays in their arrival home tonight.

'You mean you're not going to promise anything different in the future?' she asked.

He whooshed out a sigh, then groped for the right words. 'I don't feel as if I've promised the wrong things so far. I mean, I'm only here one week in four. You said it yourself. I really like being with you, Tink.' His tone lost some of its angry edge. 'I think we're good together. Great together. My life at home—I know I never talk about that. To be honest, I think the main reason I come here is not the extra money, even though, heaven knows, I need that, but the fact that I don't have to think about home...' He stopped. 'It's tough. My life at home is tough. It's so good to have you, and not to talk about it, or think about it—'

'This is your R&R, isn't it? Your time out?'

He seized on both expressions, grateful for them. 'Yes! And it's so good!'

'Not for me, Joe.' She could hardly get out the words. Sobs wanted to come out instead.

'No?' he said softly.

'The word "love" obviously means something very different to you. Not what it means if I say it. I want to be part of your life. Your whole life.'

This time his answer came quick as a rabbit trap clamping shut. 'No, you don't.'

'So you're not going to tell me anything about—'

'No. I'm not.'

OK, two choices.

One, accuse him of having a wife.

Two, storm out and slam the door.

Christina did neither. She just started shaking so hard that Joe couldn't have missed it from a distance of three hundred metres. Couldn't have ignored it unless he didn't care anything for her at all.

And he did care.

He came up to her, wrapped his arms around her, physically held her on her feet so she wouldn't subside onto the rug with her face buried in her hands.

'I am so sorry, Tink,' he whispered. 'I didn't see it coming. Maybe I should have. That crack about warning me, and the room—that probably wasn't fair. I can see how you feel. Couldn't we just try and…?' He stopped.

'Yes?'

He didn't say anything, just kept holding her. Oh, hell, and she so loved the way he smelled, even tonight when it came tinged with the faint aromas of aeroplane, axle grease and kangaroo. She didn't know what it was. Him, his soap, his clothes. He always smelled like this and she always loved it. Could have drowned in it. Could have saved her life with it.

'No,' he finally answered. 'I'm not going to argue. I've got no grounds. Nothing to promise. Nothing to offer. Hurts, it's stupid. I'm stupid. Sorry. I've been an idiot not to realise that you'd want things spelled out more clearly. I'm not in the market for something long term, for a commitment. I'm just not. I have enough of those. I just don't have room and, really, you wouldn't want me to.'

'But you won't let me be the judge of that,' she said, in a voice that managed to be hard and wobbly at the same time. 'You've just made the decision for me, without telling me—'

'Can we stop this now? Can we? I think we have to, because I don't think there's any point in saying more, or anything more we can say.' He pulled back and stood very upright, chest like a board, arms folded over it. She could see what he was doing, mentally clawing his way back to a less emotional operating mode, getting some distance.

She tried to do the same.

He was right. They'd reached the impasse she'd…only one-quarter expected, to be honest. Less than a quarter. Ten per cent. She only now fully realised that she had seriously been hoping he'd throw his arms around her and tell her it was all a mistake, he wanted everything that she wanted, and that he'd make all the right promises on the spot.

But, no, they'd reached an impasse, and there was nothing left to say.

'Are they…uh…they're not still expecting me at the house tonight?' he asked. 'At this hour?'

'If your flight had been on time, that was the plan. But now we should wait until tomorrow. I was thinking so even before the joey and the flat tyre. No one's had enough sleep over there the past week or so. I don't want to go thumping around those loud wooden floors and turning on lights at two in the morning.'

'My stuff…' Which had accumulated to several suit-cases' and boxes' worth over the past two years.

'I'll be out on the clinic run till almost dark tomorrow. Where are they slotting you at the hospital?'

'Don't know yet.' Joe was always used where he was needed. The emergency department, Maternity, Paeds, Anaesthesia occasionally.

'If you can drop me at the base, you can have the car,' she told him. 'Then if you get a break during the day you can pack and shift. I didn't…box anything up for you because…' She didn't finish.

'That's OK. Hell, that's OK, Tink. I wouldn't have expected for a second…' He didn't finish either.

'Have your shower. I'm going to bed,' she gasped, and didn't wait.

Not for an answer, not for a protest.

She knew nothing would come.

And, of course, she couldn't sleep.

At two-thirty she stopped listening for the sounds of him moving around the house. He'd obviously gone to bed, too. At three she stopped thinking about going along to his room and climbing into his bed…or hoping that he would come along and climb into hers. At three-thirty she surrendered the idea of phoning the obstetrics and gynaecology unit at the hospital in the hope that Georgie Turner or Grace O'Riordan would be there, delivering a baby.

If they were, they wouldn't have time to talk. If they did have time, Joe would hear her sobbing on the phone. And sobbing and talking wouldn't even put a dent in the pain.

At four she got up to get a glass of water in the kitchen and came back to meet Joe padding silently along the passage towards her, wearing only his black cotton pyjama pants and an inadequate cloak of darkness over his bare chest. They did one of those silent movie–type byplays where two people both moved in the same direction to try and get past each other and almost collided three times, accompanied by fervent apologies. But it wasn't funny.

'Are you married, Joe?' she said.

'No!' His protest tailed away to a rough whisper. 'Hell, no, I'm not married!'

'Well, that's something.' It sounded very bitter.

'Ah, Tink, ah, hell. Don't do this.'

'Do what?'

'Don't look for reasons.'

'Aren't there reasons?'

'Of course there are.'

'Then tell me what they are.'

But he didn't answer, because they were already holding onto each other like shipwreck survivors in a dark sea. His whole body was warm from sleep—or maybe from frustrated wakefulness—and she could feel the low ride of his drawstring waistband against her lower stomach through the thin stretch cotton of her sleeveless pyjama top.

It was so familiar. The way her breasts pressed against him. The rapid burgeoning of his arousal. The tickle of hair, the rumbling groan of need he made, the rippling sensitivity of every square inch of her skin.

Christina didn't mean to let it go as far as it did, but when he started kissing her, seeking her mouth a little clumsily in the darkness, she just didn't care about self-preservation or pride or boundaries. He felt so good, and she wanted him too much, the way she always had.

He didn't ask out loud how far he could go, but his body asked the question with every deepening kiss and every more intimate touch, and he never got no for an answer. The door to his room was only a few feet away, so that was where they ended up, sitting on his bed.

She could just see the faint swimming of light in his dark eyes, the sober expression on his face.

'Christina…' he breathed.

He peeled her top over her head and bent to kiss her breasts and her neck. She closed her eyes, letting him, just letting him do it, then she reached out and spread her fingers in his thick hair, pulled his head up and kissed him so hard they were both grateful for breath at the end of it.

He stood, pulled her up, slid her pyjama pants down then his, taking his own nakedness and state of arousal for granted. She'd seen it before. She'd responded to it in a hundred wonderful ways. This time it would be as good and as powerful as ever. Still standing, he touched her, gliding his hands lightly over her body, all the expected places and some unexpected ones as well. The backs of her knees, the knobs of her spine.

He was taking inventory, storing up memories, as aware as she was that this was the last time. It really was. It had to be. No secret hopes in her heart this time. 'Christina…' he breathed again. His hands grew slower and lighter on her skin, hardly touching her breasts, whispering down her body.

Suddenly she felt angry and impatient and didn't want to wait, didn't want to linger over this as if it was some great elemental parting, made unavoidable by war or destiny. This was his choice, and it didn't have to happen. She had set the challenge, but he had failed to rise to it, so how the hell could he act as if they were playing out some twenty-first-century version of *Romeo and Juliet?*

Let's just do it, Joe, slake our needs and move on, if that's all you've ever wanted from me.

She grabbed his hips and rolled them both onto the bed so that he was on top of her, his weight threatening to flatten her breasts and challenge her lungs. Then she wrapped her legs around him and guided him into her with rough haste, lifting her body to meet his first instinctive thrust.

'Hey…' he growled.

She didn't answer, just held him tighter with her legs, lifted herself harder against him, straining to feel that exquisite sensation of total fullness. Then she began to rock, knowing what it would do to his control, wanting to punish him and give to him and prove how wrong he was, all at the same time.

He swore, and groaned.

Then he gave in.

No turning back now.

Sensations dovetailed and began to spin like water diving into the hollow centre of a whirlpool. Christina closed her eyes. She didn't need sight. She had all the information she needed about Joe's state of mind from other sources—the whip-like motions of his body, the sounds wrenched from deep inside him, the grip of his hands.

And then she stopped caring even about those things, stopped knowing where his body began and hers ended. They clawed their way higher and higher towards release, and it was wonderful, long and hard and intensely satisfying, but seconds after it had finished, her spirits had plunged again and she wondered what on earth she'd just done.

Made everything even harder?

Given him a send-off he'd never forget?

Lost even the illusion of having taken the assertive approach?

They lay together for a few minutes, breathless and still, but she couldn't bear it and eased her body out from beneath his arm, needing the bleak safety of her own bed.

'Stay,' he growled, clamping a hand to her hip.

'I can't, Joe.'

'OK. OK.' His hand went slack and he let her go.

For the second time that night, he wasn't going to fight for her.

CHAPTER THREE

MORNING CAME way too quickly.

Christina heard evidence that Joe was already up as soon as she'd turned off her alarm. She hid in bed for several minutes, but couldn't postpone the inevitable, so she scrambled into the bathroom and succeeded in keeping clear of him until a five-minute overlap in the kitchen, when she managed to down a glass of juice. The idea of anything more substantial made her feel ill, and yet her empty stomach scarcely felt better.

'So I'm dropping you at the base?' he said.

'Yes. We can go now, if you want.'

'OK. Then I'll have time to look at the room.'

They were tense with each other this morning. The care for each other's state of mind had gone, and of course so had the comfortable teamwork between them that had been so apparent last night when they'd dealt with the joey, the flat tyre and the hitchhiker.

The emotional nakedness had gone, too—the willingness to say, *I love you.*

Joe was angry that this wasn't fun any more, that Christina had rocked the boat and changed the rules. She was angry that fun was all he wanted, that he would go to such lengths to stay inside his comfort zone, even when she'd shown him so clearly that she wanted more. That hurt so much that it had to be someone's fault.

And it's not mine, Christina thought. She felt totally drained.

She looks as wiped as I feel, Joe decided as he drove.

When he'd taken her phone number off a hospital staff notice-board two years ago and had called her about the boarder she was looking for—'reasonable rent, shift worker OK, own room, share bathroom'—he hadn't thought about the possibility of something like this.

He'd started out at the doctors' house, but had known pretty fast that it wasn't what he wanted. He didn't need the potential for clashing personalities, compulsory partying when he wasn't in the mood, minimal privacy. He was there to work, to make money and get a bit of breathing space. Christina Farrelly's place fitted the bill perfectly.

Roughly fifteen minutes after first setting eyes on it, and on her, he'd known that he wanted both the room and the woman. She was just the kind he always went for. Attractive in a natural kind of way, with a supple figure, some nice curves, bright brown eyes that knew how to laugh and dance, dark hair in a swinging ponytail and a smile that was more urchin grin than Mona Lisa mystique. She had a healthy energy, a bright mind and a depth of kindness that you couldn't fake.

She didn't play games.

He didn't either, so it hadn't taken him long to get across to her how he felt and what he wanted. It had been easy, not planned. One morning they'd been in the kitchen together, making silly little apologies to each other every twenty seconds as they'd crossed paths, preparing their separate breakfasts. She'd been standing by the toaster, waiting for it to pop up, with her hand leaning on the benchtop, and he'd just come up to her and laid his own hand on top.

She hadn't taken hers away—he hadn't seriously feared that she would—and it was all the communication either of them had needed. Their arms had gone around each other, their lips had met, they'd pressed their bodies together, they'd whispered a few things.

Oh, that feels so good. You knew I wanted this, didn't you? I think your toast is burning.

Two years later…

He might have been way too slow over the past couple of months to pick up on the fact that she wasn't happy with the state of their relationship anymore, but the blue shadows beneath her brown eyes and the tight muscles in her face this morning were concrete details impossible to overlook.

Her body language said a lot, too—the way she was hugging up against the passenger door, her legs angled away from him and her shoulder in a tight, protective curve.

Yeah, he felt angry about it.

Angry with her, angry with himself.

And anger was what he dealt with at home so much of the time. It was exactly what he loved about coming here, about the time he spent with Christina—that he could relax and laugh and get out and have fun, revel in that whole side of himself, bring it out in her, and just not have to feel angry and responsible and overwhelmed.

Well, the illusory sense that Crocodile Creek was a different, safer, happier, easier and more benign universe had been stripped away now. When he glanced across at her, he didn't see safety and peace any more, he saw only a whole new set of problems. He wanted to grab her by the shoulders and yell, *Why did you have to rock the boat, when it was all so good?*

But it wouldn't be fair.

When they reached the Remote Rescue base, nurse Grace O'Riordan was just zipping into a parking place out front in her battered little car. Tink made a little sound and sat up straighter when she saw her. A spark of relief, Joe realised. She and Grace were friends. They'd talk.

In fact, everyone would talk. It was that kind of hospital, that kind of town.

His heart sank. He got enough of this at home, especially when he was out anywhere with Amber. It was an anonymous kind of attention then, way less personal than this, but still it brought the same neck-crawling awareness that you were being talked about behind your back. Amber was fantastic, the way she dealt with it. Joe was the one with issues.

He said tightly to Tink now, 'We can talk about keys and things later in the week, can't we?' He'd be flying home on Sunday. It seemed like a long time away, and he had no idea if the time would drag or rocket by.

She nodded in reply, tried to smile, gave up on the attempt and just climbed out of the car. He watched her walk over to Grace, then wheeled the car around and sped towards the hospital, his whole being in rebellion against the way everything had changed.

The doctors' house was a hive of early morning activity. Cal was still in residence with his rediscovered love, Dr Gina Lopez, and their little boy, CJ, although they were looking for a place together in town. Hamish McGregor was mooching around, complaining about the weather, which was a bit rich coming from a Scotsman. His contract would be coming to an end very soon, and he'd be going home. Charles Wetherby, the hospital's almost legendary medical administrator, had a few staffing problems on his hands at the moment.

'So you shouldn't all be bloody looking at me,' Joe muttered under his breath as he opened the noisy back veranda screen door and stepped into the kitchen.

He fielded the chorus of greetings, managed a couple of jokey, blokey lines, ignored the undercurrents and asked, 'Which room's for me, does anyone know?'

Emily Morgan hopped up from the table. 'I'll show you, Joe.'

Chatting about plumbing quirks and shopping rosters, she led him along to a cool, dark space that opened onto the side veranda about halfway along. Those French doors in each room were what saved this place, he considered. You could actually come and go through them without the whole world being aware of the fact. Provided you learned where the creaking boards were, he revised, stepping onto the veranda and hearing an agonised groan from the wood beneath one foot.

'No one minds if you put a chair or two out here,' Emily said. 'It's peaceful when no one else is around.'

'Does that ever happen?'

She laughed. 'It's been known. There's even a degree of tact involved, occasionally.'

Hamish appeared out of the next door along at that moment, wearing scrubs and in a hurry. 'Lucky,' he flung back at both of them.

Emily made an anxious sound and watched him go.

'It's OK,' Joe said. 'I can do without tact. You're right, I don't feel particularly lucky right now. I thought Christina was happy to—Yeah. Anyhow.' He stopped suddenly as he saw the stricken, embarrassed look in Emily's grey-blue eyes.

'Oh,' she said. 'Joe. Gosh. He was talking about the baby. Not you and—I'm sorry, did Christina fill you in?'

'Fill me in?' he echoed.

Fill me in? Oh, by the way, Joe, I'm ending our relationship and you're moving into the doctors' house. *Of course she filled me in!*

'That's why I'm here, isn't it?' he said bleakly. 'Looking at the room.'

This whole thing was awkward enough, without him and Emily talking at cross-purposes. Who was being slow here?

Me, probably, he thought. My head's a mess.

'Th-the baby from the rodeo,' Emily said, stammering with remorse. She was quite shy at times. 'We didn't have a name for him at first, so we called him Lucky and it stuck, even though he's officially Jackson Cooper now. And I'm just a bit worried, seeing Hamish go haring off like that.'

'It's unexpected?'

'Yes, and we all have so much invested in the little guy now. Megan and the baby have both been doing so well, adjusting to each other nicely. They'll be discharged once we can sort out the family situation a little better, and the feeding. At the moment, her parents don't even know she has him, and she's refusing to go back home. She's only nineteen. If something's gone wrong…'

'Right.' That was all he could say. 'That wouldn't be good.'

Emily touched his arm. 'Listen, about you and Christina. I'm sorry I misunderstood. People are going to talk, of course, and *not* be tactful, but it's only because we care about both of you. It's none of our business, I know.'

'That's OK. It was my fault.'

She nodded, looked as if she was about to say something more, then decided against it. 'I'll let you settle in. You're working today, aren't you?'

'Should get across there in a couple of minutes,' he told

her, so that she would go away. They both knew he didn't have to be in that much of a hurry.

When she left, he took a proper look at the room.

Ah, hell, this was so typical!

Christina had made up the bed. He recognised sheets she sometimes used at home. She'd stacked some books on the bookshelf. He knew she must be the one who had done it and that these weren't simply the discards of a previous resident, because he recognised the names of authors he liked. No one else here in Crocodile Creek knew him that well.

No one else knew what brand of toothpaste he used, and that he was finicky about not getting a thick, dried-up collar of minty green stuff around the top of the tube. No one else knew the music he listened to on a lazy Sunday morning. No one else knew the silly voice he put on when he talked to friendly cats.

Because it was *rubbish* what Christina had said about her not being a part of his life! Even if he never talked about home, they knew each other. And what they had together was important, even if it was part time and focused purely on the present. How could she accuse him of not being a part of her life?

She'd even put flowers on the bedside table to relieve the slightly spartan atmosphere—some bright, trailing things that came from her own garden. He knew that because she always made the effort to have flowers around her own house, too.

His heart twisted and he hated himself because of how much he'd hurt her, because of the way this had hit him out of the blue, and because he still didn't believe that he had it in him to offer her more. It wouldn't be fair on either of them.

* * *

It was impossible to talk in the plane. Without earphones, the noise level was too high, and with them…well, who wanted to bare their soul into a plastic headset? On the ground during their pre-flight routine, Grace had given her a pat on the shoulder and a sympathetic smile, which had told Christina that word had begun to spread about her break-up with Joe.

And my face must be a front-page headline all on its own, she realised.

They only had two clinic stops today. The first one would be the shortest, at a cattle station to the north-west owned by a huge pastoral company. At around eleven-thirty, they'd make the hop from there to Gunyamurra, the tiny town not far from the rodeo ground where baby Jackson Cooper had been found eleven days ago.

'It was like one of those earthquake miracles, Christina, don't you think?' Grace said into the headphones as they flew. 'You know, when newborns are found alive after days buried under rubble?'

'I guess it was,' she answered, obedient to the need to respond to Grace's happiness about it. Grace was a great nurse.

The clinic at Amity Downs was uneventful, a textbook extract on the kinds of problems they encountered in these isolated regions. Stress-related illnesses exacerbated by the drought, minor injuries that hadn't been taken care of so that they'd become infected, routine check-ups, including prenatal care for women who faced the prospect of a long journey to hospital when their babies were due.

Arriving at Gunyamurra, they set up some equipment in the tiny Country Women's Association hall that doubled as a clinic during the visit they made here every second week. The air in the building was rather musty. The CWA ran a mini lending library, and as well as a handful of current paperbacks there was a larger selection of old Australian classics—Mary Grant Bruce's 'Billabong' series, and lots of Ethel Turner. They were lovely books, but rarely borrowed these days and probably filled with mould spores. As usual, Christina opened all the windows.

Then it was time for a break for lunch before the first patients were due. Since the dusty town didn't run to a café or sandwich shop, everyone had brought their own.

'And I've got a flask of hot water for tea,' Grace confided to Christina.

She betrayed her Irish heritage in her fondness for it—strong and milky and sweet. The same heritage was clear from her freckled skin, blue eyes and amazing laugh. You had to be in a pretty bad way if you didn't find Grace O'Riordan's laugh contagious. It burst beyond the confines of her slightly too plump torso and cascaded like a musical scale, and Grace could find a reason to laugh at almost anything.

'Let's not sit in this stuffy clinic building, drinking the urn water out of mugs that predate the invention of radio,' she said.

'And probably haven't had a proper wash since.'

'Exactly. We can find a tree to sit under. And I thought, you know, you might—'

'Yes, Grace, I do want to talk!'

'That's the spirit.' Grace's eyes were twinkling and sympathetic at the same time. 'Bring it all up, like a dodgy meat pie.'

Christina laughed. The sound ended on a half-sob. 'Oh, bloody hell, Grace, this just feels so bad! I knew it would. But it feels even worse than I thought it would.'

'Well, you know, when you ditch a perfectly good boyfriend, who doesn't want to be ditched, for no valid reason that the grapevine's managed to work out yet...' She wagged her finger, but then recognised that Christina wasn't quite up to tough love yet, even in a teasing way. 'Come and tell Auntie Grace all about it.'

Which was absurd, because Grace had to be the younger by at least five years.

They sat in the only nearby shade they could find, beneath the rainwater tank stand at the back of the little CWA building, where several pepper trees clustered. Christina fiddled with a sprig of pinkish corns, breaking them off and letting them trickle through her fingers, bringing a hot scent to her nostrils.

Normally she loved crossing the Dividing Range into this dry outback country. It was such a contrast to the steamy heat of the coast. Most people who lived in Crocodile Creek looked to the ocean—for employment, for recreation. Out here, you had the same wide horizon and yawning sky, but there was a quality of silence and stillness that brought you face to face with yourself like nowhere else.

Christina launched into the whole story—everything she loved about Joe, everything he blocked off, her decision, the thing about the room, and how she'd wanted to do this properly, make it as easy as possible on both of them, but the room had felt like a mistake, because he'd been angry about it.

'And the fact that it took us over two hours to get home from the airport didn't help.'

'What, you walked on your hands?'

She told Grace about the series of fated delays. 'I mean, they were minor. We delivered the joey to the park ranger, we fixed the tyre, we dropped the hitchhiker where he wanted to be let off. And then we got home and I couldn't put it off, because if I'd had it hanging over me until to-night, or if Joe had heard from someone else today about the room…'

Grace had questions. Had he tried to argue? Did Christina have any theories?

They finished their sandwiches and their tea, and were still talking about it.

'And I've even thought, yes, maybe he is married,' Christina said, 'but that there are mitigating circumstances so he doesn't want to tell me, even though if they were the right circumstances, I think I could…I'd try…to under-stand.'

'Yeah?' Grace made a sceptical face. 'The great myth about married men—that there can be a good excuse. Like, for example?'

'You know,' Christina's tone was self-mocking because, yes, was there ever a good excuse? 'Like his beautiful blonde wife turns into a swan during the hours of dark-ness…'

'Right.'

'And if he ever leaves her the spell becomes irreversi-ble and she's condemned to remain a swan forever. That kind of thing.'

Grace tut-tutted sympathetically. 'Yes, I've known a lot of men over the years with swan wife issues.'

'All right, all right, so I haven't been able to think of a reason I'd accept.'

'It would be a stretch,' Grace agreed. She paused, and her tone changed. 'Have you ever asked him?'

'If he's married?'

'Yes. Just straight out. "Joe Barrett, are you married?"'

'Yes, I asked him at four o'clock this morning,' Christina said bluntly. 'When we met up in the passage outside my room because neither of us could sleep.' She didn't elaborate on what had happened after that.

'And what did he say?'

'He said he wasn't.'

'But he could be lying.'

'Except that I have to believe my judgement of character is better than that!' she burst out. 'Wouldn't I know?'

'Ugh. Thousands of women in history haven't.'

'Vote of confidence there, Grace.'

'Sorry, but you were thinking it yourself, weren't you?'

'Of course I was.'

'There's more water in the flask—want the last cup?'

'No, thanks.'

They heard the chink of metal and the creak of leather and a woman came round the corner of the building, leading a horse. 'Can I tether him here?' she said. 'I'm here for the clinic. Am I early?'

'Yes, tie him up here,' Christina said. 'Is that what you usually do when you come into town?'

The woman made a face. 'I usually drive. And I don't come in often.' She looked hot and tired and driven by much more than just a need to find a place to tether her horse. 'Would there be a bucket inside? I'll need water for him, too.'

She eyed the metal tap protruding from the tank, and then the tank itself. This part of the country hadn't had much rain. Banging the flat of her hand on the corrugated iron, she listened to the sound. 'Still something in there,' she said. 'Water. That's what I'd want if I had the Midas touch, for everything to turn to water. Gold, you can keep—useless stuff!'

'I'm sure there's a bucket,' Grace said cheerfully. 'Wait right here!'

She disappeared through the back door of the building,

and the woman—she must be in her late forties, Christina thought—leaned her forehead against the satiny neck of the horse. It seemed a bit odd that Christina couldn't place her. She was clearly local, and not a new arrival. That practised way she'd banged on the water tank to judge its level by the sound suggested someone born and bred on an outback property. But Christina had been flying these clinic runs for several years and hadn't met her before.

'You'd work at the hospital sometimes, wouldn't you?' she asked Christina, after a minute. 'You'd have colleagues there?'

'Yes, we rotate the workload a lot,' Christina answered. 'I know pretty much everyone.'

'And patients? My daughter's there at the moment. Megan Cooper.'

'Oh, Megan!' The conjectures dissolved and reformed themselves in a different pattern—one which gave answers and raised new questions. 'We all know Megan. And the—' Christina stopped abruptly, horrified by what she'd almost given away.

The baby.

Little Lucky, now officially known as Jackson Cooper. Christina had filled Joe in on the dramatic story of the little boy's secret birth and miraculous survival after she'd picked him up from the airport last night, and Grace had marvelled aloud about the whole thing again during their flight this morning.

Megan was still refusing to give her consent to her parents being told about the baby's existence. Her mother— this tired woman right here, with her yearning for rain—thought that Megan had miscarried a stillborn child. The girl's father didn't even know that much. And medical ethics regarding patient confidentiality prevented any of the hospital staff from telling them.

If only the two of them could get into Crocodile Creek to see Megan, everything would surely come out in the open and the teenager's fear about her parents' reaction would recede, but the Coopers' cattle property was so crippled by drought that neither Honey nor her husband would consider making the long drive to the coast just yet. As far as they were concerned, they'd come and pick their daughter up when she was discharged, and life would go on as before.

It wasn't going to happen.

'And—and the difficult time she had,' Christina continued awkwardly, praying that Mrs Cooper hadn't noticed her gaffe. 'You must be very happy that she's doing so well now.'

'I haven't even seen her, have I? It's just…impossible, at the moment.'

'Seems like you don't travel very much.'

'Not unless we have to. I'm like a cat on hot bricks just coming this far. That's why I'm on Buckley, even though it's a two-hour ride on horseback. If I'd taken the car, Jim would have wanted to know what I was going into town for, and he would have stopped me.' She caught sight of Christina's face. 'I'm not a prisoner.' She gave a tired laugh. 'Well, I might as well be, I suppose, but it's not Jim who's keeping me in chains. It's this drought. And the work. And— Listen to me!'

Yes, I am listening to you, and I want to start treating you for depression and stress without so much as taking your blood pressure first, Christina thought. She said gently, 'Want to wait until we're comfortable inside and I've had a look at you, and tell me the rest of it then?'

'Oh, I'm not here about me, Doctor,' Mrs Cooper said. 'It's Jim, my husband.'

Grace appeared with the bucket, and the horse's needs were seen to. They were far simpler ones than Honey Cooper's, Christina realised again when she'd introduced herself properly as Dr Farrelly and asked about why Mrs Cooper was there.

'Jim won't get himself checked out,' Honey said in a weary voice. She was now seated in the little office they used for examinations and treatment. 'He had a prescription for something to keep his blood pressure down, but that's run out. Can I get another one for him if he's not here?'

'You really can't, Mrs Cooper, I'm sorry. He has to come in himself.'

'I'm cooking with less salt, like they told us at the hospital after his heart attack last year, but it's no good, because he just adds it at the table. Says he sweats too much of it out to go without. And as for the stress…! He's working too hard, his heart's in terrible shape, we know that. He's been told he should have a bypass eventually. What can I do, Dr Farrelly?'

'You have to get him to come in. I really need to see him and give him a proper check-up before I prescribe any kind of treatment, even if it is just a question of renewing prescriptions he's had before.'

Honey Cooper closed her eyes and shrugged. She was a woman who carried her burden with her wherever she went, her tortured heart right there on her sleeve.

Joe had hinted at his own burdens last night—burdens he left behind in New Zealand and was glad to escape. Christina was his temporary haven, and maybe he needed it, had the kind of problems at home that meant he deserved it, but she didn't want to be used that way any more.

She thought about prescribing a casual, part-time affair to Honey Cooper. The Joe Barrett solution.

It'll really take your mind off your troubles, Mrs Cooper. It'll do wonders for you, as a bit of R&R.

The idea was so ludicrous that she almost laughed...and then she felt angry with Joe all over again.

'Let me give you a good check-up while you're here,' she told Honey, and discovered that her blood pressure was higher than it should be, just like her husband's.

Honey's expression lightened at the news, and Christina knew quite well what would happen. The medication she prescribed for Honey would get taken by her husband instead.

'Please, try and get him to come to our next clinic,' she said as Honey rose to leave. 'Or if you can get into town over the next couple of days. Megan...' She hesitated, pulled in opposite directions by the complexity of this family's tribulations. 'Needs help working out her future,' she finished, knowing that it was inadequate and yet still probably more than she should reveal.

But Megan's mother was too weighed down by other concerns to pick up on any hints. 'Into town?' she echoed.

'Yes, when she's ready for us to bring her home.'

A high-riding four-wheel-drive pulled up at the front of the little hall as Christina ushered Honey back into the larger space that served as a waiting room. She heard a male voice over the squeak of a vehicle door whose hinges needed lubricant. 'Come on, you lot, out you get. We're late and we'll have to wait two hours at this rate.'

Honey peered out the window and froze, her renewed tension going unnoticed by Grace, who'd just called in a mother and baby for a check-up and immunisations. A couple of the other waiting patients were aware of it, however. Distances might be vast out here, but neighbours were still neighbours, and they knew each other's business.

'Philip.' A sun-weathered man in his fifties growled the greeting and stuck out his hand as the owner of the four-wheel-drive stomped confidently into the hall.

Christina knew the new arrival, although they'd only met a handful of times. Philip Wetherby. He was Charles Wetherby's younger brother, aged around forty, and he ran a huge cattle station not far from here. The two brothers weren't close—barely spoke, she gathered—but town gossip was silent as to the reasons why. Whatever the source of their grievance, it had happened a long time ago.

'Greg,' Philip said to the man who had greeted him. 'Good to see you. Your dams holding up?'

'Getting pretty low. If we don't get rain soon…'

Philip looked around the room. Honey had turned her back, and was studying some health posters pinned to the wall. His eyes fell on her but stayed blank. There was recognition, but no acknowledgement, and his gaze quickly chased through the rest of the space.

'Stupid to use this first-come-first-served system,' he said. 'I don't have time to sit around all afternoon.' He speared Christina with his impatient expression. 'Look, can't you apply some kind of triage? Lynley, my wife, had a migraine and I've had to bring these people in.' His voice dropped as his gaze flicked to the three indigenous men who'd accompanied him. They were presumably employees on the Wetherby property. 'You have to treat them like children half the time, they don't look after themselves.' He didn't wait for her agreement, just took it for granted. 'If we could get seen first…'

'I'm afraid that's not possible,' Christina replied coolly. 'As you've said, we operate on a first-come-first-served basis, unless someone needs urgent treatment.'

'My cattle need urgent treatment, but you're telling me that doesn't count.'

'Sorry.' She gave a short, polite smile then turned away from him to call her next patient.

She knew that Philip Wetherby would be fuming behind her back. Hard to believe the man was Charles's brother. Although Charles was the one with health problems, thanks to his confinement to a wheelchair, Philip looked like the weaker man—the kind who put others down in order to feel superior in his own estimation. He had a ropy build because of the physical nature of his work, but brute strength didn't equal strength of character.

Where Charles's compassionate eyes saw straight into people's hearts, Philip's critical ones took in only enough detail to give him ammunition. His mouth turned down slightly at the corners, and his top lip was too thin. You wouldn't notice it on someone you liked, someone who smiled, but on Philip Wetherby, you noticed at once.

He sat down with a grunt on the opposite side of the room to where his men had stationed themselves, and when Honey slipped out the door, he uttered an impatient snort that could have meant anything.

And even though Christina was determined not to give in to the man's I'm-too-important-to-be-sitting-here vibe, she was on edge as she saw each successive patient, and relieved when she'd dealt with the three from Wetherby Downs.

'I want you back in two weeks to see if that chest has cleared,' she told the last of them, knowing Philip Wetherby wouldn't be happy about it. Maybe he'd trust the man to get here on his own next time. Or he'd send his no doubt under-appreciated wife.

It was after four-thirty by the time she and Grace finished, having referred two patients for further tests in Crocodile Creek. They'd need to pack up their equipment quickly, as their pilot, Glenn Corcoran, would want to be in the air again within half an hour in order to get back before the light went.

Grace was in a chatty mood. Perhaps she was being kind, taking Christina's mind off Joe. 'Mrs Strachan is getting huge,' she said. 'I'm thinking she'll be early, but she said the other two have been a week late. She doesn't seem too bothered about having it at home if it jumps the gun. How did you go with the mob from Wetherby Downs? Ticked the boss cocky off, I hope.' She was talking about Philip.

'You don't like Charles's brother?'

'Do you? He's so far up himself he needs caving equipment. Which I'm sure our Charles would be happy to supply, along with a very inaccurate map.'

Christina laughed, and felt the tight fist around her heart ease its pressure just a fraction. 'You're good for me, Grace.'

'That's the plan, Chrissie. Sorry, you don't like Chrissie, do you? Or Tina?'

'Not much. Bit prissy, both of them.' Which was why Joe had soon changed Tina to Tink.

Grace dropped her voice. 'Tell me about Honey Cooper.'

'Do you know her?'

'She came to this clinic with her husband once. You must have been off that day. Who would have been doing this instead? Oh, nasty Kirsty, I suppose. The Coopers are both the type that never have a day's illness until they drop in their harness twenty years too soon. Which is about due now.'

'Grace, after that summary, I don't need to tell you a thing about Honey Cooper!'

'So why was she here?'

'For advice on her husband, who wouldn't come. They

both have high blood pressure. Jim isn't taking his underlying heart trouble seriously. His wife takes it seriously enough for both of them, but there's not a lot she can do.'

Grace shrugged. 'I could write a book on the psychology of the outback male and his partner.' She locked the cupboard where they stored a few basic supplies and surveyed the three neat rooms. 'Are we done here?'

'Looks like it.'

Mrs Considine, the CWA stalwart who ran the tiny post office and store, had closed up her premises in order to help them ferry their supplies back out to the airstrip at the edge of town, where they found Glenn frowning about a warning light on the instrument panel that was showing when it shouldn't be. He lifted hatches and checked gauges and muttered a couple of ominous phrases, then found the problem, which fortunately turned out to be an easy fix.

'Still, we've lost twenty minutes,' he said, looking at his watch.

He was a good pilot, and good at anticipating the needs of the medical personnel who flew with him, but, as Grace had said once, the sense of humour gene on the personality chromosome was missing,

'Which means he could be the best-looking man on the planet—and I'd have to say he comes close—but in my book he's about as sexy as a cardboard cereal packet.'

Christina had the same book. She spent hours with him every week, but didn't think she'd get asked to his wedding.

'What, your girlfriend can't wait that long?' Grace teased Glenn now, since she was a self-described 'woman who refused to recognise a lost cause when she fell over one'.

He raised his eyebrows and shrugged at the comment about his girlfriend, uttered a mechanical laugh since

Grace's twinkling eyes had telegraphed that he was supposed to, and went through his pre-flight routine exactly as usual.

Christina hid inside her headset and looked out the window as she waited for take-off. The late sun had begun to glow a darker gold on the rust-coloured rock and hard ground. A trail of dust boiled behind a vehicle racing along the road into Gunyamurra from the west. The town always looked so small in all this vastness, as if a giant had thrown a handful of matchboxes onto an empty table.

She tried to appreciate the grandeur of it all, to tell herself that her infinitesimal place in the universe simply didn't warrant this amount of pain in her heart about one incomprehensible New Zealander, but it didn't work.

Nothing worked today.

The dust trail from the approaching vehicle got closer. Glenn revved his engines to the moment of juddering and screaming that came just before he launched into the taxi down the airstrip, and a second later they set off, gathering ground speed rapidly. They'd shake off the earth in a few moments, and in about an hour they'd touch down in Crocodile Creek.

That vehicle and its dragging parachute of dust still nagged in the centre of Christina's vision. A service track ran parallel to the airstrip just beyond the fence, and the battered four-wheel-drive careened along it as if in a race with the plane. Crazy driver, hadn't he heard about the fatal game of chicken between two vehicles out at the Wygera settlement a week and a half ago? Racing a plane made even less sense as an adolescent game.

Then she saw that it was an older woman at the wheel, glimpsed her frantic face and manic gestures, recognised her and understood that if this was a race, it was a race for someone's life.

'Glenn!' she yelled into her headset. 'Abort take-off! Abort it now!'

CHAPTER FOUR

'ANY THOUGHTS, Joe?' Hamish McGregor said.

They stood in the tiny nursery that formed part of the obstetrics and gynaecology ward. There were two babies in it. One was a healthy, full-term girl who would go home with her mother today. She'd had a fussy night, so her mother was tired and taking a break and a nap while she could. The other baby was Jackson Cooper.

Aka Lucky.

Joe had plenty of thoughts. Not quite enough of them were about this little boy. He couldn't get last night's talk with Christina out of his head, that was the problem, couldn't believe that what they'd had was really over.

He grabbed at the mental puzzle pieces Hamish had given him. Low-grade fever, fussy and listless, not wanting to feed. Newborn babies were hard to read and important to take seriously, and this one had already endured more than his share of problems.

'It has to be an infection,' he said. 'Not at the incision, that's looking great. The cord stump is nice and dry. You said the blood and urine tests came back clear. It's just one of those non-specific things. Do everything, I'd say. IV fluids, something to bring the fever down, another course of antibiotics. Is the mother feeding him?'

'Trying to now, with some ambivalence, and they haven't got the hang of it, yet, I'm told. I won't be surprised if she chucks it in.'

'It would be really, really good if she could not chuck it in, wouldn't it?'

'You're the one with the winning smile, Joe. Convince her!'

So Joe met Megan and Jackson, the patients everyone was talking about—the ones who'd made Christina's voice go eager and soft and satisfied all at the same time last night in the car—and they had a chat, and he shamelessly ratcheted up his Kiwi accent, which often greased the wheels of conversation with Australian patients.

'Breast-feeding's the best thing for him, Megan,' he told her.

'I don't think I can.' Her sense of defeat seemed habitual.

'Yes, you can!' He crouched down beside the chair where she sat with the baby hemmed in by pillows. 'You know, with kids—with anyone you love, really, parents and siblings and friends—there are so many things that are out of your control, things you try to do for the best that can backfire. But breast-feeding's not one of them. Breast-feeding is the number one, simple, no ifs or buts or downsides, best thing you can do for your newborn baby. I'll tell you something. My mother tried so hard, but she couldn't do it for my sister.'

I'm saying too much, he realised. He was running on at the mouth. Too emotional today. Didn't quite have it all where he wanted it.

'She couldn't?' Megan said.

'My sister has some health problems.' He waved a hand, regretting that he'd gone in that direction. He hardly ever mentioned his family to a patient, let alone Amber's health. His personal life felt too close to the surface today, a professional liability. 'Point is, you can do it for Jackson, if you decide it's important to, and there are people here who'll help you with it, just a buzzer away, any time you need them.'

'There was that nice doctor…the woman…'

'Dr Farrelly?'

'No, Dr Turner. She showed me. And a nurse. I don't think she's on today. Listen, I'm not dumb, you don't need to talk down to me.'

'Sorry if it seemed that way.'

'I get what you're saying. I do want to keep trying with this, but he doesn't seem interested today, and I don't think I've got his mouth positioned right.'

'We'll find someone.' He looked at her more closely as he spoke, saw beyond the chronic air of defeat, and realised she was right. She wasn't dumb. 'Meanwhile,' he went on, 'he has a bit of a fever and he's not feeling good, that's why he doesn't seem interested. We've given him something to bring it down, and his tests have come back clear, but we're going to start him on a couple of different antibiotics, just in case. You could also try a breast-pump, because he wouldn't have to suck so hard on a rubber teat, and sucking's too tiring for him today.'

'I get help with the breast-pump, right?'

'Yep.'

'Yip? You sound like my dog!' She actually managed a smile, and he could understand why this girl and her baby had the whole hospital community holding its breath.

'Take-off is aborted.' Glenn was still wrestling the aircraft to a controlled taxi speed, with the end of the airstrip rapidly approaching. 'Another ten metres and we couldn't have done it, Christina, do you realise that?'

'I know.' Christina's voice was shaky. She didn't mind flying, but didn't like the drama of an aborted take-off or a difficult landing.

'So this should be important.'

'I think it's going to be. That's Honey Cooper on the track beside us—Lucky's grandmother—and I don't think she's screaming after us like this just to wave us goodbye.'

Grace was craning to see as the aircraft wheeled around. 'It is Honey!' she confirmed. 'She's stopped. She's going back towards the gate. Something must have happened out at the station, and not long after she got back there from our clinic, too. With that ride, she's had a rough day, and a long one.'

'She'll want to meet us as close to the plane as she can get,' Glenn said. As everyone did around the hospital, he knew Lucky's name. 'I'll have to tell Base we've got a change of plan.' He got on the radio.

'It has to be urgent,' Christina said. 'After what she said to me this afternoon.'

'It's Jim,' Grace answered. 'I can see him there in the passenger seat beside her.' She added, more to herself than to her colleagues, 'Oh, lord, it's probably his heart again.'

It was.

The air from the propellers whipped Grace's and Christina's clothing as they ran from the plane. Honey had parked crookedly beside the end of the airstrip and opened the passenger door. Jim was slumped stiffly there, grey-faced and sweating profusely, still clearly in the grip of great pain.

He was gasping for breath, and gripping the top of his arm.

'Jim?' Christina urged him. 'Can you speak? Tell us about the pain?'

'Killing me,' he groaned. 'Help! Help me!'

'Jim, we're going to get you onto the ground.' It was dusty, but it was flat, and if they needed to start CPR…

'Why? What are you doing to him?' Honey demanded in the background. She looked as if she'd aged ten years in the past hour. 'I've got a blanket.'

'Roll it up for us, Honey.' It would help to support him in a position that made breathing easier.

'Yes… Yes.'

Glenn always seemed to know when he'd be needed, and he was there now. 'Help me get him onto the ground,' Christina said to him, and he nodded. Then to Jim, she said, 'Could you swallow an aspirin, Jim? It'll really help if you can. We're taking care of you now, and you're going to be fine.'

'I have aspirin in my bag,' Honey said, and started a panicky rummaging in a chunky, home-made leather contraption which Megan must have made for her as a child.

'Could you take it, Jim?' Christina repeated. 'Chew it up for us and swallow it down?'

He made a strangled sound which she took as a yes—*wanted* to take as a yes.

'What kind is it, Honey?' Mentally, she debated getting out their own supply, but if this was a 300 mg soluble type, and Honey had it right there, it could actually reduce the size of the infarct and make a big difference, just in the crucial window of time while their far more sophisticated equipment was brought from the plane.

Brought from the plane.

She jerked her head around too fast and found Grace. 'Grace, I want the life pack, the oxygen.' She paused for half a second while her mind raced. Suction equipment? They'd need it if the worst happened. Get Grace to bring it now, in case? She wouldn't be able to carry all that gear.

'Glenn, help her. Suction gear, medication kit. Fast, or Jim's going to think we're just slack and messing around here, aren't you, Jim?' The jokey tone didn't work, but it got her meaning across to her colleagues. 'You're doing really well, OK? We're onto this now, and you're going to be all right.'

Golden rule of heart patient treatment. Never let them think they're in trouble, even if they are, because the fear only made it worse.

She felt for Jim's pulse while Honey produced the aspirin and coaxed him to chew and swallow. It began to fizz in his mouth as it dissolved. No perceptible pulse at the wrist. That wasn't good. It meant his systolic pressure was below eighty, and she couldn't give nitroglycerine because that would only lower it further.

She found the carotid pulse in the neck and even that was weak, erratic. He was barely conscious. Telling him again that he was safe in her hands, she addressed Honey. 'Tell me about the previous trouble he's had.'

Honey's summary was confused and jumpy. It had only been a mild attack but tests had shown he should have a bypass. No, he hadn't had it yet. There just hadn't been the right chance.

'What was he doing when the pain started?'

'Seeing to the horse. Yelling at me for going into town behind his back. Turned out he'd been feeling bad all day, but he didn't tell me. If he had, I never would have left him to come to see you. To come and see you *about him*.' She gave a sob of bitter laughter at the irony.

A fatal irony, it might yet turn out to be.

Christina wasn't under any illusions here. This man was in a bad way.

Grace arrived with the portable oxygen. The cylinder

was only about fifty centimetres in length but it was still heavy. 'Want me to do it?'

'Yes. Full tilt.'

Christina's vision seemed to cloud for a moment as she spoke. Hell, was the light fading already? No, it was just the shadow from a fluffy ball of cloud, but the cloud was low in the west and while the sun floated behind it the light stayed purple and dark like a warning about the approach of dusk.

Glenn had the life kit. Christina sent him back to the plane for a stretcher, then ripped open Jim's shirt and slapped the three electrodes into place, one beneath each collar-bone and the other low on his left side roughly level with the umbilicus. She switched on the machine, saw an initial fuzz of static on the screen and then a rhythm—the wrong rhythm, the one she'd hoped not to see, with its bizarre QRS spikes indicating a complete heart block.

After getting the oxygen mask in place and the oxygen flowing, Grace wrapped a blood-pressure cuff around Jim's arm to try and get a measurement but when Christina looked at her she just shook her head.

Unreadable.

This patient could arrest at any moment.

And he was still in terrible pain.

She worked to set up an IV, needing the access for pain medication and life-saving drugs if he arrested, as she feared he would. The needle went in cleanly, followed by the plastic cannula. Grace drew up some saline to flush the line as a check, while Christina prepared morphine. With Jim's pain still at a crippling level, she gave the entire first dose at once, along with more reassurance.

'We have the drip in now, Jim, and that's going to help us medicate you and get this under control. You're going to be fine. The pain should ease very, very soon.' She added an anti-emetic to the IV because of the strong possibility that the narcotic drug would make him nauseous. 'We're going to get you into the plane now, and get you to the hospital.'

Glenn came into his own at this point, strong, adept and rock-faced. Timing their actions together, they got Jim onto the stretcher and pushed its sturdy wheels over the hard, dust-coated ground to the aircraft, while Grace took care of the equipment.

Shakily Honey asked, 'I'm coming in the plane?'

'Yes, of course.' Grace touched her arm. 'But better move the car first, Mrs Cooper.'

'Yes. Yes.' She added in a frightened tone, 'Don't— don't go without me.' She didn't trust anything right now. It wasn't rational, but it was human.

A few minutes later, Glenn launched into his pre-flight routine for the second time. Honey had left the Coopers' ancient farm vehicle parked just beyond the airstrip. She had nothing with her but the clothes she wore and that funny leather bag.

'I'm here, Jim,' she whispered to her husband, in a cracked voice. 'Jim, it's all right.'

This time their take-off proceeded without incident, and there was that sense of relief which came when the wheels had lifted and the aircraft seemed to shake off the pull of the earth. The relief was an illusion, Christina knew. There was an hour of flying to get through yet.

She barely took her eye off the ECG trace, willing it to stay in a pattern that was acceptable, if barely. Those QRS spikes were still way too wide.

Thirty minutes to go.

Twenty.

Honey hid her face against the window and silently cried. Christina could almost sense the shaking of her shoulders even when she wasn't looking in that direction. Grace comforted the woman stealthily, because no one wanted Jim to see that his wife was so upset, Honey least of all. She was doing everything she could to hide her panicky, emotional state in order to lessen her husband's own fear.

'Doing great, Jim,' Christina said. 'Nearly there now. Getting close.'

Close, but not close enough. The trace deteriorated. Ectopic beats appeared and Jim lost consciousness completely as his heart went into ventricular fibrillation, which showed on the ECG as wild, patternless wiggles. He'd gone into full cardiac arrest and his heart wasn't going to start beating again on its own.

'Glenn, we need to put down,' Christina said into her headset.

'Descent's started, Doc.'

'I can't see the coast.'

'That's because it's getting dark.'

'How far out are we? I'm really thinking we should put down.'

Was Honey listening? How much could she say about how urgent this was?

'Do we have a situation?' Glenn asked.

'Yes.' And it was against protocol to defibrillate or intubate a patient while in flight. With the powerful current in the defibrillator and the tricky technique required for intubation, it was just too dangerous, both for the patient and for the personnel working around him. CPR was possible, but less effective in the plane's confined space.

What she wanted was to drop into a level, grassy paddock in sixty seconds flat so she could work to get his heart going again, shock him and intubate, but she understood Glenn's reluctance. It was getting dark, they were just a few minutes out of Crocodile Creek, where there was a hospital, equipment, staff, even an experienced heart specialist, although not the facilities Jim would need for bypass surgery or angioplasty.

'Your call, then, Doc,' Glenn said. 'I'll find somewhere if you say we have to.'

Oh, lord, did they have to?

'Can we push up the schedule?'

'I've already requested emergency landing clearance. I can ask for a better flight path, come in faster, on a steeper descent. You won't gain much time with any of that at this point. Can't promise you'd gain much time if we drop short either, and in this light there are risks.'

'We'll go all the way,' she decided out loud. 'You'd better tell them to close the runway because we won't be getting clear of it just yet. When you're on the ground, just stop. I want the ambulance out on the tarmac right by us as soon as it's safe. Make sure they know this is happening, *stat.*'

They all felt the renewed speed and then, a little later, the steepening of Glenn's descent. He confirmed it through their headsets. 'Not long now. Bit of a pressure change coming up.'

Yes, Christina could already feel it in her ears. She swallowed, worked her jaw up and down, and felt her head clear a little. Grace began to do the same.

It was going to be a hairy landing. The seconds ticked by in slow motion, while her pulse raced and that wild electrical heart activity zig-zagged across the screen in front of her like the visual equivalent of gunfire. She had put in an airway, sliding it upside-down past the ridges on the roof of Jim's mouth and then rotating it 180 degrees to curve down over the tongue. Now she put on a bag mask and began ventilating him at twelve to fifteen breaths a minute, knowing the actions could all be futile. Handing over the bagging to Grace, she began chest compressions, struggling for effectiveness in the plane's cramped space.

'Hold his hand, Honey,' she said through her effort. 'Squeeze it and let him know you're here.'

Because you might be saying goodbye, only I don't want to tell you that.

The descent felt rough, fast and steep, and at this moment she wouldn't have exchanged any amount of a sense of humour for Glenn's steely expertise with his controls. She knew he wouldn't crack a smile at any point during this but, then, he wouldn't break a sweat either. He'd just get them onto the ground.

There was a thud and a groan as the landing gear came down. It sounded too loud and too violent, and then there came another thump, even louder, and she held her breath, terrified. If she'd pushed Glenn to make this landing too tight…

Bump. There it was, thank God, the touch of the wheels on the tarmac, crooked but not violent. A little lift came, then another bump, and they were down, careening along the runway, slowing as they went. Christina felt queasy, and Honey looked it. She still had tears squeezing from her closed eyes and her hand gripped Jim's.

As soon as their taxi speed began to feel like a car on a country road instead of an out-of-control train, Christina told Grace, 'I'll put the pads in place.'

'Your own ticker's resumed normal operations, then?' Grace said.

'You're not joking!' Christina answered. 'I was thinking just now, here we are, we're all going to die, and it's already been a *seriously* below-average day.' An unsteady sob sneaked its way into the middle of her laugh. 'It really isn't fair.'

The plane slowed…slowed…stopped. She didn't even look up to see where they were, if the ambulance had arrived, who had come with it, although she was dimly aware of Glenn skipping through most of his final procedures and jumping out onto the tarmac.

She had the pads on Jim's chest, one under the right collar-bone, the other lower down on the opposite side. The hum of the life pack charging up to 200 joules hit a crescendo then it beeped its readiness.

'Everybody clear?' she called.

Grace held onto Honey to make sure. They couldn't touch the patient or anything around him made of metal at this point. 'Yes, we're clear,' she said.

'OK, shocking now.' Christina pressed the buttons on both paddles with her thumbs to release the charge.

Jim's body jerked and the ECG trace disappeared. They waited and watched. It was like a jury sequestered before revealing its verdict. You didn't yet know the outcome. You just had to wait. Christina recharged the paddles while she did so, ready for a second shock if it was needed, and when the rhythm re-formed on the screen it was still horribly wrong.

Grace handed Honey down the aircraft steps to Glenn. There'd have to be someone on the ground to take care of her. She needed it at this point. What she didn't need was to witness any more of this.

'Shocking again at 200,' Christina said as soon as Honey had gone and the charge had built again.

No go.

'And again at 360.'

No.

She felt movement—a vibration and some thumps as someone entered the plane. In the warm tropical air of the coast, she hadn't even realised the rear door had been opened.

'How long since he arrested?' Oh, lord, it was Joe! She would have known it in another second even without hearing his voice, just by the aura of his body next to hers, just by the way he smelled.

Flooded with an impossible mix of emotion—relief… way too much of it was relief…just that physical relief she always felt at being with him, like an addict getting a drug—she answered, 'I've lost track. Too long. They sent you from the ED with the ambulance?'

'Yes. You've shocked up to 360?' He leaned closer and she felt his solid upper arm brush hers, bare beyond the short sleeve of the surgical scrub suit he wore. The sensation was so familiar, but it didn't belong to her any more.

He didn't belong to her.

He never had.

'Yes,' she answered, after drawing in a breath. 'I'm going with adrenaline and I'm going to intubate. CPR and bag him for a minute, just to get some air and circulation pushing through.'

'Then shock him again…'

'Yes.' If his heart hadn't produced a rhythm by then… Well, you still kept going, another cycle of three shocks followed by CPR, you tried everything for thirty or forty minutes, and you watched for the miracle, but the chance of it got less and less.

Grace was already drawing up the adrenaline. Joe

started CPR, pausing only long enough for Christina to intubate with Grace's help.

'OK, standing clear, please. Shocking now at 360 joules.'

Jim's body jumped again. The trace went static, then a rhythm resolved.

'Sinus pattern,' Joe said.

'Thank God for that!'

'Forty. It's too slow.'

'I'll give atropine.'

'Hopefully it won't come up too far or we'll be back where we started.'

'We?' Every muscle in her body tightened. 'It's not *we*, Joe. Don't use that word, please.'

Oh, hell, where had that come from? Unprofessional and stupid and just wrong. She set her face hard, willing herself to forget the rash personal reference, and willing him to ignore it.

He did, and Christina hardened her control so that she didn't risk letting down the barriers again.

She drew up the dose, hoping it wouldn't speed the heart up too fast and send it once more into the wild electrical rhythm that couldn't translate into the right beat. Unfortunately, a patient's reaction to the drug couldn't be predicted.

'OK,' Joe said a few minutes later. 'Looking better, now. He's up to sixty.'

'Gag reflex is back. I'm taking out the airway.'

'Give him the high-oxygen mask and see how he goes.'

They watched and waited. Jim stirred and groaned through his mask, his depth of unconsciousness lightening. They would be able to move him soon.

'Who else do we have on the ground?' Christina asked.

'Ambulance and two officers, one is driving, one's with

the patient's wife. That's Nick Brady. You'd know him, he's pretty good. She seems…'

He stopped, tilted his head in the direction of the tarmac and listened. Christina heard voices, but didn't take her eyes from the heart monitor. Joe leaned out the door and came back half a minute later to report quietly, 'She's done a bit of a dive.'

Christina made a stricken sound. She knew Honey must be on the edge of a complete nervous collapse.

'Nick doesn't think it's serious.' That was partly for Jim's benefit, Christina knew, because it was just possible that he could hear and take in what was going on. 'Low blood sugar, exhaustion, stress. But they're going to send for a second ambulance and check her out.' He dropped his voice even lower. 'What do we know about these two?'

He'd said it again.

We.

Such a little word, but it hurt so much, the way it mocked their current status.

Christina ignored it and just answered the question. 'Patient is Jim Cooper, Megan's father. Remember, I told you last night about—'

'Right.' He gave a short, efficient nod, which made his jaw look very strong and square, and murmured, 'I got introduced to Megan and the bub today.'

Grace—who must be aware of the undercurrents—leaned closer to Christina and said, 'Speaking of which, there's a family reunion coming up. Thought about that yet, Christina?'

'Uh…' Lord, no! She hadn't! In the few moments when she hadn't been focused purely on the technical demands of Jim's care, she'd been thinking about a very different reunion. Her own, just now, with Joe. Which had been every bit as difficult as she'd known it would be.

But Grace was right. Honey would want to see Megan as soon as she could, once she'd regained her own strength a little and satisfied herself that Jim was stable. And when Honey saw Megan, she would see her new grandson as well, unless they called ahead to the unit and got an express refusal from Megan to allow her mother through the door. Would the girl go that far? Would Honey take any notice?

'Let's take it one step at a time,' Christina answered. 'For now, for us, this is just about Jim.'

'You think so? Tell you what, we'll swap jobs for to-night,' Grace murmured back, smiling wryly. 'I'll do the life-saving and you can clean up the family mess.' She was a good enough friend to get away with the challenge.

Christina said, 'You're saying it's going to get dumped on you?'

'I'm saying nurses have the sticky bits sometimes. I'm not looking forward to it, because if it gets stuffed up somehow and they all end up permanently estranged…'

'They'd all lose out,' Joe cut in, as if he knew something about such a prospect.

'And I'll feel to blame,' finished Grace.

'Don't, Grace,' Joe said. 'Whatever's going on, it must have started months ago, before anyone at this hospital was ever involved.'

Grace nodded. 'You're right, of course. But feelings don't operate on logic, do they?'

'Heck of a lot easier if they did.' He looked tired and stressed suddenly.

The skin around his big, dark eyes was tight, and his hair stuck up at the back as if he'd run his hand through it too many times since its morning brush. Christina wondered what kind of a day he'd had, what kind of a month he'd just come from in New Zealand, what kind of a *life* he had there, for heaven's sake, and how much work he'd put in to settle into his room in the doctors' house this morning.

She'd done most of it for him yesterday, of course. Made the bed, hunted up the books, picked those flowers. Had she tried too hard? Said too much, with all these gestures?

Stop.

Just stop.

'Heart rate up to sixty-five, respirations are coming up, too,' she said. 'I think we should move him now. We've been hogging this runway long enough.' She changed her tone a little and spoke directly to Jim, even though he still hovered on the edge of unconsciousness. 'We're going to get you into a hospital bed now, Jim, where we have some better machines for reading what's going on with your heart. We'll give you something more for the pain before we go.'

He could take another dose of morphine at this point, she judged. When she'd delivered it through the port in his IV she asked him how he was doing and was rewarded with the flickering of his closed lids and the faintest nod.

The transfer to the ambulance went well. An onlooker wouldn't have sensed any drama, or any frantic hurry. Still, the danger wasn't over, and possibly the journey wasn't either, if he needed to go south for the kind of surgery they weren't equipped for here.

The hospital seemed quiet as they turned into the ambulance bay, a reassuring edifice with its modern design and clean lines. Glimpsing the waiting room that opened off the emergency department entrance, Christina saw two or three patients waiting, and there were lights in the windows of the main building, of course. If you looked closely, you could glimpse a couple of TV screens. Darkness had fallen while they had been working over Jim on the airport tarmac, and from somewhere she could smell hot, savoury food.

A quick, smooth journey along a corridor brought them to a bed in the resuscitation section of the ED. Honey had been given a bed of her own in the adjacent area of the unit. She was in the care of a nurse and Christina saw she'd been hooked up to a drip. She had a cup of tea in her hands also, but hadn't made much headway with it.

She reacted as soon as she saw them, struggling to sit higher and breaking into rapid speech. 'I'm sorry. This is so stupid. I don't need this. Jim, I'm here,' she called, 'but they've got me in a bed. Can I bring this thing with me?' She gestured, impatient and agitated, towards the drip stand.

The nurse raised her eyebrows in a question and Christina and Joe both nodded. Honey would only fret herself into a worse state if she couldn't get closer to her husband. Grace took over, helping her out of bed and making sure her IV line wasn't wrapped around her. 'This way, Mrs Cooper.'

'We're going to put him on a better ECG machine,' Christina explained. 'It has more leads, which might feel a bit scary, Jim, all these things stuck to you, but it's only so we can work out what kind of heart attack you've had. We'll be taking some blood as well, giving you more medication through your drip and monitoring you very closely.'

We.

She was doing it now, too.

It was the way medical personnel often talked. Safety in numbers, or something. But until last night 'we' had meant something much more personal in a context like this. Herself and Joe, working together, understanding each other, getting the team-work right, feeling good about what they did because they knew they did it well…

Then planning a night out afterwards. A crazy night sometimes. Mad races along the beach, kicking up the foam with their bare feet. Lighting a campfire in the back garden and toasting kebab sticks threaded with marshmallow, banana and pineapple pieces, then dipping them in melted chocolate.

Filling a kid's wading pool on a hot summer night once, and setting up the television and video player on the back veranda in front of it because Joe had said, 'Hey, feel like a naked spa movie marathon?' They'd both been pretty inventive when it had come to making entertainment. They'd had so much fun.

Yes.

Fun.

Rest and recreation, just the way Joe had wanted.

Focus, Christina.

She was supposed to be taking blood.

Now.

Because they needed to measure the cardiac enzymes to get a definitive marker of infarct size. They'd get a result within minutes and a clearer answer on whether they would need to ship him south to Brisbane for surgery, and what medication he should be given in the interim.

Honey watched them like a hawk as they worked to set up the ECG and take the blood. Jim opened his eyes as the needle went in.

'Hey, you're back with us,' Joe said. 'I'm Dr Barrett—Joe, if you want—and you're safe here in Crocodile Creek Hospital, Mr Cooper. We're going to take good care of you.'

'Are you in much pain now, Jim?' Christina asked him. The thin plastic cannula began to fill with blood as she spoke, and it was flowing nicely. Wouldn't take long to fill the test tubes.

'Much better,' Jim managed to reply, his voice thin.

'Oh, Jim!' Honey bowed her head and pressed his hand between hers. Her IV tubing snaked across his arm.

'Tracing's looking a lot better, too,' Joe said quietly. He drew Christina further away from the bedside, into the adjacent and almost empty section of the department. 'What are you thinking? I guess technically he's my patient now, but you probably want to follow through.'

'What I'm thinking? It's definitely an inferior infarct and the pain's settling already, so that's good. We'll see what the enzyme levels are like and start thrombolysis. Hopefully the ECG changes will settle and we won't have to transfer him for more invasive treatment. We'll get Dr Lopez to see him, discharge…' She stopped.

'Cross that bridge later.'

'I'm too tired to iron out all their family and financial problems tonight, that's for sure.'

'I'm going to have a better look at his missus, but it seems best to keep her in overnight, too,' Joe said. 'She's looking a wreck.'

'What time do you get off?' The question slipped out of Christina's mouth all by itself, pure habit.

She saw him stiffen. 'Hamish is on tonight,' he said. 'He's in here already, in Paeds, pretty busy with a couple of sick kids. Lucky spiked a fever this morning, by the way, but we couldn't find a specific problem and he seems much better now. I'll go when Hamish tells me things have quietened down, but I'm on call, so if things get hairy… Did you want—?'

'I didn't want anything,' she cut in quickly. 'I was just asking.'

'Because I do want to talk,' he told her.

He bent his head, only moving a few inches closer with the gesture but still it had the effect of locking out the rest of the world and flooding her with all her painful awareness of him. How could she ever get used to this? To being close to him without touching, to hearing his voice when the words weren't meant only for her, to pretending to him and herself and everyone else that this was OK, they were friends, they were fine, she wasn't breaking apart inside.

'Tonight?' she said, wanting it and dreading it at the same time.

He was so big. Like a wall. She had to look down, inspect her fingernails for life-threatening cuticle splits or something, because anywhere else she looked she'd only see his body, his face, his eyes.

And even when she didn't look, she could still feel.

'I know we're both tired,' he said. 'Maybe it's a mistake. But there were a couple of things you said. A couple of things I should probably say. Not feeling that patient about waiting.'

'I'm not sure, Joe.'

'Will you be home?' he pressed.

She nodded. There was nowhere else she wanted to be.

Not that she wanted to be at home much either, when her place would seem so...so...

Joe-less.

Oh, hell!

'So when I'm done here, or even if I'm only grabbing a break, I'll be over.' His voice rumbled in his chest and she wanted to do what she'd done so many times in the past and press her ear there—half her body, really—so she could feel the vibration. 'It might be late.'

'All right,' she answered.

'There are some things I want you to understand, even

though they won't change anything about…what you've said.'

It sounded ominous, not something to look forward to.

But she looked forward to it all the same, because as he turned to go back to their patient and she got slammed yet again with all the familiarity of his body—the way he moved, the shape of him—she knew she wouldn't forgive herself if she didn't give him—give herself?—just one more chance.

CHAPTER FIVE

'CHRISTI-I-I-NA! How goes it?' said the hospital administrator.

'Hi, Brian.'

She didn't like the way he said her name, or his frequent jaunty mannerisms with his voice. Having left a much more stable and comfortable Jim and a resting Honey in the care of Joe and a nurse in the emergency department, she'd gone in search of Grace before leaving the hospital for the evening—and she hoped Charles Wetherby might be around, too—but maybe Grace had already gone. The two of them were both overdue to clock off, after a longer than usual day.

Unless Grace had gone to see Megan and the baby.

Heading that way, Christina had had to pass Brian Simmons's office and he'd caught sight of her, unfortunately. She always felt petty in her response to him. He seemed like a perfectly decent guy, had helped her more than he'd really needed to over the business of organising the room in the doctors' house for Joe.

He shouldn't rub her up the wrong way just because of a few irritating mannerisms, which were no doubt designed to disguise a level of insecurity and unhappiness in his personal life that she should feel an extra dose of empathy for today.

In a warmer tone, she added, 'What are you still doing here at this time in the evening? You can't be doing emergency surgery on a file folder.'

'You see, that's what everyone thinks—that because it's not immediately about saving lives, my job fits neatly into nine till five,' he said seriously. 'But Jill and I have been sweating over staffing and budget issues for the past two hours.' He dropped his voice. 'Bit of TLC, too, to be honest, but don't let that go any further, will you? Jill hates to have her private life splashed around.'

'Of course, Brian.'

Over his shoulder, Christina could see the director of nursing seated at the desk. The light from the lamp there struck the far side of her face, while the near side, in shadow, was tear-stained. She had a mature, maternal kind of beauty in the uneven lighting, but she didn't look happy.

Brian followed the direction of Christina's gaze, but didn't say anything for a moment. 'I'm glad I can count on you,' he finally replied quietly. 'Her ex-husband should be shot and dumped in the concrete for the new bridge, I'm telling you.'

He almost looked ready to do the deed himself.

Was something going on between the two of them? Christina had always found Jill Shaw uncomfortably frosty and rigid, but if Brian, of all people, had seen something else—something sadder—beneath the surface of her personality, something that reflected a dark truth about the marriage she'd ended last year...

He *was* a kind person in his way. Observant. There was more to him than the awkward, pompous bean-counter that first met the eye.

'I'll leave you to it,' Christina said, and actually found herself patting him on the arm.

Her emotions were on a hair trigger today. She knew Brian's wife had left him several years ago. It must have hurt a lot. She understood the hurt now, in a raw, physical way she wouldn't have quite known about before.

'No, it's fine, we're done. Jill?' he called back into the office. 'You're not still pushing those numbers around, I hope. I told you to go. Come in for a minute, Christina,' he invited her. 'Give me an update on tonight's admission.'

But when Jill had picked up her bag, acknowledged Christina in her usual distant way and hurried off, Brian didn't seem all that interested in Jim Cooper after all.

'Look, I know you must be having a tough week,' he said. 'I've been through it myself and, believe me, I know. The emptiness. Thoughts going round and round. Wrong-headed solutions. You shouldn't sit at home. Can I twist your arm and march you out of the house on, say, Wednesday or Thursday night for a meal?'

'Oh, Brian, I don't—'

'Very low-key and casual. Just between friends. Work colleagues who have more in common than they did a week ago. That's all.'

She didn't want to go. Not with Brian. Not with anyone, really. He was right. She dreaded going home tonight, but once she got there she knew she'd just want to sit and let her thoughts circle in her head, not make the effort to go out again. She wasn't so sure about the 'wrong-headed solutions'.

Sitting at home all week would be wrong-headed, though, wouldn't it? Knowing Joe was in town, but that they weren't together even in the hours he wasn't working? Just thinking about it, about him, with nothing new to conclude?

Lord, she felt as if she was getting flu. Her whole body ached with the effort of holding everything together.

And Brian had been through it, too.

'As long as it's low-key,' she said. 'Pizza or burgers in town. That'd be good. But I'm not up for a big evening.'

'Did I mention a big evening? Let's rewind the tape.' He pretended to listen. 'Nope. Definitely no mention of a big evening.'

She had to laugh. 'All right, then. Thursday?'

Because that would give Joe three whole days to realise how blind he was, and if she and Joe were doing something together, of course Brian would understand if she cancelled their—

Stop it, Christina!

'Thursday. Great. It's in the diary. Pick you up at seven?'

'Sounds good.' She heard sounds coming through the rather thin wall between this office and that of Charles Wetherby, next door. 'Charles is still around?' she asked.

'Is he ever not?'

'Well, true. I'm going to grab him while I can, anyhow.'

'Always happy to be grabbed,' the medical administrator said a minute later, when Christina had apologised for doing it.

She apologised again when she tried to outline Honey Cooper's request, made at a desperate gabble just before Christina had left the ED. 'I'm sorry, it sounds unnecessarily complicated, doesn't it?'

'Contact Mrs Considine-at-the-Gunyamurra-store's nephew's brother-in-law, because the nephew himself is away, but Mrs Considine has to phone the brother-in-law because Honey doesn't have the number, and Mrs Considine has cards at Fiona Donnelly's on Monday nights so you'd have to chase her up there, and Honey does have the number for the Donnellys,' Charles parroted, propelling his wheelchair towards a file cabinet. 'Just a little bit complicated, if I've even got it right.'

'Which is why I thought it might be a lot easier if you could phone Wetherby Downs and ask someone from there to go over.'

'Right,' Charles said, with his back to her.

His back communicated a lot.

A deep-seated reluctance, for one thing.

Christina apologised again. She'd known there were long-standing family tensions, but she also knew that Wetherby Downs was a huge property. There'd be a manager. She could make the call herself and speak to him, if Charles could give her the number. He would suggest this himself, surely, if he didn't want to speak to his brother in person.

'Honey isn't in good shape,' she said, pleading her case, wishing she'd just gone with the nephew's brother-in-law's et cetera. 'Aside from the anxiety, she was dehydrated, low blood sugar, underlying high blood pressure. Just exhausted, basically. She's fretting because she doesn't know if Jim let the cow and calf out or if they're stuck in the shed with no water and feed, and then there are the dogs. I promised I'd make sure that someone—'

'The Considine brother-in-law whose phone number we don't have.'

'Yes, or whoever I could get—would go over to the Coopers' and check that everything was OK.'

Charles spun around silently in the wheelchair. He was good at that, athletic and adept. Once his lower body strength would have matched the powerful build of his arms and torso, and he'd probably ridden a horse as if he'd been born on a saddle.

'No, it's about time I talked to Philip, actually,' he said, on a controlled sigh. 'Let's not go on this wild-goose chase with the Considine brother-in-law's whoever. I'll phone my brother and he'll send someone. You can tell Honey and Jim it's taken care of.'

'Thanks, Charles, I know it's probably an errand you don't need.'

'Might be an errand a few people *do* need,' he murmured, adding, 'Get yourself off home, if you're doing clinic hops again tomorrow.'

'Is he going to die, Dr Barrett?' Honey reached up from the hospital bed and clutched Joe's arm, her voice an agonised whisper. Jim lay just metres away beyond the door into the resus area.

'No, he's not going to die, Mrs Cooper.' He felt much more confident in saying it now.

The first lot of bloods had come back—more would be taken at intervals during the night—and they looked good, as did his ECG tracing. It apparently hadn't been the massive infarct that it could have been, given the drama. He was on a barrage of medication, and it was working.

'What's going to happen, then?'

Joe outlined the best-case scenario. 'We'll keep him in here for a few days, on continuous monitoring and treatment. If everything has resolved well, he can go home and he can even build his activity levels back up pretty much to where they were, as long as he feels comfortable. But he'll need more treatment. A scheduled procedure—a bypass or angioplasty—will give you both a chance to make preparations. You've been told about that in the past, I understand.'

'We just haven't been able to manage it,' Honey answered.

'Well, you'll have to manage it soon. There's still a chance he may need the surgery on a more urgent basis but, from what I'm seeing so far, I'm cautiously optimistic that he won't.'

'Oh! Oh, that's wonderful!' She blinked back tears. 'Is he sleeping?'

'Dozing.'

'I want to see my daughter. I don't know where she'd be. Which ward, I mean.'

'Want me to check for you?' Joe asked.

He knew quite well that Megan was in the obstetrics and gynaecology unit with her baby. He also knew that she didn't want to see her parents. He got the impression that no one would be too upset if Honey somehow managed to get up there on her own and thus forced the issue. But he wanted to make sure.

He went to the phone at the nurses' station and dialed the extension for O and G.

Got Christina.

'Tink?' he said automatically, and felt his stomach lurch sideways. 'What are you doing on this phone?'

'Joe? What's happened? I'm just, you know, hovering. Are you still in the ED?'

'Yes. Everything's fine. ECG tracing has improved a bit more. Bloods came back and look good.' He reported the figures. 'But Mrs Cooper wants to see her daughter. How are we handling that?'

Silence.

'I think we're not,' she finally said. 'I think it's going to be an "oops". Is that playing God?'

'Probably. But, hey, I was born for the role.'

She laughed, then said, 'Don't, Joe.'

And he knew what she meant.

Don't remind me how much we always laugh when we talk.

'Actually, Megan's having a rest now and Lucky's in the nursery,' she said. 'That might be a good thing. The two of them can talk, and—Yes, tell Honey that Megan's in Room Four.'

Grace raised her eyebrows when Christina put down the phone. 'We're letting it happen?'

'How are we going to stop it? Honey's not the type to nod politely and do nothing if she's told, "I'm sorry, your daughter has asked us not to let you see her." We're not a prison, and she's not a danger to the patient.'

'You don't know that,' Grace said, in a voice of doom.

'I do know that! They're going to kill themselves in that family, not each other!' Deliberately, she went over to Megan's bed and touched her shoulder, knowing that Grace would be watching her every move. 'You've got a visitor coming, love,' she said.

Megan's eyes opened sleepily, then went wide. 'Is it—?' She stopped. 'Who?'

'Your mum.'

'Mum? *Mum?* She—'

'Talk to her. She's had a rough day.' Briefly, Christina outlined what had happened to Megan's dad, stressing that his condition looked as if it would resolve well. 'Jackson's in the nursery, and we'll keep him there for now,' she finished. 'How you handle it is up to you.'

'Oh, he's beautiful, Megan! Just beautiful!'

After a tearful ten minutes of talking between mother and daughter, Honey held her new, sleeping grandson in her arms. He still looked frail and small following the heart

surgery he'd needed shortly after birth. He'd had a spike
of fever that morning—Christina and Grace were glad they
hadn't heard about it until a short while ago—but this had
resolved with IV fluids and medication.

'You're not angry?' Megan said.

Honey made a helpless sound. 'How could I be angry?'

'Dad was, six months ago. I thought he was going to kill
Jack, and he didn't even know about the baby.'

'Does Jack know about the baby, love?'

'No. He's gone. I thought he might write, but—I guess
he took Dad pretty seriously, and then when they sacked
him over at Wetherby Downs... I *hate* Philip Wetherby!
We're not going to tell Dad about the baby, OK?'

'Oh, love...'

Seated at the nearby nurses' station, Grace and Christina
looked at each other. It was impossible not to overhear.
Mother and daughter's voices rose as their conversation
grew more heated, and there was no other noise in the unit.
The second mother and baby who'd been in Megan's room
today had gone home, and a couple of Georgie Turner's gynae patients across the corridor had their TV sound systems
pressed close to their ears.

'Don't sound like that,' Megan said. 'Don't talk as if I'm
being unreasonable. Mum, you are the one who's said all
along that we can't upset Dad, and what could possibly upset him more than this?'

'The baby's so beautiful...'

'But that doesn't solve anything!' she burst out. The
baby in Honey's arms didn't stir. 'You can't act as if we're
all happy families now. People keep treating me as if I'm
dumb. I'm not. We're going to lose the farm because I'm
not bringing Jackson back out there, hours from a doctor
when he's had all this trouble, when he so nearly died, and

you and Dad can't manage the place without me. Unless we get a hundred millimetres of rain, like, *tomorrow,* he's the last straw.'

'Megan—'

'Yes! My baby is breaking the camel's back right now, to-day, this week. I could have given him up. I thought about it. But I made the choice. And I knew what I was doing. I've chosen my baby over the farm. We can't have both, in this drought. And I don't think Dad will ever forgive me for that.'

'He'll have to be told—'

'Yes!' Megan agreed fiercely. 'Of course he'll have to know eventually! But let me get out of this hospital and set-tled here in town first before we talk to Dad. Let his heart get better before I break it again.'

She glared at her mother, ready for a counter-attack. None came. Honey's head was bent over the little bundle in her arms. Their drip bags and drip stands—one adult-sized, one for an infant—stood behind them like sentinels.

'She's upset,' Grace murmured, frowning at Honey. 'She doesn't need this. She's supposed to be a patient her-self tonight.'

'I'll take her back to the ED.'

'Are they going to try and find a ward bed for her?'

'She doesn't want one. They're keeping Jim in Resus overnight, and she wants to stay close. No one's arguing.' Against Honey's desire to stay with Jim, Christina meant.

'Except these two,' Grace answered, meaning some-thing different.

'Yes, and you're right, they've done enough of it to-night.' She stood up and went to Honey. 'Let's get you some rest now, Mrs Cooper.'

Honey looked up and nodded, her cheeks wet with tears.

'Megan, can I give Jackson to you?' Christina asked,

and Megan held out her arms at once. They transferred the delicate baby carefully, and he didn't waken.

Honey got to her feet and Christina helped her twitch the IV tubing out of the way. 'We'll sort this out,' she promised her daughter, but it was obvious that she didn't have any answers. 'Twenty-six years!' she said as they walked along the corridor in the direction of the ED. 'Twenty-six years ago this mess started, Dr Farrelly. Who would have thought it would end up this way?'

'I don't know the story,' Christina told her.

'No, of course you don't. It was all kept pretty quiet. It's wrong when that happens. After all, it was an accident. All three of them agreed on that. You still don't know what I'm talking about, of course.'

'No, I'm sorry, I don't.'

'Charles and Philip and my Jim. It happened just after he and I started seeing each other, but he wouldn't listen to any advice of mine about how to handle what went on. The three of them were out pig-shooting. Jim and Charles were eighteen, but Philip was five years younger, only a kid. And Jim made a mistake and shot Charles, and old man Wetherby never forgave him for it. Wouldn't even believe it was an accident at first, because at one stage Jim and Charles were after the same girl. Wetherby cut off our access to Gunya Creek at the crossing. The Coopers had had an agreement over the creek water with the Wetherbys for sixty years. After the old man died, Jim went to Philip—he was running the property by then; Charles was still finishing his medical degree—and asked him, *begged* really, to give the access back, but Philip said no. It had only ever been a favour by the family in the past, and he was under no obligation. Since then…' She stopped and shook her head, too weary to go on, but Christina didn't need to hear any more.

'That's why Charles is in a wheelchair? Because Jim shot him?'

'Yes. All three of them weren't taking the right care. They never told me a story that made complete sense. Philip was mucking around, Charles was distracted. There was blame on all sides, Charles admitted that himself. Old man Wetherby thought it had ruined Charles's life, but he was a stronger man than that and he's made something of himself. Wetherby should have been proud of his eldest son, but Philip was always the golden boy for him. I know Charles hasn't had much to do with any of them since.'

Christina didn't know what to say. She finally blurted, 'Who knows about this?'

'Oh, a lot of people. Word gets around. It's no secret in Gunyamurra. But it's an old story now. Jim can be…difficult sometimes. He's too proud for his own good. He doesn't rally the support some men might get in his position. He had a pretty rough upbringing. I think I'm the only person who ever sees…' She tried again. 'Even Megan doesn't see…' She couldn't go on.

They reached the emergency department, and when he heard the sound of their approach, Jim opened his eyes. 'Honey,' he breathed, then closed his eyes again and was immediately asleep.

Outside, the night air was still warm, although a breeze from the ocean made it feel fresh.

Hometime, Christina thought.

Collect her car and house keys from the main desk in the ED, where Joe had said he'd leave them, collect her car from one of the reserved staff spaces where he would have parked, and drive home.

Something to eat. Water the plants. Check for phone

messages. Open her wardrobe and move the hangers along to fill the empty space where Joe's shirts had been until to-day. While dealing with the wardrobe, decide what she'd wear for her low-key dinner with Brian on Thursday night, because she hadn't done laundry for over a week and there might not be many clean options left.

She couldn't do it.

She couldn't go out with Brian, not even on the terms he'd proposed, not when the thought of Joe's missing shirts had twisted inside her like a rusty knife-blade. She should never have said yes.

Turning, she went back into the hospital foyer and headed in the direction of the hospital administrator's of-fice. If he was still there, she'd tell him face to face. If he wasn't, she'd leave a note.

His light was on, she found, and his door was open. Ap-parently he was still in the building somewhere. Not want-ing to be discovered in the act of cowardly note-scribbling, she waited, and realised that Charles was still there also, in his office just beyond the thin, inadequately sound-proofed wall.

He was on the phone.

'Tell me why I shouldn't despise you, Philip,' she heard. 'You had the perfect opportunity to end all this after Dad died. You told me you would. I thought you had. I never realised it had become so dire.'

There were some seconds of silence. Christina didn't know what to do. She peered out into the corridor, but there was still no sign of Brian. Charles's office door was tightly closed. She found a pad of sticky notes, tore the top one off, wrote 'Dear Brian,' and stood with the pen poised over the little yellow square while her mind stayed blank as to what to put next.

'Your standing in the community?' Charles said, in the adjacent office. 'That's—' Silence again, then, 'Yes, of course I accept my share of the blame. Dear God, we were kids, all three of us. Look, we're going to do something about this, and we're going to talk again. For now, you're telling me you couldn't have fathered this child but, to be honest, Philip, your word may not be good enough for me at this point.'

She couldn't stay any longer, Christina realised. Charles was so private about his personal life and his family history. He would never be talking like this if he knew he could be heard. And she couldn't write the note for Brian. The right, appropriate, carefully censored words just wouldn't come, while tears—along with all the wrong words—threatened to come all too easily.

Dear Brian, I've realised I can't go out with you on Thursday night. I'm still so in love with Joe that it feels like an illness. I'm hungry, but my stomach has shut down and gone queasy. I'm exhausted, but I know I'm going to lie awake all night. I know I've done the right thing, but in many ways that only makes it worse. Sorry. We'll reschedule in three years, when I'm cured.

She crumpled up the yellow scrap with 'Dear Brian' on it, shoved it in her trouser pocket, slipped out of the office and faced the prospect of her empty home.

CHAPTER SIX

AS IT TURNED out, Christina's house wasn't empty.

Or rather, her wide front veranda wasn't.

Joe was waiting for her, warm and solid, taking her in his arms as soon as she'd taken the steps that led up from the garden to the raised floor level. 'Sorry if I scared you,' he said.

'You didn't,' she admitted. 'I'd been thinking you might be here.' She pushed him gently away and he let her do it. The warmth he'd created on her skin lingered there, however.

'And I thought you definitely would be,' he said. 'I got a lift with Georgie Turner. She drove off and then I found a light on inside, but no one here.'

'I left the light on this morning, in case I got back after dark. And, Joe, you know where I keep the spare key.'

Silence.

'It didn't feel right,' he finally said.

And, yes, he was right, it didn't, not after he'd given her back his own key to the house just that morning.

'Well, I'm here now,' she said on a slight edge. 'It's safe for you.' She unlocked the front door and they went inside, their tension with each other more evident the moment they were in an enclosed space.

'What, should I really just have let myself in, Christina?' he asked, dropping his voice low. 'I'm not living here any more.'

He prowled around the living room. They both did, too ill at ease to sit or do anything logical like eat or pour a drink. It felt so weird and wrong and impossible, the fact that she couldn't just go up to him and hug him anymore, stroke his face. It slashed her confidence to the roots at one stroke. The rights you had over someone else's body when you were together, the blurring of space—she just hadn't realised it would feel so weird and so terrible when those rights were gone.

She was the faithful type. She'd known that about herself for years. Ending their relationship didn't mean she'd switched off her feelings. She'd go on loving Joe Barrett for a long time.

'Have you eaten?' he suddenly asked.

'Uh…'

'Because you look pale. I haven't either, but I bet I had more today than you did. Can we find something? Or get pizza, or something?'

'I don't want pizza,' she answered quickly.

Pizza was too cosy, too casual and sexy. Pizza was what they'd done too many times before when they'd been tired. Pizza you ate with your fingers, leaning over the coffee-table, and you watched a movie together, you didn't have some challenging 'talk' while dealing with strings of melty cheese. She loved watching Joe eat, because he had the perfect combination of mess and grace and relish, but she didn't want to watch him eating pizza tonight.

She was still thinking about it when he disappeared into the kitchen. She followed him. 'What are you doing?'

'Scrambled egg on toast. We'll bung some bacon in the sandwich press if there is any.'

He was using 'we' again. The really nice, casual 'we' that in the past had meant impromptu picnics on the carpet or fruitless fishing trips or lazy sessions in bed.

'Tell me what you wanted to talk about, Joe.'

'Not until I've got some food into you.' He was already cracking the eggs into a bowl. He pulled a wooden chair out for her at the kitchen table. 'Sit, OK?'

She did, but only because she'd begun to wonder how much longer her legs would hold her up, and whether her empty stomach would stay where it belonged. Time slowed and her will-power went walkabout. She sat there and watched him work and made no attempt to control anything about the situation.

He looked at her occasionally, as if to check that she hadn't slumped onto the table, but he didn't speak, just forked the eggs until the yolks and whites mixed, dropped bread into the toaster, heated the sandwich press and sliced the rinds off bacon.

'How come you're like this, Joe?' she blurted out when the meal was almost ready. 'So protective?'

'Is that not masculine enough, or something?'

'No, I didn't mean that. The opposite, in some ways. A lot of way less masculine men than you just don't know how to take care of anyone but themselves. My Dad.' Her parents lived hundreds of kilometres south, on the Gold Coast. They'd never met Joe. Which said something. 'I love my dad, but his idea of taking care of my mother when she's tired is to tell her it's OK if she's ten minutes late getting dinner on the table.'

He shrugged. 'Different generation.'

'It's not just that. You see, you never talk. Any time I

give you a cue to tell me about your life at home, your childhood, what's made you who you are, any of that, you head it off and turn it into a generalisation.'

'I said I wanted to talk tonight, didn't I?' On the face of it, it sounded like a belligerent, confrontational line, but it wasn't when Joe said it. It still contained the same easygoing flavour, the tiny nuance of a tease. He put down the two plates of eggs and bacon on toast, and brought a jug of water and a carton of orange juice to the table.

'Yes,' she said aggressively, not feeling easygoing at all. 'So talk.'

So talk.

Joe cut off an egg-piled corner of his toast and forked it into his mouth, buying time. He already knew that he wasn't going to be any good at this. He'd spent too much time training himself in that direction. He didn't believe that talking could change anything, and yet he'd been the one to suggest it. Nice contradiction, Dr Barrett! Why had he decided that Christina needed to know all of this stuff about his life?

To be fair, I guess, he decided inwardly.

Life hadn't been all that fair to the Barretts, but this didn't mean he had to continue the family tradition.

'My sister has Treacher Collins syndrome,' he said. He hadn't planned such a dramatic opening line, but it had come out all by itself, prompted by the life's-not-fair thing, probably.

'Treacher Collins syndrome,' Christina echoed, and he could see her flipping through a mental medical textbook. Had she hit the right chapter? Craniofacial anomalies? Yep, she was getting to it. It sat there in an alphabetical list, somewhere below Moebius syndrome and Nager syndrome and Parry-Romberg syndrome.

He helped her out, just in case she'd turned to the wrong page. 'It's genetic. Rare. One in ten thousand births. If it's carried by either parent, it's a dominant gene, so any child they may have has a fifty-fifty chance of having it, which may have implications for Amber down the track if she wants to have kids.'

She listened intently, nodding every now and then, narrowing her eyes, never taking them from his face. He could see how much she wanted his words to solve something, get the two of them back on track towards a shared future, but he knew it wouldn't happen. She looked fragile suddenly, even though he knew how strong she was, and he wanted to hold her, feel that fabulous contrast between his bulk and her pliant grace.

'And, of course, it can be a spontaneous mutation,' he went on, struggling with the detail for a moment.

Was he hiding behind all this medical stuff?

Trying to scare her off with it?

Yes, definitely that.

'On chromosome five, if you want to get technical. And that's what it was in Amber's case. No one else in the family carries the gene.'

He paused for breath, but he was ready to keep going, to answer her questions. He was pretty sure he knew what she'd ask and he had his responses ready.

Yes, unfortunately in Amber it was severe. Yes, with the characteristic undeveloped external ears, down-slanting eyes, absent cheekbones and eye-socket floors, and small, slanting jaw. Yes, she'd needed numerous surgical procedures and she still faced more. She'd almost died at birth when her condition had taken the medical staff by surprise. She hadn't been able to breathe or feed normally.

Now Amber had a conductive hearing aid and a tracheostomy which was operative at night and capped during the day to give her a voice. A jaw distraction procedure was coming up, and after that they hoped she'd be able to lose the trach but didn't yet know for sure. She might get an internal hearing device some time in the next few years.

And she was a great, terrific, fabulous kid, fifteen years old now, bright and articulate and creative, comfortable with herself, but, yes, she got stared at sometimes, she got teased, she got asked insensitive questions, and he was so proud about how she handled it.

As for how his mother and stepfather handled it…well, he'd get to all that next.

But Christina didn't go in the expected direction at all. Instead, she jumped ahead so far and so fast that he was left open-mouthed with his head spinning. She put her knife and fork down on the plate on either side of her barely touched meal and pushed her chair back. Her ponytail swung like a horse flicking a fly, and her warm brown eyes were blazing.

And even while he was shocked by her reaction, he still had time to think how gorgeous and dynamic she looked.

'That?' she said angrily. 'Something like that…you haven't told me in two years… And you tell me now, as if it totally explains why we're at this impasse with each other? It doesn't explain anything, Joe! I've read about Treacher Collins. I'm a doctor.'

'So you know it can be pretty serious.'

'You're hiding your sister just because of her facial deformity, the way people used to hide the family lunatic and believe they could never marry because there was a streak of insanity in the family? I don't believe it! I don't understand why you haven't told me any of this in two years, and why you're telling it to me now as if it explains…!'

She stopped.

Started again a few seconds later.

'No. Actually, I do understand. And that makes it worse. A heck of a lot worse.'

Her voice broke and she rushed out of the kitchen, and he knew it was because she was too upset to stay. He could hear her gasping, angry sobs, and for a moment he was tempted to let her have it her way. Leave her alone, if she wanted to be left alone. Let her be angry with him, if that was what she believed about his motivations. It would define the end of their relationship more clearly.

But then he rebelled. He'd gone along with her ultimatum so far because he hadn't felt that he had the right to do anything else. If he wasn't promising a future for the two of them, then she had every reason to turf him over to the doctors' house, every right to put her own needs first and keep her options open.

This time, though…

He couldn't let her get it so wrong.

Rising from the table, he listened but couldn't work out where she'd gone. The house seemed too quiet. Then he heard the back screen door flap and followed her in that direction. Standing on the veranda, he saw her prowling the back garden, where a streetlamp shining through from the next street gave everything the bluish-white hue of moonlight.

He went down the steps and confronted her angry, wounded expression. 'Christina, it's more complicated than you think.'

'Listen to yourself say that! Whose fault is it?'

'Mine. I know that.'

'So change!'

He laughed tiredly.

Christina drawled, 'I know. You just said it. It's more complicated than I think.'

'The reason I didn't tell you is not because I was ashamed of Amber, if that's what you're thinking. Hell, no! I'm incredibly proud of her.' He outlined the surgical procedures she'd had, the struggles she still faced. 'And it wasn't because I thought you'd be horrified about her either. I know you're not like that.'

'Then why?'

He sighed, facing the unpleasant prospect of finding the right words, picking his way through. 'Amber's birth destroyed my mother's marriage to my stepfather,' he began.

'I thought they were still together.'

'They are, but it's only because neither of them trusts the other to do the right thing for Amber. My stepfather has a drinking problem. It was always there in the background, but it got worse after Amber was born. He makes an enemy of every doctor who treats her. He doesn't trust my mother to "stand up to them". And sometimes he's been right. There have been a couple of times when, in hindsight, the wrong decisions have been made—like when they tried to take out her trach at one point, and had to put it back in because she couldn't get enough air without it. New Zealand just doesn't have enough doctors with enough experience of this condition.'

'Your parents couldn't have taken her elsewhere for another opinion?'

'There isn't the money. I'm putting in a lot to support them as it is.'

'The New Zealand health system doesn't cover all the costs?'

'When you're talking about expensive, ongoing procedures like the ones Amber has had, and still needs, no health system covers all the costs. For a start, some of her surgery is regarded as cosmetic. Or elective, and subject to waiting lists, which mean the timing ends up all wrong. And some costs are impossible to quantify, like the fact that my mother can't hold down a decent job when Amber has needed so much of her time. I know my mother would like to leave my stepfather. She married him when she was still in pieces over my father's death, and she mistook his domineering for strength. She's stronger herself now, but she believes that staying with him is best for Amber. Because of the way he alienates doctors, because his priorities for Amber aren't always right, because of the money. She fights to maintain the partnership, even if it's just on the surface. She doesn't want to rock the boat.'

'And neither did you, with me. You just wanted the R&R. You didn't trust me enough to tell me any of this, because you thought that if you did, I might not stick around for the fun times you wanted from me. Do you know how much that hurts?'

'Would you really stick around, Tink? Would you really take it on? Every cent that I save by working over here goes to my parents for Amber. To my mother, really. If I can make enough of a nest-egg to convince her she can afford to leave my stepfather, then that's hers, too. Amber has such courage. I'm not going to let her down. She's only just turned fifteen. I'm staying in Auckland, probably permanently and definitely until Amber is grown up and independent. I'm not moving elsewhere because if I wasn't in Auckland, I think the family situation would blow sky-high. I don't trust my stepfather's intentions. I don't trust my mother's strength. I trust Amber absolutely, but she has enough on her plate just dealing with the surgery and the self-image. If I left…' He shook his head. 'Bad enough being here one week in four. If it wasn't for the money…'

'Money? I have money. My grandmother left me $60,000 as well as this house.'

He laughed. 'That would have gone down well. Christina sweetheart, I love you, give me your inheritance so I can spend it on my sister.'

'When people love each other—my God, Joe, you of all people should understand this—they take on each other's lives, each other's problems.'

To Joe's ears it sounded sweet, seductive…naïve. It sounded like a siren song whose hypnotic influence he had to fight or it would weaken him and drag him under.

'I don't want this,' he said. He tried not to sound harsh, but knew he had to sound firm. 'You don't know what you're offering. Christina, it doesn't work, that whole idea of a problem shared being a problem halved. Not when it's stuff like this.'

'So you're the only one who gets to be a hero. Boy, you have tickets on yourself, don't you?'

'It's not like that. Your involvement would only compound the pressure. And I've got enough pressure. That's exactly what I've loved about being here, being with you. So much less pressure.'

She paced around the garden some more, still angry and agitated. Her breathing came in little gasps and he knew it was because of the battle inside her between yelling and crying. In the end, she did both.

'Go! Just go, OK? If you're going to keep talking like this, I don't want to hear it. I never thought I could be this angry with you. I—I can't even talk about it any more.'

He looked at her and saw that she meant it. And she was right, of course. He'd said what he had to say, what she deserved to hear—the basic explanation. Now he needed to leave her alone to digest it, and to come around to his point of view.

Love wasn't enough, if what two people needed from each other was so totally different, and in such conflict. It wasn't enough if one of them was only going to drag the other one down. He should never have said the L word, because for her it meant a future, and for him it didn't.

He just didn't have the space.

Todd had driven to the gate to pick him up, as he'd promised to do.

Promise? It had been more like a threat.

'Take your days off, then, dag-face, but if you're not back on this spot by five o'clock Tuesday afternoon, I'm not waiting.'

Jack had dropped from the cab of the truck that had given him his last lift at four forty-five. His watch read six-ten as Todd's ute scrabbled to a halt in the dirt on the far side of the gate.

'Hungover?' was Todd's cheerful greeting. He'd wound his window down but hadn't bothered to get out of the car.

'Head's splitting,' Jack answered on a drawl.

Of course it wasn't true. He never wasted too much honesty on Todd. Digger wasn't so bad. The kind of bloke who respected you if you earned it. Todd didn't have enough discrimination to respect anyone.

'Come on, fathead, climb over,' he said.

'I want my back pay first.'

Todd laughed. 'What, you think I carry that kind of cash around with me?'

'I know you do.' He pointed at the back of the ute. 'It's taped to the side of the tyre well, right there.' In a plastic

packet, and the tape was that strong cloth kind. It was a pretty obvious hiding place.

Todd's eyes narrowed, but he recovered quickly. 'And where are you going to keep it?' he jeered.

'Lend me the tape and I'll find somewhere.' Against his own chest, probably.

'Half. You can have half. Gesture of good faith.'

Jack nodded. He hadn't expected more. To be honest, he hadn't known what he'd do, what his next move would be, if Todd called his bluff and refused to give him anything, but apparently the man needed him enough that he had some leverage now.

Gotta strategise a bit more in future, Jack, he told himself.

Todd was going to shift his stash, for a start, so Jack would need to learn the new hiding place as soon as he could, or the first half of his back pay might be all he'd ever get. And he should listen to his instincts and think a bit more about what was going on here. Why did Todd carry so much in cash anyhow? And those reports he came back with from 'the boss'—they were inconsistent sometimes.

The trip down south, even though Jack hadn't got where he wanted to go, seen who he wanted to see, had cleared his head, hardened his spirit. The night he'd spent, two days ago, dossed down on some damp shrubs behind the bus shelter at the hospital, he'd barely slept but he'd thought a lot, watching the patterns of bright and dark through the hospital windows.

It hadn't been a waste of time, as he'd thought at first. It had fortified him somehow, and when he'd set off again, walking north beside the highway just before dawn, he'd felt as if he was carrying something new and good inside him. Pining and mooning and dreaming *didn't do you any good. You had to plan, and you had to take action.*

She had seen something in him that no one else ever had.

She'd told him he was strong and smart.

Time to start proving it.

On Wednesday, Christina had the day off.

She knew it would be tough. Sleeping in until nine-thirty had been a stupid strategy of denial. Now she just felt thick-headed and sluggish, only getting to breakfast at a quarter past ten. On top of it all, she felt nauseous, and two pieces of buttered toast with Vegemite didn't do enough to settle the feeling.

Yesterday, she and Glenn and Grace had done another clinic flight, one of their regular island hops. It was like a different world. Ocean instead of desert. Tourists irritated that illness had disrupted their expensive break, instead of locals trying to get on with their normal lives. The cases had all been pretty routine, no drama, no patients to bring in to the ED. She hadn't set eyes on Joe at all.

She'd arrived home before dark, but the empty house hadn't felt any better in daylight than it did at night. She'd co-opted a couple of people into going for a drink at the Black Cockatoo, but then she'd only had a single lemon squash and left after less than an hour. The smell of beer had made her feel ill, and the noise of the other drinkers had jarred.

She knew she'd have to advertise for a new occupant for Joe's empty room very soon, because she would fall into too many bad habits if she stayed on her own.

Not eating right, for example.

Those plates of congealed scrambled egg had just got

chucked in the bin on Monday night, and she'd had an evening meal of tea and chocolate biscuits instead.

She wouldn't look after herself unless she had someone here to shame her into it, she knew that. What she really needed was someone *she* could look after, someone to give her the incentive to have salad ingredients and vegetables, cheese and cold sandwich meat in the fridge, decent bread in the pantry, a bathroom she cleaned twice a week, someone she wouldn't want to appear in her pyjamas in front of at noon on a Saturday.

Megan Cooper.

Megan and her baby.

The idea came to her as if a voice had spoken it in her ear, and her brain was slow to catch up.

Could it work? Would Megan be interested?

She was almost ready for discharge. She was only still there because she hadn't got the feeding thing sorted out, and because the family situation was complicated. Jackson would need a little longer, and Megan would probably spend most of her time at the hospital by his side even once she was no longer officially a patient herself, but it would help her to have a place she could come to just to crash occasionally, do laundry, eat a home-cooked meal.

'I'm going to ask,' she decided, speaking out loud to her coffee-cup. It was a poor substitute for the conversation partner she really wanted in her kitchen right now.

Don't go down that path, Christina.

Stay practical.

What else did she need to consider?

Rent? She wouldn't charge anything. Or not until Megan was well and truly on her feet anyhow, and then only for the sake of the girl's pride.

Joe had insisted on paying for his room for the first few

months, two years ago, but it had been obvious that he had been trying to save every possible cent that he earned here. Christina had seized on a couple of leaky taps as an opportunity as soon as she'd realised.

'I'm hopeless at that stuff, Joe, and I'm not interested in learning. I'll call a plumber…or if you have the skills, could you do it? Could we make it in lieu of rent, that you'll tackle those jobs that come up from time to time?'

He'd agreed, and she hadn't had a leaky tap, a loose board on the veranda, a wayward lawn, a sticky door or a blown light bulb since.

Why did all her thought tracks come back to Joe?

She made a growling noise, put her coffee-cup on the draining-board and focused again.

Rent. The issue of rent. Megan might not be able to barter her rent with practical skills. She'd been raised on a farm, but she was young and not ready for motherhood and she had a fragile baby to take care of. But it would be great to have the two of them in the house. Especially great to have a baby…

Tick, tick, tick. Biological clock. No father in sight.

Christina Farrelly!

It was all arranged about Megan and the baby by the end of the afternoon.

'And I've put a box in the staff tea-room, Christina,' Jill Shaw told her, in her office. 'For donations of clothing and personal items for Megan and Honey and the baby. Honey had nothing when she flew in with you.'

'That's right, only her handbag.'

'She's bought some underwear in town, but we all know that money is tight for that family so she doesn't want to invest in a whole new wardrobe.'

'That's thoughtful of you, Jill,' Christina said.

'Yes, well. Some kinds of needs are obvious and easy to meet.'

Charles appeared in the doorway, having done his usual magic trick with the silent wheelchair. He was pretty magic at catching up on a conversation halfway through, too. 'We're talking about the box for the Coopers?' he asked.

'Yes, Dr Wetherby, I hope you approve.'

'Don't approve of the Dr Wetherby bit, Jill,' he said with a grin, 'but the rest of it's fine. There are three packets of nappies in there already, I noticed.'

'Oh, wonderful!' Christina answered. 'We're going to have to empty it three times a day.'

'I thought of that. It's a big box,' Jill retorted.

And finally she smiled.

Christina caught Charles's lingering look of approval at the change in Jill's face, and wondered about it. First Brian clucking over their director of nursing, now Charles. Prickly Jill had been a little softer lately. She was getting over her bad marriage, and her divorce. What might happen next? Brian and Jill? And what about Charles? Had he ever thought of marriage?

She couldn't wonder about it for long, because Charles had something to tell her.

'I've spoken to Glenn. I'm hitching a ride with you tomorrow.'

'On the clinic run? Springing a performance evaluation on us?'

'Do you think you need one?'

'Not urgently!' She grinned, and got the same approving look that he'd given to Jill.

He cares about all of us, that's all it is, she decided. Cares about his hospital and his staff. Brian's free to give

Jill a shoulder to cry on, and my dinner with him tomorrow is nothing more than filling in time. There's no mess…

Except the one between her and Joe.

No one could help her with that.

'Well, you're safe from inspection for the moment anyhow. I'm taking a day off,' Charles said. He frowned suddenly. 'You and Glenn and Grace are heading into the Gulf country, but you're going to take a detour first and drop me at Wetherby Downs.'

CHAPTER SEVEN

'How did it go today, Christina?' Charles asked as they climbed into the air, away from Wetherby Downs.

For once, his mind didn't seem fully focused where his mouth was, Christina thought. He had asked the question absently, his gaze straying back to the arid view from the aircraft window before he'd even heard her answer.

'Pretty routine,' she told him through their headsets. The twin engines droned on. 'Although I took a few bloods and tissue samples. We might have some follow-up, bringing a couple of people in for treatment.'

'Mmm,' he answered, still looking at the ground below. 'Lord, it's dry! I could see it on the way out this morning, the perceptible shading off of the green into brown as soon as we were over the mountains.'

Christina looked at the land below. It spread out like a map, the detail of the terrain clear but flattened by their increasing altitude. She saw cattle moving toward a wide, tree-lined loop of creek, and a windmill turning lazily against the backdrop of dry, red earth.

'How is Wetherby Downs?' she asked

They'd picked Charles up from the private airstrip at the huge station fifteen minutes ago on their way back to Crocodile Creek. The strip was a couple of kilometres from the main homestead, whose location was marked from the air by its groupings of desert-hardy trees. He'd just been sitting there on his own, with his wheelchair parked by a fence-post as he'd watched the approach of the plane. For some reason no one had waited with him after dropping him off, and he'd looked like a very solitary figure.

Helpless, you would have said, if you hadn't known him the way they knew him in Crocodile Creek.

'It's on the market,' he answered bluntly, his jaw tight.

'That bad?'

Christina couldn't believe it. She knew that on such a vast acreage there should still be water. Gunya Creek was spring-fed and permanent. It never dried up. Even if Charles's younger brother had had to sell off some stock to ease the burden on resources, a place of this size had its surplus capital from the good years invested—protected—elsewhere.

'The cattle are doing fine,' Charles said. 'It was my decision to put the place up for sale, since I have partial ownership, and it has nothing to do with the drought. Everyone's going to know about it soon enough, so there's no point in secrecy.'

'Why?' she asked blankly. She could see that Grace and Glenn were both listening, just as curious.

'Because even with a direct approach from me, my brother refused to help the Coopers, not in their current crisis, and not by giving them back the creek access they had for three generations. And since my father neglected to specify in his will that the family property was not to be sold in order for one of the part-owners to realise their capital share, I'm doing just that—forcing the sale. There are pastoral companies who'll be very interested, because they know they can push for a rock-bottom price in this drought.'

'But, Charles—'

He ignored her. 'I spent some time sitting with Jim Cooper last night. We were pretty good mates in our teens. Now he's a broken man. If there's any chance of him getting back on his feet, physically and emotionally, he's going to need a miracle.'

'And you've found one?' Christina asked eagerly. Everyone at the hospital wanted the best possible outcome for the Cooper family.

Charles shook his head. 'I tried. But my brother is a pompous idiot, and weak with it, which doesn't leave me with a lot of choice. If Philip isn't going to honour his obligations as part of the local community, then I'm going to put my share of the money from the sale of Wetherby Downs towards helping the community in a different way. Wygera needs a swimming pool. Crocodile Creek needs better scanning equipment. The doctors' house could do with a new fridge, I'm told. Any suggestions to add to the shopping list are very welcome.'

Well, he'd shocked all of them!

'Th-that's very generous of you, Charles,' Christina told him.

'It isn't,' he snapped back tersely. 'It's blackmail. I've used two strategies on Philip over the course of our lives. I've protected him, and I've ignored him. Both of those strategies appear to have failed. We'll see what happens with this one.'

'Is this…?' Grace began, sounding unusually tentative. 'Charles, you've told us this isn't a secret, but—'

'But does that mean I want the news spreading like wildfire? Of course I don't, but it'll happen anyway. Tell whoever you like.'

Had anyone ever seen Charles like this before?

Christina certainly hadn't. She wondered what had gone on between the two men, and whether Charles's lonely wait for the aircraft was significant. Who had driven him out to the airstrip? Why hadn't they stayed? Who had been the angriest, Philip or Charles?

Nobody felt much like talking after this, and she was glad to realise that the flight back to Crocodile Creek would soon be over.

Famous last words. They got a radio call to divert to Wygera on the way in, to pick up a patient. The rescue helicopter was transferring a young woman in pre-term labour at twenty-eight weeks gestation down south to a hospital with a high-level neonatal unit, and couldn't be spared for an emergency at the settlement right now.

Wygera.

Joe had gone out there with a nurse on a clinic visit today, Christina knew, and her body went into fight-or-flight mode when she thought about seeing him. That queasy feeling from yesterday was back, and flying through a patch of rough air didn't help.

She and Joe hadn't parted well on Monday night. She'd looked up Treacher Collins syndrome on the internet the previous day, but all that had done had been to strengthen her belief that if Joe really cared about her, he should let her fully into his life. He was so proud of his half-sister. Christina would have loved to meet her, but clearly Joe never planned to let that happen.

She had been angry, hurting about it, questioning Monday's decisions and reactions, ever since.

But no lightning bolts of clarity had hit. Was she right to feel angry? Was she crazy to keep on looking for ways to give him another chance? What could she do to prove that he was wrong?

Joe and nurse Lindsay Palmer met them beside the airstrip, in the staff vehicle they'd used to drive there from

Crocodile Creek that morning. In the back of the vehicle, stretched awkwardly along the back seat, they had a kid with his arm curled protectively around some rickety thing that looked like a school craft project.

'Appendicitis,' Joe reported, yelling over the slowly subsiding propeller noise. He flashed Christina a glance and they both forgot to smile or say hello, too distracted by how complex their feelings were.

Lindsay gave everyone a brief greeting.

'Not sure how much detail you got on the radio,' Joe continued. His habitual good cheer seemed forced today, which was no surprise. 'I'm hijacking the plane because I think he's ruptured already, and we still have patients to see. Not to mention a thirty-mile drive back being less than ideal for young Shane.'

'How bad is he?' Christina asked.

'Not as bad as you'd think. Pain-wise, that is. He had the characteristic protective walk when his mother brought him in—he didn't want to come, still doesn't. Very tender when I got him lying flat and had a feel, but the tenderness was atypical. Mildly febrile. No nausea, although his mother said he had some last night. No vomiting, though. Then when I was debating what we should do with him, he started telling us something had popped and it wasn't hurting nearly so much any more and could he keep on with his model now, please?'

'His model?' Grace queried.

'The thing he's holding. It's a design for the new swimming pool and it's got some terrific ideas, actually. I said he could bring it with him, since he wasn't one bit keen to come without it.' He stepped closer to the plane and raised his voice. 'Charles, could we swap jobs for the rest of today?'

'Me take over the clinic with Lindsay?' Charles called back. 'Makes sense. I'd like to spend a bit of time out here. They've been through such a lot lately.'

They all knew that with his wheelchair he couldn't do anything useful, medically, in the confined space of the plane, and that having Joe back at the hospital could be vital if resources were stretched thin by any other emergency. Cal would operate.

'Glenn?' Charles said.

'Yep.' The pilot knew what to do. He had soon jumped down to the hard-baked clay of the strip to unfold Charles's wheelchair for the short transfer to the vehicle. Charles's upper-body strength and agility made the shift from chair to front passenger seat smooth and fast, and the wheelchair was re-folded and put in the back, along with some equipment they hadn't needed that day.

'Am I going in the plane?' Shane asked.

He looked about ten. Straw for hair, sleeveless flannel shirt, big eyes like glossy buttons. He could have obtained gainful employment as a scarecrow, he was obviously a handful, and you liked him as soon as you looked at him.

'Yes, you're going in the plane and, yes, you can bring your model,' Joe told him.

'It's the best one,' Shane said. 'Did you see Roddie's? It wasn't as good, but he says he's making it better. Everyone's working on 'em now. It was my idea!' He sounded affronted.

'We'll have a competition,' Charles announced with dour satisfaction from the passenger seat of the car, his face still as grim as it had been since they'd picked him up. 'It's perfect. All the kids at Wygera, anyone who wants to enter. This pool is not just going to be a big cement bathtub surrounded by dirt. It's going to be properly landscaped, really attractive, almost a water park, if we can manage it. It would be great to get the kids' ideas. The prize for the best model is... Dammit, what's the bloody prize? Fast-food vouchers? It's got to be something better than that. I'll have a think. Lindsay?'

'The prize?' The older nurse looked startled and a little blank. She didn't know that her hospital administrator had decided to force the sale of his family heritage that afternoon. Grace looked as if she was tempted to give over the goss right now.

But of course there wasn't time.

'No, I mean, let's drive, finish that clinic,' Charles answered the other nurse.

'Shane, up you go,' Joe was saying. 'Your mum's coming in the car with Dr Wetherby when he's finished at the clinic. She wants to pack an overnight bag for you first.'

Back in the plane, as Lindsay and Charles drove off, Christina was already getting out the IV equipment. They would need to hit him with a barrage of antibiotics, and they wouldn't wait for confirmation that the appendix had indeed blown. Shane looked uncomfortable, in more pain than he was letting on, but still consumed with the issue of the pool design.

'If there's a competition, there should be a prize for whose idea it was to make models, as well as for the best one,' he said. 'Tell that other doctor. The weather one.'

'Dr Wetherby? We will,' Christina answered. 'But not right now.'

'He's selling, Joe,' Grace came in. 'He told us today. He's using his part-ownership to force through the sale of Wetherby Downs.'

Joe whistled.

'Yes,' Grace agreed. 'I'm pretty shocked.'

Christina didn't join in. She thought Grace was probably attempting to take the heat, distract Joe and herself from each other.

Thanks, Grace. Yes, it's tough, being shut up in a plane with Joe. You're right, I want to cry or yell, so if you can keep the conversation ball bouncing, I'm grateful. And, yes, you'd probably also like to hear, at some point, what he and I talked about on Monday night, and how angry I got.

She hadn't found the right opportunity for that conversation with Grace yet. Probably could have if it had felt easier to open her mouth on the subject. But it felt…hard. Her stomach sank with reluctance every time she thought about it.

She swabbed a patch of skin on the inside of Shane's elbow with antiseptic, coaxed a vein into greater prominence and slipped the needle in. Shane didn't flinch. He was still clutching his model, which was made out of plastic margarine containers and cereal packet cardboard and silver and gold cigarette pack paper and half a dozen other makeshift things.

'See, it has to have water jets, and a couple of slides…'

'This tube is going to stay in for a while, Shane, so I'm going to tape it in place, OK?' she cut in.

'And a wading pool for the little kids, and a deep bit for the slide to go into…'

Glenn began his preparations for taxi and take-off.

'And it has to have grass, and shade, and look like… like…you know, you *have* to go there, you can't stay away. What're those places? Oh-ay-sisses.'

'An oasis?'

'Yes. Has to be like one of those.'

'It sounds great, Shane.'

'I'll be bringing togs and towel out to Wygera myself,' Joe agreed. 'Should see the splash when I do a bomb into the water. People scatter. OK, now we're giving you some medication, Shane. But that's going through the IV so you don't need to worry about a bad taste in your mouth.'

'Speaking of which,' Grace came in, 'if it's hurting, I can give you a squirt of this stuff, Shane. It tastes OK, you've probably had it before.'

The flight was uneventful, including a textbook-smooth landing and no smiles from Glenn.

'He's a good kid,' Joe commented to Christina as the noise level in the aircraft subsided and they taxied towards the ambulance waiting beside the tarmac.

Shane was lying quietly, probably still thinking about his model. The double transfer from plane to ambulance to hospital when an emergency admission came by fixed wing aircraft wasn't ideal. The helipad was better placed, directly adjacent to the hospital, even though the cost had been higher to have it that way.

'Good patient, too,' Joe added.

'I like the model,' Christina said.

'Wouldn't want to contemplate the budget for it.'

'Charles seems very determined that it won't be an issue.'

'Do you think he'll really force the sale?' Joe looked sceptical.

'Well, he said himself, after we'd picked him up from Wetherby Downs, that it was blackmail.' Instinctively, because she was talking about something so sensitive, she leaned closer, and both she and Joe noticed, felt the familiar intimacy.

His dark gaze flicked down to her arm close to his, and lifted again, moving over her body almost like a caress. The very air between them felt different. Her skin felt different. The way her lungs filled.

She took a careful breath and continued, 'But even if the sale doesn't go through, I've had the impression that Wetherby resources could find enough capital for a community swimming pool without liquidising their major asset.'

Joe dropped his voice. Had he been listening to what she'd just said? She didn't think so. 'Are you going to the party at the doctors' house tonight?' His jaw jutted, making him look strong and stubborn.

Party? No, she was going out to dinner with Brian. But she didn't want to tell Joe about that because it sounded like a transparent piece of rebound dating.

Which it wasn't. She wasn't remotely ready for rebound dating yet.

'Party?' she echoed.

'Dora Grubb's birthday, spur-of-the-moment idea of Cal's.' Dora and her husband Walter were stalwarts on the house-keeping side of hospital activity. 'She's been a treasure lately, taking care of Gina and Cal's young CJ, and they thought Georgie could do with a nice night, too, after dealing with her mother's death. I think you should come, Tink.'

'Why?'

He didn't have an answer. Probably because her question had been sharp and angry and pointless.

'I'm sorry, Joe,' she said.

'Because you're not going to come?'

She closed her eyes. 'Because I snapped at you. I'm not angry with you about...' She waved a hand. 'Party invitations.'

'But you are angry. Still.'

'Yes.'

'We'll talk about it tonight.'

'Sheesh, Joe! Two years we don't talk about anything important—'

'No?' He looked startled.

'No! But suddenly this week talking is the magic bullet?'

'I think we talked about a lot of things that were important,' he said quietly.

She ignored him. 'We talked on Monday—'

'You know, talking about mowing the lawn can be important if there's the right spirit behind it. Saying, please, pass the milk, or did you see that goal in the last minute of the game? Talking isn't everything. It's the actions behind the talk that count. The spirit behind it.'

Christina was in no mood to listen to this kind of philosophy. 'And we ended up angrier!' she finished.

'You're snapping again, Tink.'

'Well, this time there's no apology!'

But there was a safety in feeling able to show her anger that she didn't fully understand or appreciate until she was out with Brian that night. She'd gone straight home after the flight and hadn't heard an update on young Shane, so she was happy when Brian could give her one.

'The appendix was ruptured, as Joe thought,' he said over dinner. 'It was tucked behind the bowel so Cal couldn't get it out via laparoscopy. He had to go in through an old-fashioned incision, but he didn't muck around in there and the boy will be fine once the infection's brought under control.'

'That's good to hear, Brian.'

Christina was a lot less happy about the ambient backdrop to the update.

Brian had brought her to Mike Poulos's parents' very swishy three-star restaurant, which was part of the Athina hotel.

Low-key, she wanted to protest. You promised me it would be low-key. Pizza or burgers. And that was the only reason I said yes.

With its glorious ocean views, wall-sized aquarium of tropical fish, imported chef and prices to match, the Athina's restaurant was not low-key!

And Brian didn't pretend to think it was either. He had

arrived at her door earlier with a dozen roses, and had persuaded her to change into 'something dressier' before he would head out. She'd abandoned her denim skirt and cotton shirt and put on a pair of elegant black trousers and a shimmery top in rich metallic colours that fell from thin straps to drape across her front and left her shoulders bare. She'd even put her hair up with pins.

This time she fitted the bill...which was going to be huge. Brian had called ahead to the restaurant to order some special lobster dish for two that wasn't on the menu, he'd chosen one of the most expensive Chardonnays on the wine list and he kept requesting love songs from the live musician.

Christina was furious.

But how could she say so?

It was just conceivable that you could yell at a man for treating you like a cheap date, but to yell at him for the opposite reason? Because he was lavishing a two-hundred-dollar dinner and large quantities of special attention on her when he'd insisted this was just between friends?

She would have yelled if it had been Joe.

Light-bulb moment.

She was comfortable with Joe. They were safe enough with each other to get angry. Couldn't he see how important that was?

But she couldn't yell at Brian.

And couldn't *he* see how wrong this whole evening was?

'I've always thought you were pretty special, Christina,' he told her.

No, no, no! I haven't been sending out those kind of signals!

'Well, you know,' she joked deliberately, 'I did my medical degree at Sydney University and my professors were pretty happy with me.'

'That's not what I mean, and you know it.'

Yes, darn it, I do know it, but take the hint!

He didn't.

'I know it's too soon—'

'It takes time, doesn't it? I think Jill's only just getting over her divorce. She's a terrific woman, Brian. I hadn't seen it until recently, and I think she really values your support,' she gabbled desperately.

'And, of course, I'm happy to give it, but Jill is not who I want to talk about right now. Tell me more about the real Christina Farrelly. Is she the fabulous woman I think she is?'

No, she's a complete hag, with a definite depletion of brain cells this week, Christina thought, and she should never have come out with Brian.

'She's pretty tired,' Christina said truthfully. She didn't want to hurt him. Where was the human compassion in doing that? Not to mention the career advantage.

By skipping dessert and gulping her wine, she brought the evening to an earlier finish than she'd been afraid of. Brian looked at his watch. 'I'll run you home, but let's call in at the hospital first. I have a couple of errands to take care of.'

He wanted to show off the fact that they'd been out, she soon realised.

Not to Joe.

After some embarrassing encounters with people like Cal and Georgie, which Christina was sure Brian had engineered in order to parade their date, meeting up with Joe was the one chance event of the evening, and she was so relieved to see him that she couldn't help letting it show.

Joe Barrett, I'd a hundred times rather spend an angry evening with you than a smoochy evening with Brian. Can I tell you that? Does it mean something? Will it help? Can you save me from Brian right now?

'Joe?' She grabbed his arm and steered him down the corridor towards the surgical ward, while trying to make it look as if he was steering her. 'Give me an update. You're looking in on Shane?'

'Just have. His mother's with him and he's doing pretty well. Pretty groggy from the PCA.' The abbreviation stood for patient-controlled anaesthesia. 'He's pressing the button for it a lot.'

'What's he having? Morphine?'

'Yes. He's still on oxygen, fluids, anti-emetic, antibiotics. Cal did a good job as usual. Didn't have him in Theatre too long.'

'Routine, then.'

'So far. And we're getting bowel sounds. Which means he should be back to working on his swimming-pool design in a few days.'

'I hope Charles goes ahead with his competition idea.'

'Have you ever known Charles not to go ahead with any of his ideas? Eh, Brian?'

He smiled dutifully, while Christina laughed.

'Good point,'she said. 'I'd like to see Shane myself. Do you mind coming back with me, Joe? Now?'

Please?

She turned the minimal acceptable number of degrees back in Brian's direction. 'Brian, thanks for a really lovely meal. Don't worry about getting me home. I'll thumb a lift with someone.'

He frowned. 'Christina, that's dangerous.'

She hadn't meant it literally. 'I'll make sure it's someone whose last name I already know,' she told him patiently, and didn't wait for his reaction.

Still dragging Joe with her, she took a couple more determined steps in the direction of the ward, and Joe murmured, 'I like this arm-clutching exercise. New anger-management technique?'

'Oh, Joe…!' It was almost a sob.

'Hey…Tink!'

'Don't make me laugh when I'm feeling like this.'

Brian had gone, finding some discretion at last. Joe and Christina both slowed and stopped.

'Forcible laughter induction procedure against the patient's will,' Joe teased, his voice only for her. The rest of the universe seemed to disappear. 'Grounds for a medical malpractice suit, I'd reckon.'

'Stop!' She pressed her hands to the sides of her head.

'Listen…' His voice dropped even lower. 'If I can get you to stop feeling angry, I'll do it, using fair means or foul. I never wanted us to get to this point.' He traced a soft line across her hand with his finger.

She gave a helpless sigh. 'You know what I've started to think? Being angry isn't such a bad thing, especially if we're talking about it. At least it means we have something real!' She reached out and brushed her knuckles against his forearm, loving its strength, no longer willing to surrender her right to touch him.

'Do we still have something at all, Tink?' His dark eyes wandered over her, and they stood even closer, enough to feel each other's heat. 'I thought we didn't.'

'Oh, we have something.' Her hand hovered over his shoulder, then dropped away again. If she touched his neck, he'd bend and kiss her. She knew he would, and that would be too hard to deal with.

'Great big wounds, if nothing else,' he suggested.

'Yeah? You have them, too?'

'You really think I'm breezing through the week? Living it up at the doctors' house? Cruising for chicks at the Black Cockatoo?'

If you feel the same way I do, why are we in this mess? she wanted to yell at him. *Why are we putting ourselves through this for no reason?*

Bloody heroes!

'Shall we just…go to the party, Joe?' she suggested, knowing they couldn't get into an intense and personal conversation now, pull their lives apart and put them back together again just metres from patients in their beds.

'Yeah, let's,' he agreed.

So they went, walking in silence out of the hospital and across the memorial garden in the soft night, not touching, no longer a partnership, but still with so much going on.

And it was noted by numerous pairs of eyes that they arrived together, even though they moved apart as soon as separate groups of friends greeted them.

'So?' Grace demanded, cornering Christina in the big kitchen a short while later. 'You look great. Brian took you to the Athina, didn't he?'

'Yes, but that wasn't—'

'No, I know, it was a much bigger evening than you wanted, but don't tell me about dinner with Brian. Tell me about Joe. I saw you coming across the garden with him.'

Someone had turned the music up loud. A couple of kids were dancing on the lawn, up past their bedtime. There were people in the pool, and Gina was acting as a self-appointed lifeguard. Joe was mooching around out there as well. Brian put in an appearance, but didn't stay long. Mrs Grubb had ignored her role as guest of honour and was taking charge of the food.

Joe. Grace wanted to hear about Joe, the way she had three days ago by the water-tank in Gunyamurra.

'Bottom line, Grace, it's the swan-wife issues,' Christina told her friend.

'Oh, it is?' Grace looked intrigued. And worried.

'Yep. I was right. You were right. Sticks out a mile. Incredible that no one else in town has noticed the tell-tale dropping of flight feathers.'

'But seriously!' Grace yelled above the music.

'Seriously? OK. Swan-sister issues. Family issues.' She couldn't go into details. Joe had made it clear he didn't want it all talked about. 'A family he can't leave or let down,' was all she could say.

'And that you can't be a part of?'

'According to him. He's a go-it-alone kind of man, shouldering the whole lot, with a great big suffering hero complex, Grace.'

'Which only makes you love him more, even when you don't want to, because in our line of work you come across too many men who don't shoulder their responsibilities at all.'

Yes. Exactly.

'Why does it work that way, damn it?' Christina yelled back, over an extra-loud patch in the music. 'Love him, and get angry with him, and realise that I'm not doing myself any favours with any of it.'

Grace looked at her, tilted her head to one side and frowned. 'You know what? I'm starting to think there's a better way to look at this. I think the grieving period was premature.'

'OK, what's this now?' Christina let out a weary laugh. 'You're telling me the sky isn't falling after all? Is that what you're suddenly saying? It's not what you were saying on Monday at Gunyamurra, Grace O'Riordan.'

'Give him another chance.'

'Wha-a-at?'

'Didn't you say to me that if you knew why then you thought you could deal with it? Now you know why. The swan sister. Which is way better than the swan wife. So deal with it for a while, and see how that feels.'

'Have him back in his old room? It's all settled that Megan and the baby are going to move in.'

'Good. Because you don't want him back in his old room. He can stay in his new room, here. You want to give yourself some protection.'

'The protection of the two of us maintaining separate dwellings three kilometres apart, while I open up my heart and tell him, Here, rip into it.'

'See? You understand the situation perfectly.'

'Grace!'

'Christina, Christina. We all care about you, and you're a mess. If Joe had frolicked off into the sunset without a backward glance, like a certain recent pair of doctors I could mention, I'd want you to stick to your guns on this. Well, you'd have no choice. But look at him—'

'He's—?' Christina whirled around in search of him. She hadn't realised he was anywhere near. He'd been outside ten minutes ago. She found part of an arm and shoulder, the top of his head and one hip. Her view of him kept getting obscured by other people, but she went on looking in that direction anyway.

'Yep,' Grace said, looking the same way. 'Sticking his head in the drinks fridge, wearing a thousand-yard stare. Been doing it for the past five minutes. Doesn't have a clue what he's looking for. The thing's on its last legs anyhow, and with the influx of warm air he's generating, I'm not holding my breath for the beer and orange juice staying cold next week. You see, he's just as much of a mess as you are.'

'Which, according to you, is a good thing.'

'Has to be, doesn't it?' Grace answered gently. She looked at Christina for a moment. 'Think about it.'

Joe didn't give her a chance to do that. He emerged drinkless from the fridge and caught sight of her. 'This is where you've got to?' he said, as if he'd found her under the front seat of the car, like a lost CD.

'I'm prepared to consider other locations to park myself.'

He didn't say another word, just grabbed her hand, engulfing it like a big leather glove.

'Where are we going, Joe?'

'Beach? I don't know.'

'The beach sounds good. Will anyone…?'

'No. No one will care. They might notice, but they won't care.'

There was no moonlight tonight, but the frilly white edges of the waves seemed to throw off their own luminescent glow. The sand felt cool and spongy. Joe stopped to lever off his running shoes and roll his trousers to the knees. He could never bear to have anything between his feet and the beach. Christina kicked her shoes off, too, and they walked the length of the cove to the rocky outcrop at the foot of the bluff and found a flat, cool place to sit and talk.

'I'm glad I told you about Amber on Monday night,' Joe said. 'I didn't think it would feel good afterwards, but it did.'

'Why didn't you think it would feel good?'

'Because I was getting my nice, separate universes all mixed up.' He reached out for her hand again, didn't add anything to his answer.

Christina thought about pushing. Why? Why did you want separate universes in the first place? Why won't you trust me or…or celebrate…when I say I want to be part of any universe that you're in, forever, for the rest of our lives?

But then she remembered what he'd said about talking, just that afternoon. She hadn't been in the right mood to listen at the time, but the words had stayed in her mind all the same. How you could talk about trivial, impersonal things like garden chores and TV sport and it could still mean something if there was the right spirit underneath. How actions said just as much as words. Or said more.

Meanwhile, his hand was talking to her. He had the back of it resting against the rock, his knuckles taking the roughness of the salt-crusted stone while her hand got to rest in the soft, warm bed of his big palm. The ball of his thumb slid back and forth across her skin, painting loose circles of sensation.

She looked down. Only this one point of contact. Two hands. One that was on the thin side, with a scattering of freckles and a current unmet need for moisturiser. The other built like a bear's paw, only smooth and brown. She couldn't see it, but she knew there was an old scar cutting across the pad of muscle below his thumb. Letting her gaze track upwards, she found the blue-black tattoo like a narrow bracelet on his upper arm, circling the strong muscle.

'I'm glad you told me about Amber, too,' she said at last. 'I only wish you'd done it sooner.'

'Don't go telling everyone in Crocodile Creek, will you?'

'Of course I won't!'

'She hates to think that people talk about her, even if she knows they mean well. She doesn't even like to hear me telling her too often that I'm proud of her.'

'How does she handle your parents and all their conflict?'

'I don't think she's quite realised yet that it should be different, that not all fathers are aggressive and loud and bullying, and secretly ready to put their daughters through any amount of plastic surgery necessary to make her look normal.'

'He wants that? For her to look normal?'

'No matter what the cost.' He picked up his previous

thread. 'And meanwhile that not all mothers are driven to living their most important emotions in secret, because Mum *knows* Amber only wants the surgery that's necessary for her health—heaven knows, that's extensive enough. She knows Amber doesn't want procedure after procedure in a doomed quest for the perfect supermodel eyes and nose, but she pretends to go along with Geoff, my stepfather. She sacrifices too much, tears herself in half agreeing with everyone, while Geoff rants and raves and drinks up half of what she tries to save.'

He shook his head. They'd both got tangled in what they were saying, in danger of losing the original thread. It happened when something was this complicated, emotionally.

'But you're offering Amber a different model of male behaviour,' Christina said. 'That's so good, Joe.'

'I'm just her brother.'

'She must think that brothers are pretty OK, then.'

'Hope so.'

More silence.

He eased his hand from the rock. She turned it over and traced the red indentations imprinted by the rough texture of the stone. 'Looks sore,' she said, thinking about Grace's advice to give him another chance.

'It's OK,' Joe said.

'Bloody hero!'

He grinned. 'Yeah, I'm a real nuisance.'

'You are!' She grinned back. Then she sighed.

His black eyes glimmered at her, steady and open.

Heroes had their good points.

She made her decision.

'Could I, please, kiss you, Joe?' she whispered.

CHAPTER EIGHT

'ARE you sure that's a good idea, Tink?' Joe said, even though the words felt as if they might kill him. 'Kissing me?'

'It's a brilliant idea.' She leaned in and touched the pads of her fingers to his lips. She wasn't grinning any more.

Neither was he. Her kiss felt as if it might kill him, too. He knew he shouldn't let it happen, but right now he didn't have it in him to say no when she was insisting yes. He just waited for her mouth.

It felt cool. It felt soft. She teased him, only brushing her lips against his, pressing them briefly then brushing them away. She took his face between soft hands and angled her head to one side, brushed his mouth again, angled her head the opposite way, dabbed a tiny bit of moisture with the tip of her tongue, just where his lips parted.

Then she sat back and pulled the pins out of her piled hair, combed the loosened strands with her fingers and shook them down around her shoulders, releasing a cloud of sweet, nutty scent into the air.

His groin tightened in a rush of heat. He wanted to grab her, ravish her, show her his strength, give in to his impatience as fast as a man could, and yet he held back. He'd been wanting this all week, thinking about it, remembering Sunday night and aching with loss and sheer physical frustration at the thought that it might never happen again.

Now she was offering, sweet and wicked at the same time, getting to the point as slowly, slowly as she could get away with, while his body responded lightning fast. He hid the speed and power of his reaction, still at a loss. He'd listened to what she'd said she wanted on Sunday night, and had respected her right to make that decision. Now she was saying something different—backing down, really, saying that she'd decided it could work on his terms after all.

So what was his problem?

Christina didn't know either.

'Hey!' she whispered at last, letting her breath and the light touch of her fingernails caress his ear. 'It takes two.' She kissed a trail of sensation down his neck, threaded her fingers into his hair. His spine began to tingle.

'Yeah?' he growled. His body echoed the sceptical word with an unequivocal imperative of its own.

She's saying yes, idiot, so let's make it yes. Now!

'This is what you want?' he growled. She shrieked with surprised satisfaction as he engulfed her with his arms and half rolled, half carried her from the rocks onto the sand. 'Yes?' he growled again, as they rolled. He also meant, 'Here?'

And she knew it. 'Yes,' she told him, getting breathless.

She ended up on top and he pulled her close. She lay with her head pillowed on his chest and he stroked her silky hair, giving her one last chance to change her mind. She didn't speak. Then, with his eyes closed yet still able to find her unerringly, he cupped his palm against her jaw and turned her face towards his.

No games now. Their kiss turned deep and hungry at

once. They invaded each other's mouths, pushed at each other's clothing. Their bodies were shaking and they ignored the sand. And if anyone else decided to take a walk on this beach tonight… Well, this would be over pretty soon, the way they were each pulling the other towards the brink.

She sat up, sliding up his body to straddle his chest, and he opened his eyes, wanting to see her—see the hair that fell loosely over him, the lost, blissful expression on her face, the hunger and the beauty. And it was all there.

He watched as he touched her, running his hands along the fabric-covered thighs that squeezed against his chest, loving everything about her while still knowing that this wasn't enough. Or maybe it was the whole problem. He cared about her well-being too much to rope her into the complexity of his life.

She pulled her shimmery top over her head, her raised arms lifting and rounding her breasts in their dark lace bra. He reached up for her, running his hands over those jutting forms and then down the satin of her bare skin. During all of this, her eyes stayed closed, which meant he could keep watching her.

Watching her emotional nakedness, and her trust.

Watching just how much she gave to him, now as always.

And that was when he knew that they had to stop.

His hands stilled, resting on her hips. She waited, a little frown on her forehead. She was almost smiling, anticipating, waiting for him to cup her breasts again, or pull her down so he could reach the fastening of her bra. She thought he was teasing her.

'Joe…?'

He spoke the first part of his thought out loud. 'This feels so good.'

'So why are you making us wait?'

There was a beat of silence before he answered, 'Because we can't do this.' And even while he was saying it he was mentally kicking himself for abusing his body—and hers—with this much denial.

Ah, hell, saying it wasn't enough, he realised. He had to make a move.

He did so with an immense effort, lifting her off him, coaxing her sideways onto the sand, pulling himself up to sit so that he could protect his throbbing groin. His breathing came with an effort. She was looking at him, stricken and bewildered.

'Bit gob-smacked,' she said, making light of it. 'Thought it was going pretty well.'

'But what's changed, Tink?' he burst out. 'What's changed for you since I moved into the doctors' house three days ago that makes this suddenly OK now? Because you know about Amber? Because I said I was glad that you did?'

'Thought it was a pretty good start,' she answered lightly.

He wasn't fooled.

He knew the way her thinking had travelled. She thought they were going to do this in stages. Step one, Joe talks about his family and discovers it doesn't feel as difficult and bad as he might have thought. Step two, Christina comes to New Zealand for a holiday, meets Amber and their mother and Amber's Dad and tells Joe how great Amber is, and that there's hidden strength in his mother, and even a couple of qualities in his stepfather that she can connect with and admire. Step three, she throws herself into the whole situation with a hundred per cent of her heart and Joe feels so pressured by what she's prepared to sacrifice for his sake that he forgets how to breathe.

Which means, step four, they both suffocate.

He'd seen his mother stretching herself in ten directions at once, trying to fill the bottomless well of other people's needs. She'd come close to destroying herself in the process. And it wasn't that he thought men were stronger. But he thought that they often protected themselves better. They had a streak of selfishness that meant they would always look out for number one.

He'd done it himself with Christina. He'd known from the beginning that he couldn't stretch himself far enough to give her the whole package, so he hadn't tried. He'd protected himself, by keeping their relationship light and fun and restricted to the present. And he'd thought he'd been making the boundaries clear to her all along, but that hadn't helped.

Christina wouldn't protect herself at all. She didn't want to. She wanted to jump in with both feet. She was such a giving kind of person, but he couldn't let her do it, not when he'd seen just how badly wrong it could go.

'It's a mistake,' he said bluntly. 'This isn't going to work for either of us, because it isn't what you want, and you know it. You were right on Sunday night about ending it. Now you're talking about a "pretty good start" to a rekindling, as if I'm a fish on a line and you're carefully, carefully reeling me in.'

Although they weren't touching, he felt her stiffen in anger and shock. 'That's an awful—'

'No! I don't mean it the way it sounded,' he said quickly.

'That I'm a cold-blooded manipulator and you have a—a—*fish brain?* I hope not!' Her eyes flashed at him, because she had spirit as well as kindness.

'I mean, you're hoping for more,' he said. 'You're thinking that I've—*we've*—taken one step forward, so in a couple of months we'll take another.'

'Would that be terrible?' Her tone was mild but he knew she was still angry.

'There's only one place we can end up if we keep taking those steps,' he told her, 'and it's not somewhere I want to go.'

'Where do you want to go, Joe?' By this time she was close to tears, but she didn't want it to show, he could tell. Her voice sounded unnaturally hard as she asked the question.

'Nowhere,' he answered. 'Home. That's where I want to go right now.' He stood up. 'To the doctors' house.'

Where the sheets on his bed still smelled like her laundry detergent, and the flowers she'd put in a vase on the desk were beginning to wilt.

Sand showered out of Christina's top when she'd put it back on. It tickled on her skin and ended up in her trousers. She followed Joe up to the house. He took rapid strides, clearly as angry and frustrated as she was, getting well ahead of her in seconds. But every time he realised that she'd fallen behind he would stop and wait for her, which made her feel even angrier.

You're not my white knight. Stop acting like one.

Her feet dragged in the soft sand at the top of the beach. She felt drained and exhausted, queasy with it by this point. She didn't want to go back inside, where the party was still going on, although there were fewer cars parked out front now. Someone turned the music down lower as she and Joe approached. There were probably people trying to sleep by this time. It was after eleven, and most staff had to work tomorrow.

'I'm going to head off home, Joe,' she said.

He nodded carefully. 'How're you getting there? Brian picked you up, didn't he?'

She'd almost forgotten. 'I'll walk.'

'Not at this time of night.' The white knight was back, his armour shiny and well oiled. 'Let me duck inside and see if I can borrow someone's car to run you across.'

'Don't. Grace's car is still here. I'll ask if she can give me a lift. I can hang around for a bit if she's not ready to go. And you can go to bed, if you want, because you're not my personal host here tonight.'

He looked at her without speaking, then kind of apologised for both of them. 'I guess we're both tired.'

'Think so.' She tried to say it lightly, and ignored the way her body reacted just to the sight of him—weak knees, unsteady breathing, the works.

Looking as if it was an effort to get his feet moving, Joe went directly to his room via the veranda, and Christina went inside. She soon found Grace, who was laughing loudly in a group of four. But she was happy to leave right then, she said when Christina asked for a lift.

They talked in the car.

'So…Joe's not coming?' Grace asked. 'You know, bit of late-night fence-mending, nudge, nudge.'

Christina raked her teeth across her lower lip and sighed. 'I think it was the wrong advice, Grace.'

'Oh, hell, was it?' She looked stricken, the habitual twinkle of mischief gone from her blue eyes. 'How could it be wrong? You saw him stuck in front of the fridge like a thirsty ghost. Emily says he's been like that all week, a total mess. I'm really sorry. I should keep my nose out of my friends' business, shouldn't I?'

'It was what I wanted to hear, Grace, to be honest, but he went all noble and determined to save me from myself kind of thing, and I'm…' She stopped. 'Angry?' she tried, but it didn't feel right.

Well, nothing felt right.

'No, just numb,' she corrected.

'How about if I stay over? I can sleep on the couch. Then if you want to talk some more…'

'Gosh, Grace, are you that worried about me?'

'I'm a bit worried. You look like you're not sleeping, and not quite well. You look…pooky.'

'*Pooky?*'

'It's a technical term.'

Christina laughed. 'It'd be nice if you stayed over. Just so the house doesn't feel so empty. But you can have Joe's—' She stopped. Corrected herself. 'The spare room. No need for the couch. The bed's all made up in there.'

She'd washed the sheets yesterday, had left the bed unmade during the day then prepared the room ready for Megan in the evening, even though Megan wouldn't be moving in for another few days. Nice little strategy of pretending to herself that she was moving forward.

'And would there be an offer of hot Milo and a biscuit as well, by any chance?'

'In case I need another cry on Auntie Grace's shoulder while we're drinking it?'

'Thanks to the nightly Milo and biscuit, it's a pretty well-padded shoulder. You have to admit it's well suited for the purpose.'

Having Grace there overnight meant that she was still there in the morning, and in the morning Christina got out of bed feeling fine, but felt nauseous by the time she reached the bathroom and was retching into the basin by the time she'd got the lid off the toothpaste for a freshening of her mouth. She hadn't even shut the bathroom door.

Little weatherboard Queenslander cottages didn't have

very good soundproofing. Christina had rinsed her mouth
out with plain water, since the toothpaste smelled way too
strong and didn't seem like a very good idea. She was wiping her face with a towel, wondering why she still felt so
funny in the stomach, why she'd been feeling this way for
days, if she thought about it, when Grace appeared.

'What was that? Are you OK?'

'Not sure.' Although she'd begun to have an idea.

'Did you have very much to drink last night?'

'Half a glass of wine with Brian. Lemon squash at the
party.'

Grace asked a couple more questions.

Christina answered them.

'I'm a midwife and you're a doctor,' Grace said. 'What
do you think?'

They looked at each other.

Christina said, 'No.'

'No?'

Grace asked another set of questions.

Christina said, 'No,' again, but more desperately this time.

'We're going to do a test,' Grace decreed. 'I am zipping
to the pharmacy this second, and we are doing a test.' She
looked at her watch. 'They'll be open.' Being the only one
in Crocodile Creek, the pharmacy had extended hours. 'It's
after seven. What time do you have to get to the airport?'

'Not until eight. We have a scheduled patient transport
this morning, and another one this…aagh… this afternoon.'

'Uh-oh, are you leaning over that basin again?'

'Yup.'

'I'll get you some dry biscuits. Or fruit?'

'Biscuits,' Christina gasped. 'And water.'

Grace brought the biscuits and a filled glass, then left

the house, which felt very silent and still after she'd gone. The biscuits and water helped. Christina felt better. She managed a shower, towelled her body dry, ate another biscuit and looked at herself naked in the mirror.

She looked the same.

She didn't look pregnant.

But she probably was.

The dates added up. There had been that stomach upset a month ago which she'd told herself hadn't lasted long enough to compromise the effectiveness of her contraception, but... How much wishful thinking had lain behind that conclusion?

Did she *want* to be pregnant, then?

Oh, lord, what had she been thinking a month ago? That she could force a commitment from Joe if something like this happened?

No, that implied some serious thinking about pregnancy over the past few weeks, which didn't fit where her thoughts had focused at all. Biological clock, yes, actual state of pregnancy, no. So much had changed since then.

She was shaking, nauseous again.

And still naked.

She touched her breasts, remembering Joe's hands on them last night. Did they feel fuller? Maybe a little. Something went thud in her stomach. Grace would be back with that test any moment now, and pregnancy tests now only took a few minutes to yield a very reliable result. She got dressed quickly, while her mind flooded with questions.

What do I want? A false alarm? A way to pressure Joe? No.

Not that.

Two could play the solitary heroism game.

She'd have to tell him, of course, but she would make

it clear to him from the very beginning that his involvement was not required.

A VW Beetle engine died noisily in her driveway and the front door opened thirty seconds later, while Christina was still in her bedroom. 'Here,' Grace said, handing over a paper bag from the pharmacy. 'I'm going to make you some breakfast. Toast and tea. Just show up for it when you're ready.'

'That'll be Christmas.'

Grace counted off the months on her fingers. 'Well, I guess by then I won't need to ask you the result of the test.'

Even without waiting until Christmas, she didn't need to ask Christina about the result of the test when Christina returned from the bathroom. Her whole face must have said positive.

'Oh, gosh! Oh, wow!' Grace breathed. 'Oh, I'm going to hug you!' She did. 'Oh, that's…momentous!'

'Yes,' Christina agreed shakily.

Understatement of the year. She still had no idea what this would mean, how it would change her attitudes or her plans. She couldn't focus at all. It didn't seem real, and yet at another level it felt *right*. She'd always known she wanted to be a mother, even if she'd never imagined it starting like this…

'Christina?'

'Hmm?' She blinked at her friend. She'd been miles away.

'When are you going to tell Joe?' Grace asked her gently.

CHAPTER NINE

Do WE turn the flight around?

Christina looked at Jill and saw the same unspoken question reflected in the older nurse's face. This should have been a routine afternoon patient transport from the hospital back to this boy's isolated home on a cattle station in the Gulf country.

Ben was nine, in plaster from hip to toes after fracturing his femur falling from a horse, and he'd greeted them with a grin wider than his face, just after lunch, because he'd been so happy to be out of his hospital bed and going home with Mum to his dad and his sister. His mum had looked pretty happy about the whole thing, too, hugging him and getting dithery about packing up the get-well gifts he'd received.

'So much chocolate! The balloons are beautiful, but…'

'We don't let them on the plane,' Christina had had to tell her.

Forty minutes into the flight, Ben Cartwell wasn't grinning any more and Judy Cartwell wasn't thinking about balloons.

'I don't understand why this is happening,' she said in a strained voice. She squeezed her son's hand. 'Just try and get your breath, Ben, try to relax. It's OK.'

The asthma attack had taken everyone by surprise. 'Mild asthma,' Mrs Cartwell had reported after the leg break, when staff had taken a patient history. But this attack wasn't mild. It had begun with an audible wheeze and moderate respiratory distress, and they'd quickly put up a nebuliser mask and given a dose of Ventolin, but if these were helping, they weren't helping enough.

'I've never seen him like this before,' Mrs Cartwell said. 'Ben, you don't have to be scared. Just relax.'

Turbulence rocked the aircraft once again, making equipment lockers rattle and stomachs swoop up and down. Christina didn't like the unpredictable motion any more than Ben did, and was beginning to wish she had a supply of those nice dry biscuits with her that Grace had found in the pantry this morning.

Speaking of which, Joe knew nothing about the pregnancy yet. She didn't know when she'd get the right opportunity to tell him, and she hated having to wait like this. It gave her too much time to plan out conversations that wouldn't work in real life the way they did in her head, because important conversations never did.

And was talking enough, anyhow? She craved action, but didn't know what she could do.

'This was what started it,' Jill murmured. 'It's very rough. He got scared, and that can be a strong trigger.'

'Glenn?' Christina said into her headset. 'What's the story? Do we know what weather we're coming into? More rough stuff?'

'Good chance,' Glenn answered. 'I could try flying higher.'

Jill and Christina looked at each other again. Fly higher, yes, but away from hospital care?

'What's happening?' Ben's mother wanted to know.

'What are we doing?' She sounded panicky herself, even though it was obvious she was trying not to. Ben could see the panic and it didn't help.

'How are you feeling, Ben?' Jill asked. Her voice was always much softer when she talked to a paediatric patient. 'Breathing better?'

As a highly experienced theatre nurse as well as the hospital's director of nursing, she didn't come on flight duty very often, but she liked to do it from time to time 'to keep my hand in', she said.

Grace was off today, so Jill had rostered herself for the two patient transport assignments, instead of sending another more junior nurse. That morning's trip had been quite uneventful, but Christina was grateful for Jill's level of experience right now.

You didn't want to turn a flight around for nothing. Like any medical service, this one operated on a budget that was always too tight, and flying cost money.

On the other hand...

Ben was shaking his head in answer to Jill. He tried to speak, but he couldn't. With his best, most desperate effort, nothing would come. Mrs Cartwell moaned in a shaky voice, 'Oh, Ben!'

Christina whipped her stethoscope back into her ears and practically glued the other end of it to Ben's chest, listening in several different places.

Silence. A layperson might have thought that the wheezing had stopped and that Ben's condition was improving. Christina knew better.

'Glenn, we're going to head back,' she yelled. 'Now, please. Ben, love, we'd better not take you home today after all. That's a disappointment, I know.'

But at the moment he was too distressed and frightened

to care. The aircraft lurched again as the boy kept up his panicky, desperate and futile efforts to breathe, half his face hidden by the misted mask of the nebuliser. His condition was worsening rapidly, his lungs almost completely closed. Fighting her queasy stomach, Christina found a pulse of almost 140, and a respiratory rate of forty-five. His trachea tugged inwards as he tried to breathe, using muscles that shouldn't need to be involved.

Jill had already begun to draw up the life-saving adrenaline he needed. 'Country nice and flat out here, Glenn?' she asked in a casual tone, and they all knew what she meant.

If Ben's condition didn't improve with this latest barrage of treatment and he arrested, they'd need to intubate him to maintain airway control, and that could only be done safely on the ground.

No, Christina resolved. By hook or by crook, she was going to bring this patient back from the brink before he got to that point.

'Flat? Yeah, mostly,' Glenn answered Jill, serious as ever. 'That's my problem, not yours.'

'Are we landing?' Mrs Cartwell said. 'Please, tell me what you're going to do for Ben.'

'We're heading back,' Jill said. 'Just for safety's sake.'

And, please, Christina added inwardly, let us not have to land in the middle of nowhere, on the way, so we can save this kid's life…

She had been hoping so strongly for a routine day. She would have been able to sign off at the end of it, drive across to the hospital from the flight base, find Joe, work out a time when they could talk. Nothing would make their conversation easy, but at least she'd have had some lead up, some preparation, a chance to stay calm. Now, even with the best-case scenario for Ben, she'd be jittery, awash with ebbing adrenaline, more tired than ever.

She felt the slow bank and lift of the aircraft as they turned back towards Crocodile Creek and gained some height. Jill gave the adrenaline. Christina listened to Ben's chest again, tried another dose of Ventolin. The turbulence eased.

And so, fractionally, did Ben's breathing, but he still looked desperately scared and struggling. It was so hard watching a child unable to breathe, and the time remaining until they would be back on the ground stretched ahead too far.

'Pulse rate has dropped a bit,' Jill reported. 'One-thirty. Respiratory rate at thirty-five now.' She raised her voice. 'Ben, love, you're doing a lot better. It might not feel that way yet, but you're getting better. Your chest is opening up again. Good lad!'

'We're doing the right thing, heading in this direction,' Christina said.

'Oh, absolutely!'

Their descent began at last, bumpy for most of the way. Even in the midst of his distress, Ben flinched every time, and Christina realised he was frightened about his leg.

'Your cast's protecting the break,' she told him. 'It's not going to go crooked, and it's not going to hurt.'

She wasn't sure that he believed her. His knuckles were white as he gripped his mother's hand, and she looked ill with fear.

On the ground, they made the transfer between aircraft and ambulance, and from the ambulance to the ED, with the boy's condition still touch and go.

Joe was working today, and things were busy. He always looked so energised and focused under these conditions, his big body moving efficiently, no hint of clumsiness or unnecessary noise. He turned away from an elderly woman who'd apparently taken a fall, saw the new stretcher being wheeled in, and saw Christina, too.

Be right with you, he gestured, but didn't spare the time for a smile.

My baby's going to look like him, Christina thought suddenly.

'This is a bounce,' she told him, as soon as Ben had been set up in an emergency cubicle. She meant that this patient had been discharged and had needed to come back. Joe understood the medical slang at once, and made a characteristic face. Bounce, hey? It never looked good for a hospital to have too many of those!

'Unrelated problem, though,' he said. 'Bad luck for the kid.'

'Mum's upset, too.'

'She would be!'

Joe checked Ben's vital signs. His oxygen saturation had climbed to ninety-four per cent now. There was no sign of cyanosis, no use of accessory muscles to breathe, and Ben could speak a full sentence. He'd need an oral steroid drug and monitoring for at least twenty-four hours.

'You're off the hook now,' Joe said to Christina.

'I know…' She was aware that she'd been hanging back, fiddling with Ben's notes, not really required now that the hospital staff had taken over. But she had to tell Joe that she wanted to see him. She saw Hamish coming towards them and grabbed her last chance. 'We need to talk, Joe.'

He looked at her, gave a half a smile at last. 'This talking stuff is getting to be a very bad habit between us, Tink,' he muttered.

'I know, but something's come up.' My stomach this morning, and a distinctive colour in a test window.

'I'm working a long shift today. Midnight.' And he'd be working again all day tomorrow, and flying back to Auckland early on Sunday morning. Christina was on call all weekend for emergency flights in the helicopter. How did you schedule a pregnancy conversation into a timetable like that?

And how did you follow through? She wouldn't see him for three weeks after this. From experience, she knew he was unlikely to phone. Three weeks was a long time when you'd just found out you were pregnant and didn't know what the baby's father would want.

I have to take action on this, she thought again.

'Hello, Ben,' Hamish said behind them. 'And this is Mum? Of course it is! I'm Dr McGregor.'

'Could you phone me at home, Joe?' Christina said. 'Let me know when you're about to take a dinner-break. I'll meet you somewhere.'

'I'll phone from the house and you can meet me there.'

'Let me have a wee chat to Dr Barrett,' they both heard from Hamish.

He was already coming their way. Joe's suggestion would have to do, because Christina couldn't come up with a better alternative in the middle of the ED.

She spent several agonising hours waiting at home, before reaching the earliest time at which she could expect Joe to call, and then she had to wait two hours more before he actually did, at nine o'clock. She knew it wasn't his fault, but it didn't improve her state of mind.

'I'm at the house.' Background sound half drowned his words. 'It's noisy, unfortunately.'

'I'll be right there.'

'Come along the veranda. Because if you go in through the kitchen…' Most people did, but you could get waylaid there with offers of tea or beer and never escape.

He sounded tense—irritated, probably—and she wondered what he'd picked up from her. That she was the kind of ex-lover destined to remain a nuisance?

Yes! With bells on!

'Want something to drink?' he offered when she got there.

'No, thanks.'

'I've got my dinner heating up in the microwave. I can't hang around here too long, Tink.' He said it gently, but he meant it. She felt like a nuisance again, even when he reached out and touched her shoulder, as if in apology. 'Half an hour at the most, and I have to get back.'

'That's OK,' she said. 'Get your dinner.'

He nodded and left. Christina heard voices in various parts of the house and hoped that no one knew she was there.

Joe's room felt too small with both doors shut and Christina already very on edge. She saw the flowers she'd picked for him on Sunday. They'd wilted by this time, and though the clear glass vase she could see their water had turned to a revolting cloudy beige. Her stomach had something to say about the sight.

Turning away from it, she looked at the bed, too hastily made. She could imagine his big body there, rumpled from sleep, warm, smelling just the way it should.

Joe came back with his dinner. 'This is horrible,' he announced.

'The meal?' It was one of those frozen things. He put it down on the desk next to the wilted flowers and didn't make any attempt to eat it.

'No, eating in front of you, rushing this.' He paused. 'Whatever it is.'

'It's…' As on Sunday night, she just had to say it. Creeping up on the subject—*Hey, guess what, I'm going to be shopping for a whole new wardrobe in about three months, Joe*—would be ridiculous. 'It's…'

Simple.

Only it wasn't.

'I'm pregnant, Joe.'

'Say that again?'

But she didn't. She knew he'd heard. He let out a low, rough sound, then made a jerky grab for the desk without looking at it. He hit the plate and it tipped over the desk edge and his dinner splattered onto the polished wooden floor. The plate bounced but didn't break, and landed on top of the food. They both looked at the mess helplessly in silence, then Joe gulped back a tortured laugh. 'Looked pretty inedible even before.'

'I'm sorry.'

She couldn't take this. Not the dinner. Not the vase water. Not Joe's reaction. She fled to the veranda and then on to the lush garden endowed by one of Charles Wetherby's forebears. She knew Joe would follow her, and it was a place that offered some potential privacy, if only behind screens of leaves.

He did follow, and she felt him behind her, watching and waiting until several deep, careful breaths had brought her nausea back under control. Was she going to feel this way for the next two months, or was it stress and fatigue as much as pregnancy?

'OK now?' he asked.

'Think so.'

She heard him sigh heavily between his teeth and turned to face him. She wanted to see what was written there, not imagine the worst. A cluster of frangipani leaves brushed his shoulder unnoticed, and he looked blank, struggling for steady ground, naked in his shock.

Which was probably better than pretending he was instantly happy.

Maybe it was better.

'Say something,' she prompted.

'I'm a bit stunned.'

'Yeah. And?' It sounded too hostile, too aggressive. Without waiting for an answer, she gabbled on, 'I was stunned, too. I'm not saying that it's an unacceptable response, first up.'

'If you were stunned, then you obviously didn't…' He stopped.

She knew what he'd been about to say. 'I didn't let it happen it on purpose?'

'I'm not suggesting it, Christina.'

Her body burned, and she felt compelled towards total honesty. 'You probably have a right to suggest it,' she told him in a low voice. She saw his eyes narrow, and went on quickly, 'Remember that stomach upset? Not to get too technical on the timing, but if I'd been really on the ball I would have taken a morning-after pill the day you flew out.'

'Did you think about it?'

She nodded. 'Coming home from the airport. But I thought the risk was very low.' She took a breath. 'And then I thought that even if it happened, would it be so terrible?'

Is it so terrible, Joe?

'So did you know about it on Sunday when you picked me up?' He reached up and began to shred the leaves with mechanical precision.

'No, of course not. You mean when I told you I'd arranged the room for you at the house? Of course not! Why?'

'I thought you might have been saving it up.'

'Saving it up?' she echoed blankly, before she understood what he meant. 'Oh, for heaven's sake! You mean like ammunition? A last-ditch stand?'

He whooshed out another sigh. 'That sounded bad, didn't it?'

'Yes. Very. If you really think I'm that—'

'Manipulative,' he cut in. 'I don't. I *don't*.'

'Then why say it?'

'Because I'm taking this as it comes, Tink. I didn't think you'd want pretence.' Well, he'd got that right, at least. 'Tell me…tell me what you're thinking and feeling. What you expect.' He added the last three words as if they cut his mouth.

'I don't expect anything. From you, you mean? Nothing! Only what you want. Support for my decision to keep the baby, that's all. Which was pretty instant, I should tell you.'

'Because I can't—I'm fighting to keep my head above water as it is.'

'I know that. You're hating this. It's got you terrified. This is worse than I expected, Joe.'

He threw the shredded leaves away and began to prowl back and forth. She went up to him and pinned him in place with her touch, and they managed to sit down next to each other on the ornamental garden seat. He leaned forward, resting his elbows on his knees, picking the green leaf matter from under his fingernails. He didn't say anything at first, and something told her she should simply wait.

'I was sixteen when Amber was born,' he said finally after several restless shifts of his shoulders and his legs. 'Old enough to realise straight away, and to get told, that something wasn't right. She was little and frail with such a strange, funny little face. She already had the trach in, of course, and an NG tube, and she was like…'

He stopped and shook his head, while Christina waited.

'When I was much younger, seven or eight,' he tried again, 'I rescued some baby birds from a nest that a cat had got to. They were still pink and featherless, just a day or two old, and of course they died. I couldn't manage to keep them warm or fed. And I just wasn't going to let the same thing happen to Amber. I just wasn't.'

'No…'

'Her face reminded me of those birds. Not the right shape. So naked and small. I felt so protective towards her. One of my best friends said something about her being a retard and I punched him in the stomach. Four times. This probably isn't explaining why I'm reacting this way now.'

He twisted towards her and their shoulders touched.

'I don't know if it is,' Christina said, close to tears. 'All I know is that you've had two years to tell me these stories. Now you expect me to catch up in a couple of days, understand everything about who you are, because of your life and your past, in a few days. When I've never seen where you live, met your family, heard any of this before. You're asking too much of me, Joe!'

'Yeah, that's ironic, isn't it? That's half of what I was trying to avoid. Asking too much of you.'

'And what's the other half?'

'Of what I'm trying to avoid? A horrible marriage like my mother and Geoff have. And the agony of being ready and waiting to cut off your own arm for the sake of someone you love. We were confronted with that so often in Amber's first few years of life. Time and time again I used to think, Today? Is today the day I should cut off the arm? I'm ready. Give me the signal. I mean, the thinking wasn't as concrete as that, but the feeling was there.'

'You think you're going to have to cut off your arm for me? For the baby?'

He didn't answer for a long time. 'I think I'm just tired,' he finally said.

And he needed to get back to the hospital, which meant a peanut-butter sandwich eaten standing up in the kitchen first, because his hot dinner was still splattered on the floor. 'So you should go,' she told him. 'I'll clean up.'

'Don't. I mean it, Christina. I'll be really angry if you do.'

She left it where it was.

The congealed microwave meal was still on the floor when Joe got back to his room just after midnight. He looked at it, glad that Christina had taken him seriously and hadn't cleaned it up. He unglued the plate from on top of it, tried to remember what the packet had claimed the meal to be, but couldn't. With a handful of paper towel, he scooped most of it up and chucked it in the bin. Several passes with a cleaning sponge took care of the rest.

The ED had been busy again that night, with a procession of routine cases, including a couple of difficult types—a bad-tempered drunk who'd aspirated some of his own stomach contents, a heroin overdose whose family situation would need looking into. Christina's asthma patient Ben had gone up to the paediatric ward, his chest in pretty good shape considering how bad he'd been earlier, but a question mark still hanging over the issue of his discharge after the period of observation. He seemed very nervous about another flight. Sedation was probably the best option.

Joe had looked in on Jim Cooper, too, even though he was listed as Gina's patient now. He'd brewed up a mild infection which had slowed his recovery over the past couple of days. Honey split her time between her husband and her daughter, while remaining fiercely protective of Jim's ignorance about the baby.

'Not until he's ready!'

Meanwhile, Honey fretted about whether the dogs and the other animals were really being taken care of properly by whatever help Charles had organised out there.

Hungry after such a long day but definitely not wanting another microwave meal, Joe prowled into the kitchen. No one was there. The house was very quiet. He peered into the fridge and found some Cheddar cheese on one of the crowded shelves. There was even some bread left. Cheese on toast. That would do.

Communal living wasn't his favourite thing, even though everyone in this place was pretty good. Moodiness was kept private, boundaries were respected. Food kitty money was usually paid, shopping and cleaning rosters were adhered to, and quite often someone cooked a big meal.

But he had a need for privacy and solitude that couldn't be fully met here. He also had a need to know that if he left three slices of cold pizza in the fridge overnight, they'd still be there the next day to heat up when he came in from a long stint at the hospital and wanted some supper. His life wasn't simple, so he seized on simplicity wherever he could find it, even in the little things—like where his next meal was coming from.

He'd been pushing himself too hard for such a long time. He'd worked long part-time hours while he'd studied medicine. He had a full patient load in his practice, squeezed into three weeks out of four. He worked as many hours as Charles Wetherby would let him when he was here, bracketed on either side by flights of several hours across the Tasman Sea and boring waits at airports in Brisbane or Cairns.

He'd pretended to Christina through their whole relationship. Pretended that he was this laid-back, carefree, relaxed kind of guy. Hell, it had been so good! But it had been a pretence. In his real life, there was no room for carefree or relaxed. He wished there was. He wished he could open up that part of him and let it fly, the way he'd been able to do here, with Christina…the way she'd told him wasn't enough for her any more.

'What do I smell?' said Mike Poulos, behind him.

'I can make some more,' Joe offered at once, hiding the fact that he'd rather eat alone.

'It's fine. I just wanted some water.' Mike found a chilled jug of it in the drinks fridge, and soon disappeared again. He should have been Christina—because she was the only person in Crocodile Creek Joe wanted to share a fridge with—but he wasn't.

Joe would be on a plane to Auckland in thirty hours. His flight would get in late in the afternoon, and he had patients to see in his group general practice on Monday morning, starting at nine and going through until seven. Later in the week, Amber had a medical appointment to talk about the jaw surgery that her doctors wanted to perform soon.

He and Mum and Geoff would all be present at the appointment as well. There was still some uncertainty about whether they'd be able to remove Amber's tracheostomy at this point, and Geoff would no doubt get belligerent about it. How come these supposed experts didn't have definitive answers? How come it would still take so many more procedures to get Amber looking 'right'?

'Joe, tell these idiots!' Geoff would no doubt say. 'You're a doctor! They won't talk down to you like they talk down to me!'

And back here in Crocodile Creek, Joe's own child

would be quietly growing in Christina's womb. Healthy? You had to believe so. You couldn't spend seven months or more being scared. But even the smoothest pregnancy in the world was tough to go through alone.

He felt as if someone was tearing him in two, and hated Fate for the trick it had played. He'd got himself into this situation because he'd so badly wanted time out and fun, something that was just simple and good, and now he'd ended up with more responsibility than ever.

Even if he stopped coming to Crocodile Creek out of sheer self-protection, if he never saw Christina again and never met their child, he would always know, always wonder. Boy or girl? Bright? Athletic? Artist, scientist, dreamer? Like me, or like her? He'd always know that someday Christina or the child might need or want to make contact.

At which point, he would be confronted with everything he'd put Christina through, and everything he'd missed out on.

He didn't know what to do.

Christina couldn't get to sleep, even though she was once again exhausted to the point of nausea. She found a packet of sea-salted chips in the pantry and the salt settled her stomach but not her stress levels.

She had meant what she'd said to Joe earlier. It hadn't helped their situation at this point that he'd held so much back over the past two years. That story about Amber and the baby birds… You couldn't doubt his intensity, his sincerity, but a summary of his life at home and a couple of anecdotes weren't enough.

She gave up even trying to get to sleep, went on the internet and did another search on Treacher Collins syndrome. The first time, she'd done a search of the whole Web, but this time she clicked the 'pages from Australia' button.

And suddenly, after scrolling through several screens and clinking on various links, she saw Joe himself smiling out at her in close-up, his mouth wide, his teeth very white in his bronzed face, his strong arms wrapping from behind around the shoulders of a girl who looked about twelve or thirteen.

Amber.

She was smiling, too, her trach kept in place at her throat by a plastic strap that looked like a white necklace.

Christina couldn't believe it at first. It didn't seem real, to discover Joe and his sister this way, to think that if she'd had any reason to explore TCS on the internet over the past couple of years she might have stumbled on them like this before she'd ever heard about Amber from Joe.

Why hadn't he mentioned this site to her?

Why hadn't he mentioned the poem that Amber had written?

"'I am not quite like you",' she had called it, and then the lines had gone on to describe feelings and tastes and day-to-day routines that were exactly like those of thousands of other young girls, interspersed with stark descriptions of things that were very different.

'When I wake in the night, haunted by a scary dream, I
   scream.
But it is silent. I have my trach. My breathing does not
   touch my voice.'

Christina read the poem and looked at Joe and Amber until the computer screen switched to sleep mode and went dark. She didn't know how long she might have gone on sitting there if it had stayed bright.

All night?

She knew what she wanted to do now. She just didn't know how far Charles Wetherby would be willing to go to make it possible. She'd have to see him in the morning, as early as she could.

CHAPTER TEN

THE morning felt a lot fresher than Joe himself did as he walked across to the hospital just seven hours after he'd left it.

He had a mug of coffee in one hand and a piece of stale Danish pastry in the other, because there were too many people already in the kitchen at the doctors' house, making breakfast, and he'd had to escape some well-meaning questions from people that he just didn't have it in him to fob off today.

In the quiet of a Saturday morning he could hear the waves lapping gently in the cove and some parrots squabbling in the trees. There was another sound, too, that took a few seconds to penetrate his consciousness and announce its identity. It was a low throb, getting louder.

It was the rescue chopper.

He saw it rise over the top of the hospital, coming from the helipad, which wasn't visible from where he stood. It swung out towards the dark turquoise carpet of ocean, hanging at an angle in the sky in a fashion which reminded him of how glad he was that he only ever had to go out in it on the rarest occasions—just twice, during the two years he'd been coming here.

Christina flew in it almost every week.

She was probably flying in it now.

The issue wasn't courage, it was trust. She had more trust than he did—trust in other people's competence, their good intentions, their strength. Trust in *him,* for that matter, more than he had in himself. Would he really get it remotely right with his response to this baby, who didn't yet seem real? Yes, she had too much trust, he sometimes thought… And he felt much happier when the whirly-bird rotor-blades had levelled off parallel with the horizon and the thing was at least flying straight.

It rose higher, travelling over the water, and headed directly out to sea. The Great Barrier Reef lay in that direction, roughly thirty kilometres offshore. Less than a third of that distance away floated Wallaby Island, home to one of the Reef's most extensive tourist resorts. This was its peak season, with holidaymakers going there for a break from the much harsher winter down south. The rescue chopper could easily be headed there, or to one of the other tourist islands further to the north or south. It had almost disappeared by the time Joe entered the main hospital building.

He started straight in on a morning round, wanting to fit it in before the inevitable call to the ED, where he would be mainly working again that day. In the paediatric ward, he found Cal Jamieson checking on Shane's appendicectomy incision, his pain levels and his notes.

'We'll get him off the morphine,' Cal told a nurse. 'He's looking good.'

Ben was in the next bed, his breathing further improved and his observations also better than they had been yesterday afternoon. Joe talked to his mother about giving a sedative tomorrow before they even mentioned that he'd be taking a flight home, and she nodded. 'I think that would help. Nothing too strong, though.'

'You don't have to worry, Mrs Cartwell.'

He saw a couple of other people then headed in the direction of the ED. Georgie Turner collared him on the way, striding up behind him and calling his name. Her short black hair looked sleek and shiny and she had way too much energy for a single parent who regularly got called out at odd hours to bring other people's babies into the world.

Christina's baby, in about seven and a half months?

Would he be there? Did he want to be? Would she accept him at that point?

'Listen, Joe, Christina was going to show Megan and her mother the room at her place this morning,' Georgie said, 'but she's been called out on an emergency flight to one of the islands.'

'Not Wallaby?'

'No, further than that. There was a question about needing to refuel, I think, and we don't know how long they'll be.'

'I saw the chopper going out,' Joe confirmed. 'Not that long ago.'

'She called in a message for you, in mid-air. Apparently you know where she keeps her spare key?'

'Yep,' he answered stoically, while his gut turned sour.

'Can you grab a break at some point and take Megan and her mother over there? Charles has OK'd a hospital car. He'll give you the keys for it. There are a couple of boxes of donated gear for them to take as well. It should only take half an hour or so. They just want to look around and see if the place'll work. But you know the house.'

He nodded, and Georgie made an apologetic face.

'It's gorgeous,' she continued. 'So I'm sure Megan will love it.'

'Shouldn't be a problem. Shall I phone the unit when I'm ready?'

'Sounds good. Thanks, Joe.' She walked briskly back the way she'd come.

In the ED he saw a couple of patients, ordered an X-ray on one and an ultrasound on the other. Emily was floating around as well. She glanced into the almost empty waiting room when he mentioned Megan and her mother, and suggested, 'Tell them you'll go now. We have no one coming in, other than our chopper case, and they won't get here for at least another few hours.'

'So you know where they were going, do you?'

'York Island. Fair distance.'

'Know why?'

'Didn't hear so, yes, they might be ages, depending on how much they need to stabilise the patient on the ground.'

Christina could be gone for most of the day. They'd probably see each other when she got back. She would be bringing a patient in. Shark attack, near drowning, heart problem, fishing accident, it could be anything. He might not hear any detail for a while. When she got here, they'd be snapping information and questions and instructions back and forth to each other, a glance and a word or two the only personal interaction.

He'd have to watch her holding everything together when she was tired and tense. They might get separated altogether by the demands of the day. She could get called out again tonight, or he might have to assist in surgery. His flight left next morning at six, which meant getting up in the dark, tiptoeing around the doctors' house, getting his last-minute gear together…

Hell, they might not see each other at all.

But we can't leave it like this, he thought. I have to tell her…

What? That she wasn't on her own? When he still didn't know how much he could honestly promise? He still felt weighed down. And he didn't want to lie to her.

He felt Emily's concerned eyes fixed on him. 'Everything OK, Joe?'

'Yep. Fine. You're right. Let me deal with Megan and her mother now, in case there isn't a better chance later.'

'Yes, because Christina is apparently keen to get it settled today. I'll phone the unit and make sure they're ready.'

He was told that they were, but when he got there he found that this had been an optimistic assessment. Honey was still going through the boxes of donated gear, which had been brought from Jill's office. 'You won't need this for him here,' she told her daughter.

'I might,' Megan said. 'For a coming-home outfit.'

She held up the ridiculously tiny garment and smiled at it. Both mother and daughter looked a lot happier and more relaxed than they had a few days ago.

Jackson lay sleeping nearby in his premmie cot, with its transparent sides. Megan looked at him, frowning. 'What if he wakes up for a feed?'

'He had a good one an hour ago.'

'But he sometimes doesn't go much longer than that, Mum.' Like all new mothers, she was already the person who knew more about her baby than anyone else.

'You have some expressed milk in the fridge,' a nurse reassured her. 'We can give him that.'

'Ready?' Joe suggested.

But Honey was still going through the last box. 'Five minutes?'

He knew he'd better call the ED, check that this outing

was still OK. He could envisage it getting extended at the other end, too. Waiting for Emily to come to the phone, he saw a slow, careful figure enter the doorway. Gown-clad, wheeling a drip stand, rather frail despite his wiry build...

Crikey, it was Jim Cooper.

No one else in the room had seen him yet.

The phone rattled in Joe's ear and he heard Emily's voice. 'Problem?'

'Just that we haven't gone yet.'

'That's OK. It's still quiet down here,' Emily said.

'Good. Great. Bye.'

'Joe—?'

But he put down the phone, cutting her off, wondering if he could or should try and head off the imminent confrontation. Jim had seen his daughter. He was smiling, because he could see how good she looked. She'd been to his room to see him a couple of days ago, Joe knew, but apparently she'd acted cagey and distant, hiding behind the fact that Jim had still been pretty weak and ill at that stage. Honey had supported her daughter's secrecy.

'She'll come again when you're better,' she'd told her husband.

'And you're not to try and come to see me,' Megan had told him, but two days later he felt strong enough, and it was clearly a very innocent defiance of his wife and daughter's prohibition.

Jim found Honey, still hovering over that wretched box of donations, and called out, 'Love? Couldn't think where you'd got to. Decided it was time I came to see my girl, under my own—'

He stopped.

He'd seen the baby in the clear-sided little cot.

And hospitals didn't park a tiny newborn—one who

was still attached to various bits of tubing—that close to someone who wasn't the mother.

Five people froze.

Predictably, Honey was the first to react.

'Just don't upset yourself, Jim.' She hurried forward, wringing another tiny baby garment into sweaty pleats in her hands without even knowing it was there. 'She didn't want to tell you. Didn't tell me for days. She had him at the rodeo, and she thought he was stillborn. It's a miracle he's alive, and doing so well. He's got a blood disorder, but it's all right now that we know about it. The birth is why she was so ill. She's keeping him. We're grandparents. I know you're going to be thrilled. A boy, Jim!' Her tone begged him to see the baby's existence her way. 'There's a boy in the family! Just don't upset yourself!'

She put her arms around him tightly. As if she was afraid he would fall? Or afraid he'd lash out? Joe had heard he had a temper, but not that he might be violent.

He wasn't violent.

He didn't have the intent, or the strength.

'Get me a chair,' he told his wife hoarsely. 'How could she be pregnant?'

'She—'

'It was the boy. Was it?'

'Jack? The father? Of course he is!'

'I sent him away. And his uncle sacked him. Damn that man…damn that man.'

'Mr Cooper, let's try to stay quiet, OK?' Joe came in.

The man was shaking, and his breathing was shallow. He needed a bypass sooner rather than later, and he had just made his hand into a fist and pressed it against his heart— The gesture sent out warning bells.

'Jim, are you in pain?' Joe tried again.

'No. No. Just…can't get my breath. It's nothing.'

Joe didn't wait. There was oxygen equipment already in the room. 'Wheelchair,' he said to the nurse, while he found a mask and prepared the flow. 'We'll put him on the portable supply and get him back to his own room, where we can look after him properly.' A minute later, they had Jim in the chair and Joe stood behind him, ready to push the wheelchair himself.

'I'm coming, Jim,' Honey said. She lowered her voice. 'Megan, the house visit will have to wait.'

'I know that. It doesn't matter.'

'Dr Farrelly wanted to get it settled today.'

'Don't fret, Mum.'

'You're a fine one to talk!'

Jim breathed noisily through the mask.

'Does he realise?' Megan continued, her distressed whisper louder than she knew. 'Does he understand? Is that why he's—? Does he understand that I won't be coming home?'

'Didn't even get to see the little bloke properly,' Jim complained a few minutes later, back in his own hospital bed.

'Jim…' Honey said.

'I know. All right? I heard, back there with Megan, and I know this is the end. I know we can't manage, just the two of us, and I know she won't want to come back. Can't come back. Not until the little fella's stronger anyway, and by then it'll be too late.'

'She thinks she's broken your heart, love. She was so scared to tell you. She wouldn't let me talk about it, prepare you, say anything at all, and then when we saw you looking at him… She's called him Jackson… I think she really loves the Ransome boy, Jim.'

'Lot of good that's going to do her, since he hasn't shown his face in six months.'

Honey fell silent and her head drooped. 'Yes, that's a disappointment.'

'We'll put the place on the market as soon as we can. We won't get enough for it, not nearly enough, with the state it's in, but we can set ourselves up in town. I can get work. There'll be something. It's not the end of the world. Doesn't Megan know that?'

'Jim, she thinks she's broken your heart.'

'No, Honey, love,' Jim said, his voice creaking with bone-deep fatigue. 'That happened a long time ago.'

Joe was still finishing up an addition to Jim's notes when Charles Wetherby arrived to see his childhood friend.

'I heard you gave us another scare just now,' he said.

'Someone has to keep you on the ball, Charlie,' Jim answered.

'Trust me, there's plenty happens around here to do that!'

Jim managed a half-hearted grin at Charles, but then Joe saw the expression drain from his face as he looked at the doorway. 'You!'

Charles turned, but before he could speak, Philip Wetherby—because this had to be Philip Wetherby, even though Joe hadn't encountered Charles's brother before—told him, 'I've been trying to catch up to you the whole way along the corridor. You move way too fast in that thing, and I've been driving half the night from the property. I called out, but you didn't hear.'

'Did Lynley send you, Philip?'

'No. Hell, no! I thought we needed to talk about this face to face.'

'Right. In other words, not in front of your wife?'

'That's right,' he agreed with a hunted look.

'Do you want to see me in my office?'

The younger Wetherby hesitated, giving Charles the opportunity to pounce.

'On second thoughts, whatever you've got to say, say it here. It's appropriate, with the three of us.'

'I'll catch you later, Charles,' Joe said quickly, but Charles clamped a hand on his arm as he started past the wheelchair.

'Hang about, if you don't mind, Joe,' the medical administrator said mildly. 'Think it might be handy for us to have a witness to this.'

'Sure,' he agreed carefully.

'Thanks.' Charles looked up at his brother, in no way diminished by his lesser height in the chair. 'Speak, Philip.'

Philip tightened his already narrow lips. 'It's pretty simple. I'm here to tell you that you win, Charles.'

Charles merely raised his eyebrows.

'You know what I'm saying. There's no need to force the sale. I'll do what has to be done.'

'Are you listening to this, Jim?' Charles said.

'Yeah, but I want it spelled out, if it's what I think.'

'I'll grant the access to Gunya Creek. But I won't tell Lynley the truth. That Jim didn't pull the trigger. And no one else is to be told either. You and Jim have always agreed you were just as much to blame, horsing around, not paying any attention, calling me the gun-bearer and sticking me with the guns and all the work. I was thirteen! And I think you're wrong that it should have been dealt with after Dad died. By then it was water under the bridge.'

'Not for the Coopers.'

'Do we have to?'

Charles cut his brother off. 'You continued to exact a

punishment that our father put in place at a point where it made sense for Jim and me to protect you. And, yes, I'll admit we were protecting our own backsides, too, because we knew Dad's retaliation might have been even more extreme if he'd known how careless we all were. He was a violent man. But when Dad died, your "standing in the community" wasn't an excuse, Philip.'

'Do we need to cover this ground? I've said I'll do what you want, as long as my wife doesn't have to know.'

'Because of her "standing in the community"?'

'Pretty much.'

'The creek access isn't enough. It would have been ten years ago, but it's not any more. Wetherby Downs is going to give Jim and Honey everything they need to get back on their feet, little brother, or the sale goes ahead. Restocking, equipment, labour to ride their fences and deliver their feed, until they're back in profit.'

'I'll have to work out a budget.'

'The money's there.'

'It is,' Philip conceded.

'So the budget isn't necessary. And there's one more thing.'

Philip pressed his fingers over his eyes. 'How can there be more? Isn't this enough?'

'This one won't threaten your ego too much,' Charles promised in a mild tone. 'I'd just like you to find out where that nephew of ours has got to, if you have any information.'

'Our nephew? You mean Jack?'

'Your sister Celia's boy, Philip,' Jim said. 'Took weeks for Honey and me to find out his last name was Ransome.'

'Yes, born and raised in Sydney,' Philip answered, 'and then Celia tells me he wants to be a cattleman and can I please train him up.' He shook his head. 'You surely can't hold me responsible for what happened with your daughter, Cooper. They were both over eighteen.'

'Yeah, and now they're both parents,' Jim said softly. The new light of hope that had appeared in his eyes a few minutes ago was getting brighter. 'And call us naïve, Philip, but it might make a difference. We'd just like him to know.'

An hour out of Crocodile Creek, on the return flight, Mike Poulos radioed a report to Base about the patient they were bringing in. She was thirty-four, on a reef holiday with her husband, in early pregnancy and with a history of pelvic inflammatory disease. They received a confirmation that Dr Turner would be standing by for emergency surgery when they landed.

Because it had to be an ectopic pregnancy.

Knife-like abdominal pain on one side, bloating and spotting, signs of shock… Every symptom pointed to it, as well as the patient's history. Christina had broken the bad news and the woman and her husband were both upset, mourning the loss of a planned child and the risk to future fertility.

With her own pregnancy constantly in her mind, Christina ached for them but didn't let it get personal. It wouldn't help them to hear her own story, or to have her inwardly wondering how she'd feel in the same situation and whether there was any chance that Joe would be by her side—whether she'd want him if they had no future together.

During flight, the options for treatment were standard, straightforward and limited. They were treating the shock and buying time until the surgery, basically. Christina had given oxygen, IV fluids and pain medication, and elevated the patient's feet.

'Not long now,' she told the woman and her husband, seeing the shape of the coastline take on familiar lines.

'And did you catch that message for you from Charles?' Mike asked her. 'That he's got things sorted out for this week?'

'Yes, I got it, Mike,' she answered, not yet daring to think that this was good news.

On the ground, in the ED, Joe heard the sound of the chopper blades overhead, just as he had that morning on the Remote Rescue's outward flight.

'Do we know what this is yet?' he asked Emily.

He'd been all over the hospital that morning, both before and after that scene in Jim Cooper's room. He hadn't caught up on what kind of case was being brought in, whether they'd need him.

'The rescue chopper?' Emily was writing up some notes, and didn't look up from them. 'With Christina? She has an ectopic pregnancy. It's ruptured. Georgie's going to operate, with Jill assisting and I don't know who else. Apparently...'

The world faded. The sounds of the ward, the fluorescent light overhead.

All of it.

Just faded...

Joe blinked slowly. Emily had stopped speaking. He realised that suddenly she was looking at him, and although she'd been sitting half a second ago, she was now on her feet and standing close. 'Lord, Joe, what is it?'

'Nothing.' He whooshed out a breath, willing the room to stop spinning and those blotches in front of his eyes to disappear. 'Don't worry, it's nothing.'

Although Dr Morgan did have a certain way with words this week!

Resolving the ambiguity had only taken him a few seconds. It wasn't Christina's pregnancy that had lodged in a

Fallopian tube and ruptured the narrow passage. Good grief, of course it wasn't! She was bringing in a patient.

But in that brief time when he'd got it wrong…

'Are you sure, Joe?' Emily was still frowning at him. 'You look as if your whole life just passed before your eyes.'

'It did. But it's gone now. See? Whee!' He made his hands into butterfly wings. He did not want to talk about this!

What had talking really done for himself and Christina this week?

The ebb of the momentary burst of adrenaline left him way shakier and more distracted than he should have been. In the two seconds that had ticked by while he'd given Emily's words the wrong meaning, he'd mentally cancelled his flight home tomorrow, called the other doctors in his practice and arranged for them to cover his workload for the next week, even decided that Amber's appointment to talk about her surgery could be postponed, because helping Christina through the dangerous loss of her pregnancy was much more important. Anything that Christina wanted he would give her, because it was so important.

Important and a dragging weight of responsibility at the same time, but he couldn't let that stop him. Would she let him take it on, though, when he'd made it painfully clear to her this week how much of an added burden it would be? When he knew he wouldn't be able to hide the weight?

'I'm grabbing a two-minute coffee,' he told Emily.

'Are you really sure you're all right?'

'I'm fine.' He was going to be, as long as he could find some time with Christina today.

'Have you had lunch?'

'Not yet.'

'Take lunch, Joe.'

'It's OK.'

'Look, this new patient is going straight into surgery. Georgie's already here, waiting to scrub. If you want to talk to Christina, she'll be free in a few minutes.'

'What makes you think I want to talk to Christina?' Oh, lord, if this had become everyone else's business already, when he still didn't know what the outcome would be, he'd hate it.

'Because you said her name, Joe. Didn't you hear yourself?'

'No. Said her name?'

'Just now, when I told you about the incoming case. And you sounded as if it was part of your dying breath.'

His dying breath.

Joe lost count of how many of those he took over the next fifteen hours, but they all felt that way. It had to be some kind of cosmic punishment, he decided. He hadn't talked to Christina for two years, not about the things she'd wanted to hear. Now he was desperate to talk to her, but their paths just did not cross.

He was called to an emergency admission, and by the time he'd admitted and treated the burns case that had confronted him, Christina had gone out on another urgent flight. He should have been off in the evening, but Charles asked him if he could manage to stay late. 'We've got a staffing glitch suddenly for the coming week. I'm swapping a few people around. I…uh…shouldn't give you the details, I don't think.'

'No. Fine, Charles.' He blinked. Somebody else had had some confidential emergency. He should probably spare a bit of emotional energy, hoping everything was OK for them since the medical staff at Crocodile Creek had had their share of problems lately, but he couldn't. Spare emotional energy? There wasn't any. 'Yes, I can stay on as late as I'm needed,' he said.

When Christina returned with their latest patient—a truckie who'd overturned his vehicle and had a query head injury—Joe was busy, and when he thought about her in the quieter hours of the night, wondering if he could grab a break, phone her, go over for half an hour as long as he kept his pager clipped to his pocket, it just didn't seem to make sense.

One in the morning? She'd be fast asleep. You didn't waken a woman at that hour to promise you'd 'be there for her' when you knew you couldn't hide from her just how much the promise would cost.

Four-thirty in the morning… Honey was suddenly aware of someone in the room. She'd gone to sleep by Jim's side and now she woke up, her hand in his. But someone was there. She looked up and it was Megan.

'Just checking,' Megan said, and gave a half-smile that was tentative and fearful but still better than any smile Honey had seen for months. 'Dr Wetherby says Dad's going to be OK.'

'He is, love. And such good news. I can't believe we have access to the creek. The feud is over. We'll have money to restock. We can go home…'

'I don't know…'

'There'll be money for you to go to university now,' Honey told her, reaching out in the dim light to hold her daughter's hand. 'Maybe we have to wait until Jackson's a bit older but there are distance courses… You can study at home and do the access weekends… Somehow we'll work it out.'

'We surely will.' It was Jim, awake, his half-lidded eyes watching his wife and his daughter with a joy that shone through his drugged sleepiness.

'The first thing is your bypass, Dad,' Megan said.

'The first thing is your happiness,' Jim growled. 'Megan, girl, I'm so sorry… We asked too much from you. We'll make it up to you. You'll see.'

'I'll be fine, Dad,' she murmured. 'I'll be fine.'

Honey leaned forward and kissed her husband gently on the forehead. 'We'll all be fine now,' she murmured. 'We'll be a family.'

Would they? Megan gazed down at her parents and saw the love they felt for each other and felt her heart twist. It had been such a short time… Such a short time to know her heart…

Where was he?

He was out there, she thought. Somewhere, he was out there. Please.

There were footsteps in the corridor. She heard murmured talking and looked out to see Dr Farrelly and Dr Wetherby talking urgently in the corridor. Another drama?

But Charles was tugging Christina down to give her a swift hug, and Christina was carrying a holdall.

Megan closed her eyes. Christina was going to her love, she thought. That Kiwi doctor who'd been so nice this week. Her love… She knew it.

Someday I will, too, Jack, she promised. Someday I will, too.

It was still dark when Joe got up, after a bare three hours' sleep over at the house. He had his bag already packed, didn't feel like breakfast. His whole body creaked with stiffness and fatigue. He got to the airport at five-fifteen, every muscle in his body still moving with lead weights attached.

And there was Christina, when he thought he'd lost his

last chance to see her for three endless weeks. She'd come to see him off.

'Tink!'

With the airport lounge almost empty, he'd seen her straight away, standing near the check-in desk, waiting for him. She waved and smiled as he strode towards her, his heavy bag suddenly much lighter in his grip. His stiffness faded.

She stuck out a mile in his vision, the way she always had. She'd always seemed to him to have so much *more* than any other woman he'd ever met.

More heart.

More energy.

A more beautiful smile.

'Hi,' she said as he reached her, her voice husky.

'Tink,' he said again. He buried his face in her neck, inhaling the scent of her hair in open appreciation. 'Mmm, you smell so good!' And she was the only person who ever made him feel this way when he hugged her.

Tingling.

Exultant.

Where he belonged.

He couldn't help the relief and happiness he felt, even if it was an illusion, even if the weight came down hard on his shoulders again a minute from now. At least this way he'd get to tell her face to face that she wouldn't be going through pregnancy and parenthood alone.

'What are you doing here at this hour?' he asked her, trying to keep it light. 'Seeing me off?'

'Coming with you,' she said. Her mouth pressed hard against his hair, his cheekbone, the corner of his mouth. She held him tight. 'I'm flying to Auckland with you, Joe.'

'That's…not possible.'

'It is, thanks to Charles, who cleared my roster for the week, and to the airline, which fortunately had some spare seats.'

'Wh—?'

She was still smiling at him. No, she was grinning. Laughing into his face, stroking his jaw, looking happy and excited, like a tourist on her honeymoon.

Yes, and she had a packed bag at her feet.

His heart began to lift.

It shouldn't be doing that.

Why was it doing that?

It should be sinking like a stone, weighed down with his awareness of what she was prepared to give, with his responsibility for her happiness if he let her give it. For hours he'd been expecting this sinking feeling, steeling himself against it, dreading it.

But now it wasn't happening. His heart wasn't sinking, it was lifting. Like a bird. Like a plane. Like…Superman? Except that he'd just begun to glimpse the possibility that he didn't have to be Superman any more.

'Because you said it yourself, Joe,' she said, speaking only for him. 'Sometimes talking isn't what counts. There has to be action.'

Her eyes were alight. Yes, she could see how he felt. See that weight lifting. See him about to float up in the air like an untethered balloon.

'So I stopped listening to what you said, and started thinking about everything you'd actually done over the past two years since we've been together. I know you love me,' she said, 'and I'm not letting this go. I'm not letting you shoulder everything on your own. You're not shouldering anything on your own from now on, because you have me. I'm spending a week in New Zealand with you and

your family while we make some plans for how we're going to handle our future *together*. I don't care about the details, if we live here or there, if we use my savings or keep
them, but the *together* part is non-negotiable. I'm fighting
for that. OK?'

Her eyes narrowed a little and she lifted her chin. He
suddenly saw that she was a little less confident and bull-
dozer-ish about this than she would have him believe, and
that was unbearable. He couldn't let her suffer the doubt
for another second.

'I love you,' he said, holding her tight. 'I love you and
I want you, and you're right, I'm not letting you go. I'm
fighting for it. You know what? I'm not reacting right.' He
shook his light, giddy head, grinning. 'I never thought—
Well, I never thought you'd do something like this. I
thought we wouldn't see each other for three weeks and
that when I came back it would go on being tough. But
even if I'd expected you here this morning, saying what
you've said, I would have thought it would make me
feel…loaded down. Even more than before. And that I'd
just drag you down, too.'

'That's why you wouldn't let me do it.' She understood.

'Yes. Only yesterday, something happened… it was stupid… When Emily said you were bringing in the ectopic
pregnancy she worded it so that for a few seconds I thought
the patient was you. And I knew in that instant that I'd drop
everything to be with you, no matter what. And something
clicked.'

'Yeah?' She pressed her nose against his.

'I was going to offer you everything, all my support. I
was so glad to see you standing here, because it gave me
the right chance to say it. But I thought it would feel as if
I'd put the last nail in my own coffin. Only it's not mak-

ing me feel that way. It's making me feel—Oh, lord, Tink, if you really want to do this…'

'Actions speak louder than words.' She waved her passport in his face. Through the terminal windows, the light of dawn had begun to seep higher and brighter in the eastern sky.

Joe laughed out loud. 'It feels good. It feels great. I'm…just happy. Christina Farrelly, I'm happy!'

'The way we've always felt when we're together, Joe,' she whispered. 'And it's not going to change.'

'You think?'

'I know! But I didn't know how to make you see it. Just telling you didn't help. I finally realised I had to show you. Take action. Prove it.'

'And let my reaction argue the case? It has, Tink. I'm—'

'Happy!' She grinned, then kissed him sweetly.

'Happy.'

'And about the baby?'

'So happy.'

She didn't seem to doubt him.

'I'm never going to let you go,' he whispered.

'We do have to check in.'

'Don't have to let you go to do that. I have skills. See?' He shouldered his bag and picked up her suitcase in the same hand, which left plenty of him still for her.

'Oh, Joe!' She laughed and grabbed his spare arm, and together, half an hour later, they took flight into the dawn, towards their shared future.